DEDICATION

I dedicate *The Fall and Rise of Jacoby* to my second mother, Oreatha France of Melbourne, Florida.

ACKNOWLEDGMENTS

I would like to take this time to thank the following people: Sidney Rickman, and Marguerite Lemons, my editors, and Jeff Lancashire, my graphic artist.
website: http://www.adjacentdesign

Contents

Jacoby stood in the hallway paralyzed with fear. Pockets of sweat soaked the material under her armpits. Her hand gripped the strap of her purse so hard her knuckles hurt. Forcing herself to relax her hold, she fished around in the bottom of her purse until she felt the outline of the key and withdrew it.

Transfixed she stared at the tarnished gold-colored object in the palm of her hand. The sight of it made blood rush to her head. Swaying, Jacoby planted her free hand on the wall for support. Beads of perspiration broke out on her forehead and her knees began to tremble.

From where it came she didn't know, but a burst of strength combined with resolve fluttered to life in her gut. First it was small and then the flame grew in intensity, enveloping her body. Stilling her quaking knees, she inserted the key into the doorknob. With relief she felt it turn. With the flat of the hand, she pushed the door open, letting herself inside the pitch, black apartment.

The Fall and Rise of Jacoby

MICHELE CAMERON

ISBN: 13: 978-0-9889509-1-7
ISBN :10: 098895091X

CHAPTER 1

Jacoby kneeled between the library stacks.

"Psst, Jacoby. Where are you?"

"I'm over here, Claudia," she whispered back.

"Girl, you shouldn't be bent over like that in this deserted part of the library. You might not come out of these stacks the same way you went in."

"Chile, please," Jacoby laughed. "Only you would think of something like that happening at the library in the middle of the day."

"You never know," Claudia laughed. "Bunnell is a small town with more males than females. There really aren't enough of us to go around."

"If there are so many men around here, why don't I have one?"

"They're scared of your daddy. Deacon Alexander is nobody to play with."

"Daddy's a teddy bear," she denied. "He's all roar and little bite."

"That's what you say. When you were in the ninth grade and Lorenzo Waters went to your house to see you, he told everyone your daddy took the flowers, threw them in the trash can, and said, 'Look at this door. Don't knock on it again.' "

Jacoby shook her head from side to side at the memory. "That was kind of embarrassing."

"Lorenzo passed the word around school that it would be a waste of time to try and date you."

"Daddy was just testing him to see if he had any backbone." She added with mild sarcasm, "Obviously he failed the test."

"No matter what your father does, you take up for him."

"He's my father and I love him dearly. Besides, what has daddy done to deserve your criticism today?"

Claudia's eyes twinkled merrily. "You know that I love him, too, but after your father said a few words at the close of service last week... Gee whiz. I didn't think that I had a chance of going to heaven. So since there's no hope I may as well live it up."

Jacoby put the last book in place and scrambled to her feet. "That's what you want to do anyhow so don't blame it on my daddy."

"You're right," Claudia answered good-naturedly. "Have you decided if you're going with us tonight?"

"I don't know," Jacoby answered carefully. "There's Sunday school in the morning."

"Rex and I won't keep you out too late. We have to go to church ourselves."

Jacoby's brow furrowed with puzzlement. "What is this place again?"

"It's a small town called Cassadaga."

"Cassadaga?"

"Yeah! It's a town full of psychics and they tell you your future."

"How can there be a town of psychics?"

"I dunno, but I want to go and see what my future holds."

"We already know that," Jacoby teased. "You're going to marry Rex, have a boatload of kids, and live happily ever after."

"I want confirmation," Claudia said.

"I'm amazed that you believe in that stuff."

"My cousin went there and the fortune teller told her to buy a scratch-off lottery ticket and she did. That night she won twenty-five thousand dollars."

Jacoby scoffed, "That was just a coincidence."

"I don't think so," Claudia denied. "My cousin is so cheap she wouldn't have wasted her money on a ticket unless she knew that it was the real thing."

"I don't think that I should be going to see some psychic. The bible says to stay away from witchcraft."

"It also says that a woman's place is in the home but check out where we are every day from nine to five. Come on, Jacoby," she pleaded. "It sounds like so much fun."

Jacoby gave her friend a resigned look. "Okay," she said. "I'll go. But when you and Rex pick me up don't tell Daddy where we're going. I don't want to hear his mouth."

"You don't have to worry about that," Claudia said with feeling. "I don't want to hear it either."

That evening Jacoby viewed with amusement the bickering between Rex and Claudia.

"Do you know where you're going?" Claudia asked demandingly.

"Yes, Mom, I know where I'm going."

"Don't call me Mom," Claudia said sharply. "I think we're lost. We've been driving forever. Use your GPS."

Rex quipped, "I can't hear it over your non-stop talking. Maybe this psychic will tell you that your mouth is going to get you strangled one day."

"Funny!" Claudia shot back. "Well, I'm getting ready to find out if you're the right choice for me."

Rex declared triumphantly, "There's our exit, 4116."

Rex slowed down as he drove the two lane road towards a sign directing them to Cassadaga. "This doesn't look very spooky to me," Claudia said as she swung her head around, looking at the normal-looking houses that flanked the road.

"I'm glad that it doesn't," Jacoby said, breathing a sigh of relief. "I feel like a hypocrite coming here and then going to church tomorrow morning."

"Stop your worrying," Claudia said. "God knows what a good person you are. I doubt that he'll punish you for taking a little adventure."

Rex parked the car in front of a hotel. It was a huge rambling one with a porch that ran the perimeter of the building. The window panes were dingy and there was paint peeling in some places. Weather-beaten rocking chairs sat on the front porch.

Claudia read the sign in front of it. "Cassadaga Hotel. It looks like it could have been in *The Shining*. Let's go and see what the psychics have to say."

"There don't seem to be many people around," Jacoby said with a nervous cackle. "I hope it's not because they know something we don't."

They strolled along the nearly empty street viewing signs in front of small houses. Psychic on duty. Palm readings. Tarot Card readings. "They do it all, don't they?"Jacoby said.

"Yeah," Claudia said. "Let's choose one and go in."

"I want to look around some more," Jacoby answered.

"Isn't there any place to eat?" Rex asked.

"I guess not," Jacoby said. "I mean, these are peoples' homes, not restaurants."

"I bet we can get something at the hotel," Claudia said.

"Maybe on the way out," Jacoby said. "But I'd rather get this out of the way first." Jacoby's gaze was drawn to a small gray house with beautiful roses in front of it. To its left was a garden with grape vines hanging on wire. "Let's go take a look at that one. It looks homey for a witch to be living there."

"That's just what I want," Claudia quipped, "a homey psychic."

They crossed the street to the house. "What is a certified psychic?" Jacoby asked, reading the sign on the lawn outside the house.

"I think that it means that whatever she's told people it's come true," Claudia whispered.

"How would she know that? Did they come back and tell her?"

"I don't know," Claudia whispered. "But I want to go to the psychic who lives here. It's kind of like getting a warranty on a television."

"I'll wait out here for you guys," Rex said as he plopped down onto a worn green bench.

"Don't you want to have a reading?" Jacoby asked.

"I think I'll pass," he said.

"Rex is scared," Claudia chuckled.

"I'm not scared," he denied. "I just like to be surprised when things happen to me. I think life is more fun that way."

"So do I," Jacoby said, nevertheless she followed Claudia up the cobbled sidewalk to the entrance. "Ring the bell and hold it," Jacoby said, reading the sign on the door.

But before Claudia could press the bell, the door was flung open. A slightly overweight woman with gray hair at her temples and emerald green eyes stared at them. She wore a red and green kimono that fell to her ankles. "Hello," she said in a friendly voice.

"Hello," Claudia said. "We would like a reading."

"Please come in." She stepped inside and they found themselves in a dark foyer. "My name is Zalia. I tell the past, present, and future of your life. It costs thirty dollars."

Jacoby and Claudia and looked at each other and then back at Zalia. "Okay," Claudia said.

"You will stay with me," Zalia told Claudia. "You will go in the other room and see the other psychics."

"But we didn't want to be split up," Jacoby protested. "Can't we stay together?"

"No, because when I or the other psychic tells you something we don't want the friend to react and give hints or clues about the reading. Mixed reactions could compromise the reading. Please follow that hallway," she instructed Jacoby pointing to the right.

Jacoby looked longingly at Claudia before going down a long hallway which opened into a kitchen. The aroma of lasagna cooking in the oven comforted her. As she sat down at the kitchen table her stomach growled. If I wasn't scared of these people I'd ask for a fork and a plate.

All of a sudden a man walked into the room and sat down. "I am Damien."

"You're a psychic?" Jacoby asked in astonishment.

"Yes," he said.

"I didn't know that there were male psychics. I kind of wanted a woman."

"I've been doing this for fifty years," Damien said in a solemn voice.

"All right then," Jacoby said doubtfully.

Damien handed her a deck of cards. "Shuffle them," he said gruffly.

Jacoby shuffled the cards several times before putting them on the table.

Damien picked up the deck and flipped over the top ten cards lining them up in two rows of five. He stared at them.

Jacoby uneasily shifted in her seat.

Damien's eyes seemed to roll back in his head and then his head dropped to his chest. An unnerving presence seemed to fill the room. "I see a lot of books around you. Okay. There is a man keeping a secret from you. Okay. I see turmoil, distrust. Okay. Your life will take an unexpected path. Okay. You will travel. Okay. There is illness. Okay. You will find true love but first you must weather a mighty storm. Okay." Then he raised his head looked at Jacoby. "Do you have any questions?"

Her mouth was dry. Afraid to ask too much she whispered, "Who is my true love?"

"A man that you haven't met yet." He added in an eerily sad voice, "Stay safe." Then Damien got to his feet and disappeared as quickly as he had appeared.

Jacoby dug into her purse and slapped thirty dollars on the table. She bolted out of her chair, down the hall, and outside where she found Claudia standing with Rex.

"How did it go?" Rex asked once she reached them.

Jacoby shrugged, pretending nonchalance. "I don't know."

"What did he tell you?" Claudia asked with a peculiar look on her face.

"That I'm going to travel and find my true love. How about you?"

An evasive look crept over Claudia's face. She slid her hand in Rex's. "Zalia said that I have already found my true love."

"That works for me," Rex said with a happy expression.

"Let's get out of here," Jacoby said.

"I thought that we were going to eat at the hotel," Rex said.

"No," Jacoby said as a sudden feeling of nausea swept through her. "I'm not hungry. My stomach feels kind of funny."

"Mine too," Claudia echoed.

Claudia and Jacoby lay in the front porch swing swatting away determined flies that dived towards them.

"Are you coming tonight?" Claudia demanded.

"You are such a bad influence on me."

"I just want you to have a little fun," Claudia chuckled. "Didn't you enjoy yourself just a little the other night?"

"Yeah, but it was kind of spooky," she said carefully. "I said two extra prayers in church the next day to ward off any spirits that might have followed me home."

"I thought you didn't believe Damien."

"Let's just say that I won't be going back. I agree with Rex. I think it's better to wait and see what God has in store for you."

"I guess you're right, Jacoby. But you have to come with us tonight. This club is supposed to be the bomb."

"How come I'm just hearing about it?"

"It's new," Claudia explained excitedly. "Pete's Place is past the railroad tracks on Old Ridge Road. Rex says the deejay rocks. He plays old music. None of that new stuff you can't dance to."

"Oh, so he's already been there?"

"Yep. He said that he danced all night. So you know he ain't going out there again without me."

"Don't tell me that you don't trust your fiancé?" Jacoby teased.

"I don't trust any of them," Claudia retorted swiftly. "But he's the best I can get in a town of about seven thousand citizens. My psychic pretty much told me to stick with him."

"Don't even try it, Claudia. Even if Zalia didn't tell you that you weren't going anywhere, you know that you love Rex to death."

"Yep. I wouldn't trade up even if I could. So are you going or not?"

"I'll think about it," Jacoby answered carefully.

Claudia wheedled, "Come on, Jacoby. We better go party there before the cops shut it down."

"Now why on earth would I want to go to a place like that?"

"Because, you're twenty years old and have never gone to a nightclub; because you're absolutely beautiful with your chocolate brown complexion, and if you don't get it together, your vajayjay is going to dry up."

"Well, I certainly wouldn't want that to happen," Jacoby said dryly. "What time are you and Rex going?"

"Ten o'clock," she said triumphantly. "We want to get a good table."

Jacoby punched into the computer the barcode numbers off the binder of the last book. "Here you go, Mrs. Gilbert."

"Thanks for helping me find these books, Jacoby."

"All of them are on the Florida Teens list so they should be good."

"I hope my grandkids will read them. They're driving me nuts playing those noisy video games all day. I have to record all my shows and watch them after they go to bed."

"We have story reading here every Friday. You should bring them by. It might encourage them to read."

"I'll see if I can get them out of the house. See you in church tomorrow, Jacoby."

"Yes, ma'am."

"May I help you?" Jacoby said to the next person in line.

"I'd like to check you and this book out," he said, handing it to her.

"What!" Jacoby exclaimed, taken aback.

"You heard me, Jacoby Alexander. I'd like to take you out."

"I'm sorry, but I don't date strangers," she replied firmly.

"From what I hear, you don't date nobody."

Exasperation flashed through her and it showed on her face.

"No one in Bunnell is a stranger," he said

"You're a stranger to me," she answered crossly.

"You got snap, crackle, and pop to you. I like that," he said and his eyes suggestively ran the length of her body.

Jacoby glared at him.

"Now I went and made you mad and I'm sorry for that. Let me start again. I'm Armstrong Battle. You went to high school with my baby brother Troy. I'd like to take you out."

"You're Troy's older brother?" she asked suspiciously.

"Yeah, I got him by four years. You were coming in to Bunnell High as I was going out."

"You're still a stranger to me."

"I'd like to change that," he said with a sincere look.

She looked at him doubtfully.

"If I can't come to your house and take you out, at least meet me somewhere so we can talk and get to know each other."

A loud cough from Sally let Jacoby know that she needed to get back to work. Handing Armstrong his book she said slowly, "I'll be at Pete's Place on Old Ridge Road tonight."

"See you then," he said and whistling off key, he strode out of the library.

Jacoby yanked at the paisley dress until it at least hit her mid thigh. Once she stepped into black four inch heels the dress seemed to ride right back up her long length. Giving up, she took a brush and tugged it through her long, wavy hair one more time, then, she anxiously peered at her reflection in the mirror. Kohl black eyeliner accented her almond-shaped eyes and was the perfect foil to her red lipstick. Squirming, Jacoby adjusted the cleavage of her dress, breathed a deep sigh. Without turning on the lights, she walked down the dark hallway past her parents' closed bedroom door.

Backing her car out of the driveway, she didn't turn on the headlights of her car until she had turned the car away from the house.

As Jacoby searched for Claudia and Rex in the smoke-filled club, she couldn't help noticing the surprised stares directed at her from more than one person. Eventually she found her friends snuggled together in a booth near the dance floor.

Rex was whispering in Claudia's ear as she cuddled up under his arm.

Jacoby grinned as she watched her friend possessively stroke Rex's cheek making sure every female in the room knew that he was taken.

As she approached them, they broke their embrace. Claudia stood and she gave her a big hug. "Girl, you look fantastic."

"So do you," she complimented, looking at Claudia in her black, silk mini dress.

"Jacoby, you kinda make me wish I wasn't engaged," Rex joked.

"Yeah, right." Jacoby laughed as she slid into the side of the booth across from them. "It took you three years to get Claudia to go out with you. I know that you're not going to mess that up."

"You're right about that," he said. "But you know Claudia always wanted me; she was just playing hard to get."

"Yeah," Claudia chimed in her eyes twinkling. "And he almost didn't get got."

Suddenly, Jacoby felt a presence behind her. She turned around coming face to face with Armstrong.

"How are you doing, Jacoby?" he asked, his eyes sliding up and down her body.

"I'm fine," she answered with a small smile.

"I was afraid that you were going to stand me up."

Jacoby noted the startled looks from both Claudia and Rex. She said, "We don't have a date, so I don't think that I would be standing you up if I didn't show."

"Ouch!" he said and placed his hand over his heart. Then without permission he sat down next to her.

"Claudia and Rex," Jacoby explained, "do you know Troy Battle's brother, Armstrong?"

Rex stuck his hand out. "Yeah, I do. I heard you were back in town. Where have you been?"

"I've been doing a tour of duty in Afghanistan," he answered in a serious tone.

"That's tough," Rex said.

"Yeah," he said. "That wasn't what I signed up for but that's where I wound up."

"Are things any better over there?" Jacoby asked.

"Much," Armstrong answered.

"When are you going back?" Rex asked.

"I'm not," he said quietly. "I was discharged because a part of my foot was blown off. My Hummer got blown up by a booby trap and my commander and I were the only survivors."

"That must be a terrible thing to go through," Jacoby said sympathetically.

"I'd do it all over again if I could keep women like you safe." He placed his hand her knee.

Claudia kicked Jacoby underneath the table.

A waitress in a pair of skin tight black shorts and skimpy tee shirt appeared at their table. In between chomps of gum she said, "Can I get y'all something to drink?"

"I'll have a bottle of Hennessey, a couple of cans of coke, and a bucket of ice." Armstrong looked at Rex. "What do ya'll want? Uncle Sam is buying."

"The Hennessey will work for me," Rex said. He said to the waitress, "Please get my girl another glass of white zinfandel."

Armstrong handed the waitress a fifty dollar bill. "Bring her a glass of wine also." He nodded at Jacoby.

"But I don't drink," Jacoby protested.

After she disappeared Armstrong leaned in and whispered into Jacoby's ear, "Jesus drank wine too, didn't he, church girl?"

When Claudia kicked Jacoby under the table again Jacoby jumped.

Thinking he was the source of her jumpiness, Armstrong gave a deep chuckle.

After two glasses of wine, Jacoby closed her eyes and bobbed her head to the music of The Temptations. They were alone since Claudia and Rex had been on the dance floor the last three songs.

"What do you know about this kind of music, little girl?"

She gave him a sharp look. "Don't think you're cooler than me because you've been in the army."

"There's nothing cool about killing people, Jacoby," he muttered in a morose voice. "And that's what I was forced to do."

Jacoby fell silent as she tried to imagine what Armstrong had been through defending their country.

"Still, life in Afghanistan is better than in this one horse town."

"You sound like you wish that you'd never come back," she said, looking at him from under her long eyelashes.

"I just came home to get my bearings," Armstrong said. "But I might find a reason to stay. Let's dance."

There was very little room to move on the crowded dance floor. As she danced close to Armstrong the combination of the wine and Mary J. Blige's voice relaxed Jacoby's inhibitions. She moved to the moderate beat of the music, loving the proximity of Armstrong's body. All of a sudden from behind she felt a man's hand palm her butt. She stumbled into Armstrong.

With his hand he steadied her.

Her heart fluttered. She moved closer to Armstrong in an effort to distance herself from the mauler, and she felt Armstrong's hot breath on the top of her head. One song led into two, then three, then four. It was hot on the dance floor and sweat dripped into the valley between her breasts, making her dress cling. Suddenly the tempo of the music changed from fast dance to the melodic voices of Earth, Wind, and Fire. Vaguely, Jacoby noticed several couples leaving the floor. But Armstrong drew her closer into his arms. He whispered, "Maurice White must have read my mind. The only reason why I came here tonight was to see you."

She melted, loving his possessive embrace. She tightened her arms around his middle and laid her head on his chest. After what felt like an eternity the music ended. In a sort of bemused state, she let herself be led back to their table.

Suddenly the lights in the club went up. Claudia said, "Well, I guess that's our cue. Rex and I were just waiting for you to get off the dance floor because we're ready to leave."

"I guess I am too," she said, giving Armstrong a soft smile.

"Are you okay to drive?" he asked with concern.

"Sure I am. I haven't had anything to drink in over an hour."

"I think that I should follow you in my car to make sure you get home safely."

"That's a good idea," Rex chuckled. "Just don't knock on her daddy's door."

Jacoby eyebrows furrowed and she gave Rex a dirty look.

"Oh, I'll knock on her daddy's door all right," Armstrong said, "but not tonight. I'll come in the daytime so I can make a good impression."

Jacoby hid a small smile of anticipation.

The fifteen-minute drive took longer because Jacoby drove with extra caution. Finally, dimming her car lights, she pulled into her driveway.

Armstrong did the same. He purposefully strode up to her car, opened her door, and roughly pulled her out and into his arms, then kissed her.

Reveling in the mastery of his touch, Jacoby sank into his kiss. But when she felt his hands wandering to cup her buttocks, she squirmed in his embrace trying to loosen his hold on her.

Armstrong released her. He ran his tongue around his lips wanting more, but he tamped down his urge and stepped back. "Go on in the house." With a glint in his eye, he said, "I'll see you soon." Then Armstrong got into his Dodge Charger, backed out, turned on his headlights and tore down the street.

"Come in," Jacoby said when she heard the knocking on her bedroom door.

Her mother entered the room with a glass of juice. "It's time to get up or you're going to be late for Sunday School."

Jacoby groaned.

"What's the matter?" She placed the glass of juice on the coaster on the nightstand. "Are you sick or something?"

"No, ma'am. I'm just kind of tired."

"If you want to stay home from church today, I guess it's okay."

"No it isn't," her father said coming into the room. "If it was Monday and you had to go to work you'd already be up and dressed. Didn't I hear you go out last night after your mother and I went to bed?"

Yawning, she replied as she covered her mouth with her hand, "I met up with Claudia and hung out."

"Why didn't you say earlier that were going out?" Abraham frowned.

"I didn't really decide until the last minute," Jacoby hedged.

"Leave her alone, Abraham," Sarai said. "Her choir isn't singing today so if she wants to stay home and rest, let her alone." She gently pushed her husband out the room. Before she closed the door, she gave her daughter a wink.

Jacoby heard her father grumbling from the other side of the door. Then she heard her mother say, "Hush, Abraham. Finish your coffee. Maybe then you won't be so cranky."

Jacoby grinned as she turned over and fell back into a deep sleep.

Hours later, the ringing of the telephone roused her. She grabbed the receiver. "So do you like him or not?" Claudia demanded.

"Him who?" Jacoby retorted playfully.

"Armstrong. That dude was all over you last night."

"Yeah, I think that he's kinda cute."

"I don't usually go for yellow men, but he'll do. He looks like a Maxwell impersonator."

"Claudia," Jacoby chuckled, "you are so crazy."

"And at least he's tall. You're only five eight but you tower over most men in those heels you wear."

"Armstrong has good manners. When we left the club he stepped back and held the door open for me. He even did that when he walked me to my car."

"Rex never does that," Claudia complained. "I'm going to have to get on him about it too. So, do you think that Armstrong might be the one?" she drawled.

"The one what?"

"You know what." Claudia drawled, "To pop that cherry."

"None of your business," Jacoby retorted. "And if he is the one I won't be telling you." As Jacoby replaced the telephone receiver in its cradle she could hear Claudia's tinkling laughter.

CHAPTER 2

There was an unsettled air at the dinner table. Jacoby couldn't put her finger on it, but something was amiss.

"Pass me the rolls, Sarai." Once he had another one in hand Abraham asked in a casual manner, "Jacoby, where did you and Claudia go last night?"

Jacoby gave a start of surprise. "I already told you daddy. We hung out."

"Hung out where?" he asked.

She drew in a long breath. "We went to Pete's Place."

"That's a bar, young lady, and I heard you were drinking with some guy."

"Abraham!" Sarai said. "What were you trying to do? Trick her into lying to you?"

"No, I just wanted to hear what she was going to say. Deacon White told me all about it after church."

"What was he doing there?" Sarai asked sarcastically.

"He wasn't," Abraham shot back. "His daughter was there and she told him."

"Then he needs to worry about his daughter and not mine," Sarai retorted just as quickly.

"All I had was wine, Daddy." Trying to lighten the atmosphere she quipped, "Jesus drank wine with his disciples."

"Don't get flip with me, young lady. You deliberately misled us."

Sarai interjected, "She didn't mislead me because I didn't ask."

Jacoby carefully placed her linen napkin on the white tablecloth. "Daddy, I didn't say anything to you for this reason. I didn't want the hassle. Pete's Place lets eighteen-year olds in there. I'm almost twenty-one, so I don't see the big deal."

"I don't want you to get into any trouble," Abraham said. "There's a lot of temptation out there."

"Abraham," Sarai gave her husband a penetrating look. "Leave her be. You haven't always been saved and going to church every time the door opened."

A brooding look settled on Abraham's face. He got up, his chair scraping the tile on the floor, and he stormed off.

###

Early evening, Jacoby lounged on the front porch swing as it creaked back and forth. The smell of fresh cut grass wafted to her nostrils and gave her a sense of peace. Her long legs were stretched out in front of her as she thumbed through the pages of Essence. She paused, tore out an ad for a hair care product, and placed it on the others. The sight of Armstrong's Charger pulling into the driveway diverted her from her task.

Armstrong got out. He looked like a model from a J.Crew ad in a pair of skinny Levi's, Polo shirt, and red, white, and blue checkered canvas shoes.

Jacoby sat up in the swing, pulling her shorts down.

He grinned as he walked towards her. "How are you doing today, Jacoby? No hangover from last night?"

"Shush," she said. "My parents are in the house."

"Gotcha. I told you that I'd be back and what I was going to do once I got here." Armstrong took the front steps two at a time and banged on the screen door.

"What are you doing?" she asked in a shocked voice.

Abraham Alexander opened it and stepped out onto the front porch.

Armstrong stuck his hand out. "I'm Armstrong Battle."

Sarai came to the door and watched through the screen.

"Are you the man who had my daughter drinking last night?" Abraham demanded.

"Daddy!" Jacoby exclaimed.

Abraham held his hand up to silence her interruption.

Armstrong cleared his throat. "Yes, suh, I must admit that I bought Jacoby wine last night."

With a stern look on his face Abraham said, "She's not of drinking age. Obviously they didn't card her. If it happens again I'll have Pete's Place shut down."

"I apologize, suh. It won't happen again."

"You say your last name is Battle. Are you Mary Beth's son who's stationed in Afghanistan?"

"I was, suh," Armstrong answered.

"And you have a brother named Troy who's also in the military?"

"Yes, suh. He's still enlisted and stationed at Fort Bragg."

"And what are you doing here?"

"I came to see you, suh. I'd like permission to date your daughter."

A fleeting look of admiration passed across Abraham's face, but it quickly disappeared. "How old are you?"

"Twenty-five."

He frowned. "Five years is a big age difference when you're young. And you saw a lot of horror over there. Sometimes war makes people hard. Jacoby has been sheltered and I don't want you taking advantage of her."

"Daddy!" Jacoby said mortified.

Abraham held his hand up again.

"That is not my intention, suh," Armstrong said.

"That's what they all say. But it's her choice whether or not to see you. She has a curfew here and we have rules. Break them and you'll answer to me."

Armstrong stuck out his hand again. "Yes, suh."

Abraham slowly shook it. He looked at his wife. "Sarai, I have to go to the prison and look at my schedule for next week. See you later."

Claudia screeched over the phone, "No he didn't."

"Yes Armstrong did. He stood up to Daddy without an ounce of apparent fear."

"Gee! I wish I could have been there."

"I know my daddy inside and out, Claudia. He admired the way Armstrong handled himself."

"I guess the hell he did!" Claudia said in wonder.

"Stop that cussing. I can tell from your conversation that you didn't make it to church today either."

"No the hell I didn't," Claudia chirped.

Jacoby laughed uproariously and was joined by Claudia.

A couple of weeks later they lay on the blanket and stared up at the sky. Jacoby pointed at the stars and counted, "Five, six, seven, and eight."

"You're going to be here all night if you're trying to count all of them up there," Armstrong said.

She turned over on her side and smiled at him. "I don't think that I've ever seen a more beautiful night."

"I think that you're the reason why the stars are so bright," Armstrong said. "They're trying to outshine you, but they've failed."

"You say the sweetest things to me, Armstrong," she whispered.

"I really feel what I'm saying, Jacoby. You've made Bunnell a decent place to live. I thank you for that."

"Unfortunately I don't have a lot of good memories about this place. Troy and I were raised on the poor side of town and I always felt as if people were laughing at us. I couldn't wait to get away. That's why I enlisted. It was a spur of the moment decision."

"Do you regret it?" she asked softly.

"Yes and no." He lay on his back, his hands cradling his head. "When I was at war I felt useful. Now," he shrugged, "I don't know what I'm going to do with the rest of my life. I need to find my niche."

"You're young, Armstrong. Why are you in such a hurry to plan your life out? I think that life has lots of surprising twists and turns and wonderful things have a way of happening when you least expect it."

Armstrong gave her an appraising look. "Give me an example."

"Well," she said slowly, "the day you came into the library. I'd just agreed to meet Claudia at Pete's Place and I'd never been to a club before. So when you approached me and asked if you could see me later the words seemed to tumble out of my mouth."

"But what you don't know is that my showing up there wasn't by chance."

"It wasn't?" she asked, her eyes wide with speculation.

"No. The minute I got back in town I asked around about you."

"Why?"

"I saw you at the gas station the day after I enlisted into the army. You had on a pair of navy shorts and a nautical shirt. You stopped me dead in my tracks because I thought that you were the most beautiful girl that I'd ever seen. I was going to try and talk to you, but I was afraid."

"Afraid of what?" she whispered.

"Afraid that it was a waste of time because I might not make it back," he said with a solemn look.

Jacoby placed her palm soothingly on his chest.

"I thank God that I did."

"So do I," she echoed.

All of a sudden Armstrong pulled her head towards him.

She closed her eyes and leaned in. As their lips touched, she inhaled the musky, male scent of him.

Armstrong's hold on her was insistent as he leisurely explored her mouth with his tongue.

With the relaxing sound of lapping water as a background, she breathed deeply. Then she felt herself being laid back onto the blanket. She barely noticed that Armstrong was removing her shirt.

Armstrong unhooked her front closure bra. He kneaded a breast with one hand while the other played with the nub on her other breast. When the fullness of his mouth closed over it she groaned and clasped his head.

He licked his tongue down from the valley of her breasts to her belly button, inserting his tongue inside and holding it there. In the deep recesses of her mind Jacoby felt her shorts being unsnapped.

Finally, when his lips left hers she felt his hands between her legs, sliding the edge of her panties to one side. He probed inside her with his index finger.

"Oh, Armstrong, you make me feel…" Then she stopped.

"I make you feel what, little church girl?" he growled.

His words were like a drenching of cold water. Jacoby grew still and pushed him off her.

"What happened?" he asked with a stunned look on his face.

"There's nothing wrong with being a church girl, Armstrong."

Armstrong wanted to grab her hand and pull her back to him yet he didn't want to frighten this doe-like creature into bolting.

"I may not always do the right thing, but at least I try," she added with a tremble in her voice.

"I know that."

"I need more time," she said quietly.

"Come on, Jacoby," he begged. "I don't want to pressure you, but we've been going out for a couple of weeks now. I thought that you were ready."

"There you go again trying to rush things. You've been waiting only a couple of weeks yet I've been waiting my whole life."

"What!" Armstrong exclaimed, sitting up. "Jacoby, are you trying to tell me that you're a virgin?"

She defensively took her hands and crossed them over her naked breasts.

"Well, I'll be damned," Armstrong said in awe.

"Don't act like I'm a freak or something," she declared in a heated voice. "I've had my chances, but I hadn't met the right guy."

"I'm glad as hell you let me go this far," he said in wonder.

"Shut up," she whispered.

"Oh my God! I can't believe I found a twenty-year-old virgin who looks like you!" he added gleefully.

"You didn't find me because I was never lost," she said brusquely. Jacoby hastily shrugged into her bra and shirt. "I'm ready to go."

"Please don't get mad, Jacoby." He gave her a searching look. "Seriously, I'm glad you told me. Your first time needs to be just right." He paused. "I'll give you more time."

"You sure will," she said as she stood pulling her shorts in place.

When she let herself in the dark house, the hallway was suddenly flooded with light.

Her father stood there glaring at her. "You're fifteen minutes late."

"I'm sorry, Daddy." She stammered, "I lost track of the time."

Abraham pointed at Jacoby.

She looked down. In her haste to get dressed she'd buttoned her shirt up wrong and part of her stomach was exposed.

"He could have been respectful enough to give you time to get dressed before he kicked you out of his car," he said harshly.

With a defensive look on her face she said, "Daddy, it's not what you think it is."

"Don't lie to me, young lady," Abraham's voice boomed, seeming to shake the pictures on the wall.

Sarai came scurrying out the bedroom in her nightgown. "Whatever is going on out here?"

"Your daughter is coming in at all times of night like some hoochie." Again he pointed at Jacoby. "Look! And she's running around half dressed after laying up with that boy."

"Abraham!" Sarai shouted.

"How could you say that about me?" Jacoby said as she brushed past him. "I'm a good daughter to you," she screamed before she slammed her bedroom door. Once inside she threw herself on the bed, buried her head in her arms, and cried a fistful of tears.

The next morning, when Jacoby shuffled into the kitchen her mother sat at the table absently stirring a cup of coffee. "Jacoby, I want to talk to you," she said quietly.

Jacoby took a cereal bowl out of the cabinet and half slammed it on the counter. "Nothing happened, Mom."

She searched her daughter's eyes. "I believe you," she said. "But, I made you an appointment with Doctor Sellers. I want you to protect yourself."

Jacoby stared at her. "I just said that nothing happened."

"And I just said that I believe you. But your clothes were in disarray so that means that you're on the verge. I don't want a relationship that may not be lasting to have a bearing on the rest of your life." She heaved a deep sigh. "Don't tell your father about your appointment," she advised. "It'll make life easier."

Jacoby looked around when she heard a loud cough.

Abraham stood in his work uniform. He held a lunch box in one hand and his car keys in the other. "I heard you're going to the fair in

Jacksonville."

"Yes," she replied in a distant voice.

"I hope you and Armstrong have a good time."

"You can relax," she said in a miffed voice. "We won't be alone. Claudia and Rex are going with us. They're not very good chaperones, though."

"So you're still angry," he acknowledged in a pained voice. "Jacoby, I'm sorry for what I said to you last week. Will you accept my apology?"

"Yes," she answered, not looking at him.

Abraham gave a suspicious snort. "I don't think that you really mean that."

"Daddy, I always mean what I say." She asked challengingly, "Do you?"

Abraham looked down at his feet.

"And I've never lied to you. You hurt my feelings by calling me a 'hoochie.' "

Abraham sat down on the swing next to her. "I guess it's hard for me to see you as an adult. Since you got with Armstrong we don't talk the way we used to. We've always been very close and I miss that."

"Daddy," she said with feeling, "Armstrong hasn't interfered with us. You're never here. You're always at church or work."

"I have been working a lot of hours at the prison lately," he admitted. He put his arm around her shoulder and held her close. "I love you, Jacoby."

"I love you too, Daddy." She chuckled. "I know that you're so possessive of me because I'm an only child." She felt her father's arm tighten around her. She loved his strength. "Relax, I'm not going anywhere anytime soon."

###

With one hand Jacoby held Armstrong's hand and with the other a vanilla ice cream cone she was licking. Some of the ice cream dripped out of the corner of her mouth.

Armstrong leaned over and licked it off.

"That's so gross," Claudia chimed from behind.

"Oh, leave us alone," Jacoby laughed.

"I wonder how long your honeymoon phase is going to last," Claudia continued.

"As long as we're together," Jacoby retorted.

"Man," Rex said. "I remember my early days with Claudia. I used to wait by the phone hoping she would call."

Claudia lightly punched him in the arm. "You still do that," Claudia said. "Don't try and play hard in front of Armstrong."

"Hey, Claudia," he said rubbing his arm. "That kind of hurt."

"You need to check your woman right now," Armstrong said caustically. "Show her who's boss otherwise she'll be wearing the pants."

Claudia gave Armstrong a sharp look.

"I'm not worried about that," Rex said. "Claudia knows what time it is." And then to soften his words he put his arm around her shoulder, pulling her closer to him as they walked.

Jacoby grinned at her friends so obviously in love.

Armstrong said, "Do you guys want to do another ride?"

"Not me," Jacoby said. "I just ate that ice cream cone, and I don't want to get sick."

"Come on and stop being such a baby. We're here to have fun."

"I've been having fun," she protested. "But we've been on every good ride once and that locomotion roller coaster three times."

"I was surprised that you agreed," Claudia said. "You've always been kind of afraid of heights."

"I know," she said. Giving Armstrong a shy look she said, "Lately I've decided to try new things."

"Good," Armstrong said. "That means you'll go on the rollercoaster one more time."

Claudia watched as her best friend was dragged through the crowd.

Rex said, "Do you want to ride again?"

"No," she said with narrowed eyes. "I've had enough for the day."

"Fine by me," he said. "Let's find a place to sit and wait for them."

On their way out of the park Armstrong stopped at a duck shooting booth.

"Step on up and try your luck," an elderly carnival worker said.

Armstrong pointed to a huge panda bear. "How many ducks do I have to shoot in order to win that bear for my girl?"

"Young man, you've got to shoot a perfect score five times."

"And it costs five dollars to play each time?"

"You got it," he said.

Armstrong reached into his wallet and handed the man a wad of dollars.

The man shouted in an attempt to rev up the crowd, "Here we go, people. We have a confident man. Step on up to see the show."

Armstrong picked up the rifle and turned it around, examining it. Suddenly a flush of red flooded his face, making his complexion look ruddy. "You cheat! This rifle is unbalanced. No one could win with this rifle."

Jacoby touched Armstrong's arm. "Baby, get your money back and let's go."

"Yeah, come on, Armstrong," Rex urged.

"I ought to take this rifle and ram it down your throat," Armstrong threatened.

"Whoa, boy," the man said, holding up his hands as if warding off a coming blow.

"I ain't your damn boy," Armstrong growled.

"My apology." He nervously picked up another rifle and handed it to Armstrong. "Sometimes they get worn out from use. Try this one."

"Be glad that I don't shoot you and put your eye out."

The man stepped back warily.

Armstrong aimed at the traveling ducks and shot all of them. When the next group popped up, he quickly annihilated them also. Then he demolished the rest. After he put the rifle down he pointed to the huge panda bear. "Is that the one you want, Jacoby?"

"Yes," she said as she avoided the eyes of the spectators.

Once the panda bear was cut down, Armstrong snatched it from the man, handed it to Jacoby, and then stomped off in the direction of the car.

Claudia looked at Jacoby. "Armstrong needs an anger management class. That scene he just made over a game should raise a red flag for you to stay away from him."

"Claudia, he just doesn't like cheaters," Jacoby said defensively. "Come on. It's been a long day."

"Too long," Claudia murmured quietly to Rex as they followed her.

Jacoby walked out of the ladies' room in the church vestibule.

Armstrong stood in the vestibule clad in a black suit, crisp white shirt, and black tie.

Startled by his sudden appearance she said, "Armstrong! What are you doing here?"

"I thought it was about time I heard my girl sing."

"I'm so happy that you came." She smiled. "Will you come over for dinner after church?"

"Only if you sing good," he teased.

"Oh, I'm real good," she replied.

"Then I'll see you after church."

Jacoby watched with head held high, as Armstrong strode to the front of the church and slid into the pew next to her mother. She couldn't see her mother's face, but she had to stifle a giggle at the way the back of her head bobbed at the shock of him sitting next to her. Then her attention was drawn to her father. From his seat next to the pastor, the rigidity of his gaze as it dwelled on Armstrong was unsettling.

As Jacoby took center stage, every member of the choir stood to attention. The organist and piano player started the prelude to Jacoby's solo. Taking a deep breath, she burst into song. Jacoby's clear voice floated to the ceiling and made everyone feel as if their eyes were on the sparrow.

Sister Sims screamed, "Thank you, Jesus." Then she fell off the front pew onto the floor. An usher ran to her and threw a white sheet over her legs. Deacon White started running up and down the aisle shouting, 'Halleluiah!' over and over again.

As Jacoby belted out the lyrics her eyes locked with Armstrong's and he gave her a wink.

At the close of the announcements Sister Gant asked, "Are there any more announcements for today?"

One of the ushers went to the pulpit, handed Pastor Leroy a check, and with finger held up in the air scurried away.

Pastor Leroy walked to the podium. "Will Armstrong Battle please stand?"

A hush fell over the church.

Armstrong stood.

"Young man, you've given the church a sizeable donation."

"Yes, suh," Armstrong said loud and clear. "I heard that you wanted to start a vacation bible school program for the kids next summer and you needed funding for books."

"That's quite true." Pastor Leroy studied him. "You're a war veteran?"

"Yes, suh. And the good Lord has made it possible for me to donate that to you."

"Then Holy Baptist Trinity Church thanks you for your donation of five hundred dollars."

A gasp reverberated throughout the room.

"Thank you, Jesus!" someone shouted out and then everyone applauded.

Tears of pride streamed down Jacoby's face,

Jacoby's father nodded approvingly.

"Would you like any more potatoes, Armstrong?" Sarai asked.

"No, ma'am," he said, patting his stomach. "I haven't eaten this good since my mother passed."

"I remember your mom. It was sad that she died so young. She was a beautiful woman," Sarai said.

"Thank you."

"So I take it that you're back in Bunnell for a while," Abraham said.

"I don't know about that. I've always wanted to go into business for myself. I'm thinking about getting some training and opening a mechanic shop."

"We have schools like that not too far from Bunnell."

"I know, suh. But if I get my certificate I can make a lot more money elsewhere."

"What are you going to live off until you get that?"

"I get a sizeable disability check from the military every month. I also got a lump sum from the government. For the time being I'm living in my mother's old house, but I'm going to buy some property."

Abraham visibly relaxed. "At least you have a plan."

"I do have a plan. As soon as I get things straightened out, I plan on marrying Jacoby."

A deafening silence filled the room.

Jacoby's mouth went dry.

Sarai's jaw dropped.

Abraham's lips tightened.

Finally, Jacoby found her voice. "No you don't."

A relieved Sarai stared at her daughter.

"I mean," Jacoby stammered, "I'm too young to even think about that."

Armstrong's eyes were diamond hard and his eyes snapped as he stared at Jacoby.

"Good," Sarai said.

"You two haven't known each other long enough," Abraham said in his blustering voice. "Divorce is a sin. So you better think carefully before you get yourself into something that you can't get out of."

The conversation was stilted throughout the rest of dinner.

Soon thereafter Jacoby walked Armstrong to his car.

His harsh profile made her feel uneasy. She said gently, "I think that you should ask a woman to marry you and not make an announcement like that in front of her parents."

He sneered. "As holy as they say they are, I'd think that they'd appreciate me wanting us to have a committed relationship."

"It's too soon."

"Just admit it, Jacoby. You and your family think that you're too good for me."

"That's not true," she protested, trying to smooth his ruffled feathers.

"You're just hangin' out with me until something better comes along."

"Stop being silly. But in the future, if you plan on asking a woman to marry you, don't take for granted that all you have to do is ask." She tried to soften her words by reaching up and planting a soft kiss on his lips.

Armstrong grabbed her. His kiss was rough from pent up sexual frustration.

Jacoby returned it with as much sympathy as passion.

After they broke their kiss, Armstrong said, "I guess I better hurry up and get into the car before I scare you off for good." He climbed inside.

She leaned down and said, "I'm not afraid anymore, Armstrong. I'm ready."

His response was a low growl.

"My parents are going to a church convention next weekend." Jacoby looked down at the ground and muttered, "It would be easier then."

Armstrong beamed. "I'll book us a room in a nice hotel. I want it to be special for you."

"I'm not going to see you until then?" she asked, disappointed.

"Of course. You know we planned to eat meatloaf at the diner on Wednesday."

"I'll meet you there after work."

Jacoby was locking up the library doors, when Claudia appeared out of nowhere. "I'm glad that I caught up with you. Guess what!"

"What?"

"Stefan Wagner has four tickets to go and see Alicia Keyes in Jacksonville and he wants you to be his date."

"Stefan Wagner?" she said doubtfully. "We've never talked so what would make him think that I would go to a concert with him?"

"He and Rex were playing ball. Stefan said that he and Vickie broke up. That means Vickie's sister Jenny can't stand him. It was supposed to be a double date. So he has three extra tickets."

"I don't think so, Claudia. You know that I'm dating Armstrong."

"But this may be your only chance. At the end of the month Stefan goes to go back to North Carolina A & T State University to finish his pharmaceutical degree. He's going to make a lot of money after he graduates."

"I don't care about that."

"You're crazy. Stefan is fine as wine and he's going places."

"I can't go."

"Why?" Claudia glared at her. "Are you and Armstrong exclusive?"

"Yes. Why would you even ask that?"

"I don't know," she said. "Rex hinted at something."

"What did he say?"

"He just said that he hoped you weren't serious about Armstrong."

"Why does Rex care who I date?"

"He doesn't, but I do," Claudia retorted. "Rex was a good friend of Troy's during high school. He seems to know something about Armstrong."

"I don't want to hear any dirt about Armstrong. And Rex shouldn't encourage me to step out on Armstrong. How would he like it if I influenced you to see other men?"

"Rex isn't encouraging anything." She pointed her finger to her chest. "I am."

"Why?" Jacoby asked bluntly.

"Because I don't think Armstrong is right for you."

Jacoby rolled her eyes. "Here we go again! You're never satisfied. Before you were nagging me to get a man and have fun. Now you don't like my choice."

"I just think that there's someone better out there for you."

"Armstrong treats me good and he hasn't pressured me for sex. Guys usually give up on me after a month of waiting. Armstrong's been waiting a lot longer than that."

"Maybe it wouldn't be so easy for him if he wasn't doing someone else."

"Give me a name," Jacoby demanded hotly.

"I don't have one. And I don't know anything about it." She hunched her shoulders. "I just have a feeling that something about him isn't quite right."

"Armstrong is a good man. You saw what he did in church last Sunday."

"But why did he do it?" Claudia wore a cynical look. "He could have put cash in the envelope. He knew that Pastor Leroy was going to make that announcement and he'd get a whole lot of praise. He needed it since your daddy hasn't exactly been rooting for him."

"You look for drama, Claudia. Who walks around with five hundred dollars in cash? Besides, he'll need proof of his donation come income tax time. I'd certainly count it on my taxes."

"Okay,'" Claudia admitted grudgingly. "You're right about that. But still... He comes to church and sits next to your mother and all. He's just a little too slick for me."

"I'm tired of this conversation. Now I have to go to the diner and meet Armstrong."

CHAPTER 3

Jacoby watched Armstrong as he finished up the last of his meal. He had a roll and was sopping up the extra gravy with it.

"Are you seeing anyone else?" she blurted out.

Armstrong choked and grabbed his water and gulped it down. Once he'd regained his composure he said, "Of course not. What would make you ask something like that?"

"I've heard a few whispers," she said, averting her gaze.

"The only person you talk to is that big mouth Claudia," he said with distaste. "Tell her to stay out of my business."

"I'm not saying that Claudia said anything to me," she said, defending her friend. "But Armstrong, look me in the eye and tell me the truth. Are you talking to any other girls?"

Armstrong put his napkin down and folded his hands. "I'm not seeing, dating, sleeping with, or talking to another girl. Females come and go, Jacoby. But you're special. The only reason I'm still in Bunnell is because of you. I love you."

She looked into his eyes and they unflinchingly met hers. She relaxed. "I love you too, Armstrong."

A naked Jacoby stood in front of the mirror and nervously viewed her body. The midnight nipples on her breasts protruded prominently in anticipation. She reached into her dresser and pulled out black lace thong underwear. After ripping the sales tag off she slid into it, braless, she grabbed a black halter dress off the bed, and shrugged into it, finishing her ensemble with black wedge shoes. Jacoby stepped back and took a deep breath.

The doorbell rang.

Grabbing her overnight bag she went to meet Armstrong.

He was dressed in black from head to toe. The only contrast to his attire was a silver dog tag that hung from his neck.

Jacoby took her hand and fingered it. "I've never seen this before. What is it?"

"It's a memory dog tag that I had made for my friends that I lost in battle."

Her heart went out to him. "You're so sweet, Armstrong."

"I try to be," he said as he drew her into his arms.

Jacoby searched Armstrong's mouth, seeking reassurance that she was doing the right thing. Once he freed her mouth she clung to him.

Armstrong took his hand and loosened the knot at the top of her head.

"Armstrong," she protested. "It took me an hour to get that right."

"I like you with your hair down," he said gruffly. "That way I can run my fingers through it." He took his hands and combed through her hair. "I have a booth reserved for us at the Seafood Shack. Are you in the mood for shrimp?"

"Always," she said.

They sat munching on shrimp and hush puppies. "The food here is always delicious," she said. "Daddy and I used to eat here every Wednesday."

"Why?"

"Because Mom usually had choir rehearsal and it would be his responsibility to feed me."

"You and your dad seem really close."

"We are. I'm more like Mom, though. I look like her and talk like her. But Daddy's the disciplinarian of the family, so I had to find ways to get along with him."

"I can't believe that you needed much discipline."

"I had to learn how to get things out of him," she chuckled. "Every time there was a school dance, which was something that he didn't approve of, I'd make him sweet potato pie. He'd know immediately that something was up."

"I love sweet potato pie, too," he said.

"When I want something out of you, I'll make you one."

Armstrong pinned her eyes with his. "I should probably make you one, Jacoby, since I definitely want something out of you."

Sexual tension enveloped the table.

With very cool deliberation, Jacoby wiped her mouth with a napkin. "I'm ready to go. Are you?"

"More than!"

Jacoby looked around the hotel room. "This is nice, Armstrong."

"I want only the best for you, Jacoby."

"I know that."

28

"I'm going to get some ice from the machine down the hall."

Once she was alone, she turned on the radio on the nightstand. Manipulating the dial she found her favorite radio station. Immediately the weekly broadcast of love songs filled the room. She went into the bathroom and quickly divested herself of her dress. Then she slid into a nightgown with a matching silk robe she'd ordered from a Victoria Secret catalogue. When she reentered the room, Armstrong sat at the small table.

He was shirtless and his bare chest glistened in the meager light coming through the drapes. He'd lit a small scented candle and a bucket of ice, a bottle of rum and two small cans of pineapple juice sat on the table.

"Come join me," he said.

She posed in front of him. "You're a bad influence on me Mr. Armstrong Battle."

"You're going to be twenty-one next week, so I don't see the harm."

"Well, since I'm not driving I guess it's okay."

Sitting down across from him she quaffed the drink he prepared. "This is really good, Armstrong."

"That's because yours is mostly juice. I don't need chaser myself." Draining his glass he said, "I've made plans for us for your birthday next weekend."

"You have?" she asked excitedly.

"I thought that we might go to Disney World for the weekend. But you'll have to take two days off from work in order to make the trip worthwhile."

"That sounds like fun. I haven't been since I graduated from high school."

"I've never been," he said.

Jacoby took her forefinger and smoothed his furrowed brow. "Can Rex and Claudia come too? I know that they'll pay their own way."

"I don't like you around Claudia," he said curtly.

"The two of you need to learn how to get along. She's been my best friend since elementary school and is very important to me. And I thought that you liked Rex."

"He lets Claudia have her own way too much. But go ahead and invite them. I'll make all the arrangements."

Keith Sweat's melodious voice floated into the room. Armstrong stood and stretched out his hand. "I want you, Jacoby."

Without hesitation she walked into his arms. They swayed to the music and she soon felt Armstrong's hands slide down to cup her round buttocks. Armstrong squeezed them before taking her hand and guiding her to the bed. He sat on the edge of the bed and removed his shoes and socks. His right foot was oddly shaped in comparison to the left. And he was missing two toes. Armstrong kept his head bent, avoiding her eyes. There was a palpable tension in the air around them. "I didn't come back from the war the way I went, Jacoby."

"I know," she murmured. "But it doesn't matter." She slid closer to him and leaned her head on his shoulder. "It's a badge of honor. I've never seen a foot more beautiful, Armstrong."

He drew a sigh of relief so deep it seemed to come from his bowels. "You're lying, Jacoby. But I love you all the more for saying it." Then he flicked off the lamp and gently pushed her to her back.

Jacoby's arms crept up around Armstrong's neck.

"You're very beautiful." He pulled up her nightgown.

Jacoby raised her arms and her breasts popped free.

Armstrong reached down and bit her breast.

"Ouch!" she said.

"Your skin is soft," he growled. "That's good." Then he licked the skin he'd just bitten.

"That feels better," she moaned.

"What's my name?" he demanded in a thick voice.

"Armstrong," she answered.

"You belong to me, Jacoby." Then Armstrong covered her body with his. With his fingers he probed her until she was wet. Then he pushed inside her.

Jacoby felt a sharp pain and then, enjoying the feel, she relaxed.

Armstrong pummeled her and she clung to him for survival. After endless pumping he exploded inside her.

Jacoby cradled him to her and soon she heard his deep breathing. Sliding free, she turned onto her side and fell asleep.

Hours later, Jacoby felt herself being pulled close to Armstrong. His breath fanned her cheek. "I want you to climb on top of me. We'll get more friction."

"I don't know what you mean," she said.

"I'll guide you." Armstrong rolled onto his back dragging her on top of him. He straddled his thighs with hers.

"Sit up," he whispered.

Once she did he guided her over his manhood. "Start slowly, and move up and down."

Once she got her rhythm, Jacoby enjoyed the sensation and she was soon rewarded with a gushing wetness that sopped between the two of them.

A look of rapt pleasure was plastered on his face as Armstrong's hands steered her movements.

She increased her speed, then she slowed again tightening her vagina walls around his shaft. Jacoby slid up and down Armstrong's slick manhood.

"You're a natural, baby," he shouted.

She threw her head back, loving the feel of control she had over his body. She took her hands and planted them on his thighs circumventing his body movement. Jacoby wiggled up and down pleasuring herself and him. Finally, she was ready to allow their wet bodies time to rest. "Oh! Oh! Oh!" Jacoby screamed right before she came. Satiated, she snuggled next to Armstrong and fell into a deep sleep.

Armstrong possessively slung his arm around her middle before he drifted back to sleep.

"Nope," Claudia said. "I don't want to go."

"You're supposed to be my best friend," Jacoby said in a mournful voice. "You've got to try and get along with my man."

"Oh," she said. "So now he's your man. Does that mean…"

"I'm not going to discuss it," Jacoby replied firmly.

"How was it?" Claudia asked with a crooked smile.

Jacoby looked over her shoulder to see if her parents could overhear them from the front porch. Since she couldn't get a visual of them she whispered, "It was good."

"Good? What the hell is that supposed to mean? You should be running around grinning like the Cheshire Cat."

"I don't want everyone in my business like you do. Good grief! The first time you and Rex did it you told everyone at school."

"It was something to crow about," Claudia said defensively. "I just couldn't keep it to myself."

"You better be glad that he's marrying you. In this small town…the boys talk."

"Who the hell cares what they say? They tell it anyhow. You can best believe Armstrong told someone that he popped your cherry."

"Shut up with that mess, Claudia." A look of irritation was on Jacoby's face. "I can see why you and Armstrong don't get along."

"We don't get along because he's too controlling. He wants your total attention every minute and if he's not around, he expects you to sit around and wait for him to show up."

"That's not true," Jacoby denied. "It's just that we enjoy each other's company so much we don't need anyone else around."

With a sad look Claudia said, "It won't be long before you don't have time for me at all."

"That's ridiculous," Jacoby scoffed. "You'll always be my friend and I'll always make time for you. Now please, will you and Rex go to Orlando with us this weekend?"

Claudia heaved a long sigh. "Okay. I'll check with Rex, but I'm sure he won't mind. We were trying to figure out what to get you for your birthday anyhow."

"We're going to leave Friday night after I get off from work and travel back on Tuesday. Armstrong's booked adjoining suites."

"What's our half of the bill going to be?"

"Armstrong's paying. He said that I'm his girl so he should front the bill."

Claudia admitted, "I guess he's good for something."

That evening Jacoby sat in the den watching the news with her parents.

Abraham changed the channel in disgust. "Another star is in rehab. Then they come out and get a reality show. To think, Sarai, these young people are going to make decisions for us one day."

Sarai chuckled, "They're not going to make any decisions. In order to do that you have to vote and I somehow doubt that's on their priority list. Thank God we have Jacoby to look out for us." She gave her daughter a gentle smile. "And I think she's pretty smart."

"Our daughter is smart. Jacoby, your birthday is Friday. Are you taking the day off from work?"

"Yes. I'm going with Armstrong to Disney World for the weekend."

A tense silence enveloped the room.

"Jacoby," Abraham said in a stern voice. "I don't think…"

"Don't start, Daddy," she said quietly. "If I want to spend the weekend in Orlando I will."

"I won't have you coming and going as you please. Or staying the night in some hotel with a man you're not married to," he growled. "It's a sin."

"I'm a grown woman. I'll be twenty-one."

"Being grown is not just a number," he said angrily. "And you live in my house."

"But I don't have too," she said carefully.

"As long as you live here you'll abide by my rules."

"Don't force me out," she said with a stubborn tilt to her chin.

Abraham jumped to his feet. He looked pointedly at his wife. "I'm going to the prison."

The slamming of the front door shook the pictures on the wall.

Sarai looked at her daughter. "Are you sure that you know what you're doing?"

"Absolutely," Jacoby answered.

Jacoby was shelving the last of the books for the day when her cell phone rang. She smiled when she saw that it was Armstrong. "I'm just on my way to meet you at Claudia and Rex's."

"I can't make it."

"What?" she exclaimed.

"I got a phone call last night. The army wants me to do a commercial pumping up the military."

"Are you serious?"

"I know," he said excitedly. "I'm at Patrick Air Force Base in Melbourne shooting it right now. I thought that I'd be back in time, but they need me to stay another night."

"But we have plans," she wailed.

"I'll make it up to you."

"But it's not just me you're disappointing," she said angrily. "There's Claudia and Rex too. We can't even go without you because you made all the arrangements and have the paperwork and everything."

"Jacoby," Armstrong said in a contrite voice, "I know that you're disappointed but my country needs me."

"Needs you for what?" she said derogatorily. "A commercial that tricks people into thinking they should join that madness overseas."

"America is doing great things over there," he retorted sharply. "This is my chance to continue to be supportive."

"Are you going to take your shoe off and let them film your foot too?" she demanded sharply.

Armstrong said in a quiet voice, "That was mean, Jacoby." Hurt reverberated through the telephone connection.

Once Jacoby realized that Armstrong had hung up, she burst into tears. Wiping them away, she redialed Armstrong's cell but it went to voicemail. "Honey, I'm sorry I said that. Call me."

When Jacoby pulled into the driveway she spied her dad sitting on the front porch reading the paper. He lowered it in surprise when he saw her. Grabbing her suitcase out the back seat she slowly walked up the sidewalk.

"I prayed that you would change your mind and you did," he said quietly.

"Prayer didn't change my mind," she said gloomily. Without another word she went into the house.

Her mother met her in the hallway. She stared in her daughter's eyes that were red from crying. "Why are you here? What happened?"

"Armstrong had to go out of town on an emergency."

"What kind of emergency?"

"I don't want to talk about it."

"I'm sorry to hear that, honey," Sarai said. She took the palm of her hand and rubbed Jacoby's back in a soothing gesture. "Your gift is on your bed and I made you a cake."

"I don't want any right now, Mom." She went into the room and slammed the door. Then pushing her gift aside, she threw herself face down onto the bed and curled up into a ball. Less than an hour later she heard a banging on her door. "I'm resting!" she shouted.

Her door was pushed open and Claudia stalked in.

"I don't want to hear it right now," she said morosely.

"I got your message, but Armstrong called before you did. Actually he called Rex. I didn't talk to the jerk."

"Don't start," she said with a miserable look on her face.

"Okay. Besides, I don't want to be a part of ruining your birthday. Get up. We're going to the movies."

"I'm not in the mood," she grumbled.

"Don't let Armstrong ruin your special day," Claudia said and her eyes were hard. "Rex and Stefan are in the den putting up with, I mean, talking to your dad."

"Stefan Wagner?" Jacoby asked surprised.

"Yes," she answered smoothly.

"I don't know about that, Claudia."

"So you're going to stay home and pout on your birthday?" Claudia protested, "You only turn twenty-one once. You should enjoy yourself."

"You're right," she said, sitting up. "But I need thirty minutes to freshen up."

"Make it twenty-five. I'll go and wait with the others."

When Jacoby walked into the room in a lace camisole shirt, tight fitting jeans, and heels, her eyes went straight to Stefan.

His eyes widened in appreciation when he saw her and he stood.

Out of the corner of her eye she saw Claudia elbow Rex, who then stood.

Stefan also wore jeans which he's paired with a green IZOD shirt, but on his feet were a pair of black leather oxfords. "Happy birthday,

Jacoby."

"Hi," she said shyly. "I hope that I didn't keep you guys waiting too long."

"It was worth the wait," Stefan replied in a smooth voice.

Rex cleared his throat. "If we're going to make the eight-thirty show we better get going."

"I'll walk y'all to the door," Abraham gushed.

After the others walked out the door, Jacoby turned to her father who smiled approvingly at Stefan. "Bye, Daddy," she said and kissed him on the cheek.

He flushed with pleasure. "When your momma gets back from her mission department meeting at the church I'll tell her where you are."

"Thanks," she said. A truce settled between the two.

"Well," Claudia said as they sat on a bench at the movie theatre, "what do you think of Stefan?"

"He doesn't talk much, does he?" she said as she watched Rex and Stefan in the concession line.

"I'd rather a quiet man than one that talks a lot of nonsense." All of a sudden Claudia grew very still. Her lips protruded and she began tapping her foot nervously as she glared across the room.

Jacoby followed Claudia's line of vision.

A tall girl with light brown eyes stared. Then she began to saunter towards them.

"Do you need to go the restroom?" Claudia asked hastily.

"Not really," she said. "You go ahead and I'll wait here for you."

"Never mind," Claudia said.

"Hello, Claudia," The girl stood in front of them and planted her hands on her hips. "Long time no see."

An awkward silence hung between them. "Hello, Alexandria," Claudia said.

"You must be Jacoby. I've heard a lot about you."

Jacoby felt the hairs on her neck rise as she stared into the light brown eyes. "Really?" Her eyebrows rose in surprise. "From who?"

Claudia interrupted Alexandria's answer. "Are you going to be in town for awhile?"

"Maybe," she answered mysteriously. "Jacoby, you look like your mother."

"You know my mother?" Jacoby asked.

"Yes. You know how small Bunnell is. Even if you don't know

someone you know something about them." She said with a smirk, "Isn't that right, Claudia?"

"Today is Jacoby's birthday and we're trying to have a good time," Claudia said roughly.

"It is?" Alexandria said, a look of antagonism appeared on her face briefly. A throng of people pushed past them heading into the dark theatre now that doors were open. "It looks like the movie is starting. Maybe I'll see you around. And by the way, Jacoby," she said in a heavy northeastern accent, "Happy Birthday."

As they watched her saunter off Jacoby asked, "How do you know her?"

"I don't," Claudia snapped. "And you don't want to. Let's go. The boys are coming with our food."

###

After the movie, Jacoby sat in the front bucket seat of Stefan's Acura as he navigated through the queue of cars in the theater parking lot.

"That was a good movie," Rex said, "but I wish Angelina would get naked once in awhile."

"She's a big star," Stefan laughed. "She doesn't have to do that anymore."

"I like action movies but the fact is they kind of lose something for me because I know body doubles really do all the work," Jacoby said.

"The studios won't let them do their own stunts because of insurance," Rex said.

"It's kind of like back-up singers. They make the star sound good and a lot of times people don't even know their names. I like people to get the praise they deserve."

"That's an admirable quality, Jacoby," Stefan said.

Jacoby saw the glint of his pearl white teeth in the darkness.

"A lot of people would think that it shouldn't matter as long as they're getting paid."

"Money isn't everything," Jacoby said.

"I hate to interrupt this highly intelligent conversation, but is anyone else hungry?" Rex asked from the back seat.

"I thought that we'd go and grab something to eat at the Red Lobster," Stefan said.

"You can't be hungry again," Jacoby teased.

"I'm like a camel," he replied. "I gorge myself all summer in order to store up for the winter while I'm away at college."

"Okay," Jacoby laughed. "Claudia?" Jacoby turned around and

peered at Claudia in the back seat. "What's going on with you? You've been awfully quiet."

"I'm going to opt out of going to get something to eat," she said quietly as she stared out the window. She paused, "I don't feel very well."

"Claudia," Rex asked with concern on his face, "what's the matter?"

"Nothing," she said still not looking at them. "I guess that hot dog I ate at the movie theatre didn't agree with me. I'm sorry to mess up your birthday, Jacoby."

"You didn't mess up my birthday," she protested. "If you're sick, you're sick."

After they watched Claudia and Rex go into the house, Stefan turned to her. "I guess it's just you and me."

She shifted nervously in her seat. "I'd like to call it a night, too, if you don't mind."

Stefan hesitated before saying, "If that's your wish."

In Jacoby's driveway, they sat in the dark confines of the sports coupe. "Jacoby, I know that I have to leave for school in a week, but I'd like to see you again."

"Stefan," she said carefully, "I don't think that's a good idea."

"Why," he asked, "because of Armstrong Battle?"

"Yes."

"Rex told me how he let you down."

"Armstrong didn't mean to disappoint me but something important came up," she retorted heatedly.

"More important than you?" Stefan queried gently. "I can't see it."

"He'll make it up to me," she said with a stubborn thrust to her chin. "Listen, Stefan. You seem like a really nice guy, but I'm not going to dump my boyfriend, someone I love, just because he disappointed me one time."

"I understand, Jacoby, and I won't press you." He said in a sincere voice, "I hope things work out for you."

"Thank you, Stefan." She leaned over and kissed him on the cheek. "Have a good school year."

"It's my last so it should be the best," he said. "Take care of yourself, Jacoby."

"I intend to," she said before opening her door. She turned on the front step, and waved goodbye to Stefan who'd waited to make sure that she was safely in the house before leaving.

CHAPTER 4

When Jacoby and Sarai exited the doors of the church, Armstrong stood by his car with a rose.

Jacoby's heart palpitated.

"I guess that means he's sorry," Sarai whispered.

"He better be," Jacoby whispered back. She halted her footsteps and her mother did the same. "I'm not going to him."

Armstrong shuffled over to them. He said to Sarai, "How are you doing today, ma'am?"

Sarai grunted a reply.

He handed Jacoby one red rose. "Please don't hit me with it," he said humbly.

At Jacoby's side, Sarai smothered a chuckle.

"I can't behave like that on church grounds," Jacoby said. "And you knew that when you came here like this."

"I just got back."

"And…"

"I hoped that you and I could go somewhere and talk. I know that it's a little late, but I'd like to take you out to celebrate your birthday."

"I'll think about it," Jacoby answered with a bland look on her face. "Call me later."

"I have everything all set up and waiting." He begged, "Please let me make it up to you."

"You can't buy back time," Sarai interjected with a negative shake of her head.

"I know that, ma'am. But I can promise not to disappoint your daughter again."

"We'll see," Sarai said with a touch of sadness.

Jacoby looked at the remorseful expression on Armstrong's face. "Oh, all right." Shrugging out of her choir robe she handed it to her mother. "Please take this home with you. Are you okay by yourself?"

"I'm feeling kind of poorly, but I'll be okay. I'm going to go home and take a nap."

Jacoby gave her mother an anxious look. "I can wait with you until Daddy comes out."

"I'm fine. Go have fun."

"Well, if you're sure."

"Scoot."

Jacoby gave her mother a peck on the cheek and then walked towards Armstrong's car.

He rushed past her to open the door and she slid inside.

Al Greene crooned about love and happiness as they rode through town. As Armstrong pulled up to his house Jacoby shot him a dark look. "I thought that you said you have something planned for me."

"I do," he said. He stared at Jacoby who had her arms folded defiantly in front of her. "Give it a chance, Miss Grumpy."

Jacoby eyed Armstrong's rundown house. The grey paint was peeling and the floorboards on the front porch were broken in several places. A feeling of pity enveloped her. "I'm sorry, Armstrong."

"Me too, Jacoby."

Once they were inside the small house she looked around. "It looks better in here."

Armstrong grinned. "I cleaned up because I knew that you were coming. While I was at Patrick Air Force Base I went to the commissary. I bought a tablecloth, a set of dishes, wine glasses, and candles." He grabbed a Bic lighter and lit the tapered candles in the middle of the square table in the kitchen.

"Don't tell me you cooked?" she joked.

"Of course not!" he grinned. "But I did pick up two dinners from the Silas's Soul Food Restaurant on Baker Drive."

"It's not Disney World, but it's not too bad an apology."

"I'll take you another time," he promised.

"I'm going to keep you to that," she replied in her most serious voice. She gave him a peck on the cheek.

Armstrong's hands wandered down her body. Once they reached her buttocks he cupped them grinding her into him.

After awhile Jacoby withdrew her mouth from his. "I'm hungry," she said.

"Me too," he said suggestively.

After they finished the meal of fried chicken, garlic mashed potatoes, candied yams, and corn, Armstrong sat back and patted his stomach. He gave Jacoby a possessive look. "While I was away, all I did was think about you."

"Same here," she said. "Let's not fight anymore."

"Let's not."

"Why didn't you call me back?" she lightly scolded. "I left you a message."

"The director was calling me and I didn't have time to straighten things out the way I should have. I did call you later that night but your cell went straight to voicemail. "Where were you?" he demanded.

"I went to the movies with Claudia," she answered, avoiding his penetrating gaze.

There was a tense silence. "Was it just the two of you?"

"No," she said evasively. "You know that Rex doesn't let her go anywhere without him." Guilt at her omission of Stefan made her jump to her feet and start clearing the dishes.

"Claudia leads him around like he's Rex the dog," he said derisively.

"Don't badmouth my friends. I don't let them say negative things about you."

Armstrong frowned. "What have they been saying behind my back?"

Flustered, she said, "Nothing. I just told you that."

Armstrong's eyes narrowed in concentration as he watched Jacoby's averted face. "I have some news you might like."

"What?'

Armstrong handed her a letter from the counter behind them. "This was in the mailbox when I got home."

She skimmed the paper. "This is great. You got accepted into tech school."

"Yep," he said. "I didn't know if they'd let me in because my grades from high school were so bad. But I blew the aptitude test out of the water."

"Does this mean you're staying in Bunnell?"

I guess so. I'm going to stay put till I graduate. Then I'm going to open my own mechanic shop. There's a lot of money in that."

"I'm so proud of you, Armstrong."

He grinned. "Thank you, Jacoby. I wouldn't have even applied if it hadn't been for you."

After they cleaned up the kitchen, they cuddled on the couch watching a rerun of *Scandal*.

"I hate this show." Armstrong grabbed the remote control. "Let's watch something else."

"Nope," she said grabbing it back and holding it out of his reach. "It's my belated birthday, so I get what I want. I'd rather watch this instead of *Band of Brothers* again," she drawled.

"Hey! That's based on a true story of those soldiers' lives."

"There's not one black person in that series."

"That's because back then the military was segregated."

"How do you feel about that?"

"That's the way it was." Armstrong shrugged. "We can't rewrite history. In spite of that it's a great show. It's better than that *Scandal* mess. That black chick screwing those white men is disgusting."

"I don't mind that so much," Jacoby said. "But that president isn't a nice guy."

"Are you trying to tell me that you'd sleep with a white man?" Armstrong sneered. "I'd beat your ass half to death if I ever found out."

"How dare you say that to me?" Jacoby demanded. "I'm not married to you and even if I was, the fact that you think it's okay for a man to hit a woman..."

Armstrong cut her off. "Gee whiz, Jacoby. I was only kidding." He grabbed the remote, and turned off the television.

She continued to glare daggers at him.

Armstrong patted her cheek lightly. "You know that I'd never hurt you, Jacoby. I love you too much for that." He lifted Jacoby into his arms and headed towards his bedroom. "Let me give you your birthday present." Armstrong laid her on the bed in the darkened room. He impatiently stripped her of her dress.

She heard a rip.

Shocked, she said, "You tore my dress."

"I'll buy you another," he promised.

Armstrong took his hands and tugged off her panties. Then he spread her legs and entered her with his fingers. Jacoby relaxed and let him do his magic as he explored every bit of her desire. When he finally withdrew his fingers he licked the moisture off. "You taste as good as candy." With one quick motion he undid the front closure of her bra. He stared at the mocha colored breasts that thrust towards him. "Every time I see you naked, you seem even more beautiful, Jacoby. I love you very much."

Not replying, Jacoby mentally pushed away the sourness of evening.

Armstrong got naked and joined her on the bed. As he covered her body with his, Armstrong devoured one ripe breast.

Jacoby flung her hands over her head and let him have his way. "Oh, Armstrong," she panted, "yes, yes, yes."

Armstrong then began to lick the nipple on the other. After an eternity he stopped. "Are you ready?"

"Yes."

Armstrong rolled onto his back taking him with her.

After he was wet she straddled him and grabbing his member slid it inside her moistness, she began to move. Jacoby worked her muscles, clutching him, riding him, shimmying up and down on him. Sweat poured down her back in the hot, steamy, room.

Armstrong shouted, "Oh, my God!"

Only then did she collapse on top of him.

The next morning, Jacoby lay on her back staring at the crack in the ceiling. Then her eyes shifted to Armstrong's flat stomach.

His manhood lay limply to one side and she took her fingernail and grazed it. Drowsily, he opened his eyes. "Do you want some more?"

"I knew that would wake you," she teased. "I have to be getting home. You know how Daddy is."

Armstrong grunted. "He's going to be mad already. What's another couple of hours?"

"I have to go so I can get ready for work. And since my car isn't here you have to take me."

"I'm tired. Why don't you take the day off so we can sleep in?"

"Sally depends on me."

"I know. Every time I come to your job she's in the back on the computer and you're up front doing everything."

"But it works for us. I like helping customers and reading to the kids on Fridays. Computers aren't my thing."

"But they don't pay you a damn thing. You can't move out from your parents' house because you can't afford it."

"I admit that I'd like it if they paid me more, but at least I have a steady job in today's job market. The public library isn't going to close."

The ringing of Armstrong's cell phone interrupted them. "Hello? Yes, this is Armstrong Battle."

Jacoby stood and picked her clothes off the floor and began dressing.

"No," Armstrong said. "I never thought about it. Are you serious? Of course I'll meet with you. I'll be back there tomorrow morning. Yeah! I know where that is. Thanks, Mr. Baylor." After closing his phone he looked at Jacoby. "Guess what?"

"What?"

"That was an agent."

Jacoby's head jerked in surprise. "An agent?"

"He saw the trailer for the public announcement commercial and wants to talk to me about signing with his agency."

"Get out of here!"

"He wants to meet with me tomorrow." Armstrong got out of bed and began pulling on his underwear. "He thinks that I have talent."

"But you never said that you want to be an actor."

"I loved doing that commercial. It was kind of exciting."

"But what about school?"

"This isn't a sure thing, Jacoby. But I'm willing to check it out. I mean, how often does something like this happen to someone from Bunnell?"

"Where do you have to go?"

"I have to go to Miami. That's where his office is."

"How long will you be gone?" she asked quietly.

"Just a day or two. I'll call you."

Claudia chortled so long she got the hiccups. In between deep breaths she stammered, "Oh my God! Armstrong thinks that he can be an actor?"

"Shush, Claudia. You act like you're not in a public library."

Claudia took her hand and covered her mouth, trying to smother her laughter but it was no use.

Jacoby couldn't help chuckling too.

"When is he coming back?"

"He called me right before you got here," Jacoby answered. "He'll be gone until the weekend."

Finally subduing herself, Claudia asked with a hopeful look that she couldn't disguise, "Does that mean that he'll be moving there?"

"He might. I don't know why he hates Bunnell so much. I like the small town feeling. Our town reminds me of Mayberry but with black people."

"Rex said that Armstrong had a really miserable childhood. After his mother died, he and his brother were so poor, that sometimes they wore the same clothes to school three or four days in a row. One time this kid was making fun of him and he broke his nose."

"What?" Jacoby's mouth dropped open from surprise.

"That's why he joined the army the minute he graduated. He sent Troy a check from his allotment every month but hardly ever visited."

"Gee!" she said in a sad voice. "No wonder he hates this place."

That evening, when Jacoby walked into the kitchen, her mother sat at the table. Her hands covered her face and she was sobbing.

Stunned Jacoby asked, "Mom, why are you crying?"

Sarai picked up a paper towel and wiped her tears. "Your father will talk to you about it when he gets home."

"Where is he?"

"He had to go to the prison on an emergency."

"But today's his day off."

"He had something he had to handle down there that couldn't wait."

Jacoby pursed her lips in displeasure. "Obviously something has upset you, so he should have stayed at home."

Sarai stood and went to the kitchen and began to fill the sink with water, adding dish detergent. "You know how your father is," she said in a tired voice. "Once he gets something in his head there's no changing his mind."

"Why won't you tell me what's upset you?" Anxiety made Jacoby's voice shrill. "I don't see why I have to wait to hear it from daddy."

"It's not my place," Sarai said. Fresh tears streamed down her face. "It is what it is."

"Mom, have you and Daddy been fighting about me and Armstrong again?"

"No," she denied. "Now go and change while I get dinner ready. Put on something nice. We're having company."

"Company! You're not in the mood to cook for company."

Sarai said in a small voice, "Your father insists."

In a huff, Jacoby stomped to her bedroom.

Afterward, Jacoby sat in the swing on the front porch. When her father drove up she rushed over to him. "What's going on?" she demanded. "Why is Mom so upset?"

"Let's go into the house, Jacoby," he said, avoiding her eyes. "I need to talk to you about something."

Jacoby sat on the couch close to her mother. Her father sat in the chair across from them. He cleared his throat. "We're going to be having a house guest for an undetermined length of time."

"A houseguest?" Jacoby asked in a perplexed tone. "Who is it?"

"She's a girl who's been incarcerated at the prison for petty larceny. They released her last week and she got into some trouble again. I thought that they were going to let her out today, but they're going to keep her for another thirty days."

"Thank God for small reprieves," Sarai said in a broken voice.

Abraham gave his wife a reproachful look. "She broke her probation by drinking so they're also fitting her for a SCRAM bracelet to wear once she's released."

A sense of foreboding filled her gut. "Why are you bringing some prison bird here to stay?" Jacoby asked apprehensively. "You and I are at work all day, but mom will be here alone with her. How do we know that it's safe to have her here?"

"Sometimes people need a helping hand, Jacoby," he said quietly.

"Don't mom and I have any say in this? I pay bills here too, Daddy. And I don't feel like feeding some stranger."

Abraham drew in a long breath. "Alexandria's not really a stranger, Jacoby. She's your sister."

Jacoby felt as if the wind had been knocked out of her. She jerked spasmodically and her arm knocked a candy dish that was on the end table to the floor. It shattered into pieces on the tile, "Alexandria?" she gulped. The light brown eyes of the woman who'd approached her and Claudia at the movies resurfaced.

"Yes, she's named after me."

Sarai jumped to her feet, covered her face with her hands, and ran out the room.

Jacoby's eyes filled with tears. "You cheated on Mom?"

He hung his head and admitted, "Yes, I broke my marriage vows."

"How old is Alexandria?"

"She's six months older than you, Jacoby."

"You've been a deacon for twenty-five years," she shrieked, "and going to church every Sunday!"

"Your mom and I were having a tough time."

"That's no excuse. You fix things with your wife and not turn to another woman," Jacoby said in utter disgust. "So all this time you were spending at the prison was because of her?"

"Yes."

"You were sneaking behind our backs so you could be with her."

"After all these years of neglecting Alexandria I felt that I needed to bond with her."

"What would make you think that this is okay?" she asked stridently. "Why should mom and I have to deal with your infidelity?"

"You're old enough to understand these things happen sometime, Jacoby."

"I don't have to understand a damn thing! Why after all this time are you bringing her here to live?"

"Watch your mouth," he admonished her. "She has nowhere else to go."

"Where's her 'hoochie' of a mother?"

Abraham looked at the disgust in his daughter's eyes and lowered his. "Shirley passed many years ago."

"Tough break," Jacoby retorted harshly.

"Don't speak ill of the dead."

"Don't chastise me," she said sharply.

"I'm a godly man. I can't deny my firstborn any longer."

Jacoby felt as if she'd been punched in her gut.

"I have to help my child or God will punish me."

"I think I'm going to be sick," Jacoby said and placed her hand on her stomach.

"I know that this is upsetting to you. But I'm a deacon. I have to set an example."

"It's too late for that," she sneered.

"I've repented to God." He looked at his daughter's stricken face. "Now I'm begging you. Please forgive me, Jacoby."

She shook her head no.

"I hope in time that you'll understand." Abraham searched Jacoby's eyes for a glimmer of understanding and found none. "Sometimes people get roped into situations and they don't know how to get out of them."

"Are you now going to blame a dead woman for making you cheat on your wife? Could it get any worse?"

"I'm not blaming Shirley," Abraham denied. "I'm the one who was married. She's gone now, and hopefully she's at peace with God."

She snorted loudly in disbelief.

"Jacoby, once Alexandria comes to live here, please don't blame her for being your sister. She's innocent, just like you. This is my shame and no one else's."

"I don't want this girl here. And mom doesn't want her here. I'm going to find an apartment for us to move into. You stay here with your firstborn." Jacoby said in a stone cold voice, "I don't want any part of this."

The next morning Jacoby woke to a silent house and went in search of her mother. She pushed her bedroom door open and saw the outline of her mother lying alone in the bed. Jacoby crept over to her and crawled into the bed next to her. She slid her arm around her mother's waist. "Mom, I'm here for you."

"I apologize, Jacoby."

"For what?" Her surprise reverberated throughout the room.

"I should have told you about this a long time ago, so it wouldn't have been such a shock."

Jacoby whimpered, "Why didn't you leave Daddy when you found out what he'd done?"

"Because I understood why he sought comfort in another woman's arms."

"There's no excuse for what he did."

"Jacoby, your father and I were married for seven years before I got pregnant. We'd been trying over and over and I couldn't seem to conceive."

"So what! That happens to a lot of couples. Maybe it was Daddy's problem and not yours," she said caustically.

"It got to where I became very despondent, and I wasn't good company."

"Then Daddy should have comforted you, not run the street like a single man."

"I felt like a failure," Sarai said in a sober voice. "So when I found out about Alexandria, I didn't have the will to keep him from his child."

"You didn't keep Daddy from her. Obviously he didn't want to own up to his responsibility."

"But he did. Once she was born Alexandria lived with us for a couple of months."

"What!"

"I was going to raise her as my own, but I got pregnant with you and all my prayers were answered. I didn't want her around."

"So a lot of people know about this," Jacoby said with shame.

"It was the talk of town. I'm embarrassed for the part I played. I could have raised you and Alexandria as sisters, but I didn't want to. I made your father take her back to her mother. She had a very rough childhood, and I feel guilty."

"Don't. I'd have done the same thing."

"Now the chickens have come home to roost and I have to accept it."

"No you don't. Before Alexandria gets out of prison," Jacoby said with distaste, "I'll find a place for us."

"I'm not going to leave your father, Jacoby. He begged my forgiveness many years ago and I gave it."

Jacoby was on her way out the front door headed to work.

Her father was climbing the porch stairs. "Hello, Jacoby."

"Don't speak to me," she said coldly before she got in her car and sped out of the driveway.

Sally peeked over her computer monitor. "There are customers at the desk that need to be checked out."

"Do you think that you can work the desk today? I don't feel like dealing with the public."

Sally gave her an appraising look. "What's the matter?"

"Nothing," she said her eyes sliding away Sally's. "I just don't feel very well."

"Okay," she said, obligingly. "We'll do role reversal." Sally handed her a list. "This list needs to be entered into our data base. That should keep you busy without being bothered."

"Thank you, Sally." Jacoby took the list and began entering the numbers on the Excel spreadsheet. After a couple of hours she had completed the task. Hmm. That was easier and more fun than I thought it would be. At lunch instead of eating Jacoby stared blankly into space. 'I don't know her and you don't want to.' Claudia's words reverberated in her head. She picked up the phone and called her. "Claudia, do you have to close at the bank today?"

"No."

"Good. Can we get together around six? I need to talk to you about something."

"Okay," she said. "Do you want me to come over to your house?"

"No," she said. "Meet me at the park."

"Okay," Claudia said, wariness creeping into her voice. "Is something the matter?"

"I don't know," Jacoby said. "I'll see you this evening."

The balmy October breeze blew the leaves backward and the smell of the park's flowers infiltrated Jacoby's senses. She grabbed another handful of Fritos corn chips and waited.

Claudia's gait was hurried as she crossed the street. A car blew its horn as she dodged through the cars waiting at the light.

Breathless, she plopped down on the bench next to Jacoby. "Hey, girl, what's so urgent?"

"What do you know about Alexandria Spooner?"

Claudia froze.

"Why did you tell me at the movie theatre that I didn't want to know her?" Jacoby asked accusingly.

"I just kind of heard stuff about her, that's all, Jacoby."

Jacoby's face flushed with anger and she clenched her teeth. "What kind of stuff?" she demanded.

"You know how Bunnell is," Claudia said evasively. "You don't need to pay attention to the rumor mill."

"But have you paid attention to it?"

A squirrel started up the oak tree in front of them and Claudia seemed engrossed in its progress. "Jacoby, I don't want to be caught in the middle of anything. I find it best to keep my mouth shut about things and mind my own business."

"Since when?" Jacoby asked harshly.

She put her arm around her friend's shoulder. "I can see you're upset, Jacoby. But I don't think that you should come to me for answers. Talk to your father."

"So you do know that Alexandria is daddy's... I don't even know what to call her because love child is a compliment and this is bullshit," Jacoby spat out with rage. "Why didn't you tell me? I thought that you were my best friend!"

Claudia winced and moved away from Jacoby.

"You and your father have always been close," she whispered. "I didn't want to ruin that."

"Well it's ruined now. And I feel as if the whole town's laughing at me and my mother."

"That happened so long ago, Jacoby. Your family isn't the only one to have skeletons in the closet."

"But I thought we were different," she wailed.

"Just because your father has another daughter doesn't mean he doesn't love you."

"Don't take up for him. He's a hypocrite taking his ass down to the church all the time."

Shocked Claudia said, "Jacoby, don't be so harsh. He did what he did but maybe he's changed."

"How do we know that? He's been going to church since before I was born. When did he get redemption?"

"It's not up to us to be convinced," Claudia said. "God knows."

"Oh," she sputtered. "Give me a break. You don't even like church."

"But I go out of respect. I don't know what's out there and I want to make sure He at least knows who I am."

Jacoby crumpled up her half empty bag of Fritos and threw it in the trash can in front of them. "When did you find out about Alexandria?"

"Come on, Jacoby. Is this really necessary?"

"How long have you known and not told me?"

Claudia drew in a deep sigh of resignation. "Since I was about ten years old."

"What!" Jacoby shouted. "You've known all this time?"

"Think hard, Jacoby." Claudia gave her a long, measuring look. "You met Alexandria before. One time we were playing hopscotch on the sidewalk in front of my house. Alexandria came and asked us if she could play and we let her."

"What!"

"She was good and beat us. We had a lot of fun that day. Then her mother came and got her. Alexandria was supposed to come back the next day for a rematch."

Jacoby screwed her face up trying to remember. After a few seconds the memory slowly surfaced.

"My mother was watching out the window. That night she told me that she didn't want me to play with Alexandria any more. I asked her why and she wouldn't say anything except she didn't want her mother hanging around because of Daddy. The next day, Alexandria arrived before you did and I told her that I couldn't play with her. She was crying as she walked away. When I got older, I found out who she is."

Aghast Jacoby said, "I played with her…"

"It's not her fault, Jacoby."

"Well, it sure as hell isn't mine," she screamed. "And you lied to me. If anyone other than my parents should have told me it was you."

"I wasn't going to tell you that!"

"After we went to the movies, you should have taken me aside and told me the truth. 'I don't know her and you don't want to,' she mimicked. "You knew her all right."

"I thought you might figure it out anyhow. Damn, Jacoby. She looks like your daddy spit her out, right down to her eyes."

"Don't say that!" Jacoby ordered.

"I'm sorry, Jacoby," Claudia said in regretful voice. "I thought since she and her mother don't live here anymore it was best for you not to know. Life is hard enough without seeking drama that you can't do anything about."

"Her mother died, and she's moving into my house."

Appalled, Claudia covered her mouth.

"Does Rex know about all this?"

"Yes," she whispered.

"And he didn't tell me either."

Claudia said tearfully, "It's not fair to blame us."

"I thought that I could count on you for anything. You were the sister I thought I didn't have." Jacoby's stormy eyes seared Claudia's apologetic ones. She declared harshly, "I don't want you or Rex in my life anymore. Our friendship is over."

###

"Mom!" Jacoby shouted. "Where are you?"

"I'm in the guest bedroom."

Jacoby went to the doorway. Her mother had a can of Pledge in one hand and a dust cloth in the other. "What are you doing?"

"Getting this room ready for your…" Sarai's eyes fell from her daughter's.

"Don't you dare say it!"

Sarai freed her hands and held her arms open wide.

Jacoby went to her.

"I love you with all my heart, Jacoby."

Since she was taller, Jacoby she rested her head on top of her mother's. She sniffed her mother's scent. "I know that you do."

"And your father loves you."

She stiffened and moved away. "I don't want to talk about him. I thought you should know that I put in for an apartment today. I'll be out before the end of the month." She said gently, "I'm offering you a chance to get away from this, Mom. You can come with me."

"I can't run from this situation any more, Jacoby. And you can't run either."

"I'm not running," she denied vehemently. "I just don't want to be around it."

"You're an adult now and free to make your own choices." After a tear trickled out of one eye and she wiped it away. "I just hate to lose you."

"You'll never lose me, Mom." She pulled her cell phone out of her pocket and held it up. "I'm just a phone call away." All of a sudden her phone rang shrilly, breaking the tension in the room.

"Hello."

"Hey, baby!"

Armstrong's booming voice made Jacoby hold the cell away from her ear.

"Hey, back."

"I've got the best news. I signed with the agency. I actually did head shots and everything for them to send out for me."

"That's good, Armstrong."

"What's the matter? You don't seem very happy for me."

"I'm happy for you," she replied. "It's just a lot has happened in the last couple of days."

"Like what?"

"I don't really want to go into it now. But I'm looking for an apartment."

"You are?" he exclaimed. "Since when?"

"Since you left," she said. "When are you coming back?"

"I'm on the road right now. I should be home in an hour."

"Can I meet you at your house?"

"Sure."

CHAPTER 5

Jacoby leaned on her car waiting for Armstrong. Once she saw his headlights she breathed a deep sigh of relief. She ran to greet him and as he exited the car she flung herself into his arms and burst into tears.

Armstrong held her steady. "What's going on with you, Jacoby?"

She didn't answer. Instead, the tears continued, drenching Armstrong's black silk shirt.

Steadying her, he held her at arms' length and stared at her in amazement.

Finally she forced herself to stop.

"We're going into the house and you're going to tell me what the hell happened while I was in Miami." He put his arms around her shoulders and led her inside.

Jacoby sat on the couch and said, her voice quivering, "Do you know a girl named Alexandria Spooner?"

There was a heavy silence in the room. Armstrong handed Jacoby a bottle of beer and said, "No. Should I?"

"She's my sister."

"How is she your sister?" he asked carefully as he sat on the couch next to her.

"Daddy cheated on Mom before I was born and now he wants to have a relationship with Alexandria."

"You're kidding."

"I wish that I was. Claudia and Rex knew about Alexandria and kept it from me."

"That's a lousy thing to do," Armstrong said. "Some friends they are."

"Yeah!" she said bitterly. "From the time I can remember I've trusted Claudia with all my secrets. But I don't trust her anymore. I told her I don't want her or Rex in my life."

"I'd feel the same way," Armstrong said in a hard voice. "She knew about this and kept it from you. She and Rex have probably been talking about it behind your back and laughing at you."

"Please don't say any more, Armstrong," she begged.

"Okay," he said, and soothingly rubbed her back.

"Daddy wants to move Alexandria into our house."

"Ain't that some shit?" Armstrong exclaimed. "So when is this supposed to happen?"

"I'm not sure exactly, but I know that I'm not waiting until the last minute to get the hell out of there. I've applied for an apartment in the Catalina Apartments. I'll be moving as soon as one of those opens up."

"You can't afford a decent apartment on your salary."

"I'm going to pick up another job," she said. "I applied at Winn Dixie grocery store."

"But I'll never get to see you if you work two jobs." Armstrong took his hand and lifted her chin. "Why don't you move in here?"

Jacoby automatically surveyed the dismal house with peeling paint and outdated furniture.

"I know it's not much to look at," Armstrong said defensively. "But we can fix it up."

Still she hesitated.

"I don't think that you should be living alone and trying to deal with all this emotional stuff that you're going through, Jacoby. Let me be here for you."

Jacoby slid closer to Armstrong and leaned on him. "Armstrong, I would love to move in with you."

"You can trust me, Jacoby." He put his arms around her. "I'll protect you from all harm."

Jacoby was packing the last of her things when she heard a cough at her bedroom door. She didn't look up from her task.

"Jacoby," Abraham said. "Your mother told me that you're moving out today. I'm sorry that you feel that you can't live here anymore."

She slammed her suitcase shut.

"You've got to understand that Alexandria can't take your place."

"She already has," Jacoby said in a wooden voice. "You said it. She's your firstborn."

"I shouldn't have said that. It makes it seem…"

"Seem like what?" Jacoby placed her hands on her hips and stared challengingly at him. "The truth?"

"Can't we work this out?"

"You're my father and I love you," she said in a broken voice. "But right now I can't stand to look at you." Jacoby blinked away tears, refusing to let them fall. "If you had told me when you weren't forced to, I wouldn't feel so betrayed. But you hid this from me for as long as you could. But it's not even about me. Mom has been a good wife to you. She shouldn't have to look at your betrayal day in and day out."

Abraham's Adam's apple jumped agitatedly. "Your mother

understands."

"No she doesn't!" Jacoby screamed. "She's just bending to your will the way she always has. What are people going to say when they find out that Alexandria is living here?"

"I hope that they'll say it's about time that I owned up to my past."

"Yeah," she spat sarcastically, "you keep hoping that."

Abraham said glumly, "Since you insist on moving, I want to pay your first and last month's deposit on your apartment. It's the least I can do."

"I don't need it," she declined. "I'm moving in with Armstrong."

Abraham's light brown eyes seemed to darken right before her very eyes. "You're going to live in sin with that man?" he said disparagingly.

"Don't you dare talk to me about sin," Jacoby warned.

"This is different. Having a sexual relationship with someone other than your wife is a sin, but living day to day with a man that you're not married to is a practiced sin."

Jacoby raised a brow in disbelief. "Are you trying to tell me that you only slept with Shirley one time and that's when Alexandria was conceived?"

Abraham visibly struggled for a response yet gave none.

"Thank you for not lying," she paused for effect, "this time."

"Have you forgotten the way your mother and I raised you to behave?" Abraham whispered.

"No."

"Have you lost all respect for me and my feelings?"

"Yes," she said adamantly. Jacoby grabbed her suitcases and stomped past her father.

Jacoby stepped back and viewed the furniture. "What do you think?" she asked Armstrong.

"I didn't know this place could look so good," he admitted grudgingly. "It's beginning to feel like a home should feel. You have excellent taste."

"Once you painted these walls I knew that I had to do something. It looks like a new house."

"The inside does but the outside needs some work."

"I'm going to plant flowers in the spring. Have you decided whether or not you're going to install central air before next summer? I didn't want to complain before because I was only here a couple of nights a week, but the heat in this place was excruciating."

"I don't know," he answered noncommittally. "A couple gallons of paint are one thing but central air? I don't know that I want to spend that kind of money."

"Well we're going to have to buy a couple of AC window units. My asthma acts up when I get too hot."

"Is your asthma acting up today?"

"No? Why?"

He swatted her behind. "Because you look real hot in that skimpy dress you're wearing."

"Oh, Armstrong," she said, "you're so nice to me."

"That's my job," he replied. At the dinner table, Armstrong bit into a chicken wing. "Jacoby, everything you cook is good. We ought to market your dirty rice."

She laughed. "I think everyone in Bunnell can make that."

"Then maybe we should move somewhere where it'll be a novelty."

The house phone rang and Armstrong grabbed it. "Yes. That's great! For what? When? I'll be there." Armstrong hung up the phone. "That was Simon Baylor. He got me an audition in Miami for a commercial."

"That's fantastic! What kind?"

"It's for dog food."

"That's kind of funny since you don't like animals."

"I'll like them for ten thousand dollars."

"That's what they're offering you?"

"Yes," he said proudly. "And that's just the beginning."

Sarai looked up from the ironing board. "Your father misses you."

Jacoby stared into her glass of sweet tea with a lemon wedge in it.

"When are you going to forgive him?"

"I don't know. Since he took his time telling me about all this, I should be able to take my time getting used to it. By the way, where is he?"

"He's at the prison."

"So he's down there with her?"

"No," she said. "He was scheduled to go in."

"Before she gets here we need to make other arrangements for our visits. You have to come over to Armstrong's house. I bought a lot of new furniture."

"Do you think that's wise?"

"I financed it four years same as cash so I have plenty of time to pay the bill. When I get my income tax checks I'll pay chunks of it off."

All of a sudden Sarai grabbed onto the back of a chair. She breathed deeply trying to catch her breath.

Jacoby stared anxiously at her mother. "What's the matter?"

"My joints hurt."

"You should go to the doctor."

"I already did," she said.

"And what did he say?"

"He told me to stay out of a lot of sunlight."

"When were you in the sun?"

"Last week I cleaned the borders around my flowers." A look of relief crossed her face. "I feel better already." She resumed her position in front of the ironing board. "It was really hot that day. He gave me a prescription so I should feel better soon." Sarai picked her husband's shirt up and hung it on a hanger along with the others. With her back to Jacoby she said, "There's nothing to worry about." Turning, she gave her daughter a searching look. "Are you happy living with Armstrong?"

"Very much so," she said honestly. "Under other circumstances I would have never done that so early in our relationship," she murmured, "but he treats me well."

"Are you two getting married?"

"He hasn't asked again. But I'm not worried about that right now. We're still learning each other."

They heard a shout. "I'm home."

"He's early," Sarai said with a perplexed look.

"That's my cue to leave." Jacoby stood, and as she and her mother walked into the foyer they simultaneously stopped dead in their tracks.

Alexandria stood next to Abraham.

Jacoby's saliva dried up.

Abraham's eyes held a pleading look. "Hello, Jacoby."

Jacoby stared at the female version of her father. Since seeing her at the movies, Alexandria had changed her hair to long braids yet those eyes remained the same.

Sarai, too, stared. Finally she said, "I didn't expect you until next week."

"Abraham pulled some strings and got me out early," Alexandria replied in her northern accent.

"I didn't know that it would be today," Abraham hastily explained.

"Hello, Jacoby," Alexandria drawled.

"I was just leaving." Jacoby kissed her mother on the cheek. "Call me if you need anything," she instructed before flouncing past Abraham and Alexandria.

Jacoby and Armstrong arrived home at the same time. With a brief nod in his direction, she stormed into the house and threw herself face down on the bed. Her eyes burnt so hard from anger she buried her face into the pillow.

"What now?" Armstrong asked from behind her.

"She's at the house."

"I knew she was getting out this week."

"How did you know that?"

"They were talking about it in the barbershop."

"So the gossip has started already?"

"I think it's always been there, Jacoby. You've just been shielded from it."

"Well," she said. " 'It is what it is.' "

"But it doesn't have to be this way," Armstrong said.

"There's no way to rewrite history," she echoed sourly.

"But there's a way to change your future." He paused, "You didn't ask me how the commercial went."

Jacoby sat up. Contrition was written all over her face. "I'm sorry. I've just been so caught up in my own thing."

"I got the commercial," he said smugly. "And Simon said that there's more work to come."

"I'm very happy for you," she said sincerely. "You did it."

"Simon thinks that I should move to Miami and I agree."

Jacoby's heart plummeted. "What! When?"

"As soon as possible."

"What about us?"

Armstrong clasped her hands in his. "I want you to come with me."

"Oh, I don't know about that," she said. "I don't have a job in Miami."

"You don't need a job. You have me."

"I can't be totally dependent on a man," she protested. "That's not my way."

"Do you know how many libraries there are in Miami? I'm sure that you can get a job at one."

"Why Miami? I wouldn't think that there's much acting work there."

"Are you kidding? Miami's got it going on. Two movie studios have pictures that are supposed to start filming there soon. Simon thinks that I might be able to get a part in one if not both of them."

"I thought that you were going back to school?"

"I can go there. It would be more convenient than me having to drive forty-five minutes to school each way if I stayed here."

"This is very sudden, Armstrong. I can't make such an important decision with my life in such a tangle."

Hardness crept into his voice. "This is the best choice for my career. I can't keep driving back and forth for auditions."

"Can I remain in the house if I decide to stay in Bunnell?

"I think I should rent it out. I shouldn't have any problem with that now with the new carpet and paint."

But that was my money.

"Has Claudia called you?"

"Not lately. After our big fight she left me a couple of messages that I didn't return."

"Oh," Armstrong said meaningfully.

"What do you mean by that?"

"Rex was at the barbershop when I was there. He said that he and Claudia have set their wedding date."

"They did!" she exclaimed.

"Claudia asked someone else to be her bridesmaid."

"Oh," Jacoby said, and a lump clogged her throat.

"Rex said, that Claudia said, it's not her fault that your daddy is a Ho."

Jacoby sputtered angrily, "How dare she say that about my father! I'm going to call her."

"You can't," Armstrong said. "I promised Rex that I wouldn't tell you."

Jacoby seethed inside and out.

"What you were exposed to this afternoon is only the beginning. I haven't said anything, but people all over town are laughing about Alexandria moving into your house and your mother having to do for her. I thought that you'd want to get away from this."

"I don't want to abandon my mother," she moaned.

"You'll only be moving a half day's drive away. Besides, she can visit. She'll probably need a place to get away also."

The image of Alexandria standing next to her father nauseated her. Jacoby unconsciously shook her head to dispel it. "Okay, Armstrong. I'll move to Miami with you."

He put his arms around her. "We can start a new life," he promised.

Damien's words echoed in her mind. " 'You will travel and find the true love of your life.' " Jacoby breathed a sigh of acceptance.

CHAPTER 6

Jacoby stared disconsolately out the window. It was the hottest March Jacoby ever had to live through. Even the palm trees bowed from the humidity. "What have I done?" she whispered. She picked up the telephone, hesitated, and placed it back on its cradle. "If I call Mother again today she'll get worried."

"Jacoby! Where are you?"

"I'm in the bedroom folding laundry."

"I signed my contract for the commercial," Armstrong said excitedly. "I begin filming tomorrow."

"That's great," she said, trying to inject enthusiasm.

"And I signed up for acting classes. I begin next week."

"Gee!" she said. "It seems like you're going full steam ahead and accomplishing things."

Armstrong looked at Jacoby's downcast face. "So I guess no calls yet from the library system?"

"No," she said. "It seems as if everyone has been at their job for over twenty years and isn't going anywhere."

"Maybe you can try doing something else."

"I'm going to have to. I'm bored to death."

"I have an idea. We haven't gone to the beach since we've been living here."

"You want to go today?"

"Sure. I'll be busy for the rest of the week. An actor I met recommended Haulover instead of South Beach. Do you know where your bathing suit is?"

"Yeah. It's in the box labeled Things I Shouldn't Wear."

"You have a great body, Jacoby. Thirty-eight, twenty-five, thirty-eight. That's just the way I like it."

Jacoby's mood lightened as they crossed the bridge that led to the beach. The smell of the sea invigorated her senses. She'd pulled her hair back into a ponytail and the breeze from her car window made it bounce around.

She looked over at Armstrong. He'd donned a pair of board shorts and wife beater tee shirt, but as usual his feet were completely covered with a pair of rubber swim shoes.

She took her hand and slid it in his. "You look hot," she whispered.

"So do you in that bright, blue bikini."

59

Once they parked, Armstrong dropped coins in the meter. "I put in enough for a couple of hours."

They walked hand and hand down to the beach. Armstrong carried a picnic basket with beer and sandwiches while Jacoby carried their beach towels.

The beach was teeming with people.

"This is why I love Miami. It's March and is hotter than July." Armstrong took off his tee shirt and Jacoby stared at his six-pack.

"Armstrong, you can always tell a military man,because their bodies are the bomb."

He beamed from her compliment. "Take off your coverall and join me in the water."

Once she'd disrobed, Armstrong picked her up and carried her towards the water.

Terrified she stammered, "I can't swim!"

Armstrong dropped her and there was a look of displeasure on his face. "What can you do?" he muttered.

Hurt, she responded, "That's a mean thing to say."

"You're right, Jacoby. I shouldn't have said that. You do a lot of things well."

The water lapped around their ankles. "Like what?" she asked. Jacoby folded her arms across her bosom and her lips protruded irritably.

"You're a real good housekeeper. And," he said with a smug look, "you were a virgin when I got you. A man doesn't forget that. Now I'm going to go into the water and cool off. Then we can eat the food you made."

In the hot sun sweat dripped down her neck. Enviously she watched Armstrong swim in the waves as the water crashed about his head.

Eventually Armstrong rejoined her and she handed him a sandwich with a cold beer.

They sat on their towels as they finished their sandwiches and quenched their thirst. "Let's take a walk down the beach."

"That sounds like fun. Besides, I need to walk off some of that food that I ate."

After about six minutes, they came upon a small wire fence. "This is what Irving told me about."

"What do you mean?"

"From here on out everyone is naked."

"This is a nude beach?" Jacoby exclaimed.

"You don't have to be naked but everyone else is."

"I don't want to see that," she protested.

"Stop being such a prude." As Armstrong walked off he was

swinging his head around as if he'd just gotten the lead in a remake of The Exorcist.

Jacoby stood indecisively. After realizing that Armstrong wasn't coming back any time soon, she went after him.

Naked people were everywhere. Jacoby couldn't help stealing looks as she tried to catch up with Armstrong's long stride. A very overweight woman played volleyball with others and a midget jogged past her. Good grief. What were they thinking? Partially nude is more sexually appealing than this mess any day of the week. She shouted in a harried voice, "Armstrong wait!"

He stopped and as she caught up with him she saw he was staring at a leggy, blonde with obvious breast implants.

Then he focused on her. "Take off your suit," he ordered.

"Hell no!"

"You're sexually repressed," he said in a disgruntled voice.

"I am not," she said hotly. "I just don't think that everyone should have the right to see my body. I would think that as my man you wouldn't want that either."

Armstrong stared at her for an interminable time. "You're right. You're for my eyes only. We should go."

Armstrong ran into the room waving a contract in the air as he danced around the kitchen. "I got the part!"

"Let me see it," she said, snatching it from him. She quickly skimmed the paperwork. "You certainly deserve it. You auditioned enough for it."

"I know. I went on call back after call back and they finally made a decision."

"When do you start filming?"

"Next week. I never thought it'd be in a movie with Gerald Butler."

"How many lines do you have?"

"Ten."

"Ooh," she teased. "You're coming up in the world. You only had two in that commercial."

Anger flashed across his face. "Are you making fun of me?"

"No," she stammered. "I'm just saying that some people never get an acting job and you've already gotten two."

"That's right," he said proudly. "I'm doing better than everyone else I know from Bunnell."

Jacoby said gently, "You can't say that, because as small as Bunnellis you don't know everyone."

"I know you."

"What do you mean by that?"

"I mean that you haven't found a job at a library when there must be over twenty in the city."

"You're right, Armstrong," she retorted sharply. "Since you finally got a job I guess I'll have to find something to do, since now I don't have to pander to you all day."

Jacoby sat across from the administrator at Kelly Services.

"So you're computer literate?"

"Yes," Jacoby answered. "I worked at the public library in my hometown from the time I graduated from high school. I kind of wanted to stay in the same field."

"We're not tied to them because they hire from within. But this morning we were asked to send an employee to the Powers Public Relations firm. They need a receptionist. It's a temp job, but if they like your work they'll bring you on full time. Are you interested?" she said, looking at Jacoby over her spectacles.

"Very," she answered.

When Jacoby parked in the complex she spied Armstrong's Charger. What's he doing home? Anxiously she let herself in the apartment.

Armstrong sat staring at the television even though it wasn't turned on.

"Hey, Babe, what are you doing home?"

He took a swig from his Pabst. "They cut my part."

"Gee! I'm sorry, Armstrong." She said consolingly, "But there will be other chances."

"How do you know that?" he snapped. "I go on fifty casting calls and finally get something and they drop me without even giving me a chance." He drained his beer and slammed the can down on the coffee table. Getting up he stumbled into the kitchen and grabbed another out the refrigerator.

Jacoby followed him. "Don't you think that you should cut down on your drinking?" she asked tentatively.

"Don't tell me what to do." He brushed past her and went back into the den.

Deciding to let that pass she said, "I have some news. I got a job today. So now I can help out financially around here."

"Good," Armstrong snapped. "Because I'm tired of covering all the bills."

###

The next morning, Jacoby peered at the number on the building through the pouring rain. I think this is it. Bracing herself, she bounded out the car and clutching her leather binder in her hand trotted towards the glass door. With head bent she ran into something rock hard. Had it not been for the hands that steadied her, she, instead of her folder, would have fallen into the puddle. Jacoby was bent over one arm, and the other encircled the small of her back. The smell of musk wafted to her nostrils and she inhaled. With parted lips she looked up at her savior.

The man who held her in his arms stared startled into her eyes. She's absolutely stunning. One of his hands was caught in her flowing tresses. Gently, he freed it, and in one fluid motion set her upright and released her.

Jacoby could not look away. Her mouth hung open and her throat felt dry. Nervously she bent for her folder.

"Let me get that for you." His voice was deep and sensual.

There should be a law against a voice like that. Dumbly she took the binder.

"Here," the man said and stepped back, drawing her inside the building to shelter. "Ms?" he said hopefully, looking at her bare ring finger.

"Miss Jacoby Alexander," she said softly.

Inside he breathed a sigh of relief.

Jacoby couldn't stop the flow of words that tumbled out of her mouth. "Who are you?" she breathed.

White teeth flashed invitingly at her. "My name is Noah. Noah Powers."

"Oh," Jacoby stammered, nonplussed. "The temp agency sent me over to meet with you."

A slow smile spread across his face. "I think that they sent you to see my father, Bradley Powers."

"Oh," Jacoby said and her expression didn't hide her regret.

There was a gleam in his eye. "I know," he replied with the same sentiment.

###

"Mom, I won't be coming home for Thanksgiving."

"Please, Jacoby. I need you."

63

"What's wrong? Is it about Alexandria?"

"No," she said, "But she doesn't help matters."

"Why don't I send you a ticket and you come to Miami? I'll fly you out of Jacksonville."

"I would, but the doctor doesn't want me to travel."

"The doctor? What's going on?"

"I didn't want to say anything, but…"

"What is it?" she asked, alarmed.

"I have lupus."

"Lupus. How do you get that?"

"No one ever knows the cause. It's something that mainly African Americans, Hispanic, or Asian women get."

"Is there a cure?" she cried.

"No. I'm just supposed to stay out of the sun, try to be stress free, and not overtire myself. I have medication that treats it."

"Mom, how long have you known about this?"

"I found out right before you moved to Miami."

"And you're just now telling me!"

"I didn't want you to change your plans because of me. I knew that you needed to get away from Bunnell. Besides, it wasn't much of a problem then. But lately, my joints ache all the time."

"It's probably the stress of having Alexandria there." She asked scathingly, "Did she get a job yet?"

"No, and your father isn't demanding that she get one. I know that life has been hard for her, but she's so lazy. She's not supposed to drink alcohol, but the minute they took that SCRAM bracelet off of her she was at it again."

"She drinks in the house?" Jacoby said derogatorily. "I couldn't even have a glass of wine."

"Your dad is so guilt ridden that she completely runs this place."

"Put her out."

"I can't."

"Then I'll come home for Thanksgiving and do it."

"Your father won't allow it." She begged, "Jacoby, please come. Just pretend that Alexandria isn't here. She's gone a lot anyhow. I miss you so much."

"All right, Mom. I'll come."

That evening Armstrong declared emphatically, "I'm not going."

"Please. I need you."

"No. I can't believe that you're going," he said angrily. "You're going to stay in the house with your sister?"

Jacoby flinched. "My mother needs me. I'll just ignore Alexandria.

That will be easy for me since in my mind she doesn't exist."

"Humph! I knew that you'd let your father get away with it," he said in a snide voice.

"I've never stopped loving my father," she whispered. "I just needed to put some distance between me and that situation. Besides, he's not getting away with anything. I haven't spoken to him since I left Bunnell."

"Well," he said sarcastically, "you'll have to talk to him when you get there. Take a few pictures of y'all around the dinner table so I can see them even though I won't be there."

"Stop being nasty," she ordered. "You know how hard this will be for me." She stressed, "I need you to come."

"I couldn't even if I wanted to. I have an audition the day after Thanksgiving."

Jacoby rolled her eyes.

"Don't act like that's not a big deal. I want to do something with my life other than answer telephones like you," he said cuttingly.

"That job you disparage pays for half of everything around here." She kicked his shoes out of the middle of the floor. "And since you're here more than I am the least you could do is pitch in and clean up once in a while."

"I put the first and last month's security on this apartment. You couldn't live in a place like this without me. You should clean it up."

Jacoby stared around in amazement at the clutter in her mother's living room. This place has never been in such disarray.

"Jacoby? Is that you?" Her mother's faint voice reached her down the hall.

"Yes, Mom." When she entered her mother's bedroom Sarai was struggling to sit up.

"Oh, Mom. You should have told me that you were this sick. I'd have come home sooner."

"I'm fine," Sarai denied. "This is just one of my bad days. Tomorrow I'll probably feel as good as new."

"What can I do to help?" she asked, helping her mother sit up in the bed.

"You being here is help enough. I've missed you so much."

"I feel so guilty leaving town. I'd have stayed if you'd told me."

"That's why I didn't," Sarai said and gave Jacoby a genuine smile. "So how are you enjoying Miami?"

"It's grown on me." She planted a kiss on her mother's cheek and sat down on the bed. "I applied at the University of Miami. I'd like to go to college part time."

"I always knew that you'd go one day," Sarai said gleefully. "Some people just take a little longer than others to figure out what they want to do for a living. Tell me about your job."

"Powers Publics Relations creates publicity campaigns for major stars and corporations that want to clean up their image. You wouldn't believe how much goes on. It's more than issuing a statement to the media if they get in trouble. There's trying to wangle them invitations to the best parties, what kind of limo to rent, where they'll be seated at an event. "

"That sounds interesting."

"It is. Every day something fascinating happens."

"Do you do any of that stuff?"

"No, not yet." She added with a determined look, "But I'd like to be a part of it. That's why I want a degree in public relations."

Sarai watched her carefully. "How's Armstrong's acting thing going?'

Jacoby hesitated before blurting out, "Not good at all. He's only gotten a tiny part in a commercial. Armstrong has way too much time on his hands to brood. Every day he gets more and more depressed. I feel so sorry for him."

"A man without a job is a sad thing," Sarai said. "He should find something else to do until he gets what he wants."

"I told him that and he got angry. He said that I don't believe in his dream, so I just let well enough alone."

"Acting may not be the career for him."

"Don't tell him that!"

"A hard head makes a soft ass," Saraii quoted softly.

"Tell me about it. By the way, where's Daddy's daughter?"

"Who knows? When she's gone all day like this she usually shows up around dinner time."

"What a lazy piece of trash," Jacoby said distastefully.

"The two of you have the same father but look at the differences between you. The reason I don't say anything to Alexandria is because I'm partly the blame for this mess. I should have never sent her away. She's had no upbringing. I hope one day she gets it together."

"I don't care nothin' bout that," Jacoby grumbled. "My concern is you. Are you really okay? Mom, I can move back to Bunnell if you want me to. I'm sure that I could get my old job back."

"I wouldn't hear of it," Sarai said emphatically. "You're going places, girl. I could tell from your telephone conversations and now your style of clothes how much you've matured since you moved. I want you to continue to grow."

"Well," Jacoby said with a pensive look, "even if I don't live here I think that I can make your life a little less stressful."

"What do you mean?"

"Nothing," she said standing. "I'm going to run a couple of errands. Do you need anything from the grocery store?"

"Just a loaf of bread, because I planned shopping tomorrow. Thanksgiving is in two days, and I haven't even bought my turkey or anything else for dinner."

"Lay here and rest. I'll be back."

###

Jacoby assessed the immaculate house of Betty Porter. "How do you manage to keep your place so clean with three kids?"

Betty grinned. "I stay on them to pick up after themselves. But I actually enjoy cleaning. It's therapeutic for me."

"When I picked your card off the bulletin board in the grocery store, I didn't know what to expect."

"I have references from other employers. I'm an early riser so after I send the kids off to school, I'm ready to go to work. Usually I'm done in time to pick my little one up. The other two ride the bus."

"I don't mean to be nosy, but are you married?"

"Yes, but I feel like a widow. My husband is a long distance truck driver. With gas prices the way they are, it's cut into our profits. We're barely staying afloat."

"Times are hard," Jacoby said sympathetically. "What do your cleaning services include?"

"I do it all. Windows only once a month though."

She cleans windows once a month!

"How large is your mother's house?"

"It's about seventeen hundred square feet. How much would you charge me?"

"If you want me to clean once a week, I'll charge you only eighty dollars a visit."

"Betty, if your references check out I'd like you to start next week."

"I thank you," Betty said relieved. "Christmas is right around the corner."

"My mother might not want you there at first."

She nodded her head understandingly. "Stuck in her ways and all, huh?"

"You just do your thing and ignore her. I'll give you my phone number to call me if she cuts up too much. But remember, Mom can't fire you because she didn't hire you. I'll be mailing your check from Miami. Which days are you available?"

"Friday's."

"That's good," Jacoby said musingly. "That way my mother's house will be relatively clean on the weekend."

"It'll stay clean longer than that. You might not even need me every week."

"I don't know about that. My parents have a house guest. She's real lazy and sloppy. Just shut the door to her bedroom and leave it as is."

"Yes, ma'am."

After Jacoby left Betty's, she drove to Silas's Soul Food Restaurant.

Silas came from the kitchen. A huge grin spread across his face, making him look like a black Santa Claus. "Miss Jacoby, how nice it is to see you."

"Same here, Silas," she smiled back.

He gave her a look of compassion. "I heard you'd left town. We sure miss you around here. Are you back for good?" he asked hopefully.

"Naw," she said. "I'm just home for a couple of days. I wanted to order a Thanksgiving dinner to be ready tomorrow night."

Silas picked up his notepad. "How many are you feeding?"

Jacoby bit back her first impulse to reply two. But instead she said, "Four adults."

"Turkey and all the trimmings?"

"Yes," she said. "But make sure that it's enough food for a couple of days."

He winked at her. "I'll supersize it."

Jacoby poured her mother a cup of herbal tea.

"I don't want her," Sarai exclaimed.

"Too bad," Jacoby said resolutely.

The slamming of the front door and the sound of feet let Jacoby know that her father and Alexandria had arrived.

Abraham entered with a happy smile on his face. "Jacoby," he said, extending his arms. "I've missed you so much."

Hesitantly she went to him but the minute his arms closed around her she felt a chink in her amour.

"I've missed you too, daddy," she said truthfully. She let her head remain buried in his chest.

"Welcome home, Jacoby." Alexandria's words interrupted the family reunion.

Jacoby stepped back and acknowledged her with a curt nod.

"How long are you going to be in town?" Alexandria asked. She leaned on the doorjamb with her arms folded in front of her in the exact manner Jacoby had observed her father do.

"I'm leaving on Friday," she replied stiffly.

"Good that you're here for a visit. Mother and Father really miss you."

Alexandria's familiarity referring to her parents made Jacoby's heart constrict and she glared at them.

They dropped their eyes from her wrathful stare.

"Maybe you and I could go check out a movie."

"No thanks," she said. "Mom is the focus for my visit. Every time I talk to her on the telephone she's exhausted."

Alexandria plopped in a chair across from Sarai. "I'd help her do some of the housework. All she has to do is ask."

"Just start keeping your room clean," Jacoby retorted. "I've hired someone to do the rest."

"Hired someone?" Abraham asked.

"Yes," Jacoby answered. "Betty Porter is going to come once a week and do the heavy cleaning."

"Don't you think that's a waste of money?" Alexandria asked.

Jacoby shot a look of contempt at Alexandria. "Mom needs help."

"I'll start helping out more," Abraham said with a look of chagrin on his face.

"You should," she said mockingly. "There's a whole book in the bible that tells you that at least you should make coffee for your wife."

Abraham's eyes drew together in a frown. "What book is that, Jacoby?"

"Hebrews," she answered sarcastically.

"Jacoby, your attitude is so bad."

Her response was just to stare at him.

Abraham cleared his throat. "Your mom keeps me updated on how you're doing down there. It seems as if you've found you niche."

"I like it. And I just got a raise," Jacoby responded with a proud tilt to her head.

"Good for you. But instead of you paying for a housekeeper, I'd rather you use your money to get your own place and not shack up with Armstrong," he said with a sober look.

"Abraham," Sarai said in a cautionary voice.

"I got this, momma," she retorted anger flooding her face. "If living with Armstrong is a mistake it's my problem and not yours." Her eyes rested on Alexandria. "I promise not to bring my mistakes into this house and burden you."

Alexandria's eyes narrowed. "Are you calling me a mistake?"

"Well, you're certainly not what I ordered," she said, standing. "Mom, I'm going to start cleaning the den."

"I'll vacuum," Abraham offered as a way of apology to Jacoby's retreating back.

Jacoby couldn't stop herself from looking over her shoulder. She had to tamp down the urge to go back and slap the smirk off Alexandria's lips.

The next afternoon they sat at the dining room table stuffing their faces with the Thanksgiving feast Silas had prepared.

"This is delicious, Jacoby," Sarai said. "I never thought that I'd eat such tender turkey from a restaurant."

"It's not better than yours, but it sure is a lot less trouble," she replied.

"So do you like Miami?" Alexandria asked between bites of stuffing she shoveled into her mouth.

"Yes."

"Do you party much?" Alexandria persisted.

"I'm in a relationship, so I don't feel the need to club hop trolling for men."

Alexandria's eyes hardened. "Why are you punishing me for something that isn't my fault?"

"What?' Jacoby replied caught off guard.

"You act like it's my fault that I'm on this earth."

"I don't wish to discuss it," Jacoby said dismissively.

"You haven't even given me a chance."

"Girls," Abraham said, "don't argue at the dinner table."

Jacoby ignored him. "Maybe if you got a job and I didn't have to hire a housekeeper I might be inclined to be kinder."

"I got a job," Alexandria snapped.

"You did?" Sarai and Abraham exclaimed in astonishment.

"It took me awhile with my record and Bunnell being so small, but I start at 7-eleven next week."

"Great!" Sarai exclaimed. "I mean, you must have been bored sitting around the house all day."

"I was. And I got tired of asking you and daddy," she stressed the word," for money.""

Jacoby's stomach lurched at Alexandria's use of the word 'daddy'.

"That's good news, isn't it, Jacoby?" Abraham said enthusiastically.

Jacoby stared at her father's eyes that seemed to constantly beg for forgiveness. Relenting she said, "Alexandria, I hope it works out for you."

"Oh," she said with a casual flick of her hand. "I'll make sure that it does."

The next morning, Jacoby threw the rest of her belongings in the backseat of her Honda Accord.

"Did you go and see Claudia while you were here?" Sarai asked.

"No."

"And you didn't run into her?"

"No."

Her mother gave her a quizzical look "What did you two fall out about? You never told me."

"I'd rather not talk about it," Jacoby answered with a somber expression.

"You two have been friends for a long time. That makes the relationship worth trying to fix."

'Claudia said it ain't her and Rex's fault that your daddy's a ho'. Jacoby shook her head no.

Eyeing her daughter's stubborn features Sarai took a resigned breath. "Your father didn't want to wake you up before he left for work, but he told me to give this to you." She held out a white envelope.

"What is it?" Jacoby asked eyeing it.

"It's money for your travel expenses and Thanksgiving dinner."

"I refuse to take it."

"He'll be upset if you don't," Sarai said softly.

"Then keep it. Treat yourself to a trip to the beauty salon."

Sarai put her hand to her hair self-consciously. "Since I've been ill I have sort of let myself go."

"You always look beautiful to me, Mom. How are you feeling today?"

"I'm feeling no pain. That's how it is. I never know what to expect from one day to the next."

Jacoby threw her arms around her mother and gave her a bear hug that was returned.

Her mother patted her on the back. She murmured, "Things should be better around here with Alexandria gone all day."

"It should be," she said dryly. "And she needs to work overtime."

"Maybe she'll get her own place," Sarai said with a look of

anticipation.

"I doubt it," Jacoby said musingly. "I get the distinct impression that she's quite content to live here forever."

"Jacoby, I wanted to explain that bit about her calling me mother."

Immediate bitterness resurfaced inside Jacoby.

"I never asked her to call me that. As a matter of fact she started just before you came. Alexandria can't take your place in my heart. You're my only daughter."

"I know," Jacoby said as she blinked back tears. "But she's Daddy's firstborn and even though I know that I'm old enough to deal with life's complications, I don't like her and I resent Daddy."

That evening when Jacoby let herself in her apartment Armstrong ran to her excitedly.

He picked her up in his arms and swung her around. "I got it! I got the part! I'm going to be a big star."

Laughing at the look of happiness of his face she said, "Congratulations. I knew that you'd do it."

Armstrong planted a sloppy kiss on her mouth. "Thank you for having my back."

"I'll always be here for you," she promised.

CHAPTER 7

A week after her twenty-third birthday Jacoby entered her cubicle, and the ringing of her telephone diverted her attention from her dour thoughts. Recognizing Allie's extension she picked up the receiver to hear the words, "What happened to you at lunch today?"

Allie had the annoying habit of dispensing with the normal niceties such as, "Hello, how are you doing?" She also frequently cut people off before they could finish what they were saying but Jacoby had gotten used to it and cherished their friendship.

"I had to work through lunch today to avoid staying late."

"You could've called," Allie responded with an admonishing tone.

"I did and you didn't answer the phone. I went to the snack room towards the end to get a soda out of the machine and didn't see you."

"Oh, that's right. Before lunch, I ran a quick errand to the daycare to check on KeKe. She was crying this morning as I got her ready for school and said she didn't want to go. I felt horrible leaving her there today."

"How was she when you went to check on her?"

Allie breathed a sigh of relief before saying, "That little minx was hanging upside down on the monkey bars. And she has a dress on. Normally, I would have told her to get down, but I didn't want her to know I was spying on her, so I just crept away."

Jacoby laughed, "Four–year–olds are totally unselfconscious about their bodies. I wish that trait would stay with us while growing up."

"Well, you don't have anything to worry about," Allie said with a touch of envy. "All the men's heads turn when you sashay into the conference area to see if they need anything else. Coffee, tea, or me?" Allie mimicked Jacoby's sensual voice.

"Yeah, right," Jacoby laughed. "That's what I say. I'm so thrilled to wait on all of those men."

"I know that's right," Allie chuckled. "Our jobs aren't so bad. It's the bullshit that goes along with it. Why in the hell should I be the keeper of the coffee pot? That was not listed in the job description when I applied for this position."

"I know," Jacoby agreed. "Do you notice how happy they get over a fresh pot of coffee? Oh my God, when I splurge and bring a box of donuts, they gobble them up as if they couldn't afford to buy them and treat us once in a while."

"It's true what they say; a full stomach is the way to a man's heart. I know that it is with mine."

"How is Lenny by the way?"

"He's Lenny. Tired of the bull at his job at the semiconductor plant, but sticking it out, hoping one day that he'll be recognized for the asset that he is and maybe they'll give him more money."

"As smart as he is, Lenny should go back to college. A degree doesn't prove that you're smarter than someone else, but that certificate does prove that you have the ability to complete a program, and that piece of paper puts to rest doubts as to your ability."

"I tried to tell him that, but he's so tired at the end of the day, all he wants to do is relax at home in the evenings with me and KeKe."

"I understand that. If I had kids, I'd probably leave it at that too. I feel as if it's taking me forever to finish school."

"How many more classes do you need for your degree?"

Jacoby answered in a tired voice, "Another two and a half years."

Allie said, "Jacoby, you're twenty-three years old and not getting any younger. You could and should have a family of your own. When are you and Armstrong going to tie the knot?

"Not any time soon," Jacoby stated emphatically.

"You've been living with him for too long without a ring. Marry him or move on."

"Move on to what?" Jacoby asked.

"How about that fine ass Noah Powers?"

"Yeah, right. Like I really have a chance with a man like that," she scoffed.

"Don't underestimate that big ass of yours, Jacoby," Allie retorted. "I've caught him staring at it several times when your back was to him. But he may be into white women."

Jacoby said chidingly, "You are so crazy, Allie. You have never seen this man with a woman, black or white, yet you have these wild theories about him based on absolutely nothing."

"I'm not talking crazy here. I peeked in his personnel file."

"Why would there be a personnel file on him? He's the owner's son."

"So what? The IRS needs paperwork on everybody. He's thirty-four years old, never been married, and has no children. That's strange."

"You know you ought to stop," Jacoby warned. "If someone finds out that you were snooping in his personal business like that, you'll get fired."

"Not hardly since the head of personnel showed it to me. I wanted to see what the deal was with him was before you went for it."

" 'Went for it.' I'm not going for anything." Jacoby was aghast at the very thought of her approaching Noah Powers about anything.

Allie pressed, "Since I can't dig up any real dirt on him, the next time he's in town I think that you should ask him out to dinner. The only thing that he can do is say no."

"Not on your life," Jacoby protested. "I wouldn't even know how to go about it. Besides, I live with Armstrong."

"I don't like him," Allie said in a plaintive voice.

"I know you don't," Jacoby retorted.

"He doesn't like me either."

"That's not true, Allie," Jacoby said weakly.

"It is true. Every time I have a get-together at the house he doesn't show. I wouldn't care about that but he keeps you from coming too."

"That's not true," Jacoby denied.

"Armstrong is like a warden. And you're like an old married woman without any of the benefits."

"I have benefits," she protested.

"Like what? You pay for your own health insurance. You have to split all the bills, yet you sleep with him like he's your husband."

"Armstrong is the only man I've ever known."

"Damn, Jacoby," she exclaimed. "I didn't know that. You're missing out on so much by living with him!"

"I can't afford my own place with paying for school and all. Besides, since my mother's condition worsened, I've been paying for her medication every month."

"Then get yourself a female roommate," Allie said bluntly. "You can still sleep with Armstrong if you want."

"If I moved out I wouldn't think of sleeping with him anymore." The minute the words were out Jacoby wished that she could retract them.

"Good Lord." Allie drawled, "Don't tell me it isn't good."

"It's good," Jacoby stammered. "This conversation about my personal business is closed."

"Okay, okay. Have you noticed anything unusual around here?"

"No."

"The firm is in trouble."

"Why on earth would you think that?" she exclaimed.

"There's been a team of lawyers circulating around lately. I heard that Noah's coming back to town to straighten out the mess."

"What mess?"

"Do you know Whitney Davis?"

"Yes. She's the junior assistant to Bradley Powers."

"Whitney printed a publicity story about Isadora Leblanc and she's raising a ruckus about it."

"Good Lord! What did Whitney print?"

"Whitney was told to do a press release and she unearthed information that Isadora is adopted. Isadora was adopted at birth, but she didn't know it. Now there's an estrangement between her and the only parents she's ever known."

Jacoby sucked in her breath remembering the secret that had moved her from Bunnell to Miami. "Her parents should have told her. Information like that is always digested easier if one knows from an early age."

"Isadora built her image on that Creole background from Louisiana which now is a farce. And now that the details are out the natural mother has contacted her."

"Uh oh."

"You bet. You know how a lot of adoptive kids want to find their real parents because they might be something great?"

"Yeah."

"That rarely happens in real life. It seems as if Isadora's mother is a drug addict who lives in a trailer park."

"What about her father?"

"It appears that he was a john. The story is about to be printed on the front pages of all the tabloids."

"But that's not Whitney's fault. She was told to work up a story on her."

"She was supposed to run it by Isadora before she released it. If Whitney had done that, Isadora would have been able to adjust to the information in private instead of it being played out in the media."

"So now Isadora's out for blood. What will suing the agency do for her?"

"I think that she just wants revenge. Noah is on his way back to straighten this out."

"How do you know all this?"

"Mr. Powers' secretary told me. She also said Noah is going to take over the firm."

"What about the branch in New York? Who's going to run that one?"

"Noah's vice president is going to take control of it."

"What's their father going to do?"

"After this fiasco, he's tired and ready to retire."

###

Jacoby let herself into her apartment and thankfully found it empty. Kicking off her shoes, she padded barefoot into the bedroom. After changing into a housedress she went back into the kitchen and started preparing dinner. Soon she heard a key turn in the lock.

"Hey."

"Hey back," she answered without looking around. "Where have you been?"

"I went to the beach to get some sun."

"Again?" her lips pursed in displeasure.

"I didn't go to the nude part."

"Yeah, sure," Jacoby muttered in a disbelieving voice.

"I'm going to take a shower," Armstrong said in a disgruntled voice. He opened the refrigerator, grabbed a beer, and headed towards the bedroom.

Jacoby sashayed down the firm's hallway. As she walked by the conference room, her eyes briefly rested on Noah Powers. He was speaking with Isadora Leblanc's lawyer in muted tones. Her heart palpitated at the sight of his smooth, chocolate complexion that contrasted with his royal blue shirt and navy blue suit. The sheen of material battled for spotlight against his sparkling coal black eyes. Just the sight of him, made Jacoby dash into her office. Once the door was closed, she leaned back against it trying to tamp down the butterflies that were tap dancing inside her. She reminisced about the day he'd held her in his arms and saved her from falling. The ringing of her telephone roused her from her reverie. "This is Jacoby."

"They fired Whitney," Allie said.

"Oh no! I feel so sorry for her."

"So do I, but Noah didn't have a choice. Powers Public Relations was able to keep Isadora as a client, but the firm has to send a message to its employees and let other clients know the firm doesn't tolerate mistakes like that." She paused. "Tomorrow is Powers senior's last day and Noah is here to stay."

"So it's official?"

"Yep. Did you see the memo?"

"What memo?"

"There's going to be a meeting at three o'clock. I guess that's when they'll make the announcement that Noah is commander-in-chief."

At two-fifty Jacoby filed in the conference room with the other employees. Spotting Allie, she made a beeline to the empty chair next to her. "Hey," she whispered.

"Hey back," Allie replied.

Della Mcavoy leaned in from behind them. "This is just a formality. Everyone knows that Noah Powers is now our boss. I wonder if his girlfriend is moving to Miami with him."

Girlfriend! Immediately a feeling of disappointment filled Jacoby.

"What girlfriend?" Allie asked.

"I had to call him in New York one time," Della said. "He was supposed to be flying in for an important meeting, but it was cancelled. She answered the phone."

"Just because a woman answered the phone, that doesn't mean that she's his girlfriend," Allie said.

"That's how she identified herself when we spoke."

"Long distance relationships never work." Allie snapped, "As far as I'm concerned, he's a free agent."

A hush fell over the room as Bradley and Noah entered.

Jacoby watched them. *Noah Powers has the gait of a jungle cat.*

The two men stood side by side at the podium and faced the employees.

The room was charged with energy as everyone waited for the announcement.

Bradley Powers cleared his throat. "I'm sure that everyone knows why we're all here. I'm retiring from Powers Public Relations. I'm an old man," he said with a gruff smile. "And I'm ready to play golf five days a week."

Laughter filtered throughout the room.

"For some time, my son, Noah has been flying back and forth between New York and Miami. He has managed to make our branch in New York very successful. As of tomorrow, my son Noah is the CEO of Powers Public Relations."

A round of applause erupted in the room.

"I have been very happy working with all of you," Bradley continued in a sincere voice. "I will miss all of you. However, I have no regrets, because I know that Powers Public Relations will go even further under the guidance of my son."

"We'll miss you, Mr. Bradley," Della's simpering voice rang out in the room.

"Yeah," Andrew Brown echoed from the back.

"I'll be checking in from time to time to make sure that y'all are treating my son right."

More laughter emitted.

Then Bradley stepped back.

Noah moved to the mike. "I'm very happy to be working with all of you."

A few people began clapping and then everyone joined in. In the medium sized room the sound was deafening.

Jacoby clapped along with the crowd. She stared at Noah, noting his smooth countenance. He held the mike in one hand and his other was in his pants pocket, pulling the material taut.

It's hot in here. Jacoby fanned the air in front of her.

Noah's eyes zoomed in on her motions.

Their eyes locked across the expanse of the room.

Jacoby felt almost giddy from the connection.

Noah smiled and when he did, one side of his lip curled up more than the other. His eyes then traveled throughout the room, encompassing everyone. "I will be meeting individually with each of you. I'd like to get to know you, your vision of your future with the company, and your vision for Powers Public Relations. But that's enough for today. After you finish what you were working on before the meeting, please feel free to call it a day."

"Whoopee!" someone shouted from the back of the room, bringing about more laughter.

"That's my son," Bradley said, again taking the mike. "He's a man of few words but definite ideas. All of you will be just fine without me."

The next day Noah Powers leaned back in the black leather chair and read the file of one of the firm's employees. Closing it decisively, he hit his intercom. "Selyna."

"Yes, Mr. Powers."

"Please have Jacoby Alexander come see me as soon as possible."

"Yes, sir," she said.

Noah absently chewed on the tip of his pencil as he continued to sift through files. Soon three discreet knocks on the door got his attention.

Jacoby stood in the doorway. She wore a navy blue skirt and white ruffled blouse. Her smooth legs needed no stockings and the heels she wore made her look ready to walk the runway. Her long hair was pinned in a chignon at the nape of her neck and her makeup was flattering yet unobtrusive. Her only jewelry was a watch and small gold hooped earrings. She nervously shifted from one foot to the other.

Noah stood and extended his hand, indicating that she should sit in the vacant seat in front of his desk. "Thank you for being so prompt, Ms. Alexander."

Jacoby gratefully sank in it. "You needed to see me, Sir?"

Noah walked past her to close the door but left it slightly ajar. "This is sort of a private meeting yet protocol insists that I leave the door slightly open."

"Of course," Jacoby answered.

Noah smiled at her hoping to ease her look of anxiety. "I'm making some changes now that I'm taking over. There are employees whose services will no longer be needed, and others will be given different positions."

Jacoby's heart sank. *Dammit! I'm out of a job.*

"You've been a receptionist here for almost two years."

"Yes, sir," she said quietly.

"Do you like working here?"

"Yes, sir," she answered in a clear voice. "I truly enjoy my job."

"Have you thought about doing something else?"

"I don't know what you mean," she said slowly.

"Your file states that you're in school at the University of Miami. What is your major?"

"Public relations with a minor in journalism."

Noah rubbed his chin thoughtfully. "I think that you're being wasted as a receptionist. Whitney Davis has left the firm. She's moving on to other things," he said diplomatically, "so there's an opening as a public relations specialist. I'm offering you the job."

"Me!" she shouted.

"On my numerous visits, I've noticed how competent you are. You're a real people person with clients when they come to the firm. That's half the battle of being a successful public relations liaison. This move is your choice. If you'd like to remain a receptionist you can."

"Will I make more money?" she asked. Then she clamped her hand over her mouth because she felt so gauche.

Noah chuckled and the cleft in his chin became more pronounced. "You already make more money than an intern, so I can't give you a raise, because it wouldn't be fair to others. However, if you sign a good faith contract, that you'll continue to work at Powers for at least three years after you graduate, the firm will give you a stipend each semester to help pay for the rest of your education."

"What exactly would my duties be?"

"You'll be reporting directly to me, but you'll be doing everything a public relations liaison does."

"I don't know that I'm ready for that yet," she said in a subdued voice. "I don't want to fall short of your expectations and then be completely out of a job."

"I will be working closely with you, making sure that you make the right decisions."

Still, Jacoby hesitated.

"If things don't work out you can go back to a clerical position. Now do you want to make the move?"

Jacoby had to stop herself from jumping up and down. "Yes."

"Excellent! You'll move into Whitney's office. Your minor in journalism should help you with press releases, but to be honest, half of the job is common sense."

He reached into a file cabinet and pulled out a large folder. "This is Isadora Leblanc's dossier. At this time, she's your only client. We need to reinvent her and redo all of her PR. I need you to make her unexpected sad news into something positive. Work up some ideas for promoting her and be ready to present them to me no later Wednesday."

"Yes, Mr. Powers."

"Mr. Powers is my father," he said suavely. "Call me Noah."

"Thank you, Noah," she breathed. "I'm very grateful for the opportunity."

"Have some business cards made up with your new job title on them." Then he grabbed two more files and handed them to her. "These are contacts that we use for the firm of caterers, limo services, and paparazzi that we can count on to show up when we need them. Don't use the same ones all the time. Mix it up so that you can have a relationship with all of them."

"Yes, sir," she said.

"Yes, Noah," he said with a smile.

"Yes, Noah," she echoed as a feeling of anticipation sent shivers up and down her spine.

"Hello."

"Who is this?" Jacoby asked.

"Who do you want to speak to?" the voice snapped.

"This is Jacoby Alexander," she snapped back, "and I'd like to speak to my mother."

"Hold on," the surly voice said.

Jacoby's jubilant mood continued to sour as she held the phone and waited.

"Hello, honey," Sarai said in a tired voice.

"Who is that answering the telephone?" Jacoby demanded.

"Lydia is one of Alexandria's friends."

"What is she doing there?"

"She's hangs out here all day with Alexandria."

"Why isn't Alexandria at work?"

Sarai lowered her voice. "She got fired because she didn't write her criminal record on her employment application. Someone saw her working there and told the supervisor her history."

Jacoby said in disgust, "It figures that she'd lie and get caught. Where's Daddy?"

"He went down to the church."

Jacoby rolled her eyes.

"Pastor Leroy is down sick so your father is running things."

"He needs to run things at home. Things seem out of control up there."

"Don't fuss, Jacoby. It aggravates me even more to think about it. How are you doing?"

"I was doing great, but the chaos up there just ruined my day."

"Tell me why you were doing great," she pushed gently.

"I got a promotion," Jacoby said, excitement beginning to bubble inside her again.

"You did!"

"Yes." As she explained the details of her promotion, Jacoby had a mental picture of her mother puffing up with pride at every word she spoke.

"Jacoby, I may have not liked the circumstances surrounding your move to Miami, but I really think it has been the best thing in the world for you."

A visual of her meeting that afternoon with Noah made a chill run up and down Jacoby's spine. "I believe that too, Momma."

Jacoby was dressed and waiting when Armstrong arrived home.

He gave her a bright smile that was returned. "Acting class ran over later than usual. We better hurry so we don't miss the opening credits of the movie." He gave her a sheepish smile. "I've never seen me or my name on the big screen before."

"Maybe this is just the beginning," she answered.

As they sat in the dark movie theatre, Jacoby absently munched on popcorn and waited for Armstrong to appear on the silver screen. "When is your scene?"

"In about five minutes," he whispered back.

After about ten minutes the movie ended, and the theatre lights flashed on.

Jacoby looked at Armstrong.

He sat motionless in his chair. His fists were clenched and he gritted his teeth.

"What happened?" she gently asked.

"What the fuck do you think happened?" he screamed.

People leaving the theatre glanced at them and hurried towards the exit.

Jacoby shrank back against the seat, shaken at the sight of the throbbing muscle on Armstrong's temple.

"They cut me out!" Armstrong stood, picked up his empty beer cup and hurled it at the movie screen. "Come on. I want to get the hell out of here."

Armstrong sped through the Miami streets, dodging in and out of traffic, cursing violently each time he had to apply breaks.

"Slow down before you kill us," Jacoby cried out as she braced her hand against the dashboard in front of her.

But it wasn't until Armstrong reached their apartment complex that he broke his speed. Once inside the apartment he paced back and forth, holding his head with his hands. "They didn't even roll my name with the credits!"

"That's probably because you weren't in the picture," she said quietly.

"Shut up!' he screamed.

"I know that you're disappointed, Armstrong," she said tearfully, "but don't take it out on me."

" 'I know that you're disappointed but don't take it out on me,' " he mimicked. "I think that we should move."

"What?" she exclaimed in a shocked voice.

"I'll do better in L.A.," he said in a harried voice. "I'll get a different agent. They have all sorts of open casting calls out there so I'll have a better chance getting some work."

"I'm not moving to L.A.," she said firmly.

"You didn't want to move here either," he said sarcastically, "but now I couldn't get you to move back to Bunnell if someone gave you a million dollars."

"I like Miami."

"You'll learn to like L.A. too."

"Listen to me. I'm not moving." She counted off reasons with her index finger one by one. "I'm in school, and I have a job that I enjoy. I just got a promotion."

"What kind of promotion?" His eyes were narrowed suspiciously.

"I didn't tell you when you got home because I wanted tonight to be your night, but I was promoted to public relations specialist."

"Please," he muttered derisively.

"Please my ass. It's true. I'll be reporting directly to Noah Powers. Powers Public Relations is also going to help financially with my education, if I promise to remain there three years after I graduate."

"Why would he offer you that?"

"He thinks that I have potential." She got up from the chair and as she walked by Armstrong, his hand shot out and he gripped her wrist.

"He thinks he sees some potential pussy," he sneered.

"Ouch," she said trying to twist her arm out of his grasp. "That hurts."

"Are you fucking that Noah Powers? Is that the potential he sees in you?" He growled menacingly.

"Let me go, Armstrong," Jacoby said with a look of warning.

He released her.

She rubbed her wrist, wincing from the pain. "If you manhandle me like that again I'll leave you," she threatened.

Armstrong towered over her. "Ever since you started college and began working at that place you think that you're the shit."

Jacoby said in a tired voice, "Grow the fuck up!'

Armstrong's nostrils flared angrily and he pointed his finger in her face. "Don't talk to me like that."

Jacoby felt his hot breath on her face. She took a step back, putting space between them. "I'm going to sleep in the spare bedroom tonight," she said in a trembling voice. She hurried to the room and slammed the door. Then she turned the lock.

Noah read the proposal that Jacoby presented to him. "I really like your idea about her supporting a cause. It gives her image grounding."

"She might be interested in being a spokesperson for adopted children or maybe even something along the lines of the Big Sister program."

"I doubt that she'd be ready right now but she might be open to it once the dust clears." Skimming the list again Noah said, "Have you contacted any of these promotional events yet?"

"No. I wanted to okay it with you first."

"Call Isadora and find out when she's free for a meeting. I'll make sure I'm there. That off the cuff remark she made really hurt her image."

"I kind of hoped that she was misquoted."

"She wasn't. It's a bad thing to call someone 'trailer park trash.' Especially if it's your mother. That's a stereotype because there are some really nice mobile homes and nice people that live in them."

"But I saw in the National Enquirer a photo of the trailer her mother lives in and I'm afraid that one is pretty bad. Maybe Isadora will help her mother out financially. That would help clean up her image."

"I doubt that she'll be ready to help her any time soon and don't suggest it to her."

"I won't," Jacoby promised. "There's a charity function on Saturday night that I think that I can get her into."

"Make sure she's seated at a front table or she should pass on it." Noah held the file out to Jacoby.

When she reached for it, the cuff on her French shirt rode up her arm and the scratches on her arm were exposed.

Noah's hand stilled in midair and he stared at them.

Jacoby hastily pulled her shirt sleeve down. She muttered, "I'll get to work on this," and hurriedly left.

That afternoon, Jacoby systematically called the vendors of upcoming social events. Each time she secured an invitation for Isadora she put a check mark next to the event.

"Look at you with your big fancy office."

She grinned at Allie as she walked into her office. "It's not that big, but it sure beats my cubicle."

"By the way, I'm healthily jealous."

"Don't be. I just happened to be in the right place at the right time."

"I don't think so," Allie mused.

"What do you mean?'

"Don't get me wrong. You deserve this job, but how many people actually get what they deserve?"

"Meaning?"

"I think that Noah Powers has taken a liking to you," she said and her voice was laced with innuendo. "And I must say, it's about time someone looked out for you instead of the other way around. We need to go out and celebrate. There's a group going to happy hour Friday night at the Blue Martini. Let's hang with them and party."

"What's the occasion?"

"Oreatha from payroll is retiring. And Noah is going to be there. I know this because I overheard him discussing it with Sam Shultz. Come on and go, Jacoby. This is the perfect opportunity for him to see you outside of work. If he thinks that you look hot in that navy blue skirt you're wearing, wait until he sees you all gussied up after hours." Then to top it off, Allie whistled.

"You're nuts!" Jacoby laughed but her mind was working overtime as she thought about what Allie was suggesting.

"That's how I got Lenny. I found out where he hung out and casually stopped by. I haven't regretted it once."

"I have a paper due next week. If I can get it done by Friday, I'll join you guys."

That evening Jacoby was putting the finishing touches on her paper when Armstrong got home.

"Hello," he said. He held out a red rose.

She ignored him.

He stomped off to the kitchen and instantly reappeared. "Didn't you cook when you got home?"

"There's a bucket of chicken on the counter. Help yourself."

A few minutes later Armstrong reentered the den with a plate of food. He turned on the television and sat down. Jacoby glared at him. "Since you never wash a dish, you should start using paper plates. I'm tired of cleaning up after you all time."

Armstrong's eyebrows met together in a frown. "You certainly are getting full of yourself."

Armstrong went over to the stereo and turned it on. Rap music blared making a reverberating sound throughout the room.

"Armstrong," Jacoby shouted in frustration. "You don't need the stereo and television on. I can't concentrate."

"Too damn bad," he shouted back.

Jacoby slammed her laptop shut. She stomped into the bedroom and climbed into the bed. She pulled a pillow over her ears and tried to no avail, to shut out the din coming from the other room.

Jacoby was dressed in a pale yellow suit, and she looked as charming as the late Jackie Kennedy. She and Noah sat across from Isadora.

"So you're taking the place of that idiot Whitney?"

Noah said in a smooth voice, "Jacoby has been given the task of revamping your image. You're the only client whose portfolio she's in charge of."

"Good," Isadora said. "I certainly don't want any more slipshod management or I will follow through and take my business elsewhere."

"Ms. Leblanc," Jacoby said.

"Call me Isadora. That Ms. title makes me seem old."

Jacoby gave her a smile. "Isadora, here is a list of events that you've been invited to attend."

Isadora scanned the list. "This is pretty good."

"I've already arranged for black Hummer limousines on these dates.

You'll have to let me know exactly what time you want to arrive and I'll relay to them the information. You need not be too early nor too late. We want the paparazzi to have plenty of opportunities to take pictures of you."

"Why must I go to three charity events in one month?"

"People like to see stars give back to society," Jacoby said.

"You're right," she agreed.

"Also, I suggest you find a cause that you want to be a spokesperson for."

"I like dogs. What about the Humane Society?"

Noah said dryly, "I think that's already taken."

"Oh," Isadora said and took a sip from the cup of coffee that Jacoby had provided for her.

"You don't have to make up your mind today," Jacoby said. "If you come up with about three or four that you wouldn't mind doing public service announcements for, I'll send out feelers and see if they'd like your assistance supporting their cause."

"I like her," Isadora said to Noah. "She's smart."

CHAPTER 8

Wearily, Jacoby leaned her head back and closed her eyes. She massaged her throbbing temples and drifted off to sleep. When she awoke hours later, she stumbled into the kitchen and grabbed a bottle of water, went to her desk and withdrew her memory stick. Sliding it into her laptop, she her pressed the on button of her computer. It didn't come on. She withdrew the memory stick and looked at it. Nothing seemed out of place. She tried to turn her computer on again and still there was no power. Jacoby placed her hand over her heart to try to stop it from thumping so hard. Grabbing her memory stick, computer, and purse she practically ran out the door. Jacoby stopped at the first Office Depot that she saw. Following the signs she went to the computer services department.

"I'm Clark. May I help you?" the clerk asked.

"I can't get my computer to come on and I need to load my college paper on this stick and print it," Jacoby said in a panic-stricken voice.

"Let me take a look and see what's going on." Clark pushed various buttons but could get no response. "Hmm," he said. "I'm going to have to take it apart."

"How long will that take?"

"You're going to have to leave it. I'll call within twenty-four hours with an estimate on how long it's going to be in the shop."

"Please, Clark. I need it by Monday evening. I have a paper due and it's on the hard drive."

"Didn't you back up?"

"No," she said despondently. "I was just so tired last night I figured that I'd do it later. I usually print my papers at work."

Clark said chidingly, "You should always back up."

"I will in the future, but please can you help me?"

"We're getting ready to close, but I'll look at it first thing in the morning. Do you have a number where you can be reached?"

Jacoby handed Clark one of her new business cards. She scribbled her cell phone number on it. "Call me at this number."

"I'll see what I can do," he said soothingly.

Jacoby tossed and turned all night. What the hell happened to my computer? It was fine last night when I turned it off. She stared at Armstrong's still form on the other side of the bed.

As if he sensed her eyes on him, he opened his eyes and reached for her.

Jacoby turned her back to him. "Leave me alone, I'm tired."

Jacoby pushed her half-eaten sandwich away. She said tearfully, "Clark said that the hard drive got wet so all the information was damaged."

"That's terrible," Allie exclaimed. "How do you think that happened?"

"I don't know because I never drink liquids by my laptop. Now I'm going to have to buy another."

"That sucks, Jacoby."

"That's just one of my problems. I have to rewrite my paper that's due Monday."

"So are you going to go and purchase another laptop?"

"Not this paycheck. This is the week that I have to pay for Mom's medicine."

"But what about your assignment that's due?"

"I'm going to stay after work and use the computer. Whatever I don't finish, this weekend I'll have to use one of the computers at the public library."

"Damn! That's a lot of trouble."

"And you can't always get one," she wailed.

"So, I guess that you won't make it to happy hour tonight."

"Why would I go to happy hour, when I'm so unhappy?"

The office was quiet as Jacoby pounded away at her keyboard. As she shuffled through her notes, she felt that she was being watched.

Noah leaned on the doorjamb and stared at her. His expression was inscrutable.

Flustered by his appearance, Jacoby pushed the monitor button, darkening the screen.

"What are you working on so late at night?"

She blurted out, "I thought that you were going to Oreatha's retirement party."

Noah flashed his bright smile. "I had a business meeting downtown, so I couldn't make it. But that doesn't answer my question." She saw the glint of his teeth again. "It's after seven o'clock on a Friday night, and I don't pay you overtime, so what's so urgent that couldn't wait until

Monday morning?"

Jacoby bowed her head. "My computer is in the shop and I have a paper due on Monday."

"When will yours be fixed?'

"It won't be," she said dolefully. "They said that I could come and pick it up but I don't see what the use of that is."

"You're probably better off. Once they break they usually never work right again."

Jacoby's stomach growled. With a look of discomfort, she put her hand on her stomach.

"Don't be embarrassed," Noah said. "In a minute my stomach is going to answer yours. Do you like ribs?"

"Name me a black person who doesn't."

"Well, I'm going to go and pick up a dinner for myself. I'll bring you something to eat. I have things to finish here before I leave for the weekend myself."

Jacoby reached for her wallet. "Thank you so much, Noah. I'm starving."

"Don't insult me by giving me money. Now what do you want, chopped pork, or pulled?"

"Chopped," she said gratefully as she slid her wallet back inside her purse.

"I'll be back," he said.

Jacoby rested her chin on her hands and stared through the doorway Noah had just exited.

About an hour later, he returned with a huge bag of food. The minute he entered her office the smell made her stomach growl, and again, she placed her hand over it in an effort to still its rumbling.

Noah's lips twitched in amusement.

She saved her work on her memory stick and shut the computer down.

Noah said, "Let's eat in the break room."

"That's a good idea," she said. "I don't want barbeque sauce on the keyboard." Once they were inside, Jacoby washed her hands at the sink. After she dried them she said opening Styrofoam cartons, "Let me do this. It's the least I can do."

They sat across from each other and chomped down on ribs, chopped barbeque, garlic toast, baked beans, and macaroni and cheese. "Oreatha is going to be disappointed that you didn't make it."

"It couldn't be helped," he said, sipping from his bottle of water. "Selyna is going to make my apologies and she has the retirement gift from the firm."

"That was very thoughtful of you."

"Word of mouth is very important in this business."

Jacoby surreptitiously perused Noah from under her long eyelashes. He wore a pair of black pin-striped dress slacks, a white shirt, and had loosened his tie. Black loafers with a tassel completed his outfit. He looked like an ad for "Black Enterprise".

"What I wouldn't do for a beer," Noah said as he finished up the last of his food.

"Me too," Jacoby grinned. "But I think that I've broken enough company rules for the night."

"What do you mean?" Noah asked as he wiped his mouth with a napkin.

She gave him a guilty look. "I know that I'm not supposed to be using the company computer for my personal use. Thank you for not making an issue of it, Noah."

"I think that I have a remedy for that." Noah reached behind him and opened a cabinet door. He pulled out a box and placed it on the table. "This is for you."

Stunned, Jacoby stared at the box. "I can't accept a laptop from you."

"You can and you will," he said firmly. "There will be times that you'll have to work at home so you can't be without one."

"I can't accept it. It's too much."

"I'll write it off as a company expenditure," he said quietly. "The firm is counting on you to do your job well, Jacoby."

Jacoby opened the box and lovingly touched the plastic covering. "It's a MAC," she breathed.

"That's what I use since they don't get viruses," Noah explained. "You shouldn't have any trouble for a long time."

That night, Jacoby secured her new laptop in the closet of the spare bedroom. When she went to bed she turned her back to a snoring Armstrong and fell into a deep sleep.

The next morning she walked into her office and stopped dead in her tracks. On her desk was a new color laser printer with a note on top of it.

If you're printing at work, you must not have one at home.

Enjoy, Noah.

Noah was watching the news when he heard his front door open.

"Noah, I'm here."

He went to greet her.

Monique was dressed in her stewardess outfit. She released her overnight bag and threw her arms around his neck

He dutifully kissed her.

"You must be tired," she said. "I expected more passion that that."

"You're right," he said. "I am tired." Grabbing her luggage handle he said, "Let me get this for you."

Monique followed him with an apprehensive look. "So how do you like living in Miami full time?"

"I don't have an opinion since I haven't done anything but work since I got here." He wearily passed his hand over his face. "I'm going to take a shower. Then we need to talk." He dragged her luggage and put it in the spare bedroom.

She stared after him with a fearful look on her face.

Noah planted his hands against the shower walls and let the steaming water pelt him. He felt cold air behind him and opened his eyes. "What are you doing in here, Monique?" he asked in his husky voice.

She grabbed a washcloth and applied shower gel on it. "Let me wash your back," she said throatily.

Noah remained passive as she began to scrub him in small circular motions. His manhood rose and he palmed it and tried to press its long length back into place.

"Turn around," she whispered. "I want to wash your Pecs."

Noah obeyed and Monique dropped to her knees. She took her finger and traced his erect member. Planting her hands on his buttocks she scooted closer to him and drew him fully into her mouth.

Noah cradled Monique's head with his hands. All of a sudden his grip tightened and with superhuman willpower he pushed her away.

"What's wrong?" Monique asked in a confused voice.

Noah stared down at her wet body before hoisting her to her feet. "I told you that we need to talk," he said gruffly. "Finish your shower and then meet me in the den."

Thirty minutes later Monique entered the room dressed in a black, silk teddy and heels. She sat on the loveseat cushion next to him.

"When you told me that you had a flight for Miami I let you come so we could talk."

"Let me come?" She swallowed hard. "Since when has that been a problem?"

"I don't feel that a long distance relationship will work for us."

"I agree," she said. "That's why I put in for a transfer to Miami. I should hear within the next few months."

"If you get it I don't want you to take it."

"Why?"

"We're not right for each other."

"We've been together for eight years," she said her eyes filling with tears.

"Exactly. If we were meant to be I would have proposed a long time ago. Monique, I'm thirty-four years old. I want someone that I can commit to."

"And you don't think that it's me?" she said in a shrill voice.

"No."

Angry tears welled up in her eyes and she brushed them away with the back of her hand. "It's our schedule. We don't spend enough time together. We can make it work."

"I don't want to spend more time with you," he said gently.

"How dare you!" she screamed.

"There's someone better out there for you."

"You sound like a character from some dumb ass Lifetime movie."

"I probably do," he acknowledged.

"Is there someone else?"

Noah averted his eyes. "I don't know."

"Who is it?" she demanded.

"None of your business," he said evasively.

"Men don't leave unless they've got someone else in the background to replace the current with. Once you grow bored with her, don't call me!"

"Okay," Noah promised in an unruffled voice.

Sheer fury ignited in her and Monique's eyes snapped. "You string me along for eight years and then dump me! You're a horrible person."

"Monique," Noah said in a weary voice. "It's better for me to have strung you along for eight years,' he said coolly, "instead of nine. I'll sleep upstairs tonight." He climbed the spiral staircase two steps at a time.

The next morning, Noah woke to an empty house. There was a gold key on his countertop. Opening his cell he surfed the Internet until he found what he wanted.

"Safelock," a man answered.

"I need my house rekeyed. Can a locksmith come tonight around seven?"

"Yes, sir. What's the address?"

"125 Gables by the Sea."

###

"Good afternoon, this is Jacoby Alexander of Powers Public Relations."

"Good afternoon," the operator said.

"I'd like to be connected to Summer Fielding."

"Just one minute, please."

"Summer Fielding speaking."

"Hello," Jacoby said airily. "I'm Jacoby Alexander and I represent Isadora Leblanc.

"Yes."

"As you know, Miss Leblanc's movie, *Keepin' it Light*, will be released in June. I have answered many calls begging for an interview with her but Ms. Leblanc is a fan of your magazine and wishes you to have it."

"Is she willing to talk about her recent discovery that she was adopted?"

"Ms. Leblanc is still working through her feelings on this matter," Jacoby said diplomatically. "I don't think that she would feel comfortable going into all the details at this time."

"Well then what good is an interview with her?"

"Ms. Leblanc would like to encourage people who have adopted children to make them aware at an early age of the circumstances. The story of her heartbreak might save many families from the emotional turmoil that she's experiencing."

"Hmm," Summer said, "I can see an angle in that."

"We would like the interview to be printed in the magazine before her movie comes out."

"Of course you would," Summer replied in a dry tone.

"There is one thing. Miss Leblanc insists on reading the piece before it goes to press."

"That's highly irregular."

"I'm aware of that, however, in light of recent information being printed that she would have preferred been kept private, Ms. Leblanc is a bit shy about giving interviews." Jacoby added smoothly, "This is only a formality because she trusts your magazine."

"Okay."

"I'll fax over the contract to you this afternoon."

With a feeling of immense satisfaction, Jacoby hung up the telephone.

Noah was standing in the doorway. He wore a pleased look. "I heard that. Excellent job, Jacoby! You're a pro."

After he disappeared, Jacoby put her hands to her flushed cheeks. At lunchtime, she grabbed a candy bar out of the vending machine.

"How's everything going?" Della Mcavoy asked.

"Pretty well, I think."

"I wouldn't take the job of promoting Isadora Leblanc for a million dollars," she said with obvious envy.

"She's not that bad. I've already met with her several times and she's been quite pleasant."

"Don't make a mistake. If you do it's off with your head."

"I'm not really worried about that."

Della looked Jacoby up and down. Jacoby was dressed in a black knit dress that clung to her curves. "I guess you aren't."

"What do you mean by that?"

"Everyone is a little surprised that the minute Noah took over you went from a receptionist to a PR person," she stated in a catty voice.

"Do they know that I'm the status of an intern and am in college pursuing a degree in public relations?"

Della's eyes grew wide. "I don't think so."

"Noah promoted others employees also. Obviously he thought people were being wasted in their past positions and wanted to rectify that."

"Please don't say anything to Noah about what I said," Della said nervously. "It's just that the other PR persons have been talking and I thought that you should know."

"I won't say anything to him," Jacoby promised. "I just want to come to work, do the best job that I can, and stay away from the nonsense."

"Okay," Della said, drawing a sigh of relief. "Hey, a bunch of us are meeting at Chili's for lunch. Would you like to join us?"

"No thanks," Jacoby declined. "I have to work through lunch today."

Around six o'clock Jacoby was sitting at her desk pretending that she had work to do. She breathed a sigh of anticipation, when she heard Noah's footsteps heading towards her office.

He came to her doorway with a quizzical expression on his face. "Late night again?"

"Yes," she said, mentally crossing her fingers at the lie that she told.

"I'm going to go and get some take-out. What would you like to eat tonight?"

"I don't care, Noah," she replied, "Whatever pleases you."

"This is getting to be a habit for us," Noah said with a quirky smile.

"One that I enjoy."

"I too look forward to it," he quipped before he left.

After Noah left, Jacoby rested her chin on her hand and stared thoughtfully at the doorway. It's also a habit that I have no intention of breaking.

Jacoby was vacuuming when Armstrong arrived home. He tapped her on the shoulder with a small box.

Shutting off the vacuum cleaner she said, "What's that?"

"Open it," he ordered.

Armstrong sat next to Jacoby as she opened her gift.

A silver pen shone brightly at her.

"I apologize for the way I've been acting since you got your promotion."

"It's very nice, Armstrong," she said with sincerity. "Thank you."

"I've been having a tough time with me being cut out of my movie and all. I want you to know that I'm very proud of you, Jacoby. I hardly recognize you as the girl that moved here from Bunnell."

"Is that a good thing?" she smiled.

"It isn't a bad thing. Promise me that you'll carry the pen with you always."

"Promise you?" Her eyebrows arched up questioningly.

"Yes, promise me. Because every time you look at that pen I want you to remember that I support you as you move up the ladder of success."

"Thank you, Armstrong. And I promise that I'll always use it."

"Sit back and relax. I'm going to cook dinner tonight."

"You are?" she exclaimed.

"It's only Manwich, but I thought that you could use a break."

"I can," she said gratefully. "I need to work on a paper that's due next week."

She took her laptop out of its computer bag.

Armstrong's eyes narrowed angrily. "Where did you get that computer?"

"The firm supplied it because sometimes I have to bring work home."

There was a heavy silence in the room. "I guess that I'll start dinner," he said with a sour look on his face.

"This was pretty good, Armstrong." Jacoby said after she finished her dinner.

"I've decided I'm going to Bunnell for Mother's day," Armstrong said abruptly.

"You are?" she said surprised. "Why?"

"They're having my high school reunion."

"I wouldn't have thought that you'd want to go to that," she mumbled.

"Why!" he snapped. "Because you don't think that I'm successful?"

"That's not what I think at all." She covered his hand with hers. "Let's not fight."

"I also need to go and check out my house because I haven't been there since my renters moved out. I thought that you might help me clean it up for the next ones."

"I'm sure that I'll have to clean it up since I want to stay there instead of at my parents."

"Good," he said. "My high school class is having a social Friday night. Will you go with me?"

"That's the only thing I'll attend because the rest of the time I want to spend with my mom."

"Okay," he said.

Noah placed a folder on Jacoby's desk before easing his long frame into the chair across from her.

"What's that?"

"It's background information on your new client, Francois Medina."

"I'm not representing Isadora anymore?"

"Of course you are. But I think that you're ready to add another star to your portfolio."

"I've never heard much about him."

"He's new to the scene. So if you can promote him half as well as you've done for Isadora, he'll be very pleased."

"It's a little late to get him into the events that she has coming up," Jacoby said doubtfully, "but I'll try."

"Francois and Isadora want to meet us for dinner to discuss things. Do you have plans tonight?"

"No, I'm free as a bird."

"I'll have a car sent to your home at seven. They want to meet at Emeril's. Have you ever eaten there?"

"No."

"The food is delicious. The dress code is shabby chic."

"Are Francois and Isadora an item?"

"I don't know, but that's something you should ask them."

"And I don't know that I'll have anything to tell them at dinner."

"You work well under pressure. I'm sure you'll come up with something," he said with confidence. "I have a meeting. See you later."

Jacoby grabbed Francois Medina's file and started reading.

Jacoby appraised herself in the full length mirror. A dress made with black lace décolleté and spaghetti straps flattered her full breasts. The satin fabric nipped in at the waist and clung to her curves ending right above her knee. Because of the humidity, Jacoby opted to wear sandals instead of pumps. She'd swept her hair into an updo and long gold earrings to match her watch dangled from her ears.

When she stepped out of the apartment building, she spied a black town car.

A man dressed in a black suit stood there holding a placard that had the words Jacoby Alexander printed on it.

"I'm Jacoby Alexander."

"Pleased to meet you, ma'am," he said in a heavy Spanish accent. Then he opened the car door.

Jacoby slid inside. When she turned to fasten her seatbelt, her eyes met the enigmatic eyes of Noah Powers. "Noah!" she exclaimed.

"You were expecting someone else?" he asked.

"No," she stammered. "I just thought that you'd drive your own car."

Noah took a long sip from a glass of wine. "Bruno is always my designated driver. I don't drink and drive."

The sexy voice of Rafael Saadiq filled the car. *Oh my God! Noah looks so scrumptious in his black suit. What the hell am I doing? This grandeur is too much for me.*

"Would you like a glass of wine?" Noah asked in his husky voice.

"Please," she stammered. "I need something."

"Sit back and relax, Jacoby. You're in the company of a friend." He poured her a glass of white wine.

She gratefully accepted the glass and took a huge sip. "This is really delicious. What is it?"

"It's Cortese. I have it imported from Italy." Noah tapped on the glass partition and the driver set the car in motion. He eased back against the sumptuous leather.

Jacoby viewed him from under her long eyelashes. "Noah, are you sure that I'm ready for this?"

"Why do you continue to doubt yourself? You've already proven to be an exceptional public relations specialist."

"But I'm a newbie. Meeting celebrities for meetings and now dinners, I mean. Isn't that unusual?"

"From the moment I saw you, I knew that you were someone who would go far if given the chance. I'm in the place to help you be all you can be."

Jacoby bristled. "So you consider yourself Henry Higgins to my Liza Doolittle?"

"There you go again, putting yourself down. You're a smart girl, Jacoby. Do you know how many people wouldn't even be able to draw that allusion?"

"I've always loved to read," she said in a shy voice. "I guess that's why I enjoy college so much."

"I'm not helping you because I have some sinister master plan. Don't you have people in your life that let you know how amazing you are?"

"My mom," she answered quietly after quaffing the rest of her wine.

"No male role model?" he asked.

"No."

"That's a shame because girls need praise from a young age from a parental male role model."

"I used to get that from my father," she said quietly. "But now we're estranged."

"Hmm," he said in a thoughtful manner. "I don't want to pry but don't you think you can work it out?"

She looked out the window as in the carpool lane they flew past other cars. "I don't know that I want to."

Noah locked eyes with hers and sexual chemistry ignited between them.

Jacoby squirmed uncomfortably and tightened her thighs together in response.

"Whatever he's done to hurt you, it hasn't soured you and stopped you from being something very special, Jacoby Alexander."

Jacoby quivered as if hot molten lava was inside her. Hoping to douse the fire she held out her glass and it was quickly refilled.

"I'm glad you're not driving," he teased.

"I'm really a lightweight, so I'll make this one my last. I don't want to act giddy around Isadora and Francois."

"Don't worry about it. This is an informal meeting. Francois has a small part in a movie and they're filming in South beach. This restaurant is a convenient meeting place."

"So he just wants to size me up?"

"That's not needed since Isadora has been singing your praises to him. I'm sure that he probably just wants to make sure that you'll take him on."

"I don't have a choice, do I?"

"He doesn't know that. It's always best to make the client feel as if you're in demand. That means you have control over the situation."

"But it wasn't like that with Isadora. I mean, she was going to leave the firm."

"She was never going to do that. She just wanted Whitney fired."

"I feel kind of bad stepping into Whitney's shoes like that. It's kind of creepy."

"Whitney is working for an associate of mine who owns a PR firm in Vegas."

"So you gave her a good recommendation?"

"Whitney worked for my dad for three years and was an excellent employee. She made a mistake and had to pay for it. Moving is not an easy thing, but she's still doing what she loves."

"So you looked out for her. You have a kind heart, Noah. Everyone doesn't."

There was a tense undercurrent in the car.

"Tell me about your boyfriend," Noah demanded in a taut voice.

Her mouth went dry. "How do you know about him?"

"You have his name written down as your emergency contact and you're listed at the same address and phone number."

"Oh. I moved from Bunnell with him."

"Are you happy with him?"

The wine she'd consumed loosened her inhibitions. "No."

"Then why do you stay?"

"He needs me. Armstrong is a war veteran from Afghanistan," Jacoby explained. "I know that he's suffering from post-traumatic stress disorder."

"Why doesn't he get some help?"

"He doesn't acknowledge that anything's wrong with him."

"Then you tell him to get help," Noah said roughly. "There are all types of counseling services for people suffering from the ravages of war."

"Armstrong thinks that his unhappiness is career related. For years he's been trying to break into acting. When he goes to an audition and gets a call back he's the sweetest person in the world. But when things don't go his way," she sighed miserably, "he acts like a real jerk."

"Acting isn't a steady job for any person. Even if you're George Clooney you go for stretches of time without anything to do. That means that Armstrong's a jerk almost every day."

"He is," she said glumly. "He's felt pretty useless since he was released from the army. But he feels that once he gets his big break his life will be perfect."

"Most likely if he was a successful actor he'd be more of a jerk. I've rarely seen fame make a person better. People are what they are."

"You're probably right."

Noah was almost afraid to ask but he had to know. "Do you love him?"

Jacoby shook her head no. "I don't think I ever did. I was just young and thought I was in love. Armstrong was there for me at a time when no one else was," she paused, ashamed to voice her feelings, "including my mother. I've promised to be there for him, and I can't break my word. But that's enough about me. Do you have a girlfriend?"

"No," he said. "I'm available."

"It's hard to believe," she whispered.

"I was in a relationship," he said truthfully. "But I felt that I was being unfair to keep her tied up knowing that I didn't want to marry her. She hates me now, but eventually she'll be glad that I ended it. Now she can get on with her life."

"That's a good way to look at it."

"The time will come when you'll realize that you can't save someone who doesn't want to be saved." Noah poured another glass of wine and handed it to her. "Here," he said staring at her sad eyes, "from the expression on your face you look like you need it."

CHAPTER 9

As Jacoby sat across from Noah the ember flames from the candle arrangement on the table cast a fragrance that evoked childhood of the fireplace burning in the winter.

A maitre d' appeared at their table. "Mr. Powers."

"Yes."

"Your party left a message that they were running late on the set, so for you to go ahead and dine. He said that Miss Leblanc texted you."

"Let me see." Noah took out his iPhone and scrolled down the screen. "She did, but I had it turned off in the limousine." He said to the maitre' d, "We'll not wait for them. Please send a waiter over with menus and a wine list."

"Of course, sir."

"I didn't think you ever turned that thing off," Jacoby said with a wry smile.

"You just saw why I don't. I turned it off briefly because I didn't want us to be interrupted on the ride over. It's rare that I enjoy a woman's conversation the way I do yours."

"Give me a break," Jacoby protested. "What did I say that was so earth shattering?"

He said suddenly, "Don't you realize how beautiful you are?"

Jacoby dropped her eyes from the smoldering intensity of his.

"And you seem quite unaffected by the glitz and glamour that walks through our door every day at work."

"I can't compete with the beautiful actors and actress that I see."

"You don't have to." Noah shuddered. "If you want to feel good about yourself take a look at those tabloid stories with titles like 'Stars Without Their Makeup On.' "

Jacoby's tinkling laughter seemed to fill the room. Guiltily she placed her hand over her mouth. "Oh my goodness, I don't want to be gauche. You won't take me anywhere else."

"I'll take you out any time you choose, Jacoby."

She blushed and dropped her gaze.

"I hope that I haven't made you uncomfortable."

"You haven't," she said honestly.

"Good," he said, picking up the menu.

A waiter magically appeared before them.

"Would you like me to order for you?"

"I'd love that," she said handing her menu to the waiter.

Noah said, "We'd like the grilled salmon, overstuffed baked potato and asparagus."

"Yes, sir," the waiter replied as he jotted down their order. He gave them a slight nod before he departed.

"You seem to know everything, Noah."

"That would be impossible," he said. "I do have an interest in a variety of things. It's amazing what you can learn from television."

"What programs do you watch?"

"I'm a sports fanatic, but I set my DVR for *Scandal*, and watch it when I get the chance. For politics, I watch *PoliticsNation* with Al Sharpton and *All In With Chris Hayes* on MSNBC. "Chris Hayes stands by his convictions. He even rides his bike to work, because he cares about the environment."

"Scandal is my favorite show. But I rarely get to watch television any more between my school work and job."

"I'm not overworking you, am I?" he asked with a critical eye.

"Of course not. I love that I'm so busy."

"Are you happy working at the firm, Jacoby?"

"Very. You know, it's funny. I thought that I was happy being a library assistant in Bunnell and for that period of my life I was. Now, I could never see myself being satisfied with doing that for a career. I guess that I was more comfortable than happy."

Noah raised his glass and said, "Cheers to a happy life and even happier future."

Jacoby clinked her glass with his before sipping.

"I was almost afraid to do that with the waitress asking you for an I.D. and all."

"Don't let that bother you. I always get carded when I go and buy Armstrong's beer." A pall seemed to settle over the table at the mention of his name.

Noah was paying the check when a frenzied Francois and Isadora got there.

"I'm sorry," Francois said. "But I just couldn't get away."

Noah said curtly, "Normally I would have left, but Jacoby has been working so hard," he gave Isadora a pointed look, "I felt she deserved a nice dinner in a fine restaurant."

Isadora slid into the chair next to Jacoby. "I'm sorry, Jacoby. I didn't come by earlier because I had a huge lunch. So I figured that I'd just hang around the set until Francois was free."

"Don't let her fool you," Francois said. "Isadora was smoozing the director hoping to get a part in his next movie."

She playfully punched him. "There's nothing wrong with forming relationships, Francois."

"You two seem to know each other well," Jacoby said cautiously.

"Isadora used to hang out with my older sister, Jasmine."

"We go way back or I wouldn't look out for this mongrel."

"Francois, I read your biography. Is there anything in it you don't want played out in the press?"

"Nope," Francois said. "I'm an open book. I'm the typical college dropout who got impatient with school and headed out to California to try to break into acting."

"Is that an angle you want me to use?"

"I don't know," Francois said musingly. "That worked for Matt Damon and Ben Affleck."

"But they have talent," Isadora said only half teasingly.

"Ha, ha, ha," Francois retorted unperturbed.

Jacoby smiled at them. "This afternoon as I was brainstorming ideas, I kind of came up with this. Everyone loves mystery. Isadora, why don't I try to get Francois into the events you're booked to attend? I'll have the two of you arrive in different limousines, but leave together. The tabloids will start speculating right away and give you both some buzz."

"But the cougar thing is overdone in Hollywood. It's not even a novelty anymore," Isadora said.

"You're only five years older than Francois so that wouldn't really constitute a cougar relationship," she replied, eyebrows arched. "I think that because he's new to the Hollywood scene, people will be interested."

"What do I get out of it?" Isadora asked in her forthright manner.

"When you're asked about your relationship with Francois, play coy. Every time Jennifer Aniston has a drink with a man it gets play on E and all the weekly magazine rags."

"And she never discusses her personal business," Isadora said gleefully.

"No, she doesn't," Jacoby agreed. "And because of it she comes off like a class act."

"I like this idea, Jacoby. But eventually people with find out that he and I have known each other for years. That will end the mystery."

"I don't think so," Jacoby said in a diplomatic voice. "You've recently discovered upsetting news about your family history. People have a tendency to turn to and begin sleeping with a friend when things get rough."

"Are you game for that, Francois?"

"We don't have to pretend to be lovers, Isadora." He put his arm around her. "I've always had a thing for you, and I think that we'd make a cute couple."

"I don't think so, little brother," Isadora said dryly as she shrugged his arm off.

Jacoby's attention was diverted to Noah.

He'd been quiet throughout the whole conversation. Now he had his arms folded across his chest. As he viewed Jacoby, a look of pride was etched on his features.

Noah and Jacoby were silent on the ride back to Jacoby's apartment. Soft music played in the background. Sadness enveloped her when she realized that she was home. "I feel like Cinderella when it was time for her to leave the ball."

"You're no Cinderella," Noah murmured quietly, "but I think that you're going to have the same happy ending that she did." Ignoring the interested look of the driver in the rearview mirror, he kissed the back of her hand. "Good night, Jacoby. We'll wait here until you're safely in the building. Don't hurry in to work tomorrow. I'll see you when you get there."

Jacoby practically floated to the elevator and up to her apartment. She turned on the light once she was inside.

Armstrong sat in a chair and when the light came on hurriedly brushed tears from his cheeks.

Alarmed, she went to him. "What's happened? What's wrong?"

"Where were you tonight?"

"I had a business meeting," she stammered.

"Dressed like that?"

"It was at a restaurant on South Beach. Why are you crying?"

"Nothing has gone right for me since I left the service," he said in a depressed voice. "I haven't said anything to you before, but my foot hurts all the time."

Stunned, she said, "I didn't know, Armstrong."

"Maybe that's why I'm always in such a lousy mood. Now even alcohol doesn't seem to dull the pain."

"You get medication for free, Armstrong. Go to the doctor and get a prescription for pain," she urged.

"I think I'll do that, Jacoby."

"And I think that you should seek counseling," she said carefully. "You saw such tragedy in the war you might need to talk to someone to get your feelings out."

"I've been thinking about that," he said, dropping his eyes in humiliation. He stood and held out his arms.

She went to him, wanting to comfort him.

"Jacoby, I don't know what I'd do without you. Life wouldn't be worth living."

Horror filled her at his words and she felt suffocated.

Armstrong's hands wandered from around her waist to cup her buttocks. He began unzipping her dress. "I can't," she said pulling away. "It's my time of the month."

"Come on, Jacoby. Stop being so old fashioned."

She averted her eyes from his. "I am what I am, Armstrong. Some things you can't change."

Fury spread across his face.

"I'm going to a shower and go to bed," she said, avoiding his eyes. "It's been a long day."

That night as they slept back to back, her thoughts were of Noah and she rubbed the place on her hand that he'd kissed.

###

The next morning Jacoby woke to an empty apartment. With relief she went to the kitchen and made herself a cup of coffee. Holding the steaming liquid, she turned on the television. Once she set her DVR box to record *PoliticsNation* and *All In With Chris Hayes* before she went to get dressed for work.

Navigating through traffic on I-95 was worse than the usual congestion with people riding on each other's bumpers, shooting each other the bird, and dodging in and out of the three lanes at eighty miles an hour. Jacoby's nerves were wearing thin when she saw her exit.

Suddenly her car began to lurch forward as if it had the hiccups. Looking at her gas tank she saw that her car still had a half a tank. Drivers blew their horns from behind her but she steadfastly kept her focus on the road. As she sat in traffic at the red light, she smelled something burning. Should I pull off to the side of the road? Jacoby looked around frantically and realized that because she was in the middle lane it was useless to try to get to the shoulder. Bumping and grinding she eked along the next mile until she could move into the exit lane. Thankfully, it was time to exit for Powers Public Relations. After her car squeaked into a parking spot, she closed her eyes and leaned her head on the steering wheel, completely frazzled.

Taps on her window roused her.

Noah stood there with a briefcase in his hand and a look of concern furrowed his brow.

She rolled her window down.

"What's the matter?" he asked without preamble.

"I don't know," she said agitatedly. "My car started acting up on the freeway. I thought that an angry motorist was going to shoot me."

"Pop your hood." Placing the briefcase on the ground he lifted the hood.

Jacoby joined him.

He held his hand over the steaming motor. "Have Selyna call Triple A," he instructed, "and have it towed where I have my Audi serviced."

"That sounds expensive, Noah," she said nervously.

"It doesn't cost me anything to have it towed and diagnostic tests cost the same at every shop." He slammed the hood. "I'm late for a meeting. I'll check in with you later for status on your car. Try and have a good day," he said before strode off towards his car.

Jacoby stared gratefully after Noah in his SUV until he disappeared.

After she left Selyna's office she called Armstrong's cell phone.

"Yes."

"Something's wrong with my car."

"You woke me up," he snapped.

"I said that there's something wrong with my car, Armstrong!"

"What's wrong with it?"

"I don't know," she said tersely. "But it started lurching on the freeway and smoke was everywhere."

"Bummer," he said. "Do you need me to pick you up from work?"

"Probably," she said. "I'll call you when I know what time I'll be leaving." She said brusquely, "You didn't come up with a solution about my car."

"What do you want me to say, Jacoby? You'll just have to have fixed whatever is wrong with it. You can't afford a new car on what you make."

"I'm going to need to drive your car to get back and forth to work."

"I need to use it myself, so you'll have to take a taxi," he said.

"What!" she said, her frustration reaching a boiling point.

"I got a part as a waiter in a movie filming at South Beach. I'm meeting with some of the cast members at Wet Willie's around eight." He asked in a sullen voice, "Do you want me to call a tow truck and have your car taken somewhere?"

"I already did that," she said, slamming down the phone.

"Trouble in paradise?" Allie quipped.

"When was it ever paradise?" she said with a dour look. "My car's in the shop and this is just one more bill to add to my credit card debt."

"Car problems suck," Allie said sitting down. "Do you need me to give you a ride home?"

"I'd really appreciate it. I doubt that whatever is wrong can be fixed by five or six o'clock."

Jacoby's office phone rang. "Yes, this is Jacoby Alexander."

"Oh no," she said. "Are you sure there isn't anything you can do? I don't know. I have to think about it. Okay," she said in a heavy voice, "I'll call you back."

"I hate to even ask," Allie said with concern.

"My car was vandalized."

"Vandalized?" Allie shouted.

"About half a bag of sugar was poured into the gas tank."

"Who would do that to you?"

"I don't know," she wailed. "Had I not driven it the mechanic could have flushed the tank. But by me driving it the whole engine is gone. It will cost thousands to repair."

"Thousands!"

"Yes," Jacoby said bleakly. "Even with a rebuilt engine. And they'd have to look around to see if they could find one. It could take months. I don't even have that much room on my credit card with all my college expenses. I can't ride around in a taxi all the time and I can't afford to rent a car for that long."

"Won't your insurance cover you on that?"

"Some would but mine won't. That car is seven years old. I didn't want to spend a lot of money on a deductible covering it."

"What are you going to do?"

"I don't know," she said and buried her head in her hands and began weeping.

Allie put her arms around her.

Jacoby clung to her with her face buried in her stomach.

Noah made himself known by a large cough. "Allie, may I talk to Jacoby alone?'

"Sure," she said, releasing Jacoby. "Call me when you're ready to leave."

"Okay," she said, grabbing a tissue from a box and blowing her nose.

Noah sat in the chair Allie had vacated. "I stopped by the garage and my mechanic PJ told me that even if they fixed your car it might not be dependable any more. I'm offering you the use of the company car for as long as you work for Powers Public Relations."

"I can't accept," she said, wiping her nose with the back of her hand.

"You don't have a choice. You have meetings and you can't depend on a taxi to get you places on time."

"What would people say?"

"That it's my company and I can do whatever I want. Perception is everything, Jacoby. You can't drive around in…" He stopped, obviously grappling for words that wouldn't offend her.

"That raggedy ass Honda Accord."

He gave her a gentle smile. "Your words, not mine."

"Why are you so nice to me?"

"You're trying to go places, Jacoby." Noah's eyes snapped angrily. "I'm not going to let anyone sabotage your future."

"What do you mean by that?"

"You'll figure it out," he said, "eventually." Noah handed her a set of keys. "This is a spare set. By the way, there's a special lock on that gas tank so don't worry about anyone tampering with it."

As Jacoby drove the white Mercedes down I-95, Noah's face remained in front of her.

"Whose car is that parked in your spot?"

Jacoby rolled over and looked at the clock on her nightstand. "It's three o'clock in the morning and you woke me up! Even though you don't have to go to work in the morning I do."

"Whose car you got?" he leaned down and his breath stank.

"Mine." She turned her back to him.

Armstrong grabbed her arm and dragged her back around to face him.

"Where'd you get that car from?" he snarled.

"My job loaned it to me."

"For how long?" he spat out.

"It's the company car. I can keep it indefinitely."

He pointed his finger in her face. "You trying to tell me they loaned a nobody like you a Mercedes-Benz SLK."

"Maybe you think of me as a nobody, Armstrong, but not everyone does," she snapped.

"I know you screwin' someone over there."

"I wish," she muttered.

"What the fuck did you just say?" his hand grabbed her chin.

She tried to pull away, but he held her tight. "What did I tell you about that?" she ground out the words.

He released her. "I'm going to sleep in the other room."

"Good idea," she snapped.

"Guess what?" Jacoby said excitedly.

"What?" Noah stopped typing in order to give her his undivided attention.

"I've managed to get a firm agreement that Isadora will be spotlighted in the entertainment section of the Miami Herald the weekend her movie comes out."

"That's almost impossible," Noah said. "How did you manage to get that?"

"I started thinking," she said with a hint of pride.

"That's a good thing," Noah teased.

Jacoby playfully wrinkled her nose up at him. "Ha, Ha, Ha. Sally, my ex-supervisor, was always bragging about her cousin Lesley Patron who works for the Miami Herald as a copy editor. So, I emailed Sally for a way to get in touch with her. She forwarded it to Lesley and she bit."

"That's amazing. Did you thank Sally and her cousin?"

"I sent them thank you cards and restaurant gift cards as a thank you."

"That's how you do business," Noah said, his eyes twinkling. He twirled a pencil between his fingers. "I think that I'm going to up our fees for Ms. Isadora Leblanc."

Jacoby chuckled. "I don't blame you. Because of cutbacks at the newspaper I have to write the article."

"So you get a byline too. Talk about killing two birds with one stone. You get your name in print and Isadora's face in one of the country's largest readerships. I told you that you were worth every penny."

Jacoby felt her blood rush to her head.

"I should be afraid. Someone else might see your writing skills and take you from me."

She spoke her thoughts out loud, "I'll never leave you, Noah."

Jacoby and Noah stared into each others' eyes.

"I would be lost without you," Jacoby whispered.

"As would I." Noah's voice was a low rumble.

Flustered, she said, "Remember, I won't be in the office on Friday, because I'm going home for Mother's Day."

"I remembered," Noah said, not releasing her from his spell.

"I'll leave the article for you to approve before I leave on Thursday." Feeling suddenly shy, she leapt to her feet and her shirt button popped open. Her breasts strained against the fabric, longing to be freed. "Oh, my God!" She placed her hand over her breasts and fled the room.

Noah leaned back in his leather chair with a look of pure satisfaction.

When she got home, Armstrong was staring at a blank television screen. "I thought that you had an audition this afternoon."

"I've been and I'm back."

"What happened?"

"I didn't get it."

"But it was your third call back. What happened?"

"I wouldn't take off my shoes. I'm supposed to be a waiter, not in a scene of Beach Blanket Bingo."

From sheer exasperation, Jacoby rolled her eyes and went to the bedroom to work on her term paper.

Jacoby pulled into her parents' driveway which was packed with cars. Who the hell is over here? Shutting off the engine, she grabbed the bucket of Popeye's chicken and fixin's off the back seat. The front door opened and Alexandria appeared. She was followed by two girls and a guy about the same age.

Jacoby heaved a sigh of annoyance at the sight of them.

They waved airily as they climbed into their cars. Maneuvering around her Mercedes, they tore off, revving their engines as their exited.

Alexandria viewed the car, her arms akimbo.

"That's a nice ride, you're sportin', sister. How about lettin' me borrow it tonight?"

"Doubtful," she said gruffly as she climbed the porch steps. "Where's my mother?"

"In the bedroom, like she always is."

Jacoby bit back a sarcastic retort. She put the food on the kitchen table and walked the hallway to her parents' room. The drapes were drawn, but Jacoby saw the outline of her mother's body in the darkness.

"Mom," she said. "I'm home."

"Jacoby!" Sarai said excitedly and jumped out of bed. "I've been waiting for you all day."

Jacoby gave her mother a smacking kiss on the cheek.

Her mother's laugh engulfed the room.

Hugging her, Jacoby said, "Mom, I miss you so much."

"I miss you too," she said. "A holiday isn't a holiday when you're not here."."

"I can't believe you doubted that I'd be here this weekend."

"I didn't," Sarai admitted.

"I brought dinner."

"Maybe later. I'm not hungry right now. Where's Armstrong?"

"At his house taking a nap," she answered brusquely. "How would you like to get out of the house?"

"Where do you want to go?" Sarai asked, eyes twinkling.

"I don't know," she said. "We can just sort of ride around."

Sarai said eagerly, "Let me get my wig." She took off a nightcap.

Jacoby gasped. There were bald patches all over her mother's head.

"Mom," Jacoby said almost tearfully. "What happened to your hair?"

"The doctor said its stress. But don't you worry about it. Hair doesn't matter to me."

Jacoby swallowed her fears. "Mom, I'm going to start sending you money to get your hair done once a week at Elaine's. Have her do scalp treatments."

"No, Jacoby," Sarai said. "You do enough paying for my medicine."

"I insist," Jacoby said.

When they got outside Sarai exclaimed, viewing the Mercedes, "Did you buy this?"

"No," Jacoby said opening the door for her mother. "But it's mine to drive as long as I want."

Sarai leaned back into the luxurious leather, content to watch her daughter. "Jacoby, I'm so proud of you."

"Mom," she said, "I'm not a big deal. I'm just trying to make my way."

"Well, you and Armstrong seem to being doing well."

"Armstrong," Jacoby said caustically, "doesn't have anything to do with this ride. Noah hooked me up."

"Your boss seems like a really nice guy."

"He is," Jacoby gushed. "He's so smart and kind. He makes me feel as if I can accomplish anything. And Mom, he's so supportive. I know that if I went to him with a problem if he couldn't fix it, he at least would help me figure out what to do."

"What does he look like?"

"He's so fine. He is really what you call tall, dark, and handsome. He looks like a Greek statue except he's dark chocolate. And he has a butt chin. It's so cute."

"What in the world is a butt chin?"

"It's a chin with a cleft," she grinned. She took one hand off the steering wheel and took her fingers, crunching her chin together. "It makes him look so darn sexy. All the women at work have crushes on him. And he doesn't even seem to notice. A lot of men that look like Noah would be conceited, but he's so down to earth."

"If this man is so great, why don't you go for it?"

"Me!" she exclaimed. "You've got to be kidding. I work for him and I don't think that he'd ever get involved with someone under those circumstances."

"Try him and see," Sarai chuckled. "But I forgot. You wouldn't do that because you're in love with Armstrong."

"Mom, don't say anything to Daddy because I hate that he was right. But he was right about Armstrong. It was a mistake to move in with him. The minute I finish school I'm moving out."

Sarai clasped her hands together. "Thank God for my prayers. What did Mr. Armstrong say about that?"

"Nothing," Jacoby answered, "because he doesn't know. I've had some unexpected expenses so it'll take me awhile to save the money for my own place. I'll tell him when the time is right."

"Don't send me another dime. I'd rather you move out and on with your life."

"I'm going to do that, Mom, but you come first. Are you hungry yet?"

"Not really," she said. "But I'd like an Oreo cookie blizzard from Dairy Queen."

"Coming up."

Jacoby stood in line reading the menu board and felt someone tapping her on the shoulder. She turned around and her mouth dropped in surprise. "Claudia," she stared in shock. "I've so missed you so much."

"Then can I have a hug?"

"Only if you'll forgive me," Jacoby jerked out as she grabbed her childhood friend.

They broke their embrace when the clerk shouted, "Number sixty-nine."

"That's me," Jacoby said.

"Aren't you the lucky one?" Claudia teased.

"Sixty-nine is a fantasy for me," she whispered not wanting the others in line to hear their banter. "Will you join me and Mom at the booth?"

"I'd love to."

"How have you been, Claudia?"

"Pretty good," Claudia retorted jovially. "Rex and I are saving for a house."

"I heard your wedding was beautiful. I'm sorry I didn't feel well that day and couldn't make it," Sarai apologized.

"It was small," she said, sliding Jacoby a look, "but I really missed Jacoby not being there."

"I'm sorry that I was so stubborn," Jacoby said with a sheepish look.

"I sent you an invitation to Miami."

"What!" she exclaimed. "I didn't get it."

"I paid the extra fifty cents for delivery confirmation. I know that it arrived there because I checked via the computer."

There was a hostile silence at the table. Jacoby deliberately wiped ice cream from her mouth. "Obviously, Armstrong kept it from me," she snapped.

113

Claudia said nothing negative, not wanting to break the tenuous bond that had formed between them. "Jacoby," she said, "people have disagreements but they get over them and move one. That's the true test of friendship."

"Who knew that Diary Queen could turn out to be such fun?" Sarai smiled.

"Thank God you have a sweet tooth, Mom," Jacoby said rubbing her mother's arm.

After they exchanged phone numbers and e-mails and addresses Jacoby clung to Claudia as if she'd never let her go. "I'll call you," she whispered.

"You better," Claudia retorted.

As Jacoby pulled out of the parking lot behind Claudia's Camry she said, "Mom, I have to go to this party with Armstrong tonight. After that for the rest of the weekend I'm all yours."

"I love you, Jacoby."

"I love you too, Mom."

CHAPTER 10

Armstrong sat in the passenger seat with a frown of displeasure. "I don't know why you have to drive. I don't like being chauffeured around like a little boy."

"It's late and you've already been drinking," she said shortly. "Sober up tomorrow and you can keep it while I'm at my parents' house." Jacoby followed Armstrong to the entrance of the recreation center. Before he opened the door, he grabbed Jacoby's hand.

Surprised, she pulled back.

"You don't want the whole town talking about us, do you?" he said, half dragging her behind him.

The dance floor was crowded with people gyrating to songs that had been popular over a decade ago. Jacoby spied a man in a multicolored jacket and had to put her hand over her mouth to stifle her laughter. Then she saw a woman that she recognized as a patron of the library dressed in a too tight dress as she did the latest shuffle. Jacoby unconsciously shook her head from side to side as she viewed the scene.

"Let's go get something to drink," he said.

Armstrong pulled her through the crowd, laughing and grinning at people who called out his name as they made their way. He told the man behind the table, "Let me have a gin and juice and a scotch neat."

"Armstrong," someone said sharply behind them.

Finally he let go of her hand.

"Shakira!" he said with a cheeky grin, "How the hell have you been?" He absently handed Jacoby her drink.

"I'm good," she said after giving Jacoby a curt nod of acknowledgement. "But look at you being all good-looking and all."

"Don't even try it," Armstrong preened.

"I saw you on that television commercial a couple of years ago. It was like crazy. I'd just fed my dog that food and there you were on the television telling me to go and buy some."

"That is crazy, Shakira."

"You got any more television work coming out?"

Armstrong said loudly enough for the people nearby to hear him, "I just finished a commercial that was filmed in South Beach."

Jacoby coughed, sputtering out her drink the minute she heard Armstrong's lie.

He gave her a forbidding look.

Shakira pounced on that. "Why you act like that, Jacoby? Is he lying? Does he have a commercial coming out or not?"

"Don't start me to lying," she said, putting down her drink with such force some of it spilled on the paper tablecloth. "I'm going to use the ladies' room." Jacoby stared in the mirror as she washed her hands. "What the hell am I doing here?" she muttered. Once she left the restroom, she found Stefan leaning on the wall in the small alcove. "Stefan," she said, pleased. "I didn't see you out there."

"But I saw you. I've been waiting for a chance to talk to you. How are you doing, Jacoby?"

"I'm good," she said.

"I'm surprised to see you. Are you going to hang out with us old people all weekend?" he joked.

"Nope," she said. "This is it for me. I'm in town to spend time with my mom."

"I heard that she has lupus," he said with concern. "Is she doing any better?"

"Today was a good day for her. But I'm glad to run into you. Mom's hair is coming out and I don't know what to do about it."

"That's a consequence of the lupus, or it could be the medication that she's on. What's she taking?"

"Azathioprine and Plaquenil."

"That's really expensive medication," Stefan said. "You know, Jacoby," he said with a puzzled look, "your mom was diagnosed at an unusual age. Most lupus patients find out before they're forty."

"She knew for quite a while before she told me. But I think that stress has complicated her condition."

"There's no such thing as a stress free world. But do whatever you can do to make her life easy as possible, Jacoby. She'll live longer and with less pain."

"I will," she promised. "I need to go back and join Armstrong."

"So you're still with him?" Stefan said chidingly.

"Unfortunately, yes," she quipped as she walked beside him, "but not for long."

When Jacoby and Stefan reentered the ballroom, her eyes were immediately drawn to Armstrong.

The wrath that radiated from him sent a chill of uneasiness down her spine.

Jacoby placed the car keys down on the table. After she turned around, Armstrong was up on her. He grabbed her throat.

"Let me go," she choked out.

"How dare you embarrass me in front of my friends? Sneaking around with that Stefan Wagner," he said threateningly.

Because of his hold on her throat Jacoby couldn't swallow.

"You think that I don't know about you and him," he sneered. "The night of your birthday you went to the movies with him. The minute I went out of town you cheated on me with Mr. High and Mighty Stefan Wagner."

"I can't breathe," she gasped.

Armstrong tightened his hold for a while longer and then he let go.

Jacoby fell into a heap at his feet and continued to gasp for air.

"And you outed me to Shakira!" he screamed. "If you can't back me up on shit, dammit, keep your fuckin' mouth shut!" Armstrong stepped over Jacoby and grabbed the keys off the counter. "I'm going out! Bitch," he sneered, "you ruin everything."

The next morning Jacoby furiously viewed the bruises around her neck. After rummaging through her suitcase, she found a mock turtle neck shirt. After she applied heavy make-up to cover the discoloration, she donned the shirt, and called Claudia.

"Hey, girl," Claudia said.

"Will you come to Armstrong's and take me to my parents' house?"

"I'm on my way."

Jacoby sat at the kitchen table with a pad, and a calculator. With frustration she tallied her living expenses over and over again. It's not enough to leave.

"Are you ready?" Claudia asked as she walked into the kitchen.

"Yes," Jacoby said and burst into tears, finally releasing her years of emotional turmoil.

"What's wrong?"

"You were so right about Armstrong," she wept. "I should have never gotten involved with him."

Claudia looked at her friend and her heart went out to her. "I didn't want to be right, Jacoby."

"I know you didn't," Jacoby responded quietly. "He's so mean to me."

Claudia stared at her with an odd expression. It was a mixture of pain and remorse. "I have something to tell you."

"What is it?"

117

"My psychic Zalia told me that a man was going to come between us."

"She did!"

"Yeah," Claudia said. "At first I didn't know who the man was. I thought that it might be Rex, so I pushed it in the back of my mind and didn't say anything."

"Why would you have thought that it was Rex?"

"Because you hadn't yet met Armstrong. But after being around him for a short time I figured out it was him. That's why I was pushing you into going out with Stefan."

"Why didn't you just tell me?"

"I didn't think that you'd believe me. Now I feel that maybe I could have prevented all this unhappiness that you've been experiencing," she said with a guilty look.

"Claudia," she said, "you're not responsible for my unhappiness." Jacoby grabbed a paper towel from the roll and blew her nose. The noise was deafening. "Besides, I was in such a hurry to get out of Bunnell I wouldn't have listened," she admitted.

"Your eyes and face are all blotchy from crying. What happened last night?"

"Armstrong got jealous because I was talking to Stefan."

"Stefan is the kind of man to get jealous about."

"It's not just that," Jacoby said, mentally reliving the previous night's drama.

With a look of alarm, Claudia sat across from Jacoby.

"Armstrong's always yelling at me. He drinks all day every day. He's home more than I am, but he doesn't help clean up the house." She defensively pulled her collar farther up under her chin, too embarrassed to reveal everything.

"Why don't you move out?"

"I can't afford to. Don't tell anyone that I told you this because its family business but I'm paying for mom's housekeeper and medication. I go into more credit card debt each month."

"I have about a hundred dollars that I can lend you."

"Thanks but, keep your money. One hundred dollars isn't going to help me out of this mess."

"Move back to Bunnell, Jacoby," she coaxed. "I know that you don't want to move in with your parents, but Rex and I have an extra room."

"I don't want to leave Miami," she said with a determined look. "I love my job and I'm in college. I plan on going this summer and then I have another year left."

"Don't you have anyone that you can live with in Miami?"

Noah's face flashed in front of her eyes. But she said with a forlorn look, "I don't think so."

"Do you still care for Armstrong?"

"Of course not. But I do feel sorry for him."

"Why do you feel any sympathy for that idiot?" she asked with an infuriated look on her face. "Look at you. You're trembling." She placed her hands on Jacoby's arms.

Jacoby said hesitantly, "Because I know why he's such an asshole."

"I know, I know. He's an injured war veteran with a fucked up foot. Give me a break."

"That's not it," Jacoby said quietly.

"What? So he had a bad childhood. Boo hoo, cry me a river."

"That's not it either." She averted her eyes.

"Than what is it?" Claudia pressed with a baffled look on her face.

"Armstrong is the way he is because he feels inadequate. So he tries to mask his shortcomings by being a bully."

"Armstrong's inadequacies are his problems not yours. Do you know how many people are homeless and living on the street? He should count his blessings that he gets a check."

"Armstrong's problem is that he has a really small penis," Jacoby muttered.

"What!" Claudia burst out laughing. "Are you serious?"

Jacoby nodded her head yes.

"So he's trying to overcompensate?"

Jacoby nodded yes again.

"How small is it?"

Jacoby shrugged.

"Here," she said pushing the paper to her. "Draw me a picture. Make it a stick figure but show where his Mandingo would fall on his thigh."

Jacoby drew the picture and after Claudia viewed it she fell off her chair onto the floor convulsed in laughter. "Oh my God," she cackled some more. "It doesn't even reach his thigh. He makes that Asian guy from the The Hangover movies look like a stud."

"Cut it out, Claudia. That's important to a man."

"It's important to me too. Why the hell did you ever sleep with him more than once?"

"In the beginning he was nice to me."

"So what! There are other men out there that would treat you the way you deserve. And they have huge Mandingos."

"Things have gotten so bad, I stay at work until its late and I have to go home. And when I do get there I sleep in the spare bedroom."

"I can't get over it." Claudia finally got off the floor and resumed her seat. "Armstrong struts around like a peacock, frontin' like he's the man, but this is all he's working with." She picked up the picture again. In disgust, she slapped it down on the table. "And where the hell is Mr. Battle and his shortcomings?"

"I don't know," she said. "He stormed out last night and didn't come home."

"Maybe he hooked up with another woman."

"I doubt it, but I hope so."

"So you don't think that he cheats on you?"

"I don't think he's going to show that thang to any of the women in this small town," she retorted.

"You're right," Claudia said. "Bunnell girls talk about that shit. I mean, we put the word out if a man ain'thangin'. What are you going to do?"

"Armstrong has a savings account with my name on it. Do you know what a maid costs?"

"A lot of money."

"That's right. And Armstrong owes me back pay for all the time we've lived together."

"Take it all," Claudia said. "You certainly deserve it. Do you want me to come down when you move? Rex and I will be more than willing to help."

"I can't move yet. For the last few months I've been putting money away in a separate bank account that Armstrong knows nothing about. I have to save every penny that I can and find an apartment. Then I'll strike taking what I feel he owes me."

Twenty minutes later Claudia's Camry idled in the driveway. "Promise me that you'll call me if you need me. I'll come down."

"Okay," she promised.

"When are you going back to Miami?"

"I'm leaving tonight so I can be at work in the morning. What are you going to do for the rest of the day?"

"This afternoon I'm going to darken the bedroom, light some candles, and give Rex the blow job of his life. I need to show him that I appreciate him for the stallion that he is."

Jacoby still had a tiny smile on her face as she let herself in her parents' house. The smell of pot roast made her mouth water and she followed the smell.

Her father had his back to her as he stirred the ingredients in a pot. Whistling, he turned on the oven door light and peered at a tray of cornbread. With a snort of satisfaction he turned the light off again.

Memories of him completing a task that she'd seen him do so many times through her childhood shook her to her very core and suddenly she felt all of her anger at him dissipate. Jacoby crept over to him and slid her arms around his waist.

Abraham's body grew still.

"Hello, Daddy," she murmured, burying her head in his back the way she had in the past.

"Jacoby," he said and tears clouded his voice, "have you come back to me?"

"Yes, Daddy, I have."

"My nightly prayer has been answered," he said. "Thank you, Jesus."

Soon they were seated around the dinner table. "Daddy, your pot roast is delicious," Jacoby said after she swallowed more of the juicy meat.

"It should be," Sarai said. "He makes it once a week."

"Yeah, I'm the pot roast king," Abraham joked.

"Your father does all the cooking now."

"He does?" Jacoby asked.

"Your mother has done most of it throughout our marriage, so I thought that I should take a crack at it."

"It's because of my hands." Sarai held them out. Some of her fingers were quite misshapen. "Sometimes it's hard to grip things."

"Are they hurting right now, Mom?"

"Not at all," she said. "It's like arthritis. Sometimes they hurt and other times they don't."

"Maybe they don't hurt because our daughter is here. Every time Jacoby comes you're in good spirits for at least a week after she leaves. But that's to be expected. Jacoby," he said truthfully, "you've always made our life easier."

As Jacoby and Abraham stared at each other the final piece of their truce fell in to place.

Observing them Sarai breathed a huge sigh of relief.

They heard the sound of car doors slamming. Abraham said in an impassive voice, "I guess Alexandria's home."

"Happy Mother's Day, Mother," Alexandria said as she strutted into the room. She was dressed in a hot pink mini dress and looked as if she'd just left the club.

Behind her was Armstrong carrying a box of candy. "Happy Mother's Day, Mom," he said handing it to Sarai.

Abraham stared at Alexandria and his large eyes were narrowed into icy slits. His thick lips were pressed together firmly.

Jacoby refused to look at either Armstrong or Alexandria.

After a brief hesitation, Sarai took the candy and placed it on the table. "Thank you for the candy, Armstrong. How did the two of you end up here at the same time?"

"I was walking down the street," Alexandria said sitting in the seat next to Abraham, "and he picked me up."

That I can believe. Jacoby stood and held out her hand to Armstrong. "Give me my car keys. My mother's gift is in the trunk."

Armstrong dug into his pants pocket and handed them to her.

Without saying anything else and with head held high she swept past him. Jacoby was holding her mother's gift and shutting the trunk when Armstrong appeared.

"Jacoby, can I talk to you?" he said, averting her hard stare by staring down at the ground.

"Not here." Her eyes snapped and she clenched her teeth angrily. "I don't want my parents upset."

"Your parents?" Armstrong snapped angrily.

"Yes," she said succinctly. "I don't want my mother or father upset. By the way, Claudia and I have settled our differences. And I know that you threw away my invitation to her wedding. And I'm sure that you lied about her calling my father a 'Ho'."

Jacoby took satisfaction in the obvious displeasure that settled across Armstrong's face. "So now you and your daddy are all tight and all?"

"He's made his mistakes," she retorted, "but he's still a better man than you'll ever be."

Armstrong stood in the pathway between her and the house.

"Get out of my way," Jacoby said in a deadly tone.

He stepped aside.

When she looked up, her father was standing on the front porch watching them. Once she reached him she linked her arm in his. "Let's see if Mother likes the gift I brought her," she said lightly.

Sarai opened the small box. Inside there were four pairs of lace gloves.

"Jacoby," she said. "They're beautiful."

"I was watching a rerun of Sex and the City. Carrie wore a pair and she looked so elegant that I had those made for you. I thought the white pair you can wear first Sunday, and the black, peach, and beige the other ones."

Sarai pulled the black pair over her knarled knuckles. "They're perfect," she gushed.

"You've never looked more beautiful, Sarai," Abraham said in his deep voice.

"Thank you, Abraham." She looked at her daughter. "I have a gift for you, too."

THE FALL AND RISE OF JACOBY

"For me? Why? I'm not a mother."

"You're acting like a mother to me," she said. "Sit tight." Sarai disappeared so quickly that Jacoby and Abraham looked at each other and chuckled.

"Happy Mother's Day, Jacoby," Sarai said, reappearing.

Jacoby excitedly tore off the paper and opened the box. Inside was a picture in a frame. Jacoby was a toddler sitting on her mother's lap. Her father had his arm around Sarai and wore of look of contentment.

"I was cleaning out my storage box and found this. I hoped that you'd want it."

"I do, Mom."

"I have something too." Abraham strode out of the room and reappeared. He held two boxes. He handed one to Sarai and the other to Jacoby. Laughing he said, "Open them on the count of three. One, two, three."

Sarai and Jacoby excitedly tore off the wrapper. They each held a velvet box. Inside there were wedding bands. Sarai's shone brightly, but Jacoby's was a darker gold.

Abraham looked at his wife. He took the ring and slid it over his wife's arthritic knuckles. "Oh, Abraham."

"I know how upset you've been because you can't wear your ring anymore." He looked at Jacoby and said, "her fingers swell. So I bought you another and went up a couple of sizes." Then again he looked at Jacoby. "That's for you. I wanted you to have it and I knew that your mother wouldn't mind. It brought us many years of happiness."

"Thank you, Daddy." She and kissed him on the cheek. "I love you."

"Thank you, Jacoby," he replied with a grateful look on his face.

Alexandria and Armstrong stood shoulder to shoulder and with contorted looks of fury on their faces watching the intimate trio.

Jacoby put her luggage down and turned on Armstrong. "How dare you treat me like that!" she screamed.

"I was drinking," Armstrong mumbled. "I didn't mean it."

"And then you took off with my company car. What if you'd hit someone?"

"I was careful," he said. "Jacoby, you've got to understand…"

"I don't have to understand a damn thing." Jacoby demanded with a disdainful look, "Where were you all night?"

"I was at Pete's Place."

"All night?" she said with obvious skepticism.

"All night."

"I don't believe you. But guess what, Armstrong? I don't give a damn. From now on, we're just roommates. I'll keep out of your way and you keep out of mine."

"When's the last time you gave me some pussy, Jacoby?" he said heatedly.

"When's the last time you deserved some, Armstrong?" she shot back.

"When are you going to stop being a bitch?"

"When you stop being a bastard." In a huff, she picked up her suitcase and stalked off towards the spare bedroom. "Don't forget to get that counseling you so desperately need."

"Your article for the *Miami Herald* is top notch."

"So you like it?" she mumbled.

"Of course I do." Noah looked at Jacoby's downcast countenance. "How was your weekend with your mother?"

"It was good." Her face brightened. "My father and I have patched things up."

"That's great news, Jacoby. How did it happen?"

"I just came to realize that Daddy made mistakes but that doesn't define who he is."

Noah nodded his head. "Everyone has made mistakes, Jacoby."

"Yes, but his was something that took me a long time to adjust to." She said hesitatingly, "Daddy had a child with another woman while he was married to my mother."

"Oh… so that's what it is."

"Her name is Alexandria."

"Alexandria?" Noah's lips flattened in displeasure from the revelation.

"Yes. Her mother named her after daddy. Obviously she wanted to make sure everyone knew he was the father."

"How did your mother take the news?"

"She forgave him a long time ago but no one ever told me about it. I found out about a month before I moved to Miami."

"So that's how you ended up here."

"Yeah," Jacoby said bitterly. "She moved in and I moved out."

"She lives with them?" he exclaimed.

"She has nowhere else to go. She's a felon and lazy to boot."

Noah exhaled a long breath. "That must be hard on your mother with her being sick and all."

"It's taking a toll on her and I don't know what to do about it. Daddy would never let me kick out his firstborn."

"I thought that the two of you had worked things out?"

"That doesn't mean that I can talk to him about her. He's so guilt ridden. Alexandria does what she wants to with no regards for anyone else's feelings. I forgave Daddy because I had to."

"You should forgive your father, Jacoby, if not for him for yourself. Forgiving someone is easier than being angry."

"It was easier once I realized how easy it is to get drawn into a relationship that is wrong for you, and how hard it can be to get out of it." Not conscious of what she was doing, Jacoby tugged the collar of her shirt, inadvertently exposing the remaining bruises around her neck.

White hot anger consumed Noah. It ran from his hairline to the bottom of his feet. His fists were clenched as he tamped down the urge to blurt out what he was thinking. Instead, barely containing his fury he grated out, "You know, Jacoby, if there's anything that you want to talk about you can. I don't judge people."

Uncomfortable with the sudden change and tone of the conversation she stammered, "There's nothing to tell."

Noah sucked his teeth in obvious annoyance.

Discomfiture made her snap, "Is there anything else, Noah? I want to send off that article to the *Miami Herald*."

Noah continued to stare at Jacoby with a brooding look. His eyebrows met above the bridge of his nose. Finally he said, "Can you give me a ride home after work? My SUV is in the shop and they didn't have a rental available."

Jacoby jerked in surprise. "Of course I can, Noah. After all, I am driving the company car."

"Thanks," he said briefly. "We'll get some take-out before we get to my house."

"Noah," she protested, "you don't have to buy me dinner every day. I'd love to take you home."

"And I'd love for you to take me. Do you like Chinese?"

"Love it," she said.

"What's your favorite?"

"I can go with sweet and sour pork or shrimp fried rice."

"That works for me."

CHAPTER 11

After Jacoby pulled out of the drive thru of the Chinese restaurant, Noah instructed, "Take left to ramp I-95 south."

Once she was back on the expressway she slid Noah a look.

He'd let his seat back to the recline position and appeared totally relaxed.

"I love this car, Noah."

"It's all right," he drawled.

"It's the best thing I've ever driven. And that Audi you drive is really something else."

"Keep working the way you have been and one day you'll be able to buy your own Audi."

Not taking her eyes off the congested highway she asked, "Do you really believe that, Noah?"

"I know that, Jacoby. I believe in you. Get ready to switch to the left lane. Our exit to Coral Gables is next."

After another five miles or so, Jacoby veered left and after half a mile pulled up to a large stone gate.

"My code is my birthday 0810."

"I don't think that you're supposed to tell me that," she said, punching in the numbers.

"Maybe I want you to remember when it's my birthday and give me a present," Noah retorted.

I'd really like to give you a present that would be for me as much as for me as for you. But she only said, "I'll make sure to mark it on my calendar. They say that Leos act like lions, but yet, I see such gentleness in your heart. You're the most caring man I've ever had a relationship with."

Noah flushed with pleasure and she could see his chocolate skin darken even more. "Does that mean we're in a relationship?"

Realizing her Freudian slip, she whispered, "What I meant to say is even though I haven't had that many men... No, I meant to say we..."

Noah took his hand and placed it on her knee. "I know, Jacoby. Now take me home. I'm starved."

Jacoby pulled into a long, narrow driveway. Palm trees that flanked the length of the long driveway swayed in the breeze. She gawked at the huge mansion with wrought iron rails and a terrazzo roof. Beautifully manicured shrubberies lined the front of the house, connected to the sides, and disappeared in the back. "It's absolutely beautiful, Noah."

"It's too large for me to live in alone," he said quietly.

Hope flared inside her. But once again she held her true thoughts. "Look at the palm trees swaying because of the breeze."

"That's because there's a tropical storm brewing out in the ocean. I hope it peters out before it moves into the Gulf of Mexico."

"It's not hurricane season for at least another month."

"That's what happens when you have global warming. Come on inside." The chime of the alarm went off when the side door was opened. "My alarm code is the same as my gate code."

"0810," she repeated.

"That's it."

"I think for security reasons that they should be different."

"You're right. I'll probably change them later. If I do I'll let you know."

Jacoby followed Noah through the terrazzo styled foyer into a large open kitchen with connecting family room. A sixty inch flat screen television was centered in the middle of the wall. "So that's where you watch your football games."

"Yeah," Noah joked. "I'm glued to the set even for the college games."

"I love sports too. I was on the color guard in high school, and got interested in football. "

"Your looks must have distracted the players."

"I don't know about all that. I do know that's the one thing that I did in high school that gave me the confidence I so needed. Daddy got me interested in basketball. We had only one television so I kind of got dragged into it. But I learned to love it."

"You'd make a good wife, Jacoby. During football and basketball season most wives complain that they feel like widows, but I guess that wouldn't be an issue with you."

Jacoby fell silent. Wife? Suddenly a word that she'd never thought of in conjunction with Armstrong made her heart flutter.

"Let me show you the pool," Noah said, opening the French doors that led off the den.

Jacoby eyed the large swimming pool with a sea foam green waterfall them.

Noah said softly from behind, "Maybe one evening you can come by and we can swim and hang out by the pool."

She gazed at it with an expression of longing. "Maybe," she replied in a noncommittal voice.

"Follow me," he said. "When Dad moved to West Palm he gutted the house of furniture."

"So I see. But you do have one couch."

"There's also a mattress and box springs in one of the rooms." With a lopsided grin, "The master bedroom also has furniture."

Jacoby felt her heart flutter. Too bad I can't stay in it. Instead she said, "So are you going to give me a grand tour?"

"Certainly. Follow me." Noah strode off to the left and Jacoby followed. "This is the master bedroom," he said.

The mahogany sleigh bed took up half the wall. "That bed is huge!"

"I'm a large man," he explained with a smile. "I had it specially made in Italy. It's the equivalent of two king-size beds. That way I can stretch out."

Jacoby felt a tingling in her loins as she stared at the inviting bed with a white down comforter.

"The bathroom has dual sinks and a step down shower. The marble tile is the same throughout the house."

"How many bathrooms does it have?"

"There are five full baths and a half bath in each hallway. There is also a game room, media room, and exercise room." As they toured the house, Jacoby exclaimed over the nickel fixtures, sunken tubs, and huge closets that accompany the oversized rooms. When they went out on the wrought iron balcony on the top floor, Jacoby breathed, "I just love this view."

"It needs a woman's touch. Many Saturday's I'd start up here with a cup of coffee planning to read the paper. I get halfway up the stairs and remember that there's nothing up here to sit on. Look!" Noah pointed at a car leaving through the wrought iron gates. "That's one of the Miami Heat ballplayer's car leaving the development."

"How do you know it's one of them?"

"The car has a specialty plate on it."

"Which ballplayer is it?"

"I don't know. The tint on the window is too dark. But whoever it is, he lives here. The houses in this development are in demand because we have such tight security. Come on," he said, closing the French doors that led out to the balcony. "Our food is getting cold."

In the kitchen Jacoby asked, "Where are the paper plates? The least I can do is dish up the food."

"They're in the cabinet all the way to the left."

"Take a seat and relax."

"There's a bottle of white wine in the refrigerator," Noah said as he slid on a stool at the snack bar.

"Perfect," she said opening the refrigerator. She read aloud the label on the bottle. "Ménage a Trios." She teased, "Is there some hidden meaning here?"

"Not at all," he said swiftly. "When I'm with my woman, I don't want anyone else in bed with us. I don't want her distracted and I definitely don't want me distracted. My goal is to give her the ultimate pleasure for the time that we're together."

"You sound very talented," Jacoby quipped as with agitation she grabbed two glasses and began to fill them.

"I've been told that I am," Noah replied. He hit a switch and music filtered throughout the room. The melodious voices of Tony Toni Tone filled the room. "We can change that to one of those rap stations if you want."

"No," she said. "I love that song."

"So do I. I like that the man is telling his woman that whatever she wants he'll provide."

Jacoby eyed Noah with hungry eyes. "I think that you would be that kind of man for your woman."

"I intend to be," he answered quietly. The intense look he gave her spoke volumes.

Even more flustered, Jacoby said, handing him his plate, "The sweet and sour pork and shrimp fried rice look scrumptious."

"Where's my fortune cookie?"

"Here," she said swiping it off the counter behind her.

Noah broke it open. He said wryly, "It states Learn Chinese."

Jacoby laughed as she put her wine glass down.

"The other side states you are known to be an honest and trustworthy person."

"I never put much store in fortune cookies but now I know one that's true," Jacoby said.

"How do you know that?"

"People talk," she said. "No one has a negative thing to say about you."

"In front of you," Noah said with a wry smile. "Sometimes people don't understand some of the decisions that are made by the president of a company."

"There are far more happy than unhappy people at the firm."

"How would you know? I never see you mingling with the other personnel."

"I don't have any free time besides lunch. The days that we don't eat together I hang with Allie."

"She's a good friend to you?"

"She is. My other best friend, Claudia, lives in Bunnell. But in

Miami, Allie is it. You couldn't ask for a better ally," she said, grinning at her pun.

"You're quite the wordsmith," he quipped. "What does Allie's husband do for a living?"

"He just got laid off and is looking."

"What's his background?"

"He worked at a semiconductor plant."

"Give him my card tomorrow and tell him to call me. I know some people. I'll see what I can do."

"That would be great, Noah. See," she pointed at him, "your fortune cookie was right."

Noah felt gratified by the compliment. "Let's see what yours says."

Jacoby laughed after she read it. "Learn Chinese."

"How about the other side?"

"Your character is about to be tested. Hmm," she said. "That sounds ominous."

"If that's true, you'll pass the test with flying colors." Noah looked deeply into the eyes. "Never lose sight of who you are, Jacoby."

"I'll try not to," she promised.

After eating, they sat close on the sofa playing guess who the artist is for each song.

He made a fist and held it at her mouth as if it was a mike. "Who's singing that?"

"Don't insult me. That's Rick James. But you know what's really funny?"

"What?"

"I didn't know until I went to high school that Mary Jane is slang for marijuana. I thought he was actually singing about a woman he was in love with. I was so sheltered."

"You were sheltered, Jacoby," Noah said dryly.

She playfully punched him on the shoulder.

"Now who is that?"

She listened to the melody. "I don't know," she admitted. "I've heard the song before but I can't name the group."

"They were before your time." Noah said. "It's the Delfonics."

"You really know them all, don't you?"

"My dad ordered those Timeless Classic cd's from PBS. That's pretty much all he's ever played."

"How is your father since he retired?"

"He's good. My sister is looking out for him. He goes golfing every day with his cronies. He's even got himself a girlfriend since he left."

"I guess so," Jacoby said. "Your father is still a very handsome man." Her hungry eyes slid down Noah's long length. "You look just like him."

"I do?" Noah asked in his deep voice. "You think that I'm handsome, Jacoby?"

"How could I not?" she whispered.

"The million dollar question is, are you attracted to me, Jacoby?"

She couldn't lie. "Very much so," she whispered.

"Thank God," Noah whispered back. He turned to her and with his index finger lifted her chin.

Jacoby closed her eyes in anticipation.

Noah's eyes adored her. "You're beautiful inside and out, Jacoby," he murmured. Then his lips gently touched hers.

She moved closer to him and as she did, his arms closed around her.

Noah opened Jacoby's lips with his and when she felt his tongue slide inside her mouth an unfamiliar heat ignited between her legs. She moaned against his lips, "Oh, Noah."

His tongue continued to leisurely explore her mouth and she melted into a puddle of quivering emotion. Her nipples hardened and her breasts strained the thin fabric of her shirt; her arms crept up around his neck. Deliriously happy, she felt herself being pushed down on the plush leather of the oversized couch. Noah turned them on their sides facing each other.

In the background Tyrese begged his woman to stay. Noah will never have to beg me. This is what I want.

Noah growled, "I've wanted you from the first time I saw you."

Jacoby felt so dizzy she was glad that she was lying down.

Noah deftly unbuttoned her shirt. His hand grazed the smooth skin of her collarbone. He unhooked her front bra fastener and palmed her mounds.

Jacoby whimpered her desire.

Noah kneaded one breast while his mouth nibbled the outline of and gently bit her nipple of the other.

Aching with desire for him, Jacoby cradled Noah's head with her hands urging him to continue with his magic. Time stood still.

Noah's lips found her mouth again and this time she opened his mouth with hers.

After endless time, Noah asked, "Are you ready for me, Jacoby?"

"A long time ago, Noah," she breathed in anticipation.

He took his hand and touched the bruises on her neck. "Who did this to you?" He grated out the words and his eyes bored holes into her.

It was as if a bucket of cold water had been thrown on her. Her whole body tensed with humiliation.

Feeling the change, Noah stared down at her, reading the anguish in the face that she'd turned away from mortification.

"I have to go."

"Jacoby, I'm sorry. I didn't mean to upset you."

"I'm not upset with you, Noah. I'm angry with myself."

"Why," he asked with a hurt look, "because you let me in?"

"That's not it," she said. She averted her eyes. "Please let me up. It's late and I should be getting home."

Noah didn't move. "Jacoby…"

"If you do care for me, Noah, you'll let me go."

Noah stood. His shaft strained against his trouser pants, pointing at Jacoby.

She stared, mesmerized by its obvious size before shame made her avert her eyes.

"Are you okay to drive?"

She nodded yes.

"Let me help you up." Noah held out his hand to hoist her to her feet.

But Jacoby ignored it and instead searched for her bra.

Noah found it behind the couch and handed it to her.

She turned her back to him while she dressed.

"Jacoby."

She finished buttoning her white silk shirt. "Please, Noah," she said tearfully. "I feel bad enough. Just let it go."

A grave Noah walked Jacoby to the car.

After she backed out of the long driveway, he walked into the house and poured himself a glass of Hennessey. Gulping it down, he poured another and easily emptied the glass. Then, as was his nightly ritual, he went to take another long, cold, shower.

Jacoby let herself in the dark apartment. As she walked towards the spare bedroom light flooded the room.

"Where the hell have you been?" Armstrong's eyes glittered angrily. "I've been calling you on your cell and it went straight to voicemail."

"Minding my damn business." She shot back, "Besides, where do you be?"

"What did you just say to me?" His nostrils flared angrily.

"I didn't stutter."

"I'm going to ask you one more time, Jacoby," he said in a menacingly voice. "Where the hell were you?"

In a tired voice she replied, "Enough of the third degree, Armstrong.

I'm going to bed." She started to walk away.

"You won't be going to bed in there," he said and there was a lilt of triumph on his voice, "unless you want to sleep with your sister."

Jacoby turned around as if in slow motion. Stupefied, she repeated, "My sister?"

"Check your voicemail. Alexandria showed up here tonight and had nowhere else to go."

"I don't want her here!" Jacoby hissed, "How dare you let this happen?"

"This is not my battle," Armstrong said. "I don't hate her, you do."

"What would make her think that it would be okay for her to come here? What did you do with her in Bunnell?"

"Nothing," he denied crossly.

"I don't even talk to her. She wouldn't have come here unless you encouraged her," Jacoby insisted.

"I didn't encourage her," he retorted. "I ran into her at Pete's Place and we hung out drinking a few beers. She said that she couldn't find a job in Bunnell. I said that there are plenty of jobs in Miami." He shrugged. "I guess she misunderstood."

Beads of sweat popped up on Jacoby's forehead. "Get your ass in there and tell her to get out."

"I'm sick and tired of all this shit," he said gruffly. "If you have a problem with her being here you tell her. I'm going to bed."

Jacoby switched on the lamp in the spare bedroom.

Alexandria rolled over and blinked in the brightness.

"Get the fuck out of my apartment."

Alexandria sat up. Tears welled up in her eyes. "I have nowhere else to go."

"Go back to Bunnell."

"Your mother doesn't want me there."

"So when did you figure that out?" Jacoby spat out sarcastically.

"She never comes out of her room. I feel like an interloper."

"Where'd you learn that word," Jacoby sneered, "from the prison library?"

"I'm sorry you hate me, Jacoby. I really need a sister."

"I don't," she said harshly. "When I get home from work tomorrow, your ass better be gone."

"Where will I go?"

"Not my problem."

Jacoby stormed into the bedroom, grabbed a pair of pajamas and went to sleep on the couch.

###

"Mom," Jacoby said. "Do you know that Alexandria is here in Miami?"

"Is that where she is?" Sarai asked in a stunned voice. "I just thought that she was hanging out with her hoodlum friends."

"So you're telling me you didn't know."

"Of course not. I was so glad she wasn't here I didn't question it. I haven't felt this good in years."

"What do you mean?"

"She and her friends were here all day every day and I couldn't get any rest. Since she's been gone I feel like a new woman."

"How long has she been gone?"

"About a week. Since she left your dad and I have been acting like newlyweds. He took me out to dinner and a movie. We even went for a walk in the park and I haven't had the strength to do that for ages. I know that I'm not supposed to feel this way, but I've been praying that she wouldn't return and she'd find someone else to stay with."

"She thinks that she has," Jacoby said grimly. "Me."

"You don't have to house her. That girl is grown. She can make her own way the way you did. She should be able to find a job in Miami and get her own place."

'Keep your mom's life as stress free as possible.' Stefan's advice resounded in her head. In the background, Jacoby heard a car horn blowing.

"That's your father. I'm late for my doctor's appointment."

"Go ahead, Mom. I don't want you missing that."

"What are you going to do, Jacoby?"

"I don't know."

"You don't owe her anything. Miami's a big city; you'll probably never run into her again after you put her out."

That afternoon Jacoby sat at her desk with her head propped on her hand.

"I'm sorry if I offended you."

Noah's voice roused her from her state of self-pity. "You didn't," she said bleakly.

"I feel as if I've put you at a disadvantage."

"Why do you say that?"

"The sadness on your face today makes me feel guilty as hell for putting you in a compromising position."

Jacoby got up and closed her door so that that no one would overhear them. "My sadness isn't about you. There are problems at home."

"I'm your boss, Jacoby." He chose his next words carefully, "You never have to see me outside the office. Nothing will change here at Powers Public Relations."

"I know that, Noah."

He stuffed his hands in his pockets and rocked back and forth on his heels. "I'm going to put on a different hat and say this not as someone who cares for you in a way that a boss shouldn't care for an employee, but as a friend."

Hope was revived in her heart that she hadn't destroyed her chance with him, considering her childish behavior the previous night.

"There isn't anything that you could tell me that would make me lose respect for you."

Her hand shook as she twirled her pen between her fingers.

"Don't say that because you don't know," she choked out.

"I know how strong you are, Jacoby. Draw on that to get you through tough times."

There was heaviness in the air between them.

"Is it okay if I leave early today? I have to go home and take care of something."

"Certainly. Are we still on for Isadora's launch party Saturday night?"

"Yes."

"I'll be out of the office for the next few days, so I'll see you there."

"Okay," she said.

"Out in the Gulf, they've upgraded tropical storm Agnes to a category two hurricane. Bands of rain will make the roads slick so drive safely."

"I will," she promised, grabbing her purse as she followed him out of her office.

When Jacoby got home, Alexandria sat on the couch fully dressed.

"I thought I told you to get out."

"The bus to Bunnell doesn't leave until nine o'clock tonight," she said. "Armstrong said that he'd take me there when he gets back."

"Why did you come here, Alexandria?"

"Your mother does better without me around."

There was a deafening silence.

Jacoby gave her a measuring look from across the room. "You're the result of a sin that my mother and I would like to forget."

"It's not my fault that my mother and our father were lovers," she said in a pitiful voice.

Jacoby winced.

"I hate feeling like it was a mistake for me to be born."

Jacoby decided not to comment on that. "Your lifestyle is taxing,

Alexandria."

"Everyone hasn't been raised the same way, Jacoby," she said with a forlorn look on her face.

There was another long silence.

"If you know that you're a problem at my parents' house, why are you going back there?"

"I have nowhere else to go," she wailed. "I tried to call daddy and tell him I was on my way back, but no one answered the telephone."

Jacoby flinched again because of the word 'daddy'. "My mother had a doctor's appointment." Her mother's words reverberated in her head. 'Since she left your dad and I have been acting like newlyweds.' Jacoby looked at Alexandria. "You can stay here for a week and look for a job. But you have to leave in a week whether you have one or not."

"Thank you, Jacoby."

"Now I'm going to bed. I didn't get any sleep last night."

Jacoby woke around one o'clock in the morning to Alexandria and Armstrong's raucous laughter coming from the den. She cast her eyes to the heavens. A week more of this nonsense?

In his boxing gloves, Noah walked over to the speedball that hung from a leather rope. First, he did a succession of fast movements with his fists, punching it with alternate hands. Working up a sweat he relished the feeling of letting go of the day's stress. Pummeling the leather, he conjured up the face of the unseen Armstrong Battle. Noah reared his arm back and with all his might hit the ball. It bounced back and as it spun back in his direction, Noah realized that he'd flattened it. It twirled around and then broke away from its chain. He stared at his handiwork. On his way out, he stopped by the manager's office.

Deon was typing data into a computer.

Noah said with a sardonic look, "Man, I messed up your ball."

"Again!"

"Yeah. And I'd like to pay for it." Noah reached inside his bag and pulled out two one hundred dollar bills. "That should take care of it including the cost of labor."

"Thank goodness we keep a couple of those on hand," Deon laughed. He looked at the sober expression on Noah's face and his laughter died. "Noah, what are you so angry about?"

"A friend of mine is being abused and I don't know what to do about it."

Deon looked at him. "You know what to do about it. The power is in your hands."

"I don't like unfair fights, man."

"Is the abuser fighting fair?"

"No."

"Then...."

"If I have to, I have to. But it'll be my last resort."

###

"You let her stay!" Allie said right before she bit into her sandwich. She said with a mouthful of food, "Have you lost your damn mind?"

"I didn't have a choice."

"You had a choice," Allie protested.

"I didn't want her to go back to my parents' house."

"She was probably testing you, knowing that you'd cave and let her stay."

"It's so mortifying to have her at my place. I just didn't know what else to do. She's watching how Armstrong and I barely speak to each other. I can tell she enjoys it."

"Of course she does. Misery loves company. That's some toxic mess going on at your place, Jacoby. Where is Alexandria sleeping?"

"In the spare room," she answered in a sour voice.

"So that means you're back in bed with Armstrong?"

"Yeah! But I wear pajama bottoms, and a heavy tee shirt. I need to get away from that insanity, but I want her gone first. I ran from Bunnell because of her. I can't keep running."

"I think that I have a solution. Lenny got the job Noah recommended him for. The pay is six fifty an hour more and there's room for him to grow. As soon as we catch up some bills we're moving to a bigger place. I'll rent you a room."

Jacoby said gratefully, "I would love that, Allie." Jacoby placed her fingertips to her temples and massaged.

"You look terrible."

"I slept on the couch the other night and have a crook in my neck. Now I feel like I'm coming down with something. All I want to do is drink a bottle of NyQuil and sleep for about a day."

Allie took her hand and placed it on Jacoby's forehead. "You're hot," Allie said, "And not in a good way."

"I hate that I have Isadora's party to attend tonight."

"Doctor yourself up real good when you get home tonight."

"I will," she said.

###

Alexandria stared at Jacoby in her black off the shoulder evening dress. Jacoby had piled her hair high and looked like Nefertiti.

"You look beautiful, Jacoby."

"Did you go looking for a job today?" she asked brusquely ignoring the compliment

"Yes," Alexandria said. "Wal-Mart is hiring."

"Good," she said. She grabbed her wrap. "Tell Armstrong not to wait up."

"He said that he was going to a hurricane party at some beach called Haulover."

"That sounds like him," Jacoby said tersely as she stormed out of the apartment.

Jacoby could barely see through the sheets of rain. She inched the Mercedes through the water and hugged the slow lane. Her hazard lights and those of other cars were the brightest things in the darkness. The ringing of her cell phone startled her and she pulled over to the shoulder of the road.

"Hello, Noah," she said in a strained voice. "I know I'm late but I'm on my way."

"I tried to call you at home, but no one answered. The party's been cancelled due to the weather."

"Thank God," she said.

"Where are you?"

"I'm only about ten minutes from my house. The road is barely visible."

"Turn around and seek shelter," he ordered. "The storm has been upgraded to a category three hurricane and it's heading towards Miami. Stay home tomorrow. I sent out an electronic phone call to everyone that we're closed until the weather clears."

"Good."

"Jacoby."

"Yes."

"Leave your phone on and text me when you get home safely."

"I will, Noah."

After another thirty minute drive, Jacoby parked and texted Noah. I'm home. Thank you for everything you do. Not being able to hide her feelings from him any longer she added, I'll miss you while the office is closed.

Drenched from head to toe, Jacoby ignored Alexandria's closed door and went to take a shower. Hot, stinging pelts warmed her chilled body.

After readying herself for bed, she read the directions on the bottle of Nyquil. "This little plastic measuring cup just won't cut it," she murmured. Jacoby turned the bottle up to her mouth and took a big gulp. She crawled into bed and soon fell into a deep sleep.

Hours later in a drug-induced state she looked at the clock. "Three o'clock?" Jacoby opened her mouth several times trying to rid it of the bitter taste. She stumbled to the kitchen and grabbed a bottle of water. The bottle was raised to her lips when in her haze she heard Alexandria.

"Yes, baby, yes," Alexandria screamed. "You know how I like it when you do it that way!"

"What the hell!" Jacoby took a gulp of water before she walked towards Alexandria's room. Alexandria has the nerve to bring some man to my house? Jacoby flung open the bedroom door and stumbled backwards.

Alexandria was on the bed positioned doggy style.

Armstrong was behind her thrusting.

Alexandria panted, "Armstrong, you're the best I ever had."

"So you like it like this?" he crowed triumphantly.

"Yes! Yes! Yes!" she answered.

Jacoby screamed and fell back against the door.

The resounding crash against the door stopped their copulating instantly.

With a look of disgust Jacoby backed out of the room.

When Armstrong came out he wore a towel around his waist. "What did you expect me to do, Jacoby?" he asked defensively.

Jacoby stumbled away from his breath that reeked of alcohol.

Advancing towards her he said, "You drove me to this. I had to get satisfied somewhere."

"I think that I'm going to be sick." She barely made it to the kitchen sink before emptying her guts of the NyQuil and chicken breast she'd consumed earlier. Grabbing a paper towel she wiped her mouth. Then she rounded on him and shouted, "I hate you! You're a horrible, repulsive, person."

Alexandria came to stand in the doorway of the bedroom. She was dressed in one of Jacoby's teddies. Her lips were twisted triumphantly.

Fire blazed out of Jacoby's eyes. "I knew that you were a slut," she paused for emphasis, "just like your mammy."

"Shut the fuck up about my mother!" Alexandria screamed.

"Armstrong, I'm leaving. I never want to see you again," she said with loathing. "But I need to do something first." With intent, Jacoby walked towards Alexandria.

"Get in the room, Alexandria," Armstrong ordered.

Alexandria almost tripped as she scurried to do his bidding.

Armstrong towered over Jacoby blocking her path to the front door. "Now you're going to march your ass back into that bedroom and join us."

"No the hell I'm not!"

"You will or else," he said with a maniacal gleam in his eyes.

"I'm out of here." She turned her back on him to leave.

Armstrong grabbed Jacoby's arm and swung her around. "You're not going anywhere." He growled, "You haven't slept with me in like forever." He leaned into her face and his eyes were glassy from the combination of rage and spirits. "What the hell do you expect me to do for sex?"

Jacoby pointed at the area between Armstrong's legs. "I got tired of being on top trying to get some friction out of that teeny, weeney," Jacoby answered, her voice laced with sarcasm.

Armstrong's face became enraged. "Alexandria doesn't have a problem with it."

"She's faking," she spat out.

"It was so good to her she followed me from Bunnell."

"You're so gullible," Jacoby screamed. "This isn't about you. She's trying to hurt me and you're just the ways and means to do it."

"You won't even give me a blow job," Armstrong said in an accusatory voice.

"I didn't have anything to wrap my lips around," Jacoby sneered. "You can't please any woman."

The crack across her face stunned her, and as she fell, she hit her head on the edge of the coffee table.

A blinding pain shot through her temple and it momentarily clouded her vision.

"You're going to go into that bedroom and watch Alexandria show you how it's done," he said, as he stood over her menacingly. "Then it's your turn."

Blood ran down her face and gathered under her chin. Petrified, she looked up at him.

"You're so stupid, Jacoby," Armstrong sneered. "I know all about you. You've been hooking up with that Noah Powers. You went to his house, drinking, fuckin' him," he said, incensed.

"Have you been following me?" she asked and her voice shook with fright.

"I didn't have to." Armstrong grabbed her purse and pulled out the pen he'd bought her. He unscrewed the cap. "This is a transmitter, you dumb bitch. I've heard everything you been saying about me to your mother, Allie, and Claudia. Did you really think I was going to let you empty my bank account? Check it. There's nothing in there." Noah picked her laptop up off the sofa and showed it to her as if it was a prize. Then he lifted it high over his head and hurled it to the other side of the room. It crashed against the floor and shattered. There was a huge gash in the wall from the impact.

Jacoby looked up at him, trembling in the wake of his violence.

"How dare you talk about me like that!" he screamed, his face was mottled with rage. "Now you're going to pay."

Armstrong grabbed her by her hair and dragged her to her feet.

"Ouch, Armstrong," she wailed. "You're hurting me!"

Once she faced him, his hot breath fanned her face, the stench making her woozy.

Armstrong reared his arm back ready to strike her again.

Her mother's face appeared before her. With all her might Jacoby kneed him in his groin and leveled him.

"Ouch!" Armstrong screamed as he clutched his penis and went down. He writhed on the floor his face was contorted with pain.

In a haze of desperation Jacoby watched him.

"I'm going to make sure you regret that!" he threatened. As he struggled to get up the towel slid off of him.

Jacoby took all the strength she could muster and stomped him in the groin.

Armstrong yelped like a wounded animal, and subsided back onto the floor, and lay on his back grabbing the area between his thighs.

Jacoby grabbed her purse and ran from the apartment barefoot. Once she was outside, the torrential rain made it impossible to see her car. She hit the alarm on her remote. As it went off, she bolted towards the flashing lights. Her wet clothes made a squelching sound as she slid into the leather seat. Without taking time to buckle her seatbelt, she gunned the gas pedal and the car fishtailed out of the parking lot. Once the complex was out of sight, she pulled to the side of the road. Her head throbbed from pain and tears wracked her body. She sobbed until she was spent. Eventually, drained, she pulled back into the storm and drove away from danger.

She pulled up at the gate, with trembling hands and punched in the numbers 0810. The gate slowly parted. She again gunned the gas pedal, but this time plowed into the cement block on the side, shattering a headlight. Shaken, she put the car in reverse. Fresh tears streaming down her face she finally pulled in front of Noah's house. Through the downpour she stumbled towards protection. Jacoby pushed the doorbell several times before collapsing onto the stoop, curling into a ball of pain.

Right before she blacked out she felt strong arms lift her. In her semi-conscious state, nevertheless, she felt safe.

CHAPTER 12

Confused, Jacoby stared at the stark walls. Feeling something unfamiliar, she lifted her hand and touched a bandage at her temple. She looked down. She noted she was dressed in a man's shirt but was naked underneath. A feeling of hysteria began to rise inside her, and she swung her legs off the bed. Slowly she got to her feet. Feeling wobbly, she grabbed the headboard.

"Good morning," a deep, throaty voice said behind her.

Jacoby swung around, "Noah," she whispered in relief. Then her knees began to buckle.

Noah grabbed her, and lifted her back into the bed. He propping her up against the headboard. "You need to eat something before you go exploring."

"I'm at your house?" Her face was screwed up as she tried to fit the pieces of the puzzle together.

"Yes."

"How long have I been here?"

"Five days."

"Five days!"

"You had a bout of pneumonia." He scrutinized her carefully. "The doctor and I were really worried about you for the first couple of days. The antibiotics finally kicked in, and all you needed was rest."

"Doctor?"

"My family doctor. We've had a full blown hurricane, but he managed to get here when the eye was over the city."

"Why don't I remember anything?" she whispered, confused.

"It's not surprising since you had a 103 degree temperature."

As if on cue, Jacoby began to cough.

"It's time for your medicine." Noah walked to the bathroom to the right and returned with a bottle of medicine and a spoon. He carefully measured the liquid into and held it out to her. "Open your mouth," he ordered.

Jacoby obediently opened her mouth and swallowed the liquid. She screwed her face up in distaste.

"Get used to it," he said. "Doctor Meadows said that you're to finish the whole bottle, not stop when you start feeling better."

"Ugh," she groaned.

"You're okay for another four hours. It was easier getting that inside you than when you were half sedated."

"So you've been taking care of me all this time?"

Noah sat down on the bed next to her. "I didn't want to take you to a hospital. Besides, they were full because they were being used as hurricane shelters."

She looked out the window and saw a clear horizon. "So I missed the hurricane?"

"Yes, we're done for now."

Jacoby squirmed uncomfortably. "So you dressed me?"

"I bathed you, dried you off, and dressed you." Trying to ease her embarrassment, Noah gave her a wicked smile. "I felt guilty for deriving such pleasure from that when you were too ill to protest."

"That's okay," she murmured, her long eyelashes fluttering down and hiding her eyes.

"What happened to make you run out into a storm like that, Jacoby?" Now Noah's mouth was hard and his eyes glittered angrily.

She dropped her head in disgrace.

"I insist that you tell me."

She muttered miserably, "I caught Armstrong in bed with Alexandria."

"That bastard!" Noah shouted as he balled his fists at his sides.

"That's not the terrible part. He wanted me to join them. And when I refused he hit me."

Noah stood to his feet. "I'll be back," he said in a deathly quiet tone.

"Where are you going?"

"Nowhere that you need to worry about. Get some rest. I'll be back before you know it."

"Noah." She stared at him with round eyes and blinked away her tears. "Please don't leave me. I'm afraid."

"I'll lock the doors. You'll be secure."

"Don't go do anything to Armstrong," she pleaded. "If something happened to you," she whispered in a broken voice, "I don't know what I would do."

"Nothing's going to happen to me."

"Please let it go," she said beseechingly. "He's not worth the trouble."

Noah hesitated, then he said, "Okay... But you have to promise me something, Jacoby."

"What is it?"

"You'll stay away from him."

"Done."

"And you need to enroll in a self defense class. You have to be able to protect yourself. That's the only way I won't go and bash Armstrong's head in."

"I'll do it," she promised.

"In the meantime," Noah reached over to the nightstand and handed her a brown paper bag.

Jacoby opened it and pulled out a small can.

"It's mace. Use it on Armstrong or anyone else who threatens you and is in your personal space."

Jacoby held the can in her hands, gratitude for Noah shining in her eyes. "I will, Noah. And thank you."

Noah stuffed his hands, in his pockets. He rocked back and forth on his heels. "How many times has he abused you?"

For a second time she dropped her head in shame. "Too many."

"I've seen the bruises on you." He sat down on the bed again. "That's why I never showed any respect for your relationship."

"What do you mean?"

"I knew that you were living with a man, yet, I tried to show you that I was interested in you as more than a friend. I was at a loss as to what to do. But I couldn't help you unless you were willing to confide in me."

"At first it was him grabbing me by my arm or the throat. The worst thing he ever did before this was to slap me."

"And you thought that was okay?" he demanded angrily.

"Of course not," she whimpered, "but I didn't have anywhere to go. I didn't want to drop out of school, leave my job," she paused before saying in a broken voice, "or you..."

There was a long silence as each of them digested the enormity of what was happening between them. "You'll never have to be without me, Jacoby. Move in with me," he said suddenly.

The world seemed to stand still. Finally she said with regret, "I can't do that."

"Why not? I have this empty six bedroom house. You can have the upstairs and I'll take the downstairs. We'll live as roommates until..." He trailed off, not wanting to pressure her into anything she couldn't handle. "I get so lonely here, Jacoby."

Jacoby's eyes widened with astonishment. "You get lonely? There's no need for that, Noah. I can name three women from work who have a huge crush on you."

Noah took his hand and placed it over his heart. "I don't want them," he said.

Heat enveloped her lower extremities. "Who do you want, Noah?" she asked, her heart palpitating wildly.

He took his hand and lifted her chin. "I want you."

"Why do you want me?"

"You're smart, beautiful and sexy. But it's more than that. There's just something about you, Jacoby Alexander."

"Armstrong once felt that way about me too. Once he had me, his feelings for me changed and I lost him."

"But what did you lose, Jacoby? He's a nothing that's obviously threatened by you."

Her eyebrows rose in query. "Threatened by me?"

"You've outgrown Armstrong and he knows it. Think about it, Jacoby. Your laptop got ruined. He knew that you needed it to finish your education. Your car was vandalized. Someone needed a key to open the door and pop the gas cover. You needed that to get to work and school. Who else could have done that but him?"

The memory of Armstrong destroying her second laptop surfaced. Reality consumed her. She burst into tears and buried her head in her hands. "How could I have not seen it? I feel so stupid."

Noah slid closer and put his arms around her. "You're not stupid. You just look for the good in people. Everyone doesn't deserve that."

She sobbed until she was spent.

Once she was done, Noah gently eased her down on the bed and pulled the covers around her. "You need to get some rest," he advised quietly. "I'll call you for dinner."

The medicine kicked in and her eyelashes fluttered to a close.

Hours later, the smell of spaghetti roused her. She stumbled to the bathroom and stared in the mirror. The white bandage was discolored with blood seepage. She touched it in disgust, then pulled at one end of the tape. The skin underneath clung to it and she flinched as she pulled away the bandage, and then threw it in the garbage can. Green and blue bruises ran from her temple to her jawbone. In horror she stared at her reflection. *How did I let things get so out of hand?*

A cough from behind startled her.

Noah stood there and behind him, she saw several packages on the bed. "While you were sleeping, I went out and purchased some things for you. I had to guess your size. You're a ten, right?"

"You guessed right. I'm a ten."

"You sure are," he said playfully.

Jacoby blushed with pleasure at his compliment.

"Along with a housecoat there are a couple of dresses, capris with shirts, and flats.

She followed him into the bedroom. "You are such a good man, Noah."

"You deserve a good man, Jacoby. Dinner's ready anytime."

"May I have a shower first?"

"Yes," he said. "Take all the time you need."

After her shower, Jacoby felt like a new woman as she sat down to eat. She twirled spaghetti on her fork. "This is delicious, Noah. How'd you learn to cook like this?"

"I'm a bachelor. I need to know how to do something."

"This is more than something," she said. Abruptly she said, "Noah, I'm really sorry about the company car. I'll pay for the damages."

"Nonsense," he said. "It's about time the high premiums I pay are justified."

"But there has to be a deductible, Noah. I feel that I should pay it."

"Don't sweat the small stuff, Jacoby. I don't."

"How long will it be before you get it back?"

"PJ said a couple of weeks. There's no rush for you to come back to work." His brow was furrowed with worry. "Take some time to heal."

"I would like to work from home until my bruises go away. I can't stand the thought of people looking at me when I look like this."

Noah handed her a slip of paper. "This is a schedule of self defense classes in the area that are available. There's a seven o'clock class that runs for a week."

"You really did your homework," Jacoby murmured as she skimmed the schedule Noah had printed off the Internet.

"You need to be able to protect yourself."

"I'll have to rent a car, so I can go back and forth to class," she said musingly.

"I can take you," he offered. "It's only a twenty-five minute drive from here."

"That sounds great. But what if the Mercedes isn't ready when I'm ready to return to work? If we drive in to work together people might figure out that we're living together."

"Do you care so much what people think?"

"It's not about me. I don't want your employees to feel differently about you."

"It's my company, Jacoby. I'm the boss and I do what I want to. Anyone who doesn't like it knows where the door is."

"Just like that?" she said softly with one eyebrow raised.

"Just like that," he echoed. "My personal life is my own business."

"Then I would love to ride to work with you, Noah."

"Doctor Meadows called to check on you."

"Did you tell him that I'm fine?"

"I told him that you're safe. But you have to go down to the police station and file a report."

"Why?"

"Doctor Meadows notified them."

"Oh," she whispered.

"It was his duty to turn it in, Jacoby."

Again she covered her face with her hands. "It's so humiliating."

"You have to make a report of domestic violence."

She looked back at Noah. "Can't I just promise not to have anything else to do with Armstrong? That's what I want."

"Once the doctor made the report the police got involved."

"I understand," she murmured. "I'll go one day after you get home from work."

"I'll go with you."

"Do you think they'll arrest Armstrong?"

"I don't know." He watched her closely. "Would that be so terrible if they did? You're the victim, Jacoby. Not him. He should pay for what he did to you."

"I can't stand the thought of going to court. People will laugh at me. They'll know how weak I am."

"You're not weak." He gave her a chastising look. "But you did make a mistake by putting up with treatment that was beneath you. You should be cherished, Jacoby, not beaten."

"It's no excuse, Noah, but I felt trapped. I also felt sorry for him."

"That's the classic abusive relationship. The abuser makes the person he abuses feel sorry for him."

"He has issues," she muttered.

"Everyone has, Jacoby. The trick is to not let your problems become someone else's."

"I'm done with Armstrong. All I need is my jewelry and the rest of my clothes."

"Don't go over there by yourself," he warned. "When you're ready, I'll escort you."

She nodded affirmatively.

After dinner Jacoby stacked the dishwasher, and Noah wiped down the counters. Finished, they sat close on the couch. Jacoby said, "I feel as if I know everything about you, Noah, yet not enough."

"My mother and father were married for years and then they got a divorce. It devastated my mom. If it is possible, she died from a broken heart."

"That's too bad," she said. "How about your sister? Did she also take it hard?"

"I don't know. Sinclair is hard to read. You never know what she's thinking."

"I saw her once at work. She's very beautiful."

"And headstrong, and domineering, but she loves me to distraction."

"Did your parents give you a reason why they split?"

"Dad said that they grew apart. It really took me by surprise because I never even saw them argue."

"How old were you?"

"I was eleven. My father and I were very close so I took it pretty hard. After the divorce, even though Sinclair and I spent our school vacations with him it was never the same. I swore that if I got married I'd never get a divorce."

"So that's why you've never married," she said half teasing and half afraid. "You have a commitment phobia."

"No, I don't," he said. "I just hadn't met the right woman." Noah mesmerized her with his eyes. "But I'm hopeful."

As they listened to a jazz station, Jacoby grew drowsy. Once she fell asleep, her head lolled to one side and unconsciously she snuggled closer to Noah.

Noah eased her away and gently picked her up. He carried her into the bedroom and laid her on the bed. After he pulled the comforter across her, he tiptoed out. Noah climbed the stairs to the bedroom with the mattress and box springs. He stripped naked, then, took a freezing-cold shower.

Jacoby walked into the pitch, black apartment. Without turning on the light, she felt her way towards the master bedroom. From behind a hand grabbed her and threw her across the room. The black behemoth stood over her as she cowered on the floor. It grabbed her and began choking her. She gasped for air. "Someone help me!" she shouted right before she blacked out.

Jacoby! Wake up!"

She felt someone shaking her and tried to open her eyes.

"It's Noah, Jacoby. Wake up!"

His deep comforting voice freed her from the nightmare. She opened her eyes and clutched him, burying her face in his bare chest. "Noah, Noah, help me."

"You're safe, Jacoby," he said and his own tears muffled his voice as he held her trembling body close. He smoothed her tousled hair. "It was only a nightmare, Jacoby. You're here with me now."

"Help me," she quavered.

"Don't be afraid, Jacoby. I'll protect you." His body ached with desire for her.

She gripped him, her fingernails digging into his back. "Lay with me tonight, Noah. I don't want to sleep alone."

Noah lay down on the far side of the bed. "Go to sleep, Jacoby. I'm here for you."

Jacoby felt he was light years away from her. In the darkness she waited. Once she heard Noah's breathing deepen she slid over to him and buried her face between his shoulder blades. She drank in his masculinity. As they spooned in the darkness, Jacoby sent a silent prayer of gratitude to God. "Lord knows I love him, but I can't tell him yet. I have to make sure that he knows it's not love on the rebound, but everlasting love."

Jacoby's breath fanning him awakened Noah. He held very still, relishing the feeling of her presence. It's too soon to tell her that I'm in love with her. She's been through so much. I need to give her time to heal.

The next morning, donned in her new housecoat, Jacoby sashayed into the kitchen. She gave Noah shy smile.

"Hello, sleepyhead."

"I know," she said. "I can't believe I've slept past noon."

"You needed it," he said. Noah sat at the breakfast counter. A deck of cards was fanned out in front of him.

"Are you playing solitare?" she asked as she poured herself a cup of coffee.

"No," he said. "I'm what you call putting my cards on the table."

"What do you mean?" she said, sitting on a stool across from him.

"I want you to know what I'm thinking."

Her heart beat wildly. "What are you thinking, Noah?" She eyed him over the rim of her cup.

"You've been through a traumatic experience with Armstrong. I don't want your feelings of gratitude to me to be confused with those of love."

She held his eyes with hers. "I know the difference, Noah. I'm not a child."

"I want you to feel comfortable living with me. In other words, I'm not going to pounce on you for sex."

I wish that you would. I could sure use some.

"I already know and respect you from a professional standpoint. But I don't want to skip the dating ritual just because you're living here."

"Dating ritual?"

"Yes," he said. "Getting to know someone before you make love is the foundation of a relationship."

"You really want a relationship with me, Noah?"

"Very much so. I want to date you as well," he said. "I want us to live here as if we've just met. I want to learn you inside and out."

She said nervously, "You may find out that I'm not that interesting."

"I doubt that. If I really felt that way I wouldn't have waited for you to get fed up with Armstrong. I would have done one of two things."

"Such as?"

"I could have put you in a position so that you were forced out of that environment. But I didn't want you to have any lingering feelings for Armstrong." Noah gave her a steadfast look. "I think that he's managed to take care of that for me."

"He has," Jacoby declared emphatically. "What was your other choice?"

"Move on."

Her lips trembled at the thought.

"Jacoby, when and if we make love you'll have to make the first move."

She gulped away her disappointment. "Is that why last night you didn't..." Her words trailed off.

"That's why," he acknowledged. "I didn't want our first time to be with you clutching me for protection and shaking from fear. I want you sure that you know what you're doing. You'll have to let me know when you're ready."

She swallowed hard and bit back the retort, "Just let me go take a shower and I'll meet you in the bedroom." But instead she simply nodded her head in agreement. "Since I'll be living here just as your roommate I insist on paying my own way."

"You can insist, but there's no mortgage on this house."

"I need to help out with the bills."

"That's so ridiculous it's not worth discussing," he scoffed. "However, I do have a way for you to help me."

"What is it?"

"This house is practically empty. I was going to hire an interior decorator but that's impersonal and time consuming. Will you decorate my house for me?"

"But you don't know that you'll like my taste," Jacoby said apprehensively.

"I love your taste in clothes."

"I don't know about this, Noah."

"This is a house and not a home. I want you to make it a home."

Jacoby didn't attempt to quell the rising feeling of anticipation about decorating Noah's house. "Will you give me some input on your likes and dislikes?"

"Okay. But I'm sure if you like it, I'll love it."

Jacoby looked at the bare walls. "I'd love to decorate your house, Noah."

"I'd love that too, Jacoby," he beamed. "I had your name added to a credit card to use for your purchases. It should be here in a few days."

"How'd you know that I'd agree?"

"I know how good your heart is, Jacoby." Noah drained his coffee cup and stood. "Even though it's Saturday I have to go into the office for a couple of hours. Will you be okay here by yourself?"

"Yes," she said.

"Good." He kissed the top of her head before he headed towards the door.

Just as he got there Jacoby said, "Noah."

"Yes." He paused with his hand on the door knob.

"I'll miss you."

Noah exhaled. "I'll miss you too."

After the door closed, Jacoby picked up the phone and called Allie.

"Hello."

"Allie," Jacoby said. "I need you to do me a favor."

"Why does my caller I.D. say that you're calling me from Noah Powers' phone?"

"I'll explain everything. But I need you to come and pick me up. Bring a set of empty suitcases."

"Why?" she said in a worried voice. "You're not moving away, are you?"

"I wouldn't leave Miami for all the money in the world," Jacoby said. "I need to get my things from my old apartment and one set of luggage won't be enough."

"You're finally leaving that loser Armstrong?"

"Yep," Jacoby said. "We're done."

"Happy days are here again!" Allie shrieked. "What's Noah's address?"

"125 Gables by the Sea."

"I'll be there in less than an hour."

Jacoby and Allie sat in her F-150. They wore hats and sunglasses as they watched the building. Allie said, "I can't believe you were going through all that abuse and kept it away from me."

"I kept it from everybody," she said, wiping away the tears that had fallen as she recounted to Allie the mental and physical abuse that she'd kept hidden. "It's not the sort of thing one talks about."

"Those bruises on you are Armstrong's shame, not yours, Jacoby."

"But I let it go on and things escalated."

"Unfortunately a lot of women do, Jacoby. The thing is for you to learn from your mistakes and not let it happen again."

"I won't, Allie," she promised making the same point to herself.

"I'm surprised with everything that's occurred Noah let you come over here without him."

"He doesn't know," she explained. "He wanted to bring me, but I need to show him that I can stand on my own two feet. I can't expect Noah to save me over and over again."

"I understand. You don't want him to be like Noah building an ark to save all the animals," Allie teased in an effort to lighten the atmosphere. "I still can't believe that you're moving in with him." Allie said in awe, "You sure are going from the outhouse to the White House."

Jacoby said, "It's not about material things, Allie."

"I know that. But you've got to admit life is going to be a lot easier for you."

"I have to admit that life is getting a lot more loving for me."

Allie shot her a look. "So you're telling me that you love Noah?"

"I do," she replied immediately. "He doesn't know it yet. We're taking things slowly. He wants to give our relationship a chance to grow."

"Noah must really want your ass."

"I really want him too," Jacoby replied.

"So have you two done it?"

"Not yet. But I'm hopeful."

"What's the holdup?"

"Noah said that he wants us to date as if we just met."

"How cute is that?" Allie said with a pleased expression.

"I know. I just moved in, and he hasn't wanted to pressure me. His birthday is in two weeks. I plan on seducing him."

Allie chuckled, "You're going to seduce Noah?"

"It seems as if that's the only way I'm going to get some. Noah's sleeping upstairs until he thinks I'm ready." Jacoby suddenly whispered, "Scoot down." She felt her heart constrict from fear. "There goes Armstrong. Damn!" she said. "Alexandria's not with him. That must mean she's still in the apartment."

"Maybe," Allie whispered back. "But we have to find out before we go up there."

They watched Armstrong get into his Charger and leave.

Jacoby snapped her fingers. She pointed at two teenage girls sitting on the bench. "I'll ask those kids if they have a cell phone. I'll call the apartment and see if Alexandria answers the phone."

"That's a good idea."

As they approached, the girls gave them a wary look.

"I'm Jacoby and this is my friend Allie."

The girl with the braids spoke first. "I'm Brittany and this is my sister Chelsea."

"Do either of you have a cell phone that I can borrow?" Jacoby asked. "I'll pay for the call."

"I have mine," Chelsea said. "But I get unlimited free minutes so you don't have to worry." She reached into her pocket and pulled out iPhone. It's on already."

"Thank you." Jacoby dialed the number. There was no answer. After dialing the number several times, no one answered. She handed Chelsea her phone and looked at Allie. "No one is there."

"Who are you looking for?" Brittany asked.

"I need you girls to do me a favor. I used to live here and I'm moving out. I want my things from the apartment and I want to do it while my ex is gone."

"That's what my mom did," Chelsea said. "She said that it was easier that way because there would be no danger of anyone getting hurt."

"Did you notice the guy in the white charger?"

"Yeah," Brittany said. "He's fine."

"Stay away from him," Allie warned. "He's a pervert."

Jacoby couldn't chuckle at the look of terror that appeared on the girls' faces. "I'll give each of you twenty dollars if you call my friend's cell if you see him come back."

"Okay," they replied in unison.

"I also want you on the lookout for a girl. She may be walking. She's a tall girl with beautiful light brown eyes. She walks around half naked all the time."

"Oh yeah! I've seen her before," Chelsea said.

"If you see either of them call 305-279-0023. " She pointed at Allie. "That's her cell number."

"And I thought today was going to be another boring Saturday," Brittany quipped. "This is like something out of the movies."

Jacoby and Allie stood in the middle of the apartment and stared at the chaos. They put down Allie's suitcases. Allie said, "This place is so dirty. The counter has stains and food all over it. And it looks like three days of dishes in the sink."

"Alexandria is a real slob."

"Can you imagine living like this?" Allie exclaimed, "I wouldn't eat a damn thing she cooked."

"The two of them will probably be very happy together. Like hangs with like." Jacoby's laptop lay in a shattered mess in a corner. She walked over and began picking up the pieces.

"Maybe the Geek Squad can save the hard drive," Allie said soothingly.

"I hope so," Jacoby said. "If not I have almost everything saved on an external hard drive that I keep at the office." Angrily she placed the heap on the kitchen table. She went into the bedroom and grabbed one of her suitcases out of the closet. She snatched her jewelry box off the dresser and dumped the contents into her small cosmetics baggage. "It'll be easier to carry if we combine stuff," she said to Allie who'd followed her.

Jacoby and Allie packed with haste. Once all the suitcases were filled to the brim Allie looked at her. "What are we going to do? There are still clothes left."

"I think we got what I wanted."

Allie said as she closed a suitcase. "I can't believe that you're going to let him have all your furnishings," she exclaimed. "You're the one that bought it."

"I know," Jacoby said. "But to be honest, if I had the time I'd donate it all to Goodwill. I don't want any memories of my life with Armstrong."

Allie's cell phone rang. "Hello," she said. "Okay, thanks." She looked at Jacoby. "Armstrong's back and Alexandria is in the car with him. They're down the street at the mailboxes getting the mail."

Jacoby said in a voice filled with fear, "Let's put them in the stairwell. Then we'll use the stairs to leave."

"I'll call the girls. They'll help us."

Allie hit redial. "We have too many suitcases to carry. Will you come up to apartment 205 and grab the dresses out of the closet? Great! Thanks." She closed her phone. "They're on their way."

No one uttered a word as they ran back and forth clearing all of Jacoby's belongings out the apartment. With relief they caught their breath in the stairwell. Jacoby heard Armstrong's voice in the hall. She raised her hand to the group to motion them to silence.

"I don't know why you got an attitude," Alexandria said in a frightened voice.

"You ain't got no money for no damn mall," Armstrong said in a sour voice. "I had to go and pick you up. What you go out there for?"

"Just to look," Alexandria said.

"Get a job and then look," he said harshly. "I'm tired of feeding your ass."

They could hear him opening the apartment door.

"In the meantime clean up this damn place." There was a pause before Armstrong screamed, "What the fuck happened in here?"

They grabbed Jacoby's belongings and began running up and down the stairs loading Allie's truck.

Once the group was finished Jacoby reached in her wallet and pullet out two fifty dollar bills. She handed one to each of the girls.

"This is more than you said that you'd give us," Chelsea protested.

"I can't thank you enough for what you did," she said. Then she gave each of them a hug.

"Will we ever see you again?" Brittany asked.

"Not here," Jacoby replied with certainty as she climbed inside.

Jacoby's cell phone rang. She looked at the number. "It's Armstrong."

"Don't answer it."

"I won't." After Jacoby saw the message she had voicemail she played it. "Let's hear what Mr. Armstrong has to say. I'll put it on speaker." She held it out so that Allie could also hear what was said.

"Jacoby, I'm sorry for what happened," Armstrong whimpered. "Please come back. Things will be different. Alexandria's gone. She didn't mean anything to me. I took her to the bus station yesterday."

"What a pathological liar," Jacoby said with contempt.

At Noah's house Allie helped Jacoby take everything to the master bedroom. Allie eyed the Gourmet kitchen. "I'm glad that I didn't come in earlier. I might have been too jealous to help you."

"You're not like that," she said. "That's why I love you."

"I love you too, Jacoby." She looked at her wristwatch. "I have to go and pick KeKe up from her play date. Are you going to be okay?"

"Yeah," she said. "I'm going to take a nap. I can't believe how tired I am."

"It's from the mental drama of the afternoon. When are you coming back to work?"

"As soon as I can. I'm getting antsy from being gone for so long."

Allie leaned over and gave her a kiss on the cheek. "Call me if you need anything," she said before she departed.

CHAPTER 13

The ringing of the doorbell roused Jacoby from her slumber. She looked through the peephole and although she could only see a man's chest, she knew it was Noah. She grinned as she opened the door. "Noah, why are you ringing the bell?"

He took his hand from behind his back and handed her a bouquet of yellow roses. "May I call on you this evening, Miss Jacoby Alexander?"

Jacoby's pure white teeth flashed her million dollar smile. "I would be very happy to spend time with you Mr. Noah Powers. Please come in."

Noah stepped across the threshold. He caught sight of the pile of suitcases in the bedroom. Frowning, he said, "I thought you were going to wait for me to take you to get your things."

"Allie took me," she said.

Noah looked questioningly at her.

"I don't want you to think that you have to babysit me."

Noah continued to gaze at her steadily.

"I'm not going back. He can have everything else."

Noah gathered her in his arms and held her close, then lifted her chin with his forefinger.

She closed her eyes in anticipation.

His lips were warm. They moved across hers and urged her mouth open. They gently explored each others' tongues. Spent, Jacoby moved in closer and slid her arms around his waist. They held each other, and time stood still.

Jacoby counted out one, two, and fifty dollars of Monopoly money. "There," she said in a disgruntled voice. "I can't believe that you wiped me out."

"If we were playing for real money you'd be homeless," he chuckled as he began putting the pieces of the board game back in the box.

"I would be homeless in real life if it wasn't for you, Noah," she said in a sober voice.

"No matter what happens between us, Jacoby, you'll never be homeless." The air between them was thick. He added with quiet authority, "That's some real money you can put in the bank."

Later that night they sat on the couch and she curled up to him as if she was a cat. Soon she fell asleep with her head on Noah's shoulder. Eventually he picked her up and took her to the master bedroom. He placed her gently on the bed and pulled the covers up over her.

Jacoby walked into the pitch, black apartment. Without turning on the light, she felt her way towards the master bedroom. From behind a hand grabbed her and threw her across the room. The black behemoth stood over her as she cowered on the floor. It grabbed her and began choking her. She gasped for air. "Someone help me!" she shouted right before she blacked out.

Jacoby sat up and stared around the room. *I had that nightmare again.* Sweat dripped from her body, drenching the sheets. She moved over to the other side of the bed where the linen was dry. She tossed and turned, unable to sleep. Then without knowing what propelled her. Jacoby got out of bed, turned on the light, and went to her jewelry box. She moved her jewelry around. *Where is my mother's ring?* After more fruitless searching Jacoby gave up and sank to her knees in despair. Feeling an immense sense of loss she crawled back into bed, pulling the covers over her head.

"I don't usually eat breakfast," Noah admitted.

"I don't usually have the time to cook it for me or anyone else, but things are changing."

"Yeah, they are," Noah agreed, smiling.

Jacoby placed a plate of bacon, eggs, grits, sausage and toast in front of him. She grabbed a bottle of orange juice from the refrigerator and handed it to him, along with a packet of vitamins.

"You're spoiling me," Noah said.

"I hope so," she replied.

"PJ is delivering the Mercedes to you sometime today. He'll give you the key."

"It's ready?"

"There was only cosmetic damage to the car."

"Noah, please let me pay…"

"Don't start," he interrupted in a firm voice.

Silenced, Jacoby picked up a piece of bacon and began nibbling on it.

After breakfast Jacoby stood in the open doorway and saw Noah off to work. "What time are you going to be home tonight?"

A broad smile lit up Noah's face as he searched her eyes.

"What?" she asked.

"You called this place home."

"It's beginning to feel like one."

"It sure is," he agreed. "And it's nice."

Jacoby leaned forward and planted a warm kiss on Noah's full lips that met hers with desire. Finally she released his mouth and stepped back. Breathlessly she asked, "What do you want for dinner?"

Noah didn't answer, instead he just stared.

Her robe had opened exposing her breasts. Noah's gaze remained fixated on the full mounds that beckoned him to touch them. He came back inside and closed the door behind him, locking it.

The look in his eyes unnerved her and she took an involuntary step back.

With quiet deliberation he said, "Come here to me, Jacoby."

Without covering herself she walked over to him.

Noah placed a hand under each breast.

She gasped from the pleasure of his touch. Eagerly she lifted her mouth to meet his. When their mouths broke away she was breathless.

Noah's mouth closed over the black ring around her nipple and began to suckle.

As he pleasured her, the sensation buckled her knees and she slid her arms around his neck, clinging to him. A virgin liquid fire shot through her. "Oh my God!" she stammered.

"I know," Noah murmured but she heard him. With his other hand he fondled the other breast.

Jacoby cradled his head in her hands guiding it to her other nipple.

She was wet with desire.

Noah gently lightly bit its tip.

Jacoby undid his pants and slid the zipper of his pants down.

She felt his body stiffen from surprise, yet he didn't back away. She reached inside his boxers and fondled him. Jacoby reveled in the feel of the muscle between his legs.

Slowly he withdrew his lips from her breasts and buried his face in her hair.

Eagerly Jacoby cupped his shaft with both her hands. She clutched him, held him, pulled him towards her, and then released him. Jacoby leaned her head on Noah's chest. She held him still by circling one arm around his waist as she pumped him.

Noah gasped as she pleasured him. Finally, Noah, not ready to release his pleasure, stilled her hand.

She felt a liquid seeping out the side of her thong and she groaned, "Oh, Noah, Noah, I can't wait anymore."

"Neither can I," he ground out as he scooped the love of his life into his arms. Noah held her gently as he walked to the master bedroom and kicked the door shut behind him. He placed her gently on the bed.

Jacoby looked up at him half fearful, half impatient.

"Are you sure you're ready for this, Jacoby?" he asked, peering down at her.

"More than ready," she assured him.

Noah stood, loosened his tie, and threw it on the chair in the corner. Hastily he unbuttoned and took off his starched white shirt, exposing black, silky hair that fanned out across his chest and drew into a straight line that disappeared into his boxers. She stared in fascination as a shape that looked like a twisted rope lifted the front of his pants. Noah followed her eyes and a smile hovered at the corners of his mouth. "I guess you can tell how much I want you."

"No, I can't, Noah," she lied. "I need you to show me."

Noah slid out of his unbuckled trousers.

Jacoby stared at Noah's long shaft nestled in a thatch of curly hair... Seeing him for the first time completely naked she gasped, "Lord have mercy!" and then burst into tears.

Astounded, Noah watched her. To no avail he tried to cover himself with both of his hands. He said soothingly, "If you're not ready we can wait."

"That's not why I'm crying," she choked out. "It's just that the sight of you makes me so damn happy."

He dropped his hands. And relieved, he chuckled. "That makes three of us, Jacoby." Then he joined her on the bed, pulled her into the crook of his arms and held her close. He trailed kisses down her jaw line, down her neck, and between her breasts before he gently positioned her on her back.

Jacoby closed her eyes as she felt herself being divested of her robe and panties. The feel of Noah's touch once again the insides of her thighs set her on fire. When she felt the mattress lift and knew Noah was getting up, her eyes flew open in alarm.

He smiled gently at her. "I'm just going to close the drapes." Noah stalked over to the huge double window and hit the switch. The mechanical button moved the black drapes and they slowly covered the window and the room was bathed in darkness. "Next time we'll have candles, but right now I can't wait."

"Please don't," she begged.

Noah rejoined her on the bed. He leaned over and kissed her. It was the sort of kiss that a man gives a woman that makes her know that he's in it for the long haul. In a leisurely manner his tongue found hers. As they explored each other's mouth, Jacoby fought back fresh tears of happiness. And this time when they broke their kiss, Noah's lips trailed down to her abdomen.

As she felt his hands part her thighs, she automatically closed them.

Noah said soothingly, "Let me taste you, honey."

Eagerly she reopened them.

Noah slid down the bed and sandwiched his head between her legs. He parted her lips until he could only see the pink. Noah began to lick her from the top of her wet femininity to the bottom.

She squirmed in ecstasy against his mouth as Noah dominated her with his tongue. Once she was saturated, he took his tongue and probed her center. Jacoby arched against his mouth. When his tongue found her center, she let loose and it flowed through to meet him. Jacoby flung her hands over her head, and they slapped the headboard behind her as Noah made love to her in a way she'd only seen in the movies.

After an eternity he lifted away from her.

Again Jacoby's eyes flew open. Even though it was dark, she could still see the glow of his eyes.

"Are you ready?"

In the background Jacoby heard the grandfather clock strike twelve.

"Yes," she replied huskily as she slid her arms around his shoulders. "I can't wait."

Noah entered her in one slow, long, movement. He savored the moment.

She felt as if he was in her throat.

He began to move with the long, sensual strokes a man makes when his desire is to make his woman complete.

Jacoby eagerly met him thrust for thrust. Her nails were like talons, digging into Noah's back yet the pain was one he relished. He pushed harder into her because of her eager thrusts.

Noah's tempo increased and in the deep recesses of her pleasure Jacoby heard the clock strike one. Suddenly a feeling of hot, molten lava began in her abdomen and passed between her legs, wetting them. She screamed, "Noah!"

Then and only then, did he saturate her with his love.

For an interminable time their rapid breathing was the only sound in the room. Noah rolled off her, and onto his side, pulling her off the saturated bed sheets to a dry part.

"Thank you," she murmured to Noah, replete with satisfaction.

"For what?" he said and she could tell he was smiling behind her.

"For…" she whispered shyly, "for making me finally feel like a woman."

Right before she drifted into a satiated sleep, she felt his arms close protectively around her.

Later that afternoon Jacoby awoke to a soft nuzzling behind her ears. She instinctively turned towards Noah.

"I didn't mean to wake you," he whispered.

Jacoby took her hand and lightly ran it down his manhood.

Immediately it stretched out.

"I'm so glad you did, Noah." She said boldly, "I want some more."

"I'm more than happy to oblige." He pulled her up and positioned her on all fours.

"Noah," she said suddenly afraid. "I don't think that I can handle you like this."

From behind her Noah felt her clitoris. "Jacoby," he said and there was promise in his voice, "I would never hurt you. I'll be gentle."

Jacoby felt relief at the touch of Noah's fingers in her wet body. "Oh, baby, I thought…"

"What?" Noah asked with a bit of confusion.

"Nothing," she whimpered, now impatient to feel him inside her again. "Please hurry," she said, "I need to feel you inside me."

Noah placed the palm of his hands on her firm buttocks. Slowly, carefully, he entered her womanhood.

Jacoby inhaled with excitement. The feeling of her body pressed around Noah's groin made her squirm even closer.

Stroke after stroke Noah pleasured her until she couldn't take it anymore. This time when she collapsed Noah remained inside her. They lay intertwined until she felt his shaft subside.

Hours later Jacoby rolled over and breathed a sigh of contentment. She stretched, loving the unfamiliar soreness in her body. She watched Noah as he entered the bedroom clad only in a towel.

"Do you have to go in today?" she asked with a pout on her full lips.

"Unfortunately I do." He grimaced. "At four o'clock I have a meeting with Irene Hatcher."

"Who is Irene Hatcher and should I be jealous?" she asked only half jokingly.

"She's a well known publicist who is relocating from New York. She wants an interview, and no, you shouldn't be jealous."

"Just making sure that I don't need to go in today and watch you."

"You'll never have anything to worry about. I've wanted you since the moment I saw you, Jacoby."

Her heart soared at Noah's words. "I'm sorry that you had to wait so long."

"Trust me when I say it was worth the wait."

Once she could speak she said, "You never did tell me what you want for dinner."

"You," he said in his throaty voice.

"I'll make that your dessert."

"That's a dessert I'll look forward too." Noah leaned over and gave Jacoby a long searching kiss that was returned with fervor. After their lips parted, he stared into her eyes.

Jacoby worshipped him with her eyes.

He gave an almost imperceptible nod of satisfaction, pleased by what he saw in Jacoby's gaze. "You had quite a workout today," Noah said with a contrived, innocent look.

Jacoby smothered a laugh at his expression.

"Get yourself some rest."

"I will," she said, snuggling under the covers.

As Noah went out the front door Jacoby could hear him whistling off key. Smiling, she drifted off back to sleep. After Jacoby woke for the third time that day, she sat up and stretched her stiff limbs. She donned her robe and without hesitation went upstairs to the room Noah had been occupying. It took three trips up and down the spiral staircase, but finally all of Noah's clothes were hanging in the closet with hers. After she'd arranged his toiletries next to hers she happily crossed her arms. The memory of the heights Noah had taken her to came to the forefront of her mind. *Noah Powers, I ain't going nowhere.*

As Jacoby cleaned the kitchen, the ringing of her cell phone startled her.

"Hey, Mom," she said after looking at her caller I.D.

"Why aren't you at work? Are you sick or something?"

"No," Jacoby said. "I'm just taking a couple of days off."

"Why?"

"I just have a lot to do. I'm going shopping for new furniture tomorrow."

"I thought that you had an apartment full."

"I did, but I left it."

"You left it! What do you mean?"

"I moved out. Alexandria can have Armstrong."

There was a long pause. "I knew there would trouble the minute you told me she was down there."

Deciding to spare her mother the details of the abuse she'd suffered she told her the least important part. "I caught the two of them in bed," Jacoby admitted. "He was getting it from," she paused and then finished in a tone laced with innuendo, "you know…"

"Dang! The apple doesn't fall far from the tree, does it? Wait until I tell your father. But he won't be surprised."

"What do you mean?"

"After Alexandria left, he said that he was relieved. Because she's his daughter he would never have put her out, but when she decided to make the move on her own, well, his whole demeanor changed. It's like he's back to what he was before she showed up at the prison."

"Then I'm grateful she came back into his life. I guess all those years of feeling guilty will dissipate now that he's at least tried."

"So where are you living?"

"I moved in with Noah."

"Jacoby!" her mother said, shocked. "Moving out from one man and moving in with another," she chided reprovingly. "I don't know about that."

"We're roommates," Jacoby hedged.

"But I could tell from the way you spoke of him before that you have feelings for him."

"I do. But believe me, Noah has been the perfect gentleman."

"How long do you think that's going to last?"

"Forever, Mom. Noah's a good man. It's not an act."

"When am I going to meet him?"

"At this time, I don't want him to feel pressured by meeting the parents and all that."

"Okay, dear. We'll wait until you think the time is right."

"Mom, I love you."

"I love you too, Jacoby. Send me your address."

"I will," she said.

"Be careful."

"Don't worry about me." She said truthfully, "I couldn't be happier or safer."

After Sarai hung up the telephone, a peace enveloped her. She went into the bedroom, closed the blinds, and sank to her knees. She clasped her hands together in prayer. "Dear Lord," she said, "thank you for removing my daughter from harm's way."

Jacoby sat on the couch viewing *The Fashion Police* on the *E* channel. Pictures of Isadora in various outfits were on the screen. In one picture Isadora wore fishnet stockings and sneakers. And in another she had on a lace top with her nipples exposed. The worst picture was one that exposed her buttocks. Jacoby turned off the television and dialed Isadora's private line.

"Yeah," Isadora said.

Jacoby could tell she was chewing gum. "Are you still in Miami?"

"Yeah, why? What's going on?"

"One of the things I want to do is to reschedule your party that was cancelled because of the hurricane."

"The movies out already, so what good is that?"

"We can still create buzz because it's in the theatres. Also there's something else."

"What?" Isadora said as she smacked her gum.

"I'd rather discuss it with you in person," Jacoby replied. "Are you available around nine o'clock?"

"That's too early. How about eleven?"

"That will be fine. I'll see you tomorrow, Isadora."

Isadora hung up without saying good bye.

Jacoby was surfing the web on the new laptop Noah had brought home the day before when the doorbell rang. She went to the door and looked through the peephole. Not recognizing the man, she pushed the intercom button. "May I help you?"

"I'm PJ. I came to drop off the Mercedes and give you the keys."

"Just a minute." Jacoby unlocked the door and opened it.

A tall, slender, handsome man with smooth, chocolate brown skin smiled at her.

Jacoby smiled back.

"Would you like to inspect the car?"

"Since you're Noah's ace mechanic I'm sure that it's fine."

"Thank you, ma'am, for the compliment. But it's garage procedure that you look at it and sign the paperwork."

"Oh, I understand," she said. Sliding into a pair of flip flops she walked ahead of PJ towards the car. She waved at the man sitting in the pickup waiting for PJ to finish conducting his business. She slowly walked around the Mercedes and couldn't discern any flaws in the paint. The white car shone brightly in the sun. "It looks great to me," she said, holding her hand out for the clipboard and pen. She signed the paper and handed it back to PJ.

After PJ and his companion left, she went into the house and grabbed her purse. Being out of the house exhilarated her. She opened the sun roof and the wind tousled her hair. Jacoby pulled into the first Publix grocery store that she saw. Taking her time, she walked up and down the aisles choosing food that she wanted to cook for Noah. After filling her cart she went to the wine aisle. She took four bottles of Chateau St.

Michelle Riesling off the shelf.

As Jacoby watched the bag boy load her wares into the trunk of the car she felt the hairs on her neck rise. She looked over the top of the car and saw him.

Armstrong stood on the sidewalk. His eyes were narrowed into slits and she could tell from his stance that he was almost chomping at the bit, waiting for the bag boy to leave her side so she'd be alone.

"Please don't leave until I get into the car and drive off," she begged the teenager.

He gave the trembling Jacoby a startled look. Then he followed her line of vision and stared at Armstrong. "No, ma'am," he said. "I won't go anywhere until you pull out of the parking lot." He asked hesitantly, "Do you want me to call the police?"

"No," she whispered. "I'll do that."

The bag boy opened Jacoby's car, door ushering her inside. She nervously pushed a twenty dollar bill into his palm.

"Ma'am," he protested. "We're not allowed to accept tips."

"I insist,' she said. "It'll be our secret." She cranked the car and sped out of the parking lot.

Instead of heading towards home, she drove around making a series of lefts and rights glancing in the rearview mirror to see if Armstrong was following her. Once she was satisfied that he wasn't, she went to the ATM. Putting her bank card into the slot she punched in her numbers. One hundred dollars should hold me until payday. Pocketing her money in her shorts, she went back to the car. She pointed her Mercedes towards home and safety.

That evening Noah sat at the snack bar opposite to Jacoby. He took a fork and dug into the plate of shrimp pasta she'd prepared. "This is so good, Jacoby. Where'd you learn to cook like this?"

"My mom started teaching me when I was in the sixth grade," she replied in a subdued voice.

Noah assessed her. "What's wrong?" he asked, putting his fork down.

"Nothing," she said. "I'm ready to come back to work, but…"

"But what?"

"Nothing," she denied. "I have a meeting with Isadora at eleven tomorrow. But then I think that I should go by the police station and file my report."

Noah searched her face. "After your meeting we'll go out to lunch, and then we'll stop by the station."

"That sounds like a plan."

That night once Noah finished his shower and walked into the dark bedroom, Jacoby's breathing was labored as she lay on her back and she was frowning in her sleep.

He eased himself into bed to keep from waking her.

Sensing his presence Jacoby's eyes fluttered open. "Hold me, Noah," she whispered.

"My pleasure," he said, gathering her into his arms.

"Tighter," she whispered.

Noah obliged.

"Tighter," she repeated.

His arms were like bands of steel and she finally drifted back to a peaceful sleep.

The next morning Jacoby dressed in a black and white striped dress with a belt that nipped her waist.

Noah stood behind her and put his arms around her middle. "You look beautiful," he said.

"You make me feel beautiful, Noah."

Noah turned her around to face him.

Jacoby closed her eyes.

Instead of kissing her, Noah nuzzled her nose with his.

She melted. When she could catch her breath she murmured, "I'm sorry about last night."

Noah gave a start of surprise. "What do you mean?"

"I fell asleep and we didn't get to do anything."

"I got to do something."

"What was that?"

"I held the most beautiful, caring, lover in the world and watched her sleep."

"Oh, Noah," she whispered.

"Oh, Jacoby," he mimicked teasingly.

As Noah navigated the Audi through the rush hour traffic, Jacoby stared at his large hands with his long, slender fingers. *Noah's hands are powerful yet gentle. They were made to love me.*

Jacoby stared at Isadora.

Isadora wore a shirt with a barbershop collar. The shirt was cut off at her midriff. Once again she saw the infamous fishnet stockings but this time they were paired with black shorts and tan UGG boots. Not realizing she was doing so Jacoby shook her head, "Did you pick out that outfit?"

"Yes," Isadora replied. "Don't you like it?"

"I think that it's a little over the top," Jacoby said diplomatically. "Maybe you should tone it down."

"I have my own clothing style," Isadora said proudly.

"What is the look that you're trying to achieve?"

"I don't know," she said. "I'm just trying new things."

Jacoby pulled out the pictures and comments of Isadora that she'd printed off the Internet. "Have you seen these? I pulled them off the Fashion Police website." She handed them to her.

"Yeah," she said, throwing them back onto Jacoby's desk. "Who is Kelly to critique someone's style of clothing?"

"That may be true, Isadora. However, the other people on the panel were just as disparaging about your clothes. You should decide on a trend and stick to it. Your outfits are all jumbled up."

A haughty look crossed Isadora's face. "I'm an actress. That will make people want to dress like me."

"There are a lot of stars to choose from. You have to give them something that stands out from others but doesn't look ridiculous."

"Are you saying that I look ridiculous?" Isadora snapped.

Jacoby chose to not reply to the obvious. "You said that you wanted to clean up your image. Just trying to get attention in the tabloids isn't the way to do that. Do you have a stylist?"

"Yes."

"Did she pick out any of these outfits on this page for you?"

"Yes," she said with a sullen look on her face. "Two of them."

"Then you need to change your stylist. She doesn't know what she's doing," Jacoby added bluntly.

"I can't fire her," Isadora whined. "She's my partner."

"What do you mean?"

"Joey and I have been together since high school."

"Oh," Jacoby said with dawning realization.

"She wants nothing to do with the acting scene. She's only here in Miami because of me. She's my rock away from all the craziness."

"Then find something else for her to do. If she truly loves you she'll want to help you rise to the level of stardom that you aspire to be."

A stubborn look settled on Isadora's face.

"What's the image that you want to project?"

"I want to be a trendsetter. Sort of like Katy Perry."

Jacoby nodded her head. "She does have a lot of style. One of the reasons is because it's her own and she doesn't try too hard. Are you ready to come out of the closet?"

"No," she said. "My personal life is nobody's business."

"I agree. But you do give up anonymity when you become a star. The question is, how big a star do you want to be?"

"I want to be the Creole Halle Berry."

Jacoby said bluntly, "Halle Berry wouldn't be caught dead in any of those outfits."

Isadora's lips stuck out in a pout.

"Does Francois know about Joey?"

"Of course he does."

"Then I suggest the two of you continue to hang out together and keep the buzz going about the relationship."

"That's no problem."

"I'm going to rebook your party for Labor Day weekend. There's always a lot of out-of-towners at South Beach. Is that good for you?"

"Sure. But I'm going back to L.A. in a few days. I'll fly back in for that."

"That sounds cool." Jacoby handed her a list. "Here you go."

"What is this?"

"Yesterday I contacted these stylists. Each of them represents some big stars that are known to be fashionable. They're willing to work with you. You can take a look at what they have in mind for you. Pick one stylist, and stick with her or him. Don't mix it up. That should help your image."

"Okay, Jacoby." She gave her a sheepish look. "You're right, Jacoby. If I want to really make it big, I need to clean up my image."

"There's a difference between an actress and a movie star, Isadora. You need to decide which you want to be. Have you found a cause that you have a heartfelt desire to support?"

"Not yet."

"Give it some real thought. I've found that if you're kind to others in the end things will work out the best for you."

"Okay, Jacoby."

With a smile Jacoby said, "I'll call you with the details of the Labor Day party."

"Okay."

Jacoby was cleaning out her email when Allie came in the room and shut the door behind her.

She grinned like the Cheshire cat. "Everyone's talking about you and Noah."

"Why?"

"Della saw the two of you arrive together after nine o'clock. They said he was opening all your doors for you. The news spread like wildfire. As a matter of fact, I had to defend you."

"What do you mean?"

"Della said that she knew you were after Noah from the get go. She said during the announcement that his dad was retiring you had a look on your face as you watched Noah at the podium. I told her that if anyone went after someone it was Noah pursuing you."

"Allie, you don't have to defend me to anyone. I'm happy and it's no one else's business who I sleep with."

"You go, girl," Allie cheered. "Sleep with? Well then... how was it? Did Noah slap it, lick it, and stick it?"

Jacoby didn't pretend not to understand. "He did that and more," she cooed. "It was better than I ever thought that it could be."

"But the question is... is Noah holding?"

Jacoby giggled like a schoolgirl. "He could take it and sling it over his shoulder."

"Damn!" Allie said. "Please tell me that you're exaggerating."

"Sort of. But Allie," Jacoby said and leaned forward in a conspiratorial whisper, "you know you hear about it, you dream about it, and if you're lucky you might see it in a movie, but Noah is unbelievable. And his technique is to die for. I honestly think that I blacked out at one time."

"But you've only had Armstrong as a reference."

"That doesn't mean a damn thing. With Noah I felt like a virgin. He reached places inside me that had never been touched before," she said.

"Have you heard from Armstrong?"

"Sort of. He's left begging messages on my cell phone. Also..." As Jacoby recounted her experience at Publix Allie's face grew perturbed. "I only escaped by the skin of my teeth."

"What did Noah say?"

"I didn't tell him."

"Why on earth not?"

"Noah had a peaceful life before I got in it. I want to keep it as drama free as possible."

"I kind of see what you're saying, Jacoby. But he had to know things were going to change for him when you moved in."

A hard glint entered Jacoby's eyes. "I want to make sure it's for the better. Not worse." There was a long pause before Jacoby said, "There's also something else that's troubling me."

"What is it?"

"I can't find my mother's ring," she said with a distraught look on her face. "It should have been with my other jewelry when I dumped it in my suitcase, but it's not there. It must still be at Armstrong's apartment." She wailed disconsolately, "The thought of Alexandria having it, wearing it, pawning it, is killing me."

"Oh no, Jacoby," she exclaimed. "Do you plan to go back and get it?"

"I promised Noah that I wouldn't go back there."

"He'd go with you."

"I know," she said. "But I don't want that. I don't want him harmed."

"So you think that Armstrong can beat Noah?" Allie made a snort of derision. "Doubtful."

"It's not about who would win the fight. Armstrong is real dirty. Unlike Armstrong, Noah doesn't know anything about life as a thug."

"He would want you to lean on him."

"I am, but there needs to be a limit. Allie, you know how when you watch a television show there's a character that's always crying and needing help? She's the most annoying cast member on the show and she usually gets killed off."

"This isn't television, Jacoby," she said seriously. "This is real life drama."

"After work I'm going to take out a restraining order on Armstrong. That should take care of Mr. Armstrong Battle."

"I hope so," Allie said.

"Besides, Noah's birthday is Saturday. I don't want anything to mar that."

"What do you have planned for him?"

"I haven't come up with anything yet." Allie said.

"Why don't you take him to Cirque de Soleil?"

"Cirque de Soleil. I've seen the billboards. Is it a good show?"

"We took KeKe there over a year ago and she still talks about it."

"Noah isn't a child."

"But the two of you will love it. It was one of the best experiences Lenny and I ever had."

"But what if Noah has already been?"

"Even if he has it's worth seeing again. There's so much going on you don't get it all the first time."

"You know, Allie, I've never even experienced the perks of Miami with Armstrong being such a dud and all. I think that Cirque de Soleil sounds like fun."

"You can order the tickets online and they'll hold them for you at the will call window. The show is expensive but worth it."

"So is Noah," Jacoby turned to her computer and Googled Cirque del Soleil.

With a smile of happiness for her friend, Allie went back to work.

CHAPTER 14

Noah perused the application of the woman who sat across from his desk. "Mrs. Hatcher, your credentials are impressive and you are a much respected publicist. I'm surprised to find you want to move from New York to Miami."

"I'm getting a divorce," she said curtly. "That's why I missed our initial appointment. I had an emergency meeting with my lawyer."

"I'm sorry to hear that."

"I'm not. It's long overdue. I want to start a whole new life for me and my daughter."

He looked at the application. "That would be your thirteen-year-old daughter Monica."

"Yes," she said. "She loves New York and hates the idea of moving here. But I know what's best for her. Without going into details her father is involved in securities fraud and once it hits the paper she'll find out how nasty people can be. Those who she thought were her friends will fall by the wayside. I want to distance her from that."

"I see. With your name you could very easily start your own firm in Miami."

"Starting and running your own firm is a lot of work. Right now I feel the need to focus on Monica."

"I understand." Noah leaned back in his chair and twirled his pen. "Powers Public Relations is doing well. Property is a lot cheaper here than it is in LA, or New York and Florida doesn't have the high estate tax that California and New York do. Miami is also becoming a playground for the rich and famous and that benefits us. Clients want face to face interaction with their publicists and flying back and forth to New York and LA isn't always easy to do with their hectic schedules. Because of that we're building our clientele. We have five publicists who are kept busy all the time. But we have room for one more. On your application you put a question mark where it states salary expected."

"I have money separate from my husband's so I'm okay financially. But I am looking for a six figure income."

"I can't start you off with that pay because it wouldn't be fair to my other publicists." Noah took out a Post-it and wrote a number on it. He tore it off and handed it to Irene.

She looked at the slip and then back at Noah.

Noah said, "Not now. But if you bring some of your big name clients with you I'll give you a bonus contingent on who they are and what they're willing to pay the firm to represent them. In six months we'll discuss salary again."

After a very long silence Irene nodded her head in agreement.

###

As Noah parked there was an air of solemnity between them. He shut off the car and looked at Jacoby who stared at the entrance to the police station. "You'll do fine," he said.

"Please don't leave me."

"Not now, not ever," Noah promised. He opened his door and walked around to Jacoby's side. Holding his hand out for hers he gave it a reassuring shake. Noah never let it go as they walked into the station.

"I'm Detective Connors. May I help you?" The police officer at the front desk assessed them from behind his spectacles.

"We're here to file a domestic violence report," Noah answered quietly.

"Both of you were the victims?"

"I'm the victim," Jacoby said as she stood partially behind Noah, letting his big frame shelter her.

"Then you're the person who needs to fill out the paperwork."

With a shaking hand Jacoby reached for the form. As she documented the acts of violence that Armstrong had committed against her she bit her lip until she felt blood.

Noah watched her out of the corner of his eye. Very calmly he put his newspaper down, and slid his hand up and down her thigh in a soothing gesture.

Immediately she felt some of the tension in her body recede and gave him a grateful smile.

"Jacoby Alexander!"

She looked up to see another police officer with a clipboard. "At least it's a woman," she told Noah thankfully as they stood and walked to the officer.

"I'm Detective Smith," she said. She eyed Noah. "I'm afraid I'm going to have to ask you to remain here."

Noah nodded his head understandingly. "Are you okay?" he asked Jacoby.

"Yes," she whispered. "It's just so humiliating."

"I'll take good care of her," Detective Smith said as she turned and led Jacoby away.

After Detective Smith read Jacoby's paperwork she said, "One of the reasons I insisted on seeing you alone was so that you could speak freely about what's going on."

"Okay," Jacoby murmured.

"That man with you. Is he Armstrong Battle?"

Jacoby sputtered, "What!"

"I take it from your reaction that he isn't," she said dryly.

"Of course not! Why would I come to the police station with my abuser?"

Detective Smith said with a grimace, "It happens quite often. Battered women's stories change all the time. It goes something like this: 'He didn't mean to do it. I hit him first. We were both drinking. I lied on him.' Anything rather than deal with reality."

"The man with me is Noah Powers." She stated, "He's been my rock through all of this."

"Good." Detective Smith said, "I can see from what you wrote that Armstrong's violence escalated with each act."

Jacoby covered her face and spoke through her fingers. "It was only after writing down everything he'd done to me that it truly sank in how low I'd fallen. I've seen him since I left."

"Where?"

"At a Publix grocery store. I don't know why he was at that end of town because he doesn't live near there."

"Did he approach you?"

"No, but he was going to. The bag boy's presence stopped him."

"Are you afraid that he'll try to harm you again?"

"I don't know. At first I thought that he just wanted to talk to me because of the messages he's sent to my phone. But the expression on his face makes me think otherwise." Jacoby shuddered at the memory.

"After you signed in, I pulled your name out of the computer system. A Doctor Meadows had already filed a report about your bruising.

Because he documented your injuries it will be no problem with you getting a restraining order. Mr. Battle will be ordered to stay a certain number of feet away from you. I think it's something that you should think about."

Armstrong's thunderous facial expression from the Publix scene loomed in front of her. "I want to do that," she said.

"Here," Detective Smith said, opening a desk drawer. "Fill this out and I'll file it at the courthouse. Also, we'll pay Mr. Battle a visit and tell him to stay away from you."

"Thank you," she said with gratitude.

Noah's cell rang as he drove them home. "Hello, Sinclair. I know that I haven't called like I should but I've been kind of busy," he said, sliding a sidelong look at Jacoby. "How could I not remember your birthday? It's right after mine. Okay, I think that I'll be able to come down. I'll be bringing a guest. Yes, a woman. Tell daddy that he's going to be pleasantly surprised when he finds out who it is. I'll call later and confirm my travel plans." He disconnected and placed the cell in the console between them. "So are you game to go up to West Palm in a couple of weeks? Sinclair's going to have a barbeque."

"I guess, Noah. I just hope that she likes me," she added nervously.

"She'll like you," he said. "Sinclair comes on strong but inside she's a ball of mush."

"What does she do?"

"She's a freelance writer for several magazines."

"Wow!" she said. "What a cool job."

"She loves it. She makes her own hours and does a lot of traveling."

"She's not married?"

"No way. She's having too much fun being single. Sinclair modeled when she was a teenager, but she decided it wasn't for her. She doesn't take orders well."

"She sounds kind of stubborn."

"She can be," he said. "When she gets her heart set on something it's hard to change her mind. She's also spoiled rotten. When she was a teenager, neither Father nor Mother could do anything with her. However, I know how to reel her in. Don't be surprised if she has two or three guys that she's dating at her party."

"How does she get away with that?"

He shrugged his shoulders. "She's honest with them, I guess. She's having a barbeque and everyone's going to hang out at the pool during the day and go boating on Sunday."

"That sounds like fun, Noah."

"I'll make sure that it is," he promised.

Jacoby stood at the bakery counter and read the inscription on the cake.

Happy birthday, Noah,
Love,
Jacoby.

"Do you like it, Miss?"

"I didn't know a cake could be so beautiful."

"We're known throughout the city for baking the best cakes."

Jacoby fished inside her purse and withdrew a fifty dollar bill. "The sample you gave me was so delicious I could barely wait for mine to be ready."

The clerk smiled as she rang up the order and moved to hand Jacoby her change. "You keep it," Jacoby said, "as thanks for getting it done on such short notice."

Jacoby couldn't help looking over her shoulder as she placed the cake on the floor of the car. Seeing Armstrong nowhere in sight, she drove home.

Later that evening Noah said, as he patted his stomach, "I'm so full of cake I could go to bed and take a nap."

"We have to finish celebrating your birthday."

"I thought we did that this morning before breakfast," he said, his eyes sparkling from the memory. "I mean, that's the best gift that I could've hoped for."

"But that wasn't for you," Jacoby said with a smirk. "That was for us. I have something special planned just for you."

"What is it?"

"It's a surprise." She smiled. "Change into a pair of sneakers. We're going out."

As Jacoby navigated the Audi onto I-95 Noah leaned back into the passenger seat.

"So, when are you going to tell me where we're going?" Noah shouted over Charlie Wilson's latest song.

"We're there," she said taking one hand off the wheel and pointing at a Cirque de Soleil billboard.

Noah's body grew still. "You got us tickets to Cirque de Soleil?"

"Yes," she said. "Allie said that even if you've seen it before that you'd enjoy it. Have you ever been?"

A faraway look settled on Noah's face. He said quietly, "One time I went with my parents. It was right before they announced that they were divorcing. That's why I said that I didn't see it coming."

"Oh Noah, I'm so sorry," she said in a contrite voice. "I should have asked you first."

"Years later I asked Mother why they divorced." Noah spoke as if alone.

"What did she say happened?" Jacoby queried gently.

"She said that Daddy stopped talking to her. She felt that she wasn't a part of his life."

"Noah," she said placing her hand on his knee, "we don't have to go to the show."

"Yes we do. Every time I drive by one of those billboards it reminds me of the last time my folks and I did anything as a family. I didn't enjoy the show that night. I knew that something was out of sync, but I couldn't put my finger on it. I need to replace that bad memory with a good one."

The lights in the building flashed psychedelic colors against the background. As they sat in the fifth row on the floor, Noah tightly held Jacoby's hand. Enraptured, they watched the trapeze artists do three somersaults in a row only to be grabbed midflight by another on a swing.

Thank God they have nets beneath them. Jacoby slid a sidelong gaze at Noah.

His attention was focused on a very tall man standing on a platform. Suddenly the man grabbed two red ribbons, jumped off the platform holding them and flew through the air as if he were a human bird. As the bicyclist rode a high wire across the stage, she felt Noah's hands clench hers only to loosen once the performer was safely across to the other side. At the close of the show Noah was the first person in the audience to begin a standing ovation for the dozens of performers who had thrilled the audience non-stop for two hours.

As people filed out of the stadium, Noah turned to Jacoby and took both her hands in his. "Thank you so much, Jacoby. That's one of the best times I've ever had in my life."

"For me too, Noah," she answered right before his mouth descended on hers.

After her shower, she tiptoed into the bedroom. Noah lay on his back with the covers on his legs. His member hung low on his side. Jacoby saw a look of peace on Noah's face that she'd never seen before. Quietly, not wanting to disturb him, she fell to her knees and clasped her hands. God, thank you so much for this man. She whispered so softly only she and God could hear her words, "Thank you for taking me out of the life of chaos that I was in. I promise to always try to be a good person to others and myself. Please protect Noah, my mother, my father, Allie and her family, Claudia and her family. I know that I'm living in sin, Lord, but please forgive me. I truly believe in my heart that it will not be forever, Amen." Gingerly she slid into bed not wanting to disturb him.

Noah turned over and stared into her eyes. "I love you, Jacoby Alexander."

Her heart ached for him. "I love you too, Noah Powers."

He pulled her into the folds of his body and she felt his manhood rise.

Noah rained small kisses along her collarbone.

She stilled his head with her hands. "Let me please you tonight, Noah."

"You please me every night, Jacoby," he said with a small growl.

"I'd like to try just a little bit more." Jacoby took the flat of her hand and gently pushed Noah's shoulder until he lay flat on his back.

She sat up on her knees at the side of his body. Leaning forward, she gave him a long kiss. Once she released his mouth, she explored his pecs with her hands loving the smooth skin, muscular arms, and flat belly that ran down to his prized possession. Jacoby followed every place her hand moved with a soft kiss.

Noah lay back and let her hands work their magic as his body relaxed.

The she gently spread his legs.

His Mandingo stood at attention.

Jacoby lightly slid her hands up the sides of his shaft. Sliding them around his tip and reveling in its slickness.

"Oh, Jacoby," Noah whispered.

"Oh, Noah," she whispered back playfully. Jacoby lowered her mouth, letting her lips close only around his tip and worshipped him. With steady deliberation she licked him up one side and down the other.

The hissing of Noah's breath was the only sound in the room.

She gently massaged his sacks as she took him fully into her mouth. Jacoby slid into a comfortable position on her side. With her head between Noah's thighs, Jacoby with very deliberate timing, repeatedly drew his long rod completely in and out her mouth.

With closed eyes, Noah flung his head back towards the ceiling. After an eternity he began to move.

Jacoby stilled her mouth and let him freely move inside it.

Noah's tempo increased and she heard him grunt the sound a man makes when he's teetering on the edge, on the brink of losing all control. Noah took his hand and tried to push her head away.

Jacoby slapped his hand away and gently gripped him with her lips so he couldn't withdraw from her.

Noah shouted, "Jacoby, I can't..." and then he shuddered into her mouth.

She swallowed before saying, "Happy birthday, love of my life."

Noah was bereft of words.

CHAPTER 15

Jacoby sat in the black leather massage chair loving the feel of the ball running up and down her spine. "What else can I get this chair to do?

"Place your feet in these stirrups and press this button," Robert explained. "It will massage the bottom of your feet."

Jacoby touched the switch and the softly gyrating motion combined with the roller that massaged her almost to sleep. "I think this would be a perfect fit for the media room."

"I bought my dad one. He suffers from arthritis from doing construction work for many years and he swears that it relaxes his muscles and he sleeps better at night."

"Add this chair to the list of my other purchases. Can you recommend a patio store in the area?"

"We have one out back in a separate building," Robert said. "Would you like me to escort you out there?"

"That sounds like a plan."

"Miss," Robert said, looking at the list of furniture she'd chosen to buy. "You said that you needed to furnish a house, but you didn't buy any bedroom furniture."

"I'm in no hurry for that," she replied emphatically.

"Okay, let's go and find you some patio furniture."

An eager Robert practically stepped on her heels as she browsed the showroom.

Finally she halted in front of a glass table surrounded by chairs with rollers. "This is it."

"You certainly have an eye, Miss Alexander. This is one of our best sets. But we don't sell a lot of them because it's pretty expensive."

"How hard is it to clean the cushions?" she said sitting down in one of the chairs and bouncing up and down to get the feel of it.

"Mild soap and water with a brush," he replied. "Do you want the umbrella to go with the table?"

"No, it's going on a balcony not a patio."

"That must be a large balcony."

Jacoby didn't know it but a look of extreme satisfaction settled on her face. "Everything in that house is large, Robert."

Jacoby stood at the counter and handed Robert the credit card Noah had placed on the pillow that morning before leaving for work for an early meeting. "When can you have this delivered?"

"Everything is in stock in our warehouse. Is tomorrow good for you?"

"Perfect!" she said. "That way I can have everything in place by the weekend."

"Miss," Robert said gratefully. "I want to thank you so much for your business. With the economy the way it is people aren't…"

"I know exactly what you mean," Jacoby said.

Noah sized Isadora and Joey up as they sat close on the couch across from him. "Is there a reason you didn't want Jacoby at the meeting?"

"I like her," Isadora said, avoiding his stare. "But Joey feels and I agree that we don't want an intern handling my affairs."

"Jacoby is really an intern in name only. Everything she does is what my other publicists do. Actually she's gotten your name in the newspaper more than some of our other clients have had theirs."

"I know that she works hard," Isadora said with a downcast look. "But sometimes it's who you know and not what you know."

"Has there been anything that you've requested from her that you haven't gotten?" Noah asked with an icy look in his eyes.

"No," Isadora admitted grudgingly. "But when people ask me who my publicist is and I say Jacoby Alexander, I get this look."

"Then tell them that you're represented by Powers Public Relations. That should get you the look you want."

"You don't seem to be getting it," Joey interrupted in a gruff manner. "Isadora took Jacoby's advice and fired me as her personal shopper. Now maybe you should take our advice and get her a different publicist. I read in the paper that you've hired that Irene Hatcher from New York. Who did you have in mind for her to represent? Don't tell me that you think that you have a star bigger than Isadora."

"My firm represents stars that are equal to the status of Isadora and stars that have made more than ten movies, while Isadora's made only one," he said in a terse yet diplomatic tone.

"Maybe that's why she needs a better publicist," Joey snapped.

Noah gave Joey a hard stare. He then directed his gaze back to Isadora. "I work very closely with Jacoby. She has made many contacts on your behalf. There's that upcoming magazine spread with Allure Magazine. You wouldn't have gotten that had you not taken her advice about getting a new stylist. Your Labor Day party is coming up. It wouldn't be good strategy for you to change your publicist at this time."

"Then after the party will you give me to Irene Hatcher?"

"Ms. Hatcher is still clearing up things in New York. I don't know the exact time she'll be joining our staff."

"When she does get here, I want my files turned over to her."

"If I don't," Noah asked, "does that mean that you aren't willing to fulfill your contract with us?"

"I didn't say that," Isadora stammered.

"What would you do if she didn't," Joey demanded. "Sue her?"

There was a heavy silence in the room as Noah chose his next words carefully. "Isadora is just getting her image cleaned up. I don't think that it is in her best interest for the public to view her as another difficult actress who doesn't fulfill her obligations. Let's talk again after her party and see if she still feels the same way."

"That sounds great," Isadora said in obvious relief.

"I would like to keep this meeting private," Noah said. "There's no need to bother Jacoby with this in case you change your mind, after you see the dynamite event she's planned for you."

"That's a good idea," Isadora said. "I really like Jacoby and don't want her mad at me." She avoided the stern look Joey gave her. "Now we have to run. I have a meeting with Francois."

"He's next," Joey muttered.

Noah heard her and his lip curled in displeasure. After they left, with chin rested on hand, Noah stared pensively into space.

They sat on the balcony drinking their morning coffee. "I went to three different stores and wasn't thrilled with any of their furnishings. But once I got to Ethan Allan I was done. Everything I needed was there."

"That sounds good, honey," Noah said as he thumbed through the morning paper.

"And then I started looking for knickknacks and stuff for the walls. I found a specialty shop in Coconut Grove and purchased some things. They're going to deliver it next week."

"Awesome," he answered absentmindedly.

"What's the matter, Noah?" She took her hand and rubbed his wavy hair. "You're awfully quiet."

"Nothing," he said avoiding her scrutiny. "I just have one meeting after another today."

"Oh," she said guiltily. "And here I am chattering about furniture and all you probably want to do is relax before we go to work."

Noah placed the newspaper on the table. "Do you have everything set for Isadora's Labor Day weekend gala?"

"I think I got it. Yesterday channels six and four confirmed that they're going to cover the event."

"That's great!"

"And there's a spread on Isadora that will be in the Miami Herald's Labor Day Sunday paper in the entertainment section. I'm also running an ad on all the radio stations in town. The first fifty girls get in free and they get an arm band for a free drink."

Noah half smiled. "The guys are going to get mad."

"No they won't," she said. "They're used to paying for alcohol. And where the girls are, the guys will follow."

"That's true," Noah said. "What else have you got lined up?"

"I'll be right back." She returned with a black planner and pulled a piece of paper out of its inside pocket. She handed it Noah. "These are the things that I have planned. The check marks are the items already confirmed."

Noah skimmed the paper. "The Miami Heat cheerleaders are going to be there?"

"I sent them passes so that they can get in free. Those girls really like to party."

"Make sure that they don't overshadow Isadora," Noah warned. "It is her event and she should be the center of attention."

"I know," Jacoby said. "I have a ticker marquee on the outside that will run Isadora's name. That way everyone will know that she's the center of attention. On the inside, the trailer for her movie will be showing all night on big screens in the club."

"That's an excellent idea, Jacoby," Noah said his eyes shining with pride. "Did you manage to get any big name celebrities to say that they're going to make it?"

"Labor Day weekend people flock to Miami because it's considered the last holiday before the kids up north start the school year. I sent invitations with tickets to all of the players, the publicists, and their agents."

"That's smart. No one likes a party like a basketball player. If they win they celebrate all night. And if they lose they'll drink all night."

"You're too funny, Noah," she laughed. "The Miami Heat has a charity game in Atlanta, but they'll be back in town by midnight. I reserved a private room upstairs for any of the ballplayers that might show."

"Do you think any of them will make it?"

"I talked to the cheerleader captain and she said they said if they win they'll stop by to celebrate."

"That would be great press. Let's keep our fingers crossed that they do."

"I had a problem with the food. The caterer that I wanted was way too pricey, so in the end, I just decided to use the caterer that Whitney used. I heard that her events were always top notch."

"They were," Noah said.

"Do you ever regret letting Whitney go?"

"I didn't have a choice for the good of the company," Noah said quietly. "Isadora was going to walk if I kept her. A boss can't sacrifice twenty employees because of one person's hurt feelings."

"I see."

"Besides, I hear that she's doing well and happy. So things turned out for the best."

"Noah?" Jacoby said with a look of concern on her face. "Do you really think people will pay the hundred dollar fee to hang out with Isadora Leblanc?"

"No," he said. "But they will for free food, drinks, and the Miami Heat ballplayers. She'll reap the rewards as the headliner."

"I hope that I don't let you down, Noah."

Again he skimmed the list that she'd given him. "If half of the stuff that you have planned kicks off your event will be the best bash of the summer."

"I'll be glad when it's over. This is taking too much of my time away from your needs."

Noah pulled her on his lap.

His body hardened as he felt Jacoby's arms settle around his neck.

"This is all I really want to do," she murmured softly as she slid her arms around his strong shoulders.

Noah turned on to the exit ramp that led to West Palm Beach.

"Did you need anything before we get to my dad's house?" he asked.

"No," she said. "I think that I remembered to bring everything."

"Thanks for doing all the packing, honey."

"It's my job to take care of you, Noah."

"You're doing a splendid job of it too," he said, patting her knee appreciatively.

"I hope your sister likes me."

"What's not to like?" Noah quipped.

Noah pulled out of the heavy traffic and veered to the left. The road turned into a two way with a golf course and county club flanking the road.

"Is that the course where your dad plays?"

"Every chance he gets," Noah grinned. After another five miles Noah pulled up to a huge wrought iron gate. After punching some numbers into the metal box the gate slowly lifted.

"We're home."

Jacoby's jaw dropped at the sight of the sprawling, brick estate. "Gee," she whispered in awe. "I thought your house was big."

"You mean our house, don't you?"

Jacoby looked at the expensive cars parked in the large circular driveway. "Your sister sure has a lot of friends."

"She's quite the social butterfly." Taking her hand, Noah led them toward the noise coming from the backyard.

Once they walked around the side of the house and entered the backyard, Jacoby spotted a large kidney-shaped pool housed under a covered lanai.

"There's Sinclair," Noah shouted over the music playing from a sound system.

Sinclair stood chatting with a group of men. She wore an orange bikini and on her feet were six-inch heels. She looks like a Victoria Secret model.

Jacoby stared down at her own white shorts and pink and white striped tee shirt, paired with white espadrilles and felt quite blasé in comparison. But the reassuring grip of Noah's hand dissipated her trepidation.

Spotting Noah, Sinclair broke away from the group and with a wide smile strode over to them. Once she reached them she threw her arms around Noah's neck and gave him a big kiss on his cheek. "It's about time you got here, Noah! I was getting worried. Everyone's already eaten."

Noah kissed her back and replied with a grin, "We slept in this morning, and when we were ready to leave I got a conference call from New York that I had to handle." Jacoby had hung back and now, Noah pulled her forward. "Let me introduce you to Jacoby."

Sinclair's round eyes so like Noah's quickly ran up and down Jacoby's body. "It's nice to meet you," she said with a small smile. "Noah has kept you a secret from us."

"He has?" Jacoby replied and darted Noah a look out of the corner of her eye.

"That's not true," Noah protested. "I told you that I was bringing my girl with me."

"But you didn't tell me much else. Never mind," Sinclair retorted.

"She and I will spend some time getting to know each other."

"Not without me being there," Noah retorted swiftly. "I don't want you running Jacoby off with your exaggerated stories of my escapades from childhood."

Sinclair's laugh filled the air between them. "I only speak the truth when it comes to you, Noah. Now, I arranged for you to spend the night in the blue room upstairs and Jacoby is in the bedroom downstairs off the den."

"Why would you put us in separate rooms?" he said with a frown. "I'm a grown ass man."

"I know that," she retorted. "But daddy has become really old fashioned lately. This woman that he's dating is sanctified and she has been a big influence on him."

"What do they do when they're alone?" Noah grumbled.

"This is okay, Noah," Jacoby said, giving him a nudge. "You want your daddy to like me don't you?"

A pout settled on Noah's lips.

"It'll give you the chance to miss me."

"Oh, all right," he acquiesced. He turned his attention back to Sinclair. "Where is Dad?"

"He took off. He said all this is giving him a headache."

"I guess so. I could hear the music from the driveway," Noah said.

Sinclair rolled her eyes. "The food is over there," she said, pointing to a long table with a tablecloth and silver serving trays on it. "I'm glad that I had it catered. Anything else would mean a day of all work and no play. Are you two hungry?"

"Sort of. But first I'm going to take our things into the house so we can get settled in."

"I'll come with you," Jacoby offered.

"No, honey, relax and have a drink. It'll only take me a minute." Noah turned and walked back around the house.

Jacoby's eyes followed him until he was out of sight.

"Carlos will fix you anything you want," Sinclair said, pointing to the bartender behind a bar. "I'm going to tell the deejay to turn the music down a little. It's even starting to get on my nerves."

Jacoby smiled as watched Sinclair saunter over to deejay booth.

Jacoby made her way to the bartender, smiling at several people who looked speculatively at her. Once she had a glass of Pinot Grigio, she eased into a lawn chair. She gulped the wine, quenching her thirst. Suddenly someone plopped down in the empty chair next to her.

"Hello," a soft woman's voice said.

"Hello," Jacoby said, relieved that someone had approached her for a conversation.

"Sinclair really knows how to throw a party, doesn't she?"

"She sure does," Jacoby acknowledged.

"Every year she says that it's the last one, but I know to clear my calendar to be back the same time next year."

"So you've known Sinclair a long time?"

"Yes. We went to college together until she dropped out to model."

"You look like you could model yourself," Jacoby said truthfully, eyeing her svelte body in the thong bathing suit."

"I sort of do," she said with a laugh. "I'm a flight attendant."

"That sounds like a pretty cool job."

"It was before 911. But I'm giving it up. My ex-boyfriend has been emailing me. He said that he's made a mistake, loves me, and wants me back."

"Congratulations," Jacoby said, not knowing what else to say after being given such private information from a total stranger.

The woman gave a deep sigh. "In the past my job came between us because we weren't spending enough time together. But he and I have realized that jobs come and go. Even people come and go. But the bond that we've shared through the years that we were together can never be broken. So we're making our way back to each other. He just has to get his house in order, if you know what I mean."

"I wish you the best of luck," Jacoby said sincerely. "Uhmm, you never told me your name."

A large shadow loomed over them, blotting out the sun. "Hello, Monique," Noah said.

"Hello, Noah," Monique said with a saucy grin. "I got your email."

Noah said to Jacoby, "Your things are in the bedroom. Why don't you change into your bathing suit?"

"That's a good idea," Jacoby said, getting up.

"Doris is in the kitchen," Noah said. "She knows who you are and will show you your bedroom."

"It was really nice talking to you, Monique."

"Likewise," she said. Monique stretched out in the lounge chair. Her long legs with red manicured toes were an enticing vision.

Jacoby walked to the house and opened the sliding glass door. She looked over her shoulder and saw Noah had sat down on her vacated lawn chair. He was leaning in close to Monique as he talked to her. A shiver of jealousy ran up her spine, but she brushed it aside. She's been a friend of Sinclair's for years. Of course they know each other. She was then distracted by a Hispanic woman who wore her hair in a bun. She gave her a bright smile. "Miss Jacoby. I'm Doris, the housekeeper."

"Hello, Doris," Jacoby returned the smile.

"Your room is this way," she said beckoning her with her hand.

Jacoby admired the large foyer with African American lithographs hanging on the linen-colored walls and the cherry-wood furniture she saw everywhere. Her luggage was at the foot of a Canopied queen-size bed with a yellow duvet. Yellow curtains hung on the window. She spied a bathroom through an open doorway to the left.

"Do you like?

"Very much so," Jacoby responded.

"Very good, Miss. Let me know if you need anything."

"I will," Jacoby replied.

Doris gave Jacoby a reassuring pat on the arm before she left.

Jacoby took her black one piece bathing suit out of her suitcase. She hadn't wanted to wear her bikini the first time she was introduced as Noah's girlfriend. She changed into the one piece. The neckline plunged and her full breasts strained against the fabric. Then she put on a pair of white stilettos. Glancing at herself in the mirror she chuckled to herself. I'm going to do me. *Being true to yourself is always best.* She took off the heels and slid into a pair of flip flops. They had a bunch of black plastic grapes across the front. When Jacoby reentered the backyard people were putting up a net in the pool.

"Come on, Jacoby," Sinclair yelled from the side of the pool. "We're going to play volleyball."

I can't swim, but I'm sure not going to tell these strangers. "I think that I'd rather watch."

Sinclair shrugged and turned back to the task of securing the net.

"Hello."

Jacoby shielded her eyes from the sun. "Hello to you too."

"My name is David," he said, sitting on the chair next to her.

"And I'm Jacoby," she said, holding her hand out.

David's grasp was firm. "You are one of the most stunning women that I've seen in a long time."

Jacoby stared into the man's chestnut eyes. "Thank you," she murmured.

"Do you live around here?"

"No," she said. "I live in Miami."

"That's not very far. What do you think about me coming down and taking you out to dinner?"

"I'm afraid that I can't do that. I have a boyfriend." Jacoby swung her head around surveying the crowd. "I guess he went into the house to change."

"Who is he?"

"It's Sinclair's brother Noah."

He gave her a look of astonishment. "You're dating Noah?"

"Yes. Why? Do you not like him?"

There was a long silence as David gave her a steady gaze. "Noah's a likeable enough guy," he admitted grudgingly. "I'm just a little surprised that he's brought you here."

"What makes you say that?"

There was another long silence. "Nothing." David said with narrowed eyes, "Just forget I said that. Here comes Noah."

Noah had changed into a pair of blue and white swimming trunks and his chest was bare. On his feet he too wore a pair of flip flops.

Monique was trailing him with a beer bottle in her hand.

"Hello, David," Noah said brusquely when he reached them.

"Long time no see," David replied.

"We're going to play volleyball, Jacoby," Monique said. "You can be on my team."

"No," she replied. "I just feel like watching."

"Come and have some fun," Noah urged.

"You go ahead," Jacoby answered.

"If you don't play," Monique wheedled, "Sinclair and I will be the only girls. The rest of them don't want to get their hair wet."

"I'd rather watch," Jacoby countered.

Noah said, "If Jacoby doesn't want to play I'll sit this one out."

"But you always play, Noah," Monique whined.

"Go on, Noah," Jacoby urged because she was feeling guilty. "Once you're done I'll have a plate of food ready for you."

"You're the best girlfriend ever," Monique teased. Then she pushed Noah towards the pool. "Come," she said. "We're holding up the game."

Jacoby watched the two teams volley the ball back and forth. There were six on each side. Sinclair and Monique good naturedly bickered back and forth throughout the game while the men patiently watched them. The water matted the hair on Noah's chest and he looked like a pro as he hit the ball over the net each time it came in his vicinity.

David still sat next to her, and his lips twitched in amusement as he watched the game.

After about twenty minutes a man on Noah's team shouted, "This is game point."

The ball soared over the net and Noah spiked it. When the ball hit the water it splashed the other players with its drenching force.

"We won, Noah," Monique shouted. She turned to him and jumped in his arms. Monique locked her hands around his neck and wrapped her legs around his waist.

Jacoby's whole body tensed up watching.

Noah paused briefly, then slid his arms them under Monique's thighs and tossed her backwards in the water.

"Some things never change," David murmured as he watched them.

"What do you mean by that?" Jacoby demanded with a hard edge to her voice.

"I mean Noah and Monique. They lived together for years and were supposed to get married." He shot her an inquisitive look. "I thought you knew that."

Fury ran up and down her spine. She glared at Monique bouncing around in the swimming pool.

Monique's head disappeared under the water and as she surfaced, she wiped her sleek, black hair out of her eyes with one hand and with the other held her bikini top against her breasts. Grinning she said, "My top came undone." She turned her back to Noah. "Fix this for me before everyone at the party sees my business."

Noah deftly clipped Monique's top.

Then Monique turned around and planted a lingering kiss on his mouth.

With an inscrutable look Noah began to wade to the edge of the pool.

All eyes were on him as he hoisted himself out of the water.

Noah grabbed a dry towel from the iron towel rack and walked over to Jacoby. He leaned over and tried to kiss her on her lips.

Jacoby turned her head and avoided his mouth.

He turned his attention towards David. "You're in my seat, man," he said stiffly.

"Well," David drawled, "excuse the hell out of me." He lumbered to his feet. "I think that the party's breaking up anyhow."

Everyone was climbing out of the water, drying off, and gathering their things. Jacoby watched Sinclair with Monique by her side. They were hugging people and promising to call each other soon.

David said, "Jacoby, it was nice meeting you. I don't know if I'll ever see you again, but let me say that you have made a lasting impression on me."

"It was nice meeting you also," she replied in a stilted voice.

Noah sat in the vacated chair.

Jacoby didn't look at him but she could feel him watching her.

"Are you ready to eat?" he asked quietly.

"No," she snapped.

"I am. And I'm going to fix you a plate anyhow."

When Noah returned with their food he held out a plate to Jacoby.

Jacoby had her arms crossed in front of her and ignored it.

Noah placed it on the round, glass table between them.

Taking a deep breath he said, "I can see you're angry. Don't let Monique get under your skin."

Seething, Jacoby responded, "You're the one who's getting under my skin."

"Me!" His eyes grew round. "What did I do?" he said.

"Flirting with her right in front of me."

"I was not flirting with her," he vehemently denied.

"Who is she?" Jacoby demanded.

Noah grew quiet. "We'll talk about it later."

"I already know," she hissed and her eyes flashed fire. "She's the woman that you lived with all those years."

Noah heaved a sigh. "I guess David told you. Monique means nothing to me, Jacoby."

"You were going to marry her, weren't you?"

"We shouldn't do this here, Jacoby. Do you want Monique to know that she was able to cause trouble between us?"

"I don't give a rat's ass," Jacoby said. She got up and ignoring all the knowing eyes stomped off into the kitchen. Once inside she found Doris stacking the dishwasher.

"Miss," she said with a sympathetic look, "I'll fix you something. You should eat."

"Thank you, Doris," she said and her stomach grumbled as if on cue.

A grin broke on Doris' face. "That one, she is devilish, is she not?"

Not caring to watch her words Jacoby said, "Which one of them do you mean? Monique or Sinclair?"

Now Doris' smile widened. "You have fire to you. That is good. If you want to be in Mr. Noah's life you need to get used to the fact that a lot of women fancy Mr. Noah. But the softness of his eyes and the look on his face as he pointed you out to me, I have never seen that before."

"Maybe Monique was standing next to me and you misunderstood who he was pointing at," she said angrily. Then she bit into a chicken wing from the platter that Doris had placed before her.

"A man does not live with a woman for years and not marry her if he wants her."

Noah sat alone by the pool and waited. He watched Sinclair hand the deejay and caterers envelopes as they packed up their belongings. He stared at his sister and she walked towards him. Her smile vanished as she saw at his stormy countenance.

Noah's eyebrows were drawn together in a frown and his lips were tightly pressed together.

"Where's Jacoby?" she asked tentatively.

"In the house cooling off," he ground out. "Why did you invite her?"

"You said that you wanted to bring her and I said that it was okay."

"Don't even try that shit with me, Sinclair. You know that I mean Monique."

"She comes every year, Noah. I don't see the problem."

"Monique and I are no longer together. Jacoby is my girlfriend. Didn't you think that she would be uncomfortable when she found out who Monique is?"

"She better get used to meeting women that you've slept with, Noah."

"Not really! Jacoby is the only woman I've dated since I moved to Miami and took over Powers Public Relations."

"Then she shouldn't be insecure, Noah."

"It's not about being insecure, Sinclair. It's about decorum. Just because you enjoy that power trip of having several men you've slept with hanging out together don't think that I have such poor taste."

"Noah!" she exclaimed. "That's a mean thing to say."

"It's true," he retorted angrily. "Now let me tell you something. You're now going to make your future sister-in-law feel like a part of the family."

Sinclair's eyes bulged. "Future sister-in-law?"

"Of course."

"You're going to marry her?"

"If she'll have me," he ground out.

"When?"

"I haven't formally asked her yet. When the time is right I will." Noah gave his sister a scorching look. "Thank God I didn't plan on popping the question this weekend. She'd throw my ring back in my face."

"I didn't know it was that serious, Noah. Monique said..." Her voice trailed off.

"Monique said what?" he asked with a stony expression.

"She said that the two of you broke up because of her schedule, but that she was ready to give her career up, marry you and have a family."

His brows snapped together. "I will have a family, but not with Monique. It will be with Jacoby, so put away your claws."

"Hey!" Sinclair protested in a feeble voice. "I didn't know it was all that. I just thought that Jacoby was a girl you were doing from work."

"You need to correct the damage you did today. Do you hear me, Sinclair?"

"Yes, Noah," Sinclair whispered in a placating voice.

"Where's Monique?" he demanded harshly.

"Upstairs changing."

"Upstairs," he said. "She's staying the night?"

"She always spends the night, Noah," Sinclair answered in a meek voice.

"And you put her in the room upstairs next to me and Jacoby downstairs?"

Sinclair looked down avoiding Noah's glare.

"You really are a piece of work, Sinclair." He scowled at his sister. "Don't try this shit again or you won't be seeing very much of me or your future nieces and nephews." Noah stormed off and went into the house in search of Jacoby.

Doris was sweeping the floor. She looked at Noah as he stormed into the kitchen. "Miss Jacoby went to her room."

Noah stalked to Jacoby's room. He hesitated outside her door, before he bounded up the stairs two at a time. He knocked hard on the bedroom door next to his. There was no answer. Turning the knob he went inside. The room was empty but the shower in the bathroom was running. Noah opened the bathroom door. Without looking inside he shouted, "Monique. I want to talk to you."

"What!" she shouted, her voice muffled from the shower.

"It's Noah. Come out here! I want to talk to you."

"I have conditioner in my hair. I'll be out in five."

Noah sat on the edge of the bed and waited.

As Monique entered the room, she wore a white satin wrapper and was rubbing her hair with a towel.

"My girlfriend is uncomfortable with you here. I want you to leave first thing in the morning."

"I can't, Noah!" Monique exclaimed. "My flight isn't until tomorrow night."

"You're a flight attendant. You can take any flight."

"Sinclair and I have plans tomorrow. You can't just ruin our weekend like that."

"You shouldn't have come here knowing that you and I aren't together anymore." He said roughly, "Have some class, Monique."

"I'm sorry if Jacoby is upset, Noah."

"No you're not. Your antics at the pool showed me that the talk that I gave you when we were alone didn't sink into your brain."

"Noah! It's not my fault that my top came off."

"Sure. And I was the only man in the pool who could fix it for you, right?"

"If she got angry about that she needs to lighten up, and not be such a prude. Maybe the truth is that she saw the chemistry between us that still exists."

"I don't know what you're trippin' on, Monique, but what we had is over," he said in a flat voice.

"Noah," Monique said, "Jacoby doesn't fit in with our crowd. Everyone could see that."

"I don't care what you think everyone could see, Monique. I love her." He stared at Monique, pinning her eyes with his. "I'm going to marry Jacoby."

"You can't!" she screamed. "You can't humiliate me like that."

"Monique," he said in a tired voice, "we've been split for some time." He searched her face. "Did Sinclair tell you that I was bringing my girl today?"

Monique averted her eyes.

"I'll take that as a yes. You brought your humiliation on yourself, by trying to make people think that we have an ongoing relationship."

"We have something that has lasted through the years, Noah," she whimpered in a desperate voice. "Don't tell me that you can walk away from this." Monique untied the sash of the robe and let it fall about her feet. Her breasts thrust out invitingly and her pubic area was bald.

Yet the sight of her left him cold. "I can and I will." Noah picked up her robe.

CHAPTER 16

Jacoby pulled her shirt over her head. 'A man doesn't live with a woman for years without marrying her if he wants her.' Doris' words rang in her ears. I need to find Noah and give him a chance to explain. Jacoby peeked out into the backyard and saw that it was empty and Doris was nowhere in sight. She climbed the stairs in search of Noah. The door to the first bedroom was open and she could see it was vacant. She knocked on the door of the next room, but opened it before getting a reply. Monique stood in front of Noah and she was butt naked.

Noah was holding a robe. When he saw Jacoby, a look of discomfiture and a red flush seeped into his dark skin. He dropped the robe as if it had scorched his hand.

Jacoby backed out of the room, her eyes never leaving Noah's stricken face. She turned on her heels and ran down the stairs.

Noah's eyes were glaciers when he turned them on Monique. He could see the look of triumph that she tried to hide and detested her for it. "Get out tonight. If you're here in the morning, I'll embarrass you in a way that you'll never forget."

"Noah!" Monique begged beseechingly.

"Leave me the hell alone." He picked up her robe and threw it at her. It landed on her head, covering her face. He went to find Jacoby.

Jacoby was flinging clothes into her suitcase.

Noah shut the door and leaned back against it.

"Jacoby," he said in an even voice.

"Don't talk to me!" she screamed. "How could you!"

"I have done nothing wrong," Noah denied in a reasonable voice.

"I caught you, Noah," she shrieked.

"You caught me doing nothing, Jacoby," he denied calmly. "I went upstairs to tell Monique that I want her to leave."

"Was it before or after you fucked her?"

He raised his hand in the air and said, "There was no fucking, Jacoby. You of all people know that it takes me longer than that to get off," he quipped, letting his hand fall to his side.

"So you think this is funny?" She yelled louder, riled even more by his calm manner.

"No, but I want you to be reasonable. Think about it. If I wanted Monique why would I bring you here in the first place?"

"Maybe you didn't know that she was coming," she countered and her words were rushed together. "Or maybe you did, and once you saw her you couldn't stay away from her."

"Calm down and stop screaming at me," Noah ordered in an even tone.

"Get out of here until I finish packing my things!"

"Calm down," he said again. He held his hand out to her.

She slapped it away. "You were flirting with her in front of me," she yelled even louder. "And you left me alone and went off with her."

"Think about what you're saying, honey," he said patiently.

"You kissed her!" she said tearfully.

"I did not," he denied. "She kissed me and you saw that it wasn't reciprocated."

"You abandoned me in front of your friends!"

"That doesn't make any sense. I asked you if you wanted to play volleyball."

"I can't swim," she admitted.

"You can't?" he said in surprise. "Why didn't you tell me?"

There was a stony silence.

"I offered to stay with you by the pool, but you practically insisted that I join in the game," Noah said gently.

"I didn't expect you to flirt with Monique in front of me!"

"And how did I do that?"

"You were cupping her naked ass," Jacoby said shooting daggers at him.

"You mean as I threw her off me into the water?" He gave her an unwavering look.

There was a long silence.

Jacoby's chest heaved up and down as she fought to control her breathing.

"What else you got?"

"You fixed her top for her," she said accusingly.

"So what did you expect me to do, Jacoby? Stand there and gawk at her bare breasts?"

"You have an answer for everything, don't you, Noah?" She wearily passed her hand across her face, rubbing her eyes. "What doesn't make any sense is why you brought me here. Your bougie friends were rude. They don't even know how to speak to nobody. Your sister is an instigator," she spat out. "And your father isn't here. Some host he is. My family doesn't have any money, but at least they're not phonies and know how to treat visitors."

"The people here today are Sinclair's friends. They're not a part of my life."

"Call me a taxi!" Jacoby slammed her suitcase shut. "I want to leave."

"I'm not letting you go anywhere," he said firmly. "You've got to let me explain."

"Yes," Jacoby screamed again. "Explain why you didn't tell me that Monique and you lived together. I was so humiliated once David told me. When you two were cavorting in the pool, everyone was watching, whispering, talking, laughing at me, and I didn't even know what the hell was going on."

"I was going to tell you," Noah said with a look of regret. "I was shocked to see her here and didn't know what to do about it. While you were in the house changing into your suit, I warned Monique to be on her best behavior."

Tears that were a mixture of fraught nerves and the fear of losing Noah cascaded down her cheeks.

Noah went to her and with his thumbs wiped the tears from her face. "I apologize, Jacoby, for not pulling you aside and telling you. But to be honest, I didn't want it to ruin your afternoon."

"Well, you see how that worked out," she sniffled. "Monique said that you've been emailing her."

"You know that's a lie. You have access to all my accounts. Have you seen an email to or from any woman that's other than business?"

"She said that you want her back."

"The only woman in the world I want is you." Noah put his arms around Jacoby and held her close.

Her body remained rigid. "Why was Monique naked?"

"She was trying to tempt me," Noah admitted in a grudging tone. "So what if I saw her naked? I've seen her naked more times than you can imagine."

"Do you think that's going to help?" she moaned.

"And I haven't lost my mind for her yet, Jacoby." Noah took his finger and tilted her chin up. He mesmerized her with his chocolate brown eyes. "Jacoby, I only get hard for you."

She saw his mouth descending towards her. She closed her eyes as she gave in.

Noah's lips were gentle, yet firm. He kissed her with an urgency combined with fear, because he felt as if that night he'd almost lost her.

Once her lips were free Jacoby leaned weakly on Noah and she heard the wild beating of his heart. She asked, and there was a catch in her voice, "Noah, do you want me to shave my vajayjay?"

"No, Jacoby. I love you just the way you are." His arms closed around her and she felt safe again.

"I still want to leave," a mentally exhausted Jacoby murmured into his chest. "I don't want to be here."

"We can go right after breakfast," Noah agreed. "Dad called. His girlfriend isn't feeling well, so he's going to spend the night at her place. But I need to go over some business with him before we leave."

"I'll wait for you in the room until you're done," Jacoby whispered in a forlorn voice as she pushed him away.

Noah let her go, knowing that she wasn't ready to completely forgive him for the drama of the day. In a hard voice he said, "Monique is leaving tonight. She won't ever be back when we're in town."

"I can't let a man put me through any more changes, Noah," she whimpered.

"I won't hurt you, Jacoby." He held her away but held her away to stare deep into her eyes.

She searched his face for reassurance.

He gripped her arms and shook her slightly. "You know me, Jacoby."

Still she didn't answer scouring his face for a commitment from him about their future.

"I'm not like him."

Finally Jacoby whispered, "I know that."

Noah gently rubbed her nose with his.

She felt her heart leap.

"You look tired."

"I am. I think that I'll call it a night," she said in a tiny voice.

"I'm going to get my things and then join you."

"Sinclair said that we can't sleep in the same room, Noah," she said her voice ragged from emotion.

"To hell with Sinclair," Noah growled before he left the room.

In the hallway, he saw Monique and her luggage by the door. Her arms were crossed in front of her and she was angrily tapping her foot. She gave him a murderous stare. Ignoring her, he climbed the stairs two at a time. In the bedroom he grabbed his suitcases. Behind him heard a cough.

He turned to see who it was.

Sinclair hovered in the doorway. "Is now okay for me to talk to Jacoby?"

"No," he said curtly. "She's resting. Talk to her in the morning before we leave."

"You can't leave in the morning," she wailed. "We're supposed to go boating."

"Jacoby doesn't want to stay and I don't blame her." He closed his suitcase. "Make nice with her while I meet with father." He brushed past Sinclair and when he reached the downstairs foyer, it was empty.

###

Jacoby woke up, when she heard the shower running. She lay in the darkness and thought about the events of the afternoon. *He really didn't do anything wrong.* She slid out of bed and out of the tee shirt and boxers she'd fallen asleep in. She walked over to the full length mirror that hung on the door. Jacoby stared at her reflection. *I need to apologize to Noah.* And I know just how to do that. There was a boom box on the dresser. She opened it and read the label of the homemade disc inside. Kem's Greatest Hits. *This is just perfect.* She pushed play and hit the repeat button. Once Kem's harmonious voice filtered into the room, Jacoby went naked to find her man.

Noah stood under the spray in the large glass shower trying to rid him of the filth of the afternoon.

She opened the door and cut off the main light. Through the frosted glass window Noah's outline was visible in the shower light.

When the draft of cold air hit him, Noah turned around.

Jacoby was facing him.

Immediately his manhood bridged the gap that was between them. His gaze was unfathomable as he stared down at her.

"Let me bathe you, Noah." She grabbed a loofah and squirted a generous amount of liquid soap on it. She motioned for him to turn around.

Noah eagerly obliged.

Jacoby started at the base of his neck. With small, circular, motions, she lightly buffed his skin.

Noah took his hands and planted them on the tiles in front of him steadying himself.

Once she'd soaped his entire back she turned him around. The water washed away the soap that lingered on his skin.

Then she washed his chest. She rinsed him again and then cradled his manhood.

Every inch of Noah stood at attention.

Her hands closed around him and she reveled at the feel of him. "You are a true stud, Noah."

The flash of Noah's white teeth in the scarcely lit room showed her how pleased he was by her words.

Jacoby pressed her lips to his and drowned in their fullness. Slowly, she began to feather kisses all over his body, all the while clutching him. Jacoby pulled his member back and forth towards her.

Dropping to her knees she took him and began to pleasure him.

He rocked on his heels and almost slipped. But quickly he righted his position over her.

Time stood still as she loved him, assuring him by deed, that she would never leave him.

His body began to jerk and he took his hands and gently pushed her away before he gave in to the wave of sex that was beginning to run through his body to explode into her mouth.

Noah cut the water off and stepped out of the shower dragging her by the hand. He quickly rubbed her dry and then himself. Throwing the towel on the floor, he scooped her up into his arms.

Jacoby cuddled into Noah as with confident steps he strode into the bedroom and gently placed her on the bed.

"Jacoby, please stay with me," he whispered.

"Always," she promised.

"Will you forgive me for not telling you who Monique was, Jacoby?" he said, peering down at her in the darkness.

"If you forgive me for making such a scene," she replied in an apologetic whisper.

"Done," he murmured. He took his fingers and played with the silky foliage between her legs. "It's absolutely perfect." He ordered softly, "Don't you dare change a thing."

Any insecurity Jacoby felt dissipated.

Jacoby's arms crept around Noah's shoulders as he buried his face in her breast. They rocked endlessly until their loving was replete.

During the night each time Jacoby screamed it was from pleasure not anguish.

When she awoke she was alone. She turned over and saw that it was after ten o'clock in the morning. Jacoby lay there contently until she heard a quiet rapping at the door. "Who is it?"

"It's Sinclair," the voice stammered. "I hate to wake you, but Doris said breakfast will be ready in about fifteen minutes."

"Okay," she answered, her voice not giving away her true feelings. "I'll be out after my shower."

When Jacoby entered the kitchen, Sinclair was alone sipping a cup of coffee at the snack bar. In front of her were serving trays of food.

"Good morning, Jacoby," Sinclair greeted with a dazzling smile.

Jacoby grunted her response. "Where is Noah?"

"He's in the office with Daddy. Would you like a cup of coffee?"

"Sure," she said, "but I'll fix it myself." Jacoby headed towards the

Keurig machine.

"No, sit. You're my guest. Doris had to leave after she prepared breakfast, but she told me to tell you goodbye."

"Too bad she isn't here," Jacoby replied stiffly. "I liked her."

Sinclair slid out of her seat, walked over to the cabinet and grabbed a mug out of it. "How do you like it?"

"Black with one artificial sweetener," she said, sitting at the long glass breakfast table.

Jacoby studied Sinclair. She was visibly nervous as she poured the coffee and added the packet of Equal. As she handed it to her, Sinclair said, "I apologize for yesterday. I didn't mean to make you uncomfortable."

"So you really thought that having Noah's ex-lover here for the weekend would be fun for me?"

"No," Sinclair answered sitting across from her.

Jacoby eyed her as she took a gulp. "So you did plan for me to be upset?"

"Monique told me a different story. She said that Noah wanted to marry her. She'd said no because of her career but came to regret it. I thought that he'd want to patch things up with her."

"If that was the case why would he bring me here?"

"I could only wonder, Jacoby. He and Monique have been back and forth for so many years I thought that this was just another one of their break-ups."

"Even if that was the case, any woman Noah brought here would be wounded by you and Monique's little plot." There was a look of chastisement on Jacoby's face that she didn't attempt to hide.

"I just want Noah to be happy." Sinclair heaved a sigh. "I know how it is to go through life not finding someone that you want to commit your life to and I don't want that for him."

Jacoby stared at Sinclair and felt some of her resentment subside.

"You have to understand that Monique and I have known each other for a very long time."

"Not as well as you think, obviously. She lied to you. Noah has not been emailing, calling, or trying to get back in her life," Jacoby stated with conviction. "He's with me now. He loves me and I love him." Her gaze zeroed in on Sinclair. "I know that I'm not the family choice," Jacoby said, "but I'm his choice."

"She's not the family choice," Sinclair denied. "Daddy doesn't really care for her and Noah doesn't want her. He made that very plain to me last night."

"He did?" Jacoby jerked forward in surprise.

"Yeah," Sinclair said. "He hasn't been that mad at me since I ran away from home when I was eleven."

Startled, Jacoby said, "You ran away from home?"

"I was gone only a day. I wanted to go to a party and Mother wouldn't let me so I took off. Noah found me at a friend's house. He embarrassed the hell out of me in front of everyone and I never ran away again." Sinclair wore a rueful expression at the memory. "Jacoby, Noah and I are very close. I don't want to ruin that."

"You mean that you don't want me to ruin it."

"I mean that I want us to start over," she said sincerely. "I promise that I will never again purposefully be rude to you, future sister-in-law."

"Future sister-in-law!" Jacoby mouth dropped from shock.

"Noah told me that the two of you are getting married."

"Noah told you that?" she exclaimed.

Sinclair slapped her hand over her mouth. Her eyes were round as she stared at Jacoby's stunned face. She whispered, "Noah told me that he hadn't officially asked you, but I assumed that the two of you had talked about it."

A rush of excitement coursed through her body making her almost feel giddy. *Noah's going to ask me to marry him*!

"Oh my goodness!"Sinclair shot a nervous look over her shoulder at the closed door where on the other side Noah met with his father. "I just keep messing up this weekend. Please don't tell him that I ruined his surprise," she pleaded. "Please don't tell anyone that I told you. It was an honest mistake."

"I won't say anything," Jacoby promised. She couldn't help asking, "Do you know when he plans to ask me?"

"He said when the time was right." Now a broad grin spread across Sinclair's face. "I'd like to settle things between us before that happens." She held her hand out to Jacoby. "Friends?"

Jacoby stared at the outstretched hand. She thought of the estrangement between her and Alexandria and the havoc it had caused in her family.

"For Noah, Jacoby," Sinclair added with earnest look.

"For the love of Noah," Jacoby said, placing her hand in the outstretched one.

A few minutes later Noah entered the kitchen with his father right behind him.

Noah viewed Jacoby and Sinclair companionably drinking coffee. He went over to Jacoby and bent to kiss her.

"No," she protested with a laugh. "I have coffee breath."

Noah branded her with his mouth. "Uhmm," he said. "That was

good."

"Hello there, Jacoby," Bradley Powers said as he sat down at the head of the table. "How nice it is to see you."

"Thank you very much for inviting me."

"When Noah told me that the two of you were dating, I couldn't have been more pleased."

Pleasure coursed through her. "Really?" she asked. "Do you mean that?"

"Of course I do, young lady. I know all the employees that work at Powers. You're a hard worker with a good heart."

"Thank you, Mr. Powers."

"Call me, Bradley. After all, we're practically family."

"Yes," she said softly, "we are." Jacoby took Noah's hand in hers and squeezed it. Their eyes met and it seemed as if they were the only people in the room.

Bradley and Sinclair looked at each other. Bradley wore a look of approval and Sinclair had one of acceptance.

When Noah dropped their suitcases in the foyer at his house, he breathed a sigh of relief.

"Noah," Jacoby said as she dropped her purse. "We could have stayed the rest of the day if you'd wanted."

"I'd had enough of other peoples' company," he said.

"So had I," Jacoby admitted. "Even though your sister and I have sorted things out, this is where I want to be." She buried her head into Noah's chest. "You and I keeping out the world and all of its drama."

Jacoby stood in front of the mirror and nervously chewed her bottom lip. Her red dress was perfectly complimented by black stiletto opened toed sandals. She wore her hair parted in the middle, but a sweeping ponytail hung to one side and was draped over her shoulder. She was putting the finishing touches of her makeup, as Noah emerged from the shower.

Noah wore a towel around his waist and his upper body glistened from the steam of the bathroom.

He took her breath away. "You look so damn fine I hate to go out. To be honest, I'd rather stay here tonight and make love to you all night long."

"We can't. This is your coming out party." Noah grinned at her. "Besides, I thought that you might enjoy a break from my nightly ravages of your body."

"Never, Noah. I look forward to it."

Noah came to stand behind her, towering over her. "Jacoby, you are absolutely stunning."

"When I was combing my hair I found a gray one. I covered it with a little gel."

"Good Lord," Noah laughed. "You women notice every little thing."

"Seriously, Noah, will you still love me when my hair turns gray?"

"Baby," he quipped, "I'll even love you when you gain a little weight."

"I've already done that," Jacoby chuckled. "I could barely get into this dress and I just had it delivered."

"You look damn good to me," he said. "In fact, I'll show just how much." Noah went to his dresser bureau. He pulled open a drawer and handed her a navy blue velvet box. "This is for you."

Jacoby opened the box. Inside was a gold chain with a diamond hanging from it, there was also a pair of matching studs. "Noah," she breathed. "They're absolutely beautiful."

"Do you like the style?" he said somewhat anxiously. "You never expressed an interest in diamonds so I wasn't sure…"

"I love square diamonds, Noah," she exclaimed. "And I've never expressed an interest because I didn't ever think that I'd have any."

"Turn around. Let me put the necklace on for you."

After Noah had secured her necklace Jacoby put on the earrings. She looked like a million bucks and felt like it. "Thank you so much, Noah."

"The pleasure is all mine."

"Now it's time for me to please you." Jacoby unhooked Noah's towel and dropped to her knees.

###

Flashes of red, white and, blue strobe lights seared the sky over the Miami Beach Strip. Bruno inched the limo through the queue of cars illegally parked outside the club until he found their reserved parking spot.

Jacoby wrung her hands as she sat next to Noah.

He placed a hand over hers. "You'll be fine. Look!" he said, pointing to the people lined up waiting to be scanned before they entered the nightclub. "There are enough people waiting to get in to fill the club."

Jacoby anxiously looked at the crowd. "But Isadora and Francois aren't here yet. I hope they don't mess it up."

"How do you know they're not inside?"

"Their designated limo parking spot is empty."

"They're just waiting to make a grand entrance," Noah said. "Isadora wouldn't think of missing the opportunity to be the center of attention."

"I guess you're right," Jacoby sighed. "Let's go in so I can make sure everything is in place."

As if on cue, Bruno got out from behind the wheel and opened the door for them to exit.

Noah held Jacoby back and she looked at him questioningly. "In case I forget to tell you later, the smartest move I ever made was making you a publicist at Powers Public Relations. Your party will be a huge success and people will be talking about it well into the new year."

"Oh, Noah," she whispered.

"I would kiss you, but I don't want to mess up your lipstick."

"It would be worth it."

Noah placed his hand at the back of her head and pulled her forward.

Jacoby's tongue eagerly met his.

When Noah finally broke their kiss Jacoby gasped, "I can't wait to get you home, Noah Powers."

"I could not want you more."

Noah got out and held his arm out.

Jacoby slid out of the limo and slipped her arm into the crook of his.

Together they walked the red carpet into Set Miami Nightclub.

He stood in the shadows. Beads of perspiration drenched his forehead. His fists were balled in his jean's pockets. Suddenly he felt dizzy and brushing past the chattering crowd he opened the door of his white Charger and climbed inside. Armstrong reached under the front seat and grabbed his pint of gin. Opening it, he gulped down a third of the bottle. The liquid fire burned all the way down to his belly. He sat still, taking a breather. Then he emptied the bottle, threw it under his seat, and cranked up the engine. The roar of the car as it sped down the Miami Strip didn't compare to the roar in his heart.

Isadora and Francois entered the club hand in hand.

Jacoby's eyes immediately went to their attire.

Isadora wore a turquoise halter dress that was perfect against her olive skin. The back of Isadora's hair hung straight but a bang accented her large hazel eyes and full eyelashes.

Francois wore a pair of black jeans and a white shirt with a skinny tie.

Jacoby breathed a sigh of relief. "I'm going to go and let Isadora know where I am," she shouted over the music.

"That's a good idea," Noah shouted back. "Do you need me to handle anything for you?"

"No," she grinned. "It seems as if the party is taking care of itself."

It was true. The dance floor was crowded and the bartenders hustled back and forth pouring drinks for the people at the bar eagerly waving money at them. Patrons watched the trailer of *Keepin' it Light* as it replayed simultaneously on the four large screens against the walls.

Jacoby navigated through the crowd to Isadora.

As she reached her, Isadora leaned over and kissed Jacoby on the cheek. "This is great, Jacoby. You did an awesome job."

"Are you really pleased?" Jacoby smiled her relief. Her dimples made her cheeks look like she had holes in them.

"Why wouldn't she be?" Francois said. "We could barely get in the club. People are standing outside in line waiting for someone to leave so that they can get in."

Jacoby surveyed the room. "It doesn't look as if anyone is leaving."

"I had so many people ask for autographs," Isadora gushed. "Should I give them?"

"That's up to you," Jacoby replied. "But you know the more of them you sign the less they're worth."

"That settles that," Isadora laughed. "I won't sign any more."

"The buffet is on the other side of the room."

"I'm not hungry," she said. "I'm too wired."

All of a sudden people started pointing at the entrance to the club. Five extremely tall men entered.

"The Miami Heat players are here!" Isadora exclaimed.

"And so are their cheerleaders," Francois said with a lascivious grin.

"They won," Jacoby said in satisfaction, "again."

Suddenly a closed look stole over Francois's face, "Here comes Joey." She wore an oxford shirt, a pair of jeans and she was sagging.

Jacoby frowned at her appearance as she walked towards them.

Joey held a drink in her hand and gave Jacoby a curt nod right before she emptied her glass.

"Didn't Jacoby do a wonderful job, Joey?" Isadora gushed.

"It sure is crowded in here," Joey said grudgingly. "I tried to get into the ladies' room and it was so packed I got tired of waiting."

Jacoby pointed to the second floor. "There's a private bathroom up those stairs. It has two stalls in it. The combination is 8135."

"Thanks," Joey said grudgingly.

"You guys enjoy the party," Jacoby said. "If you need me I'll be over at the bar with Noah."

"What time is the party over?" Joey asked.

"We've got the club until five. Make sure that you're not the last to leave."

"I'll try," Francois chuckled.

Jacoby stood in the circle of Noah's arms and watched the antics of the people in the club. "Look!" she said. "There goes Tika Sumpter from *The Have and Have Nots*.

"I told you," he whispered in her ear.

"She's picking up your business card from the promotional table," Jacoby exclaimed happily. "Oh my God! Gabrielle and Duane just joined Tika."

"It looks like you're getting us even more work, Jacoby."

"Should I go and introduce myself?"

"They'll get in touch if they want to do business. Tonight, I bet they just want to party."

A waitress hustled over to them with a tray. She returned shortly with two glasses of white wine.

"You're so smart, Noah," she said, as she stifled a yawn. "What time is it?"

"It's after three."

"We can sneak out if you want. I have a lot of security here and the party's winding down."

"Good. It looks like Francois's ready to go also. Isadora and Joey have disappeared."

"They probably snuck away for some alone time. I want to go to the ladies' room before we leave."

"I'll wait for you outside."

Jacoby pressed the silver combination lock to the bathroom. After she closed it she leaned back on the door, casting her eyes towards the heavens, she breathed deeply. "Thank you, God, for making this such a success." The sound of the lock to the door to the bathroom startled Jacoby. Then she heard Joey's brash voice. Jacoby dashed into the stall quickly closing it not wanting to hang out with her. Thank God these doors are made European style and go all the way to the bottom so they won't see my feet.

"I don't care how great this party is you can do better!"

"But, Joey," Isadora said and her speech was slurred from alcohol.

"You have to admit that this party is the shit."

"It's good," Joey acknowledged. "But you're not looking at the big picture. You don't want to live in Miami. You have offers for two movies to come out in the next year and a half. You need someone with Hollywood connections and Jacoby Alexander is only an intern. People in the business know that."

"But I sort of promised I'd keep Powers Public Relations if she could get me in a magazine. Look at this wrap party she gave me. Could it be any better?"

"The company is fine. Besides, it would be bad press to break your contract. But you should be handled by Irene Hatcher. I pulled her bio up on line. She has connections all over the world."

"I don't want to hurt Jacoby."

"No one wants to hurt Jacoby," Joey sneered. "That's why when we met with Noah and demanded that he switch you to Irene Hatcher he declined. It's obvious he's fucking her."

"You don't know that," Isadora protested.

"I overheard some of the employees discussing it. They were saying that she gets to work with stars and she's only an intern and they don't think it's fair."

Jacoby felt her heart constrict.

"That might just be jealousy. Jacoby is a beautiful woman."

"And there's the fact that Noah wouldn't listen to a thing we said when we met with him. He's willing to lose a lot of money just to please her."

"Jacoby doesn't strike me as the kind of woman to sleep with her boss in order to get favors."

"Listen to you defending her," Joey spat out accusingly. "Do you want to fuck her too?"

Jacoby had to put her hand over her mouth because she was breathing so hard.

"No," Isadora said weakly.

"Then prove it. Tell Noah that if you can't be represented by Irene Hatcher he's not looking out for your best interests. He won't want to lose the money that you're bringing in. And if you want to be a movie star, you'll start looking out for you."

The slamming of the bathroom door eased Jacoby's breathing. She staggered to the bench against the wall and tried to regain her composure. After her breathing evened out, she stood in front of the mirror and stared at her image. The lipstick print from Isadora's earlier greeting was still on her cheek. She took a paper towel, wet it, and rubbed her face so hard it burned. Then she threw it in the trash can.

Noah stood on the sidewalk. He held the door open for her. "Your chariot awaits you," he quipped.

Jacoby gave him a weak smile as she climbed in.

Noah followed her. "I told Isadora that we were leaving. She said that she's going to set up a meeting for some time this week."

Jacoby didn't answer him.

He peered at her in the darkness, unable to discern her expression. "What's the matter?"

"I think you love me too much, Noah," she answered in a small voice.

"There's no such thing, Jacoby." He pressed the button and opened the glass partition. "Bruno," he said, "we're ready."

That night after they made love Jacoby planted her face between Noah's shoulderblades. She lay awake until daylight filtered through the shades.

CHAPTER 17

Jacoby was on the balcony sipping a cup of coffee when Noah appeared.

"Good morning, honey," he said as he tousled her hair.

"Good afternoon, Noah." Jacoby grabbed the empty coffee mug that she had waiting for Noah and filled it. After adding two packets of Equal, she stirred it and handed it to him.

Noah gave her a grateful smile. "Thanks," he said sitting across from her. "I'd forgotten what it's like to hang out at the club until daylight."

"You've become domesticated."

"Quite happily so," he answered.

"That makes two of us."

"You better be," he teased.

"Noah," she said carefully. "I have a proposition for you."

"That's a good way to start the day," he grinned.

Jacoby smiled at him before she took a deep breath. "I would like Irene Hatcher to take over Isadora and Francois as her clients when she starts next week."

Startled, he asked, "Why, Jacoby? You've made a name for yourself and them. Why give someone else the glory?"

"I'm not giving someone else the glory," she replied gently. "It's just that they're a lot of work and I have some other things that I'd like to take care of."

"Such as?" Noah searched Jacoby's face for clues as to what she was thinking and found none.

"If I continue the way that I have it will take me another year and a half before I get my degree. If I go full time I have only one."

"Oh," he said, "I see."

"And I'd like to take swimming lessons," she added shyly.

"We could start enjoying the pool together," he said with an understanding nod.

"And I want to take care of you."

"Jacoby," Noah said. "Since my mother passed no one has treated me as loving as you have."

"And I love doing it, Noah. But I don't want to rush dinner onto the table or be too tired to be good company for you at night. When I go back to school, even if it's only part-time it will be draining."

"That is a lot on your plate, Jacoby," he admitted. "I'm sorry that I hadn't thought about it like that."

"I feel that I'll be more of an asset to you, when I get my degree." She added almost bitterly, "In this business, credentials are everything, you know. I don't want your firm to suffer because you gave me a job that I shouldn't have gotten."

Noah's lips tightened. "Has someone said something to you to make you feel that way?"

"Someone like who?" she asked innocently.

There was a long silence as Noah gave her a piercing stare.

Jacoby dropped her eyes.

"Isadora or Francois?" he grated out.

Very carefully Jacoby took another sip of coffee. Then she placed her mug back on the table. She stared Noah straight in the eye and said honestly, "Neither Isadora or Francois has said anything to me. Should they have?"

"No," he muttered, his eyes avoiding hers. "Your party was off the chain. They have nothing to complain about."

"But, Noah, I do want to keep my name out there. After I get my degree I don't want to have to start completely over. I was thinking that I'd like to take over the writing aspect for the firm's clients."

"What do you mean?"

"I've made quite a few contacts with major newspapers. When a publicist's client is appearing somewhere, or doing something that warrants a piece in the paper, I'll handle it."

"That's a really good idea, Jacoby," Noah agreed. "You have a way of getting a byline."

"Plus I can work from home. Anything someone from the firm wants me to do, they can email me."

"I think that is a splendid idea. I'll send a memo out tomorrow and tell the staff of the changes. But I'll miss seeing you during the day."

"I'll come there whenever you want me too, Noah."

"Can we still do lunch every Friday?" he asked hopefully.

"I'll schedule my classes around it."

"I just want you to be happy."

She clasped his hand. "I am very happy, Noah."

"I think that you've made a good decision, Jacoby."

"Great! Tomorrow I'm going to go to the university and change my status from part-time to full."

"So are you going to go to the university and sit in class?"

"I think that might be fun," she said. "By taking all my classes online I've never had the college experience."

"Don't you go falling in love with some young buck who has more to offer you than me."

"That could never happen, Lover." She leaned over and pressed her lips to his.

"Now it's my time to speak and I don't want any argument from you."

"Okay."

"I'm going to start giving you an allowance."

"No!"

"Yes!" he argued softly. "Jacoby, books are expensive, gas is expensive. The company will continue to pay for your college because you're still working for Powers Public Relations; but your pay isn't enough."

"But I pay for nothing here. Not even groceries."

"Before you moved in I used to have Merry Maids come. For cleaning this size house they charged me three hundred dollars each visit. You clean, cook and do the laundry. I'm thinking pay for seven days a week. And you'll still be working for the firm. I'm getting a bargain at four thousand dollars a month."

"Noah," she gasped, "I can't take your money."

"My money is your money," Noah retorted. "And if it makes you feel any better I can write it off as household expenditure. It's perfectly legal."

She whispered, "It's too much."

Noah said trying to lighten the atmosphere, "Notice that I didn't include our nights together." Noah raised his eyebrows in an excellent imitation of Groucho Marx. "Because it's so damn good if you were selling it, I couldn't afford to buy it."

Jacoby smothered her laughter, but still she protested. "I can't take that much money from you."

"Jacoby, I really need the tax write-off."

She shook her head no.

"I've seen the checks that you send your mother, Jacoby. I insist."

Finally acquiescing she said, "Noah Powers, you're the best thing that ever happened to me."

"I think it's the other way around," he replied.

Jacoby was in her office throwing her belongings in a box when Allie came in and shut the door behind her. With a fearful look on her face she said, "What are you doing?"

"Packing up. I was going to stop by your office on the way out and explain."

Dismay flooded Allie's face.

"I'm going to do the majority of my work from home."

Allie breathed a sigh of relief. "You gave me the worst scare. I thought that something bad happened between you and Noah and you quit."

Jacoby chuckled. "I can't think of anything bad enough for that."

"I should think not."

"Today Noah had an impromptu meeting in Fort Lauderdale. When he gets the chance, he's going to send out an email announcing that I'll be working from home for now on. I'm starting school full time so that will be easier for me."

"That makes sense." Allie screwed up her face as she tried to figure out what exactly was going on. "How are you going to be a publicist working from home?"

"Irene Hatcher is taking over my duties, and I'm going to pitch in here, if he needs me."

"Are you sure that you want to do that?" Allie asked with a wary look.

"What do you mean?"

"You've worked so hard to get where you are. Are you sure that you want to give that up?"

"When I was a little girl all I dreamed of was being a wife and mother. Once I moved to Miami I became so driven in my career because I was with Armstrong and had nothing else. But now that I have Noah, I'm torn. I still want a career, but it doesn't consume my every waking moment."

"Don't get me wrong, Jacoby. You know that I think Noah is perfect for you. But once you drop off the scene, well, you know, there's always some aggressive, younger thing ready to take your place."

Jacoby stopped throwing her things in her last box and looked at Allie.

"What I mean to say is," she stammered, "when you were with Armstrong you wouldn't even take a day off when you were sick."

A grimace of distaste flitted across Jacoby's face at the memory of her life with Armstrong. "That's because Armstrong was there. Also, I didn't want to be more financially beholden to him more than I already was."

"But you don't mind being beholden to Noah?"

"It's different. Noah doesn't make me feel as if I owe him anything."

"For you to be so dependent on a man is unlike you."

"Allie, I run Noah's house and take care of those small things that would take up a lot of his time. He appreciates that."

"Jacoby," she said carefully, "you and Noah live as if you're man and wife. What is the hold up on the marriage or at least an engagement ring?"

"Noah will ask me when the time is right."

"Don't give him too long to make a commitment," Allie said, her voice full of warning. "Men can get too comfortable real soon."

Jacoby remembered her promise to Sinclair to keep things on the down low. So she simply said, "Allie, Noah not eventually marrying me is the least of my fears."

Jacoby drove in the twilight mist down Key Biscayne Boulevard towards the University of Miami. She spied a post office and veered into the parking lot. Grabbing the letter from her purse that held a two thousand dollar check to her mother she walked into the post office. She pushed the letter into the outgoing mail slot and after making sure that it went to the bottom of the chute she exited the building. Jacoby opened her car door.

She was grabbed from behind and swung around. The back of her head hit the roof of the car. The searing pain made her close her eyes. After she reopened them she froze.

Armstrong's hands gripped her throat. He leaned in menacingly towards her. "You really think you're the shit driving Noah's SUV and all." He hissed, "I saw you in that limousine kissing him. Have you forgotten that I'm a marksman? At Set Miami I could have shot both of you and you wouldn't have known what hit you."

"Help," Jacoby squeaked out.

"Help!" he sneered. "No one is here, Jacoby. Do you see how easy it was to get to you? I knew you'd have to come out of that ritzy place you livin' in some time." He tightened his hold on her.

She felt her eyes roll toward the back of her head.

"What would make you think that a restraining order could stop me? Do you know how many women with that crappy ass piece of paper are killed?"

Jacoby struggled for air.

"So you took a self defense class," he mused grimly. He released her and stepped back. He held his arms wide and said tauntingly, "Show me what you know."

Jacoby shrank back against the car.

Armstrong reached out and grabbed her by her shirt collar, practically lifting her off her feet. Her purse fell to the ground and all of its contents scattered, including the can of mace that rolled on its side.

Armstrong picked the can up and shook it in her face. "Do you really think that I'm going to give you enough time to get this out and use it on me?"

Her knees quaked.

"I should spray your ass to death with this shit." Once again he leaned in and a glob of snot hung out of his nostrils.

The sound of a car entering the parking lot made Armstrong look over his shoulder. "You better be glad someone showed up. Otherwise I'd drag you ass in the back seat and teach you a lesson." He pointed his finger in her face. "If you tell anyone about this, you and that chump you're living with will live to regret it." Suddenly he shoved Jacoby.

She fell to the ground and lay there in a ball of despair.

Armstrong disappeared around the side of the building. Seconds later she heard the roar of his Charger and then the sound faded.

An elderly woman slowly got out of her car and leaning heavily on her cane shuffled over to Jacoby. "What's going on? What was that man doing to you?"

"Nothing," Jacoby mumbled tearfully as she gathered her things off the ground.

"It didn't look like nothing," the lady objected in a shrill voice.

"It was just a game we were playing." Slowly Jacoby stood and clutched her purse to her stomach in an effort to keep herself from hurling. She brushed the pavement debris off her bare knees. "I have to go."

"Dear, I saw what that man was doing…"

"Please," she cried out, "leave me alone."

The woman took a step back.

Jacoby bolted into the Audi and sped towards home. She raced down the boulevard until she found what she was looking for. After the car skidded to a stop, she ran into the small, brown building. Out of breath she searched the empty office for Yaz.

An Asian man in white karate styled garb came from the back. Shocked, he stared at Jacoby. "May I help you?"

Her hair was sticking up in several places. Her shirt was rumpled and her eyes were wide from fright. "I need to see Yaz," she sputtered. "Is she around?"

"No longer works here," he replied perfect English.

"That's just great," Jacoby said and burst into tears.

"What is wrong? Maybe I can be of assistance."

"No one can help me," she cried woefully. Jacoby stumbled over to a plastic chair and slumped into it.

The man stared with concerned eyes. He reached under the counter and grabbed a box of tissues. He handed a wad of them to her.

Jacoby wiped her eyes and blew her nose into the tissues. The sound was deafening. Instead of throwing them away she clenched the wet ball of tissue in her hands.

The man sat down next to her. "I am Jimmy. What has upset you so?"

"I took a self defense class. Yaz said that I would be able to defend myself, but I froze." She added bitterly, "I just stood there like a rag doll while he laughed in my face. That class was a waste of time."

"Someone has hurt you?"

"I could have been," she answered. "It's my ex. He's just playing with me until he decides to do what he wants. No one can stop him."

"Have you called the police?"

"Yes. And I've put a restraining order on him," she wailed. Droplets hung from her long lashes. "He doesn't care. He'd rather go to jail for life than leave me the hell alone."

"This is very troubling news, young lady."

"Now I'm afraid to leave the house."

"Is there no man in your life to protect you?"

"Yes," she said. "But I don't want him hurt. I can't let him get drawn into the middle of this. I could lose him forever. Armstrong is crazy."

"You must take the power from this abuser."

"I've tried," she said. "But he's so strong. And mean."

"Strength comes from the mind," Jimmy said patiently. "He knows your weaknesses and plays on them."

"I can't beat him," she said in a weak voice. "He has nothing to do but stalk me and make my life miserable."

"I will help you. I have seen tiny women level giants."

"What do you mean?" Jacoby asked.

"Pressure points," Jimmy said. "It is mind over matter. Let him think you are afraid, and strike when his guard is down."

"I can't do it," she said weakly.

"You have to learn to," Jimmy said in a no nonsense voice. "I think your life depends on it."

When she arrived home, she was relieved to find the house empty. The throbbing pain in the back of her head made her dizzy. Jacoby dragged herself to the bathroom and opened the medicine cabinet. She shook two tablets of Aleve into the palm of her hand and without water she swallowed them. Then she stumbled into the bedroom, closed the drapes, and crawled into bed. Jacoby pulled the covers over her head, trying to shut out the world.

Noah turned on the lamp.

Jacoby rolled over to her side and pushed her face into the pillow, shielding her face from his view.

"Jacoby," Noah said as he stood next to the bed and stared down at her.

Jacoby heard the concern in his voice.

"What are you doing in bed? It's not even seven o'clock."

"I have a bit of a headache," she muttered into the pillow.

"Do you need me to get you any aspirin?"

"I already took some Aleve. Noah, I'm sorry that dinner isn't on the table for you."

"Don't apologize for that. Have you eaten anything today?"

"Not really," she muttered in a noncommittal voice.

"Maybe that's why your head hurts."

"I'll get up and fix something."

"No," he said firmly. "I'll whip something up for us."

Jacoby breathed a sigh of relief. "Thanks, Noah. I'm going to take a shower and then I'll join you."

Noah stroked her hair.

The fear that she could lose him made her nauseous.

Jacoby stood under the pelting water. I have to keep quiet. Telling Noah will only put him in danger. She stood in front of the bathroom mirror. Burning anger consumed her as once again she viewed the black and blue marks on her neck. Jacoby heavily applied makeup to camouflage it. She slipped into a plaid day dress that hit her mid thigh, and barefoot padded out to the kitchen.

Noah gave a whistle when he saw her.

"You might not feel good, but you look damn good."

She gave him a small smile. The smell of Salisbury steak cooking in the microwave stirred hunger pangs.

"I cooked some of our emergency food. The rice is simmering and after the steak and gravy is done, I'm going to microwave a bag of Birds Eye Steamfresh corn."

"That sounds good, Noah."

Noah gave her a lopsided grin. "When I was a bachelor it was my signature dish."

"When you were a bachelor?"

"I don't consider myself single anymore," he said with an air of satisfaction. "Noah Powers is off the market. Aren't you?"

"Absolutely."

Jacoby was finishing the rest of her dinner when she said, "Noah, I've decided to continue taking the rest of my classes online."

Noah's fork stopped midair. "Why?" he demanded.

"The traffic is so bad in Miami," she mumbled with her head bent as she stared at some nonexistent blot on the table. "It would take me at least an hour each way to commute back and forth."

"I don't think that it would take an hour."

"But I have a lot to do here, and I haven't finished decorating the house. Also, I want to start my swimming lessons as soon as possible."

"Why didn't you ever learn?" Noah asked with a quizzical expression.

"When I was home church took up a lot of my time. On Wednesday night there was Bible School. On Friday night I had choir practice, and on Sunday before service there was Sunday School. I was also on the hospitality committee and they always had something to do."

"Such as?"

"We were responsible for providing meals if the church had a program," she said with a wistful expression.

"You sound as if you miss all that."

"I miss the church members a lot," she admitted. "It was always fun fellowshipping with them." Armstrong's face mottled with rage surfaced and fear stabbed her heart. "I really do think that I need to find a church home in Miami."

"Have you not gone to church since you moved here?"

"Occasionally I'd go with Allie," she responded, "but Armstrong..." she trailed off, not wanting to even utter his name.

"You have a new man in your life, Jacoby. If you want to start going to church on Sundays we'll go to church on Sundays."

The memory of Armstrong appearing out of nowhere doused her enthusiasm. "Maybe once I get some things straightened out we can look around."

"Whenever you're ready," Noah said. "So you aren't afraid of the water?"

"No," she said. "I've been on a boat before and it was a lot of fun; I kind of hate that we missed that outing in West Palm."

"Me too," Noah agreed.

###

Jacoby stood at the front door and shooed Noah off to work. Once his car disappeared she hurried into the bedroom and changed from her robe to a tee shirt and a pair of sweatpants. As she washed the breakfast dishes she glanced at the clock. He should be here any minute.

The ringing of the doorbell made her drop the dishcloth and hurry to the front door. She peeked through the peephole and saw that it was Jimmy. Flinging it open she beckoned him in.

"Are you better today?"

"Much better. Thank you."

Jimmy handed her a book.

"What is this?"

"It is a guide to the pressure points in a body. Read it. Learn it. Breathe it."

"Thank you, Jimmy. How much do I owe you?"

"It is a gift."

"Thank you so much for coming here for our lesson." Jacoby placed the book on the table.

"You are still too nervous to be out and about," Jimmy said in a gentle voice. "You should also take a course in martial arts. But it takes a long time to gain the skill for a woman to match a man's strength. Do you have a computer?"

"Yes, it's upstairs."

"I would like to show you a website."

Once the computer was booted up Jimmy punched in some keys. After his website was up he pointed at the monitor. "This shows real footage of how to use pressure points as a self defense. Study it." Jimmy turned away from the keyboard. "Now show me your exercise room."

Once they were inside they faced each other. Jimmy stared at Jacoby as if she were his prey. She found his gaze unnerving and looked away.

"Do not do that!" he said sharply. "You avoiding his stare will let him know that you are afraid."

Jacoby looked back at Jimmy and locked her eyes with his.

Jimmy advanced towards her and she tensed.

"Do not draw up. Don't let him intimidate you. Keep your body loose and draw your strength from your mind."

Jacoby visualized Armstrong's face and she tensed up even more.

"Draw on your inner strength, Jacoby. Think about what you will lose if he succeeds."

Noah's face flashed before her eyes and an inner resolve to live rest of her life with him surfaced. She captured Jimmy's eyes with hers.

Watching her with catlike stealth he said, "That is better. Now lull your attacker into a false sense of security. Make him think you are an easy mark. Catch him off guard. That is the key to your survival. Now stretch out your arm."

Jacoby stretched out her arm and Jimmy moved in on her, his chest touching her fingertips. He said quietly, "When he gets in arm's length, take your thumb and third finger. With all your might, thump him in the forehead right between the eyes above the bridge of his nose. Use all the concentration that you have in your body. Your life of freedom depends on it."

Noah stood on the threshold and watched Irene personalize her office. "How's everything going?"

"Everything is just fine, Mr. Powers."

"Noah," he said.

"Noah it is."

"If you need anything call Selyna. She'll either get it or tell you where to find it."

"Thank you," she said. "I read the dossier that you gave me on Isadora Leblanc and Francois. Jacoby got a lot of press for them."

"I know," he said. "And Isadora didn't appreciate it."

"What do you mean?"

Noah came in and shut the door behind him. "I'm not sure that some of Jacoby's decision to give them up as clients isn't because of them."

"Please explain."

"Isadora, not Francois, had been on me to have you represent them. You hadn't officially started yet and I felt that Jacoby was doing an excellent job."

"From what I can see she was."

"I think they may have said something negative to Jacoby at Isadora's launch party."

"Ever since we agreed that I would begin working here I've had all your clients on my Google alert. Every time their name is mentioned on the Internet or in any press I get an alert. Jacoby's clients have more hits than any of the others at the firm. Francois was considered a 'C' actor until she got him some press. Jacoby deserves kudos for her work and you should tell her that."

Noah beamed. "I will."

"I set up a meeting with them. They should be here any minute."

"Be firm with them," Noah said.

Irene arched her eyebrow at Noah. "Ari Gold from Entourage is my hero. Need I say more?'

"No, you don't."

"Hello," Jacoby said. "May I speak to Tina?"

"This is she."

"My name is Jacoby Alexander. Allie Smith is a friend of mine. You taught her daughter Keke how to swim."

"Yes," Tina said proudly. "KeKe became a very competent swimmer."

"Allie said that you also give lessons to adults and I'm interested."

"All you have to do is call the YMCA. They'll sign you up."

"I would like private lessons at my house. Are you available to do that?"

"Certainly. It's pretty expensive, though. Fifty dollars an hour."

"That's fine," Jacoby responded.

That evening Noah sat on the sofa watching *All in With Chris Hayes*.

"Are you sure that you don't need any help?" he asked as he watched her wipe down the counters.

"Nope," she said, wringing the excess water out of the dishcloth and putting it on the rack attached to the cabinet. "I'm done." She went over to the couch and slid close to Noah. "I start my swimming lessons tomorrow."

"That's great!"

"KeKe's swim coach is going to teach me. She's going to give me private lessons here."

"Here?" Noah asked with raised eyebrows.

"Yeah," she said, avoiding his eyes. "She said that she didn't mind."

"You really are becoming a homebody, aren't you, Jacoby?"

"Is there anything wrong with that?" she asked. There was an unusually tense inflection in her voice.

Noah gave her an appraising look. "Not if you're happy, there isn't."

Jacoby settled down and nestled against Noah.

Jacoby called her mother. "Mom," Jacoby said excitedly into the phone. "I learned how to swim today."

"You did?" Sarai said.

"I'm not ready for the Olympics or anything. But I learned how to float and underneath water I can swim the width of the pool."

"What made you decide to learn to swim?"

"Noah's sister has a party every year. They play volleyball in the pool and everything." Jacoby said with determination, "Next year I don't plan to sit on the sidelines watching others have fun."

"Good for you, darling."

"So how is everything going up there?"

"Things couldn't be better. Sometimes I don't even feel like I have lupus."

"Thank God," Jacoby said, breathing a sigh of relief.

"Thank you for the money, Jacoby. It's unbelievable how much you make down there in Miami. But I want to make sure that you're happy."

"I couldn't be any happier with Noah, Mom. He's the one."

"So when are we going to meet him?"

"Soon," Jacoby said. "I'm in school full time now so I guess when we get a break."

"I don't want you to take time away from your studies. I know how important that is to you."

"I have a week off at Thanksgiving. We'll come then."

"I can't wait."

CHAPTER 18

Irene was reading a file as she entered her office.

Isadora and Francois were seated on the leather coach waiting for her.

Irene gave them a cursory look, sat in her chair, and placed the file on the desk. Taking off her glasses she said, "You're late. Our meeting was at two o'clock."

"We got hung up in traffic," François explained, a little taken aback by her Irene's brusque demeanor.

"I have back-to-back meetings scheduled with clients. I can't make them wait because the two of you are late," she responded.

"Are you allowed to talk to me like that?" Isadora asked in a sullen voice.

"I'm a New Yorker and we speak our minds. I've read the file that Jacoby Alexander left on you. Her notes were very detailed. Isadora, have you found a cause that you're interested in supporting?"

"Not really," she replied in a disinterested voice.

"Well, I've arranged for the two of you to help feed the homeless at Thanksgiving."

"I'm not doing that!" Isadora uttered in distaste.

"Powers Public Relations is willing to keep you as a client. We are in the process of branching out, and we're short a publicist. Now, at this time we do not wish to sever our business with you. However, we do insist on cooperation from clients. Serena and Venus Williams are interested in becoming clients. Do you wish Powers Public Relations to continue to represent you?"

Isadora's eyes practically popped out of her head

Francois' mouth went dry from nervousness.

"Yes," Isadora finally squeaked out.

"Good." Irene handed Isadora a business card. And then she gave one to Francois. "This is the location of the shelter. Your contact person is Ernest Santos. The two of you are expected to be there at six o'clock Thanksgiving morning. Spend the day and with a cheerful smile do anything that is asked of you. People will be watching."

Once Isadora and Francois stood on the other side of Irene's closed door, with an irate expression Francois snapped, "Thanks a lot, Isadora."

"What the hell did I do?" she retorted.

"You and Joey made us lose Jacoby as our publicist and now we're dishing up food on Thanksgiving. My mother was expecting me home for the holiday." He angrily stomped down the hall disappearing from sight.

Slowly Isadora followed him.

Noah's arms were folded as he leaned against his doorjamb watching them. A smirk of satisfaction hovered on his lips.

"Let's do lunch," Allie's booming voice demanded.

"I would love that, Allie."

"Let's meet at the Olive Garden on South Dixie Highway."

"I'd rather you come here."

"That's too far to drive. I have to pick KeKe up at four-thirty."

"Come on, I'll make us a good lunch."

"It would do you good to get out of the house. Aren't you tired of being home? You're like a hermit hiding from the world. "

"I leave the house every day," Jacoby lied.

"Come on, Jacoby. I really miss you."

"If you come and pick me up, I promise I'll spring for lunch and gas."

"Why can't you meet me there?"

Jacoby searched for a reason that didn't make her sound like a person who was scared of her own shadow. Crossing her fingers as she told her lie she said, "My car is in the shop."

"Oh. I guess that I will have to come and get you. If I didn't miss you so much I'd take a rain check. Be ready in an hour."

"I will be," Jacoby promised.

They sat in the restaurant sipping wine.

"You look good, Jacoby."

"So do you. How is Lenny?"

"He's very happy at his new job. He's making so much more money we're looking for a house. We've already saved up enough for a down payment."

"That's great. Have you found one yet?"

"No," Allie said. "KeKe goes to kindergarten next year. So we're waiting for a house to open up in an area near the Aventura Mall. They have excellent schools over there."

"That's so important with all the budget cutbacks that the schools are suffering."

"I don't know if Noah told you or not, but Irene straightened Isadora out."

"What do you mean?"

"Isadora is working with the foster care system."

"Foster care!"

"That's the cause that she picked or Irene picked out for her. And she's got her serving food on Thanksgiving for the homeless."

Jacoby's eyes grew round. "Isadora's doing that on Thanksgiving?"

"And so is Francois," Allie said as she dug into a breadstick from the basket. "Irene doesn't put up with any guff. Also, she got Duane and Gabrielle's accounts."

Jealousy coursed through Jacoby. "I know."

Allie unconsciously shook her head regretfully. "That could have been yours, but you left."

"I didn't leave," Jacoby declared hotly. "I'm doing all the press releases for the publicists. That's very important, you know."

"I know that," Allie said soothingly. "I just meant that's not an everyday thing. I really like Irene. She can be abrupt, but she gets the job done."

Jacoby didn't answer. With her fork she stabbed a tomato in her salad.

"So are you bored yet and ready to come back to work?"

Jacoby's hackles rose. "I do work."

"I mean a real job," Allie teased.

"I do have a real job," Jacoby snapped.

"I didn't mean to make you mad," Allie stammered. "I just meant something other than taking care of Noah."

"Allie," she said slamming her fork on the table. "I just don't take care of Noah. I'm in school full time. After December I only have four more classes and unlike you I'll have a four-year degree."

Stunned, Allie put her fork down. "Whatever is the matter with you?"

"Nothing," Jacoby hissed. "I just don't like you insinuating that I do nothing. Being a housewife, plus creating press releases, plus going to school is very demanding."

"But you're not a housewife," Allie softly corrected her.

"Don't you worry about it! Noah and I are very happy."

For the rest of the meal conversation was stilted. There was no conversation on the drive home. Allie slid Jacoby sidelong looks, observing her stern profile.

Jacoby was relieved when she saw the entrance gate.

"Jacoby," Allie whispered. "I'm sorry that I made you angry."

"It's not you. It's me." She added, "I guess that I'm too sensitive."

"So when are you and Noah going to Bunnell?" Allie asked, trying to get their relationship back to normal.

"We're going to spend Thanksgiving with my parents. Mom feels like cooking this year so Noah and I are going on Tuesday. That way I'll have the time to take her grocery shopping and all."

"That sounds like a fun trip," she said.

"It'll be nice to get away," Jacoby whispered.

Allie's truck pulled up to the entrance of the development.

"I'm going to walk from the gate."

"Are you sure that you don't want me to drive you to your house?"

"No," Jacoby said. "I can use the exercise." She glanced at the side mirror and made sure that no one was behind them. Feeling safe she opened her door. "Just make sure you don't leave until after I get inside the gate."

"Okay," Allie agreed with a look of puzzlement.

Jacoby held her arms out. "Give me a hug."

They briefly embraced each other before Jacoby got out of the car.

On the other side of the gate, Jacoby gripped the iron bars so hard her knuckles hurt. Turning she started home, tears of boredom streaming down her face.

The sunroof was open on the car and the autumn breeze cooled them after the months of humidity. "Why won't you tell me where we're going?"

"It's a surprise."

"Since you told me to wear my bathing suit, I'm thinking the beach."

"You'd think so, wouldn't you?" Noah said mysteriously.

Jacoby relaxed against the sumptuous leather in the interior of the car. It was exhilarating to be out and about after weeks of self imposed imprisonment in their housing development.

Noah slowed the Mercedes and took a side street. Facing them was a marina where different sized boats were docked.

"We're going boating?" she asked excitedly.

"I told you that I'd take you boating and I meant it." Noah shut the car off. "I just wanted to wait until you finished your swimming lessons. Come on," he said. "Everything is all set up."

"I didn't even know you had a boat."

"Technically it's my dad's. He took the yacht with him down to West Palm, but he left his other boat here."

Hand in hand they walked down the dirt lane to the dock. Once they reached the dock a tall man waved at them. He wore a straw hat and cut off shorts with a tee shirt.

"That's Paul. He runs the place," Noah explained.

"Hello, Noah. You're right on time."

"I try to be," he replied. "This is my girl, Jacoby."

A warm sensation filled her when she heard Noah's description of her.

Paul smiled wider. "I've heard a lot about you, Miss Jacoby. I can see what Noah meant. You are absolutely beautiful."

"Are you coming on to my woman right in front of me, man?" Noah demanded in a teasing voice.

"I'd never disrespect you like that, Noah. Besides, I have a woman of my own at home. I don't need another."

"How is Callie? Has she had the baby yet?"

"You mean babies. We're having twins."

"Twins," Noah said. There was a wistful look on his face. "That's the way to do it, two at a time."

"We're done after that. It takes over two hundred thousand dollars to raise a kid nowadays. Thank God your father set up a pension for me. If he hadn't I don't know what I'd do." Paul grimaced. "But if I live to be eighty years old I'll still be working. Thank God I love my job."

"Let me know once Callie delivers." Noah tightened his grip on Jacoby's hand. "We'd love to come and see the babies, wouldn't we, Jacoby?"

Jacoby felt her uterus lurch. A yearning for children with Noah overcame her and she was at a loss for words. But she nodded her agreement.

"I'll do that," Paul grinned. "You're all ready to go. I took it out for a run yesterday to make sure that it was running smoothly. She's anchored over there."

They walked the short distance to the end of the pier. A large speedboat was looped to the dock. On the side were the words, Noah's Ark.

"My dad named it after me," Noah said with pride.

"So I see," Jacoby said, admiring the white speed boat with blue lettering on the sides.

"Your lunch is inside and you have a tank full of gas," Paul said.

"Thanks so much for taking care of this," Noah said.

"It was my pleasure." Paul tipped his hat and left.

"He seems really nice."

"He is. Paul and I are childhood friends. During the summers we did everything together."

"Did you guys ever get in trouble?"

"Of course we did. But we always covered for each other so we got away with a lot more than we should have." Noah stepped onto the boat and held his hand out to Jacoby. "Watch your step," he said. "Your flip flops are wet from the dock and I wouldn't want you to fall."

"And ruin our day!" she said as she gingerly stepped into the boat. Noah unhooked the brown rope from around the post that disappeared into the water. "Not a chance."

Noah picked up a life jacket and held it out.

Jacoby slid into it and Noah secured it. He gave it a tug to make sure she was safe before he slid into one. Then they took turns slathering sunscreen on their faces and every bit of skin that showed. Taking the wheel, he said, "Hang on for the ride of your life."

"I can't wait." Jacoby grinned as she sat in her seat.

Noah stood at the wheel. The engine revved loudly and once it idled down, Noah backed the boat until it faced the open water. The ocean was devoid of other boats. Noah hit the gas and water spewed out the back, drenching them.

"We're wet already and we haven't left the marina," she laughed.

"That's the fun of it, Jacoby."

For over an hour, they cruised the area. The salt air made her thirsty. Reaching into a cooler, she grabbed a beer, opened it and handed it to Noah. "You always know what I want, Jacoby," he shouted over the roar of the engine.

As Jacoby was opening a beer for herself, she heard the engine cut off.

"I don't drink and drive, even on the open water."

Jacoby put a sandwich and potato chips on a paper plate. Handing Noah a napkin she smiled at the huge chunk he bit out of the sandwich.

Jacoby took a swig from her bottle and then fixed a plate of food for herself. She bit into the turkey and Swiss sub. "This is delicious."

"On the other side of the marina there's a deli stand that caters baskets of food for people that go boating."

"They must have a thriving business."

"They've been at the same location for twenty years. They seem recession proof."

After they finished their meal, Jacoby and Noah leaned back in relaxation. Watching the blue waves with white caps, they felt like they were the only two people in the world and they were content.

Noah finished his second beer and leaned back. His expression was unfathomable.

"Whatcha thinking about, Noah Powers?"

"I was just wondering if you're truly happy."

Surprise made Jacoby sputter and she spilled some of her beer. Wiping her mouth with the back of her hand she said, "Of course I'm happy. How could you even ask me that?"

"I just wondered if there is something else that you need in your life to make your happiness complete."

The vision of herself in a white wedding gown rose in her consciousness, but she shooed it away. When Noah is ready to marry you he'll ask. "I know that I want you in my life forever, Noah."

"Then I'll make sure that you have me, Jacoby." Noah reached into the side pocket of his shorts and withdrew a black velvet box.

Jacoby's mouth dropped as she stared at it.

Noah got down on one knee and opened the box.

The huge square diamond almost blinded her.

"Jacoby Alexander from the moment I saw you I wanted you. Once I got to know you I loved you. I want you to be in my life, for now, forever, for always. Will you do me the honor of being my wife?"

Tears of happiness welled in her eyes and she dropped to her knees. "Noah Powers, will you do me the honor of being my husband, for now, forever, and for always?" And she stuck her hand out.

The square diamond was a perfect fit.

"It's perfect, Noah," she breathed in awe. "Just like you."

Noah picked up her hand and kissed the ring on her finger. He stood and held his hand out.

Eagerly Jacoby got off her knees and melted into his body.

As his mouth descended towards her she kept her eyes open, drinking in every facial detail of her true love.

Returning the passion of his kiss, Jacoby felt at peace with the world. As the sun began to move to the west, Jacoby sat with her hand outstretched admiring her ring. "I can't wait to tell my parents."

"Do you think that you can wait until Thanksgiving?"

"Sure," she said, surprised. "But why?"

"I'd like to formally ask your father for your hand in marriage."

"Noah," she whispered, "I think that you must be the most caring man in the world. The secret will torture me, but I'll wait for you to do your thing."

"I have another request," he said with a rueful smile.

"All of a sudden my future husband is becoming demanding," she teased. "What is it, Noah?"

"I know most women dream of the perfect wedding date," Noah said, "and I don't know what yours is, but I'd like to be married February fourteenth."

"Valentine's Day?"

"Yes," he replied. "Valentine's Day is the day my parents were married. I'd like to do it in memory of my mother."

"I forgot to add that you're also a very sensitive man. I would love to marry you Valentine's Day."

A sudden bump against the boat startled them. They looked over the side. A small shark circled the boat.

"It's a shark!" Jacoby exclaimed.

"She's just curious," Noah said. "But I wonder where the mother is." Noah took off his sunglasses and scanned the area around them. "She must have wandered off from her family and they'll be looking for her. I'm going to head us back. When we're closer to land I'm going to let you take over."

"You are?" Jacoby said excitedly.

"I am." Noah took his hand and ruffled her damp hair.

He slowly turned the boat around not wanting to hit the baby shark, and headed back towards shore. Once land was in sight, he beckoned Jacoby to him.

She stood at the wheel.

Noah stood so close behind her that she felt his breath fanning the top of her head.

"Steer it like you would a car." Noah manipulated the controls until the boat began to move.

Jacoby loved the feeling of being in control and turned the wheel. Instead of heading back to shore she raced the boat parallel to land. After thirty minutes she made another turn and headed them to the docking station.

Once they were near the dock Noah took the wheel back, nosed them to the mooring, and cut the engine for the last time that day.

"Noah." She turned and threw her arms around his waist. Jacoby buried her head in Noah's chest and breathed in his scent. "I never thought I'd be this happy."

Noah lifted her chin and nuzzled her nose with his. "I always knew that we would be. Thank you for allowing me to apologize for our botched weekend in West Palm."

"Well, you did a bang up job of it, fiancé of mine," Jacoby replied with an ecstatic expression on her face.

"Where's your ring?" Noah asked as they drove to Bunnell.

Jacoby fingered the chain that hung between her breasts. "I put it on a chain until you talk to daddy."

"I hope your parents like me," Noah said somewhat nervously.

She rubbed his thigh soothingly. "They will absolutely love you."

"What will you do if your father says that I can't marry you?"

"Marry you anyway. And then insist that mom come and live with us because he's lost his mind."

Noah grinned at Jacoby's words.

"I told Claudia."

"You did?"

"I just had to tell someone. But she promised not to say a word to anyone."

"I can't wait to meet her and Rex."

"They'll be over for Thanksgiving."

"It's beginning to sound like a party."

"We certainly have a lot to celebrate." Jacoby said musingly, "What a difference a year makes."

As Noah turned into her parents' driveway, her mother flung open the front door.

"It looks like she's been waiting for us."

"All day long," Jacoby answered.

Sarai hurried down the front steps towards them with her arms held wide.

Jacoby hurried into them.

As Noah watched, a sudden longing for his mother engulfed him.

"So you're Noah Powers?" Sarai said with her hands folded as she eyed him.

"Yes, ma'am, I am," Noah replied.

"I have been dying to meet you," she said.

"Likewise," Noah replied.

Jacoby and Noah sat at the kitchen table and let Sarai fuss over them. "Noah," Sarai said. "Would you like a snack or something? Dinner won't be served until Abraham gets home around six."

"No thanks, ma'am. Jacoby and I stopped on the way up and had a big lunch."

"You can call me Mom," Sarai said shyly. "That is if you want to."

Noah responded quietly, "I would like that very much, Mom."

The sound of a car in the driveway surprised them. Sarai said, "I wonder who that is?"

Jacoby looked out the window. "It's Daddy."

Sarai said, "He must have gotten off work early."

Abraham held a metal lunchbox in his hand. He placed it on the counter and gave his wife a peck on the cheek. He turned his full attention to his daughter.

Jacoby went to him and they embraced. He held her at arms' length and gave her a quick perusal. He said, "You look good, Jacoby."

"I feel good, Daddy." She stepped back and said proudly, "Daddy, This is Noah."

Abraham folded his arms and leaned on the counter. He studied Noah for a full minute.

Noah's eyes met his gaze unflinchingly. Then he stood and held out his hand. "It's very nice to meet you, Mr. Alexander."

The men shook hands as they sized each other up.

"So you're Jacoby's boss?" Abraham said.

"I am the CEO of Power's Public Relations, but Jacoby and I are in a relationship."

"Isn't there some kind of rule against that?" Abraham asked gruffly.

"No, sir, there isn't."

"If there was I'd find a job elsewhere so that I could still see him," Jacoby interjected in a steady tone.

"Humph! Then I guess that I should be glad that there isn't. Since you started working there I've never known you to be so happy," Abraham admitted. "And that's all I've ever wanted for you, Jacoby." He gave her a piercing stare. "To be truly happy and not settle for less than that."

Jacoby went to Noah's side. "Then you have what you want for me, Daddy, because I have the kind of happiness that women read about in romance novels."

Jacoby said, "Mom and I are going to the supermarket for Thanksgiving food. And we've decided to bring dinner. Are there any special requests?"

"I wouldn't mind pizza," Noah said.

"That's a good idea because we'll probably be eating turkey for the rest of the week," Abraham agreed.

Noah and Abraham sat watching ESPN. When a commercial came on Noah cleared his throat. "Sir, I'd like to talk to you about Jacoby."

"So would I," Abraham replied. He grabbed the remote control and muted the television.

"Then maybe you should go first," Noah offered in a respectful voice.

"I've heard only bits and pieces from my wife. I want to know how Jacoby ended up moving in with you."

"Jacoby and I were friends," Noah explained diplomatically. "She needed a place to stay and I have plenty of room."

"Why was Jacoby in such a hurry to move out from Armstrong?"

There was a long hesitation. Finally Noah said, "That's Jacoby's story and I think that you should ask her."

"Even though the two of you started off as friends now you're boyfriend and girlfriend. That puts a whole different slant on the relationship." He clucked his tongue disapprovingly. "Living with one man and then moving in with another, that's not how I raised my daughter."

Noah pinned Abraham's eyes with his. "Jacoby is truly a lady. We're very happy together."

"But how long will that last? People grow bored and want to move on. Then what will she do?"

"I won't grow bored with Jacoby. I love her very much. As a matter of fact, I was glad that she and your wife decided to go shopping. I wanted to talk to you alone."

"Really?" Abraham settled further back in his chair

"Yes, I've asked Jacoby to marry me, and she's accepted."

"You two haven't known each other very long."

"We've known each other long enough to fall in love and realize that we want to spend the rest of our lives together."

"Humph," Abraham said as he quietly considered Noah's words.

"I am formally requesting Jacoby's hand in marriage, sir."

"What would you do if I said no?"

"Jacoby and I would still marry and it would cause another strain on your relationship. I'm sure that you don't want that."

A dead silence filled the room. Abraham's lips pressed together at the mention of the stormy relationship he and Jacoby had once Alexandria entered their lives.

"She wants your approval but she doesn't insist on it."

"So why did you even bother to ask me in the first place?"

"Out of respect for you as her father."

"Thank you, Noah," Abraham said grudgingly. "I guess I'm over-protective of Jacoby. I hated it when she moved to Miami, but I couldn't do anything about it. Now I'm in the same position again. The minute I met Armstrong I knew he was wrong for her. But I feel differently about you, Noah. When you look at my daughter, your love for her shines out of your eyes."

"It's there."

Suddenly words seemed to burst from Abraham's chest. "I don't want you cheating on my daughter. If you marry her, you keep her, and treat her right."

"I would never cheat on Jacoby," Noah replied in a reassuring voice.

"Men never think that they'll cheat," Abraham said sadly. "But things change. Times get tough. And you can be made to pay for your mistakes for the rest of your life."

"I would never put Jacoby through that," Noah responded quietly.

"Never say never."

"I know for sure that I don't want her to ever feel betrayed again."

Abraham dropped his eyes in shame. When he looked up again he said, "I believe you, Noah. You have my permission and my blessings to marry my daughter."

"Thank you, sir," Noah answered.

"You can call me Dad."

Noah looked at him.

"It would be kind of nice." Abraham added, "I never had a son."

"Then Dad it is," Noah replied.

When Jacoby and Sarai got home, Noah and Abraham were asleep in the den. Noah lay on the couch and Abraham in the lazy boy. They stared at them indulgently.

Jacoby took her finger and tickled Noah under his chin. When he awoke and realized that they were back, he sat up and rubbed his eyes.

Jacoby gave a slight nod in her father's direction. He hadn't yet awakened.

Noah smiled and nodded yes.

Sarai intercepted the look between the two.

Jacoby started clapping her hands excitedly.

"What's going on?" Sarai asked.

Jacoby lifted the chain and showed the ring to her mother. "Noah and I are getting married. He wanted me to keep it a secret until he talked to Daddy."

Sarai stared in awe at the ring, then started clapping her hands excitedly.

This roused Abraham. "What's going on?" he demanded, sitting up straight.

"Jacoby and Noah are getting married!" Sarai screamed.

"Oh," Abraham said, relieved that nothing was wrong with his wife. "I already knew that."

Noah took the chain and slid the ring off it and on to Jacoby's finger. He kissed it. "That's where it belongs," he said.

"And that's where it's going to stay," Jacoby promised.

CHAPTER 19

Sarai handed Jacoby the telephone. "It's Claudia."

"Hey, Claudia," Jacoby said.

"When did you guys get in?"

"Around one."

"Rex and I want you to meet us at Pete's Place this evening."

"Pete's Place?"

"Yeah, they have happy hour starting at seven."

"That sounds like fun. Hold on a second while I ask Noah." Jacoby shouted, "Noah! Do you want to go meet Claudia and Rex later?"

Noah came into the kitchen. "Whatever you want to do works for me."

Jacoby said into the receiver. "Did you hear that?"

"I sure did."

"See you at seven," Jacoby said before she hung up the phone.

It was Noah's turn to buy drinks. He stood a head taller than most of the other men at the bar and his silhouette stood out.

"He's so fine!" Claudia shouted over the music.

"I know!" Jacoby replied with a cheeky grin.

"This is so cute on him." Claudia took her finger and crunched in her chin so that it looked like it had a hole in it. "Is he any good in bed?"

"It would take me all night to describe how good it is, Claudia."

"You're so damn lucky. He's rich and fine. Your engagement ring is to die for. You can barely see the diamond in mine."

"Hey!" Rex said. "I can hear you."

"Don't worry about it, Rex," she teased. "You can't miss what you never had."

"Ha, ha, ha," Rex retorted.

Noah came back to the table with a tray of drinks. After giving everyone what they'd requested he slid back into his seat next to Jacoby and slid his arm around her.

Jacoby cuddled closer, leaving no room between them.

Claudia asked, "So when is the wedding?"

"Valentine's Day," Jacoby answered.

"That's right around the corner," Claudia exclaimed. "Do you think that you have enough time to plan it?"

"We're supposed to meet with a wedding planner next week."

"Oooh! Aren't we going big time."

"Actually Noah and I want a small wedding. You're my matron of honor of course. But there will be no bridesmaids."

"Really?"

"Yeah," Jacoby said, clasping Noah's hand. "We're just ready to seal the deal."

Noah picked up his drink and held it up in the air.

The rest of them followed suit.

"I toast to sealing the deal," Noah said.

They quaffed their drinks.

Armstrong was parked behind trees at the edge of the property. He slumped down in the seat his head barely visible above the dash. The muscle in his cheek throbbed angrily as he observed the happy foursome saying their goodbyes. Once they got in their cars and drove away, Armstrong revved his Charger up and peeled away. Flurries of dirt were airborne as he headed towards his house. He slammed the door once he was inside.

The noise woke Alexandria. She cowered beneath the covers.

Armstrong stormed into the spare bedroom and kicked the door shut with his dirty boot.

Alexandria heaved a deep sigh of relief.

Jacoby drove them through town pointing out different landmarks. "That's where I went to high school."

"I find it hard to believe that you weren't prom queen."

Jacoby laughed lightly. "It was purely a popularity vote, and I wasn't putting out."

"Those fellows don't know what they were missing."

"I had my chances," she said. "But I wanted to wait for the right guy. My count was off by one."

"Do you ever regret moving to Miami, Jacoby?"

"No. If I hadn't made the mistake of getting involved with Armstrong I wouldn't have ever met you." Her voice quivered with emotion. "Now I can't envision a life without you, Noah."

Jacoby made a right turn and they veered onto a small, dirt road. The rocks underneath their tires made a popping sound. Trees heavily laden with moss flanked the road.

"Where are we going?" Noah asked.

"To a place that I've always wanted to bring the love of my life." Jacoby parked between two trees with an opening to the small lake was before them.

"What a beautiful view Jacoby."

"They call it lookout point. I think every small town has a place for teenagers to come and neck," she said shyly.

"I wasn't just speaking of the lake."

Jacoby's cheeks warmed from his compliment. "Since we can't sleep in the same room while we're at my parents' house, I thought that we might want a little quiet time, just the two of us."

"Just the two of us." He turned the dial on the radio and found 94.5. The melodious voice of Luther filled the car. "The Quiet Storm is playing." The air around them filled with classic love songs. Noah opened his car door and climbed out. He walked around to the driver's side and opened Jacoby's door. He held his arms wide and Jacoby leapt into them.

They held each other as they stared at the still lake with the full moon aglow over it.

The next day as Jacoby was peeling potatoes and Sarai stuffing the turkey when Noah walked into the kitchen. "Are you sure that you don't want me to do anything?"

"No," Sarai answered. "You'll just be in the way."

"Where did daddy go?" Jacoby asked.

"I don't know," Noah replied. "He said that he had an errand to run, but he wouldn't be gone long."

As if on cue Abraham opened the back door and entered the kitchen. In his hands was a case of Icehouse and a bottle of wine.

"Daddy," Jacoby exclaimed. "You bought beer? I can't believe it!"

"There's nothing wrong with me enjoying a beer with my son," he said gruffly. "The football game should be starting any minute, Noah." Abraham handed him a beer and took one for himself. The rest he put in the refrigerator. He looked at his wife who was watching him with her mouth hanging open. "The clerk at the store recommended that wine. Let me know if you like it." Whistling, he headed towards the den.

Jacoby looked at Noah. "Daddy must really like you," she said, her eyes shining with happiness.

"I like him too," Noah said, utterly relieved.

They were finishing dinner when they heard the front door open. "Who's letting themselves in with a key?" Sarai asked.

Before anyone could respond Alexandria breezed into the room followed by Armstrong.

Jacoby's fork clattered on the table. The sight of him made her stomach churn.

The air in the room felt suffocating.

Noah's eyes narrowed as he stared at Alexandria, noting her resemblance to Abraham. Then he shifted his gaze to Armstrong.

Armstrong's eyes zeroed in on the engagement ring on Jacoby's finger. He glared at his nemesis. His heart beat rapidly he stared hatred at the man who had stolen the only woman that he'd thought he'd satisfied.

Noah's nostrils flared angrily as he finally saw the man who had mistreated his woman. *Don't react. This isn't the time or place.*

Their eyes battled each other across the room.

"Happy Thanksgiving, Daddy," Alexandria said with forced gaiety.

"Why didn't you call and tell me you were coming?" he demanded.

"I wanted to surprise you."

Abraham picked up a napkin and wiped his mouth. As he stood, his chair, made a grinding noise against the hardwood floor. "Alexandria, you're my daughter so I won't ask you to leave." He shot daggers at Armstrong. "But Armstrong, you aren't welcome here. Not now, not ever. Let me escort you out."

Armstrong's hands were clenched by his sides. "Alexandria invited me," he said stiffly.

"She doesn't have the right," Abraham retorted harshly.

Armstrong turned on his heels and stormed out the house. He slammed the front door and the picture that hung nearby fell off the wall, its glass breaking into pieces.

Alexandria said resentfully, "If my man isn't welcome here then neither am I."

"That's your choice," Abraham retorted.

In a huff she scurried after Armstrong.

"They have a damn nerve," Sarai muttered under her breath.

###

That night Jacoby was drifting off to sleep when she heard a light knocking at her door. "Come in," she said, sitting up.

Her father came into the room. "I know that you're leaving early in the morning, and I wanted to talk to you alone."

"Okay." Jacoby turned on the lamp next to her bed.

"I'm sorry Alexandria ruined our day, Jacoby."

"Yeah," she said, "me too."

"What happened down there in Miami? Did she break you and Armstrong up?"

"We already didn't have anything when she showed up. She just made it where I had to leave earlier than I'd planned."

"Are you really happy, Jacoby?"

"I am, Daddy."

"I like Noah."

"I like him too," she smiled.

"It's obvious that Alexandria is jealous of you. That's why she's hooked up with your ex."

"She can have Armstrong. He's a nothing."

"I saw you and Noah in deep conversation. What did he say about Alexandria and Armstrong's antics?"

"He's not surprised. Noah just wanted to make sure that I was okay. He knew that it would be difficult for me to see Armstrong again after the way we split."

"What happened to make you finally leave Armstrong?"

Mortification resurfaced in her gut. "I don't want to talk about it. The past is the past."

Abraham breathed a deep sigh of relief. "I'm glad that you and Noah have found each other. That's the only good thing to come out of this drama that I created." He leaned over and kissed her on her forehead.

Jacoby kissed him back in the same manner.

"Be careful down there in Miami," Abraham said.

"I will," Jacoby promised.

"I love you, Jacoby."

"I love you too, Daddy," she responded.

Jacoby was on the website viewing the pressure points video when the phone rang. She looked at her caller I.D. and read the words pay phone. "Hello," she said.

"I'm going to kill him!" the voice hissed menacingly.

Dread took her breath away.

"If you marry him, I'll kill him," Armstrong threatened in a deadly tone. "I don't care how long it takes. I'll get him. And I might just do in your parents for the hell of it."

The threatening voice took her breath away. Jacoby dropped the phone and it made a harsh sound on the tile floor. She planted her hand against the wall to keep from falling. With a feeling of hopelessness she sank to her knees, and remained on the floor, almost comatose, for a long hour. The ringing of the phone again startled her. Tentatively she picked up the receiver.

"Hello, Miss Alexander."

"Hello, Fiona."

"I' m just calling to confirm my appointment with you and your fiancé Friday evening at six."

"You'll need to cancel it," she replied dully. "The wedding is off."

A week later, Noah dropped his briefcase on the foyer floor with a thud. With a frown he went in search of Jacoby. When he entered the media room she was on the computer and seeing him she cut off the monitor.

"What are you looking at?" he asked curtly.

"Nothing," she said, avoiding the intensity of his gaze.

"Jacoby, I called Fiona Ainsley today."

"Why did you do that?"

"Because you said that she kept postponing our meeting with her."

Jacoby dropped her head, not wanting to face Noah.

"She said that wasn't the case and I needed to talk to you. What's going on? Have you decided that you want to use a different wedding planner?"

"Noah," she said. "I haven't known how to tell you this, but I want to postpone the wedding."

"But why?" Noah demanded with a baffled look on his face.

"I dunno," she whispered. "Things are moving too fast. I just need more time."

"More time," he repeated in a stunned voice. "More time for what?"

Jacoby searched for a reason that wouldn't make her lose Noah forever. "I think that I'm too young to get married."

"I thought that this is what you wanted," Noah said in a wounded voice. "I don't understand."

"You wouldn't," she whispered.

"Jacoby," he said breathing heavily, "how much time do you need?"

She didn't answer him for an interminable time. Finally she said with anguish written all over her face, "Noah, I don't want to marry you. Not now, not ever."

"What!" he shouted. "You said that you loved me. I thought that you wanted to have a life with me. Have children with me."

Jacoby winced at each sentence.

"I like things the way they are. Why do we need to change things?"

"Because that's what people do. When they love each other they make a commitment."

Jacoby didn't reply.

"You've been acting strangely ever since we got back from Bunnell." His voice was ragged from emotion. "Is it because of Armstrong? Have you feelings for him after all? Is that why suddenly you don't want to marry me?"

"Yes." Jacoby stared him straight in the eye and said honestly, "I don't want to marry you because of Armstrong."

Noah looked as if she'd plunged a knife in his heart. He passed his hand through his wavy hair. "Well, then, I don't want to marry you either." Noah stepped back, turned on his heel and stormed out of the room. The next thing she heard was the slamming of the front door.

Jacoby fell on the bed and sobbed. Once she was spent, with fists clenched she screamed in the oppressive silence, "I'm so damn tired of being a victim!" The shrill sound of the phone made her grab for it. "Noah!" she said in a hopeful voice.

"No," chuckled Sarai. "It's your mother."

"Oh."

"Excuse me for not being him, but I have some news for you."

"What is it, Mom?" she asked impatiently.

"Your father and I are renewing our vows on Mother's Day. We want you and Noah to be matron of honor and best man."

"Renewing your vows?"

"Yep. I guess your dad got the wedding bug from you two kids." Sarai said excitedly. "I couldn't wait to tell you."

"That's nice, Mom," Jacoby mumbled.

"Is anything wrong, Jacoby?"

"No," she lied. "It's just been a long day."

"You must be really busy getting ready for the wedding."

"Yeah," she said. "That's what it is."

"Then I'll let you go. But before I forget, I wanted you to let me borrow my old wedding ring. My lupus is so much better that I think that I can wear it, at least for that day."

The wedding ring.

"All right, Mother," Jacoby promised. "I'll bring you the ring."

"Okay then, Jacoby. Talk to you later."

"Yeah, I'll talk to you later."

Jacoby stared up at the ceiling. *I need to take control of my life.* She dialed Allie's number.

"Hey, Jacoby, How nice to hear from you."

Jacoby began to jabber all of her words running into each other.

"Calm down," Allie ordered. "I can't understand a word you're saying. Whatever is the matter?"

Jacoby spilled every detail to Allie, everything that Armstrong had done to her since she'd moved in with Noah. She babbled incoherently at times and Allie had to ask her to repeat herself. Once Jacoby was finished Allie said, "Whew! What a bully. No wonder you've been acting so odd lately."

"He said that he'll kill Noah."

"You need to call the police."

"I'm going to tell Noah the truth when he gets back. That is, if he comes back."

"He's just gone somewhere to cool off. He doesn't know what's going on with you and he's confused. And I don't blame him. It was crazy for you not to tell Noah about all of this."

"I'm going to Armstrong's."

Allie said, her voice high with anxiety, "Don't look for trouble, Jacoby."

"I'm going to get my mother's ring."

"Wait for Noah!"

"No," she said. "I'm tired of hiding and being afraid."

"What if Armstrong isn't there?"

"I have a key. I doubt if he changed the locks because that costs money."

"Jacoby, what if Alexandria is there?"

"Good!" she said in a hard voice. "That'll be the opportunity for me to kick her ass."

"Jacoby wait!" Allie exclaimed.

Jacoby hung up the phone, grabbed her keys, and rushed out of the house.

Armstrong's parking space was empty when she got to his complex. With purposeful steps she entered the building and not wanting to wait for the elevator she climbed the stairs two at a time. Adrenalin coursed through her as she stomped to his apartment. She pounded on his door. There was no answer. Then suddenly she was overwhelmed by a feeling of panic. Jacoby stood in the hallway paralyzed with fear. Pockets of sweat dampened the material under her armpits. Her hand gripped the strap of her purse so hard her knuckles hurt. Forcing herself to relax her hold, she fished around in the bottom of her purse until she felt the outline of the key and withdrew it.

Almost blankly she stared at the tarnished gold colored object in the palm of her hand. The sight of it made blood rush to her head and she swayed so much she needed to plant her free hand on the wall for support. Beads of perspiration broke out on her forehead and her knees began to tremble

From where it came she didn't know but a burst of strength combined with resolve fluttered to life in her gut. First it was small and then the flame grew in intensity, enveloping her body. Stilling her quaking knees, she inserted the key into the doorknob. With relief she felt it turn. Taking the flat of the hand, she pushed the door open, letting herself inside the pitch black apartment.

Noah drained his second glass of Hennessey. *It doesn't make sense. I know this woman inside and out. Jacoby loves me. Something else is going on with her and I need to find out what it is.*

The waitress said, "Would you like a refill?"

"No," Noah said pulling out his wallet and taking some bills out. "This should take care of it." Just as he slammed the bills down on the bar, his cell phone rang. "This is Noah Powers."

"Noah," the frantic voice said. "This is Allie. Jacoby is in trouble."

A ball of anxiety knotted his belly. "What kind of trouble!"

"She's gone to Armstrong's apartment to look for her mother's ring."

"What?"

Allie repeated to Noah everything that Jacoby had told him.

Noah's heart pounded at the thought of how much danger she was in. "I'm on my way to her, Allie. Don't worry. I'll take care of this once and for all." His voice was clipped and his mind reeled at how much had been going on that he didn't know about.

Jacoby tossed clothes on the floor as she searched the dresser drawers and the nightstands. Once that search proved futile she went into the kitchen and started rummaging through the kitchen drawers. Suddenly she heard the front door open. Jacoby went into the center of the room and waited.

Armstrong was alone. His eyes opened wide and then narrowed into slits. "What are you doing here, Jacoby?" he snarled.

Jacoby tamped down the urge to run past him to safety. "I left my mother's ring here," she said in a voice that sounded surprisingly calm.

"So you thought after all this time that it was still here?" he taunted her. "I pawned it."

Jacoby gulped down her disappointment. "Which pawn shop did you go to? I'd like to see if I can track it down."

"You're so damn dumb." Armstrong brushed past her.

Jacoby visibly flinched.

He went to a canister on the counter and opened it." He dug inside it and when he withdrew his hand he had her ring in his palm. "I knew you'd be back for it."

Jacoby sharply drew in her breath.

He slammed the ring on the counter. "Reach for it."

Jacoby watched her prey.

"I can't decide whether to beat your ass or take you in the room and fuck your brains out."

Jacoby pasted a bland look on her face.

"I think I'll do both."

"I didn't just come here for my ring," she said softly.

"You didn't!"

"No," she said. "I kind of miss you."

"You do?" he said doubtfully.

Jacoby said in a deliberately sexy voice, "A woman never forgets her first, Armstrong."

Armstrong's chest seemed to puff up right before her eyes. Longing was reflected in his eyes.

"You have to get rid of Alexandria."

Armstrong licked his lips with his tongue. "Done."

"Now may I have my ring?"

"You liar!" he shouted. "You think that you can play with me? Do you think that I'm some goddamned idiot? Now you're going to pay!" He advanced menacingly towards her. Once he was abreast of her he towered over her.

Jacoby looked up at him. Without moving her body, almost as if it in slow motion, she brought her right hand up. Her thumb and third finger were poised and ready to strike. Measuring the distance between Armstrong's eyebrows, with all her might she thumped him in the forehead right between his eyes.

Armstrong went down. He lay on his back and he was out cold.

Oh my God! Did I kill him? Jacoby stood over him. She took her finger and put it under his nose. There was breath underneath. *He's alive. But I won! I'm not afraid of him anymore!*

Elated with self-confidence she stepped over Armstrong and snatched her ring off the counter. She turned around to leave and saw Noah standing on the threshold.

"I stood up to him, Noah!" she said excitedly. "I knocked Armstrong out. I'm not a victim anymore."

Noah's jaw was hard and he stared at Armstrong who remained motionless on the floor. His eyes moved to Jacoby and they didn't soften. "Go home, Jacoby," he said in a deadpan voice. "I'll meet you there."

"Noah, there's no need for you to stay. Come with me," she said pleadingly. "I'll explain everything."

"Do as I say." His voice was cold and his expression withdrawn. He didn't look at her as he spoke. Instead, with a brooding air, he watched Armstrong's still form.

A feeling of foreboding coursed through Jacoby as she watched Noah. She grabbed her purse and without saying anything else bolted out of the apartment.

Armstrong opened his eyes and stared around him in confusion, his eyes coming to rest on Noah.

Noah sat in an armchair. With a contemptuous curl of his lip, he watched *his* prey.

Armstrong's tongue felt thick and he struggled to sit up.

Noah said in a stony voice, "I hear that you've been terrorizing my fiancée."

A surly look surfaced on Armstrong's face and he blinked several times trying to focus.

"I wanted to do this in Bunnell but that wasn't the time or place." Noah opened the Nike bag and took out his boxing gloves and slowly pulled the right one on. "You are to never bother Jacoby again. You are to never approach her, call her, or be in her vicinity. And stay away from her parents. Do you understand me?"

Terrified, Armstrong nodded his head in frightened compliance.

"I'm going to make sure that you do." With deliberate steps, Noah advanced on Armstrong.

CHAPTER 20

Jacoby sat at the kitchen table and waited for Noah. As she heard the garage door go up, she took a long sip from the glass of wine she'd been staring at for the last hour. She stood when he entered the room. Jacoby nervously ran her hands down the side of her pants. "Noah," she said, "we need to talk."

"So now you want to confide in me, Jacoby?" Noah threw his keys on the kitchen counter. The jarring sound of doom sliced the air.

"Yes."

"It's too late," he replied, his voice filled with disappointment.

Jacoby swallowed the knot in her throat. "You have to let me explain. I lied to you today. I made you think that I didn't want to marry you because of some crazy leftover feelings for Armstrong, feelings I never had for him in the first place," she stressed.

A thunderous look remained on Noah's face.

"I was only trying to protect you."

"Protect me from that guy?" he demanded and his voice was raw with anger. "Are you sure that you weren't trying to protect him from me?"

"Noah," she said evenly, "Armstrong was a soldier. He told me that he would kill you if I married you."

He snorted his disbelief. "And you believed that!"

"I couldn't take the chance. I wouldn't want to live if something happened to you because of me. He even threatened my parents. That's why I didn't tell you."

"Allie told me that this afternoon. You confided in her, yet you hid this from me all this time."

"I didn't tell Allie until today. I was too embarrassed to tell anyone what was going on." She admitted to Noah and herself for the first time, "I am truly an abused woman."

"You let yourself be abused," he shouted. "I was here for you! I would have protected you." He poked his finger in his chest. "In times of trouble you're supposed to lean on me. Do you know how stupid I feel? I didn't have an inkling all this was going on. You could have been seriously hurt, and I wouldn't have been able to do anything about it until it was too late."

Jacoby whispered, "I'm sorry, Noah. But can't you understand that I couldn't let you save me," she said, "again?"

"No, I can't," he replied in a broken voice. "Now it all makes sense to me. You stopped meeting me for lunch on Fridays; you'd call me at work with a huge list of groceries to bring home. You lied to me over and over again. That's why you decided to take all your classes online." He made a sweeping gesture with his arm. "How could you even feel as if you were living a life?"

"I felt that I was living a life because I was the luckiest woman in the world," Jacoby replied in a clear voice.

Noah gave her an incredulous look.

"Every evening the most wonderful and loving man came home to me. Every night I got to hold him in my arms and make love to him. It was all worth it."

"Well," Noah said in a voice mixed with pain and regret, "now you don't have to hide out here anymore, Jacoby." He said with conviction, "Armstrong will never go near you or your parents again. You can go and live your life in the outside world like a real person. "

"What do you mean, Noah?" Jacoby wailed her voice high with anxiety.

"The wedding is truly off," Noah croaked and his voice was filled with despair.

"Noah, please," Jacoby begged. "Give me another chance. I promise that I won't keep anything else from you. I know that I made a mistake not telling you," she said, "but I didn't know what to do."

"I can't marry a woman who doesn't confide in me or respect the fact that I can look out for her. Marriages never work if the people in it don't trust each other. I can't end up divorced like my parents. It was too hard. I can't go through it again."

Jacoby dashed a tear away. "Noah," she cried out, "this wasn't about you. It was about me standing up for myself. Can't you understand that?"

"No," he replied in a voice full of grief. "I can't. I'm going to sleep upstairs until we sort things out. I once told you that you'd never have to be homeless. I'm going to abide by that. We'll talk in the morning."

Jacoby watched Noah as he walked off.

His shoulders were slumped from disillusionment as he climbed the stairs.

With a stabbing pain in her heart she stumbled into the master bedroom. Jacoby got on her knees at the foot of the bed. She clasped her hands together, bent her head, and began to pray out loud, "My Dear Lord God, I need your help. I deceived Noah. I tried to take matters into my own hands. I'm sorry. Please make Noah understand that I love him and will never keep anything important from him again. I want a life with him. Please soften his heart so that he forgives me. I promise I won't mess up anymore." Once her prayer was finished she was unable to lie in the bed that she'd shared so many passionate nights with Noah. Instead, she slid to the floor and remained there. She felt too empty to weep.

All night long Noah lay in bed and stared at the ceiling. Fear clutched his heart as he thought about how much danger she'd been in. Jacoby's words played over and over again in his mind. 'I was trying to protect you. He said that he would kill you. I would die if anything happened to you. I am truly an abused woman.' Finally he drifted into a fitful sleep.

The shrill sound of the telephone ringing startled him. He looked at the clock. "It's five o'clock in the morning." He looked around and remembered there was no extension. Pulling on his boxers he went downstairs to see if Jacoby had answered the telephone.

When he entered the master bedroom she was still on the telephone. The distressed look on her face tugged at his heartstrings.

"No, Daddy. Thank goodness you let me know! I'm on my way." She hung up and looked at him. Her eyes were round with fright.

"What's wrong?" Noah asked.

"It's mom," she said slowly. "She got up to use the bathroom and collapsed. The ambulance took her to the hospital and they admitted her." Jacoby ran to the closet and grabbed an overnight bag. She started throwing her belongings in it. "I have to go to her."

"I'll take you."

Jacoby took her mother's ring off the dresser and slid it on her finger. Without looking at him she said, "You don't have to come, Noah."

"You still don't get it, do you, Jacoby?" he said through gritted teeth. "I'm not letting you drive alone to Bunnell in your state of mind. Pack a bag for me while I grab my cell phone and iPad."

Jacoby stopped what she was doing and looked at Noah. "Thank you, Noah." She admitted, "I need you."

After Noah left the room, Jacoby took her engagement ring out of the jewelry box, slid it on a chain, and put it around her neck. Although the ring was hidden underneath her shirt its presence gave her comfort.

When they entered the hospital room, Abraham slept in the chair next to the bed. Sarai was also asleep. There was a clear bag of liquid being pumped into her intravenously through a clear plastic tube.

Jacoby tiptoed to her father and gently shook his shoulder.

Abraham sat up abruptly. When he saw them a broad grin encompassed his face. "Hello there you two," he bellowed.

"Shush," Jacoby said putting her fingers to her lips. "Don't wake Mother. Let's go outside so we can talk."

The trio stood in the hallway. Abraham said, "Your mother is fine. The doctor said that she overexerted herself putting up the Christmas decorations. I called back to the house once I found out but you must have already been gone."

"Are you sure that she's okay? Why did they keep her if it's nothing?"

"Since she's in here the doctor is running tests to make sure that her lupus hasn't progressed. But her vitals are good. They might release her this afternoon."

"Why the fluid?" Noah asked.

"She was a little dehydrated, that's all."

"Daddy, are you sure that you're not keeping anything from me?"

"Honey, I would never keep anything this important from you. I don't believe in keeping secrets from you anymore."

There was a tense silence. Jacoby said looking at Noah, "I know that you won't keep anything important from me anymore, Daddy. I also know that you kept Alexandria a secret because you thought that you were protecting me." She locked eyes with Noah.

His eyes were narrowed in concentration as he carefully listened to every word she said.

"You made the wrong decision, but your heart was in the right place," she said.

Suddenly an odd feeling descended over Noah. It coursed downwards from his head to his toes. The betrayal he'd felt since finding out Jacoby's secret dissipated. Words burst from his heart. "Dad, sometimes you can forgive someone for doing something that's almost unforgivable if you know that they had your best interests at heart. Right, Jacoby?"

Jacoby saw softness in Noah's chocolate eyes as he looked at her, and she felt a surge of hope.

Jacoby was fluffing the pillows up in her mother's bed.

"Stop fussing over me," Sarai said. "I'm not an invalid."

"The doctor said that the only reason he released you today was because you promised to stay in bed."

"Humph," she said. "I want my Christmas tree up before Christmas day."

"Daddy and Noah are going to set it up in the morning."

"Good," Sarai retorted. "I'll go in and check to make sure that they're doing it right."

"Okay, mom," Jacoby drawled.

Noah stood on the threshold and watched Jacoby tend to her mother. She smoothed the covers and then began rearranging medicine bottles on the nightstand. Jacoby's a nurturer by nature. She feels it is her place to protect people. I get it. I finally get it. He coughed to make them aware of his presence.

Jacoby and Sarai looked up and saw Noah standing there with a tray.

"It's time for your medicine, Mom, and a bowl of soup."

"I don't like soup," Sarai said in a plaintive voice.

"The directions on the bottle say that you have to take it with food so you might as well stop complaining," he retorted.

Sarai looked at Jacoby as she stepped aside for Noah to bring the tray in. She said to Jacoby, "I noticed that you're wearing my ring."

"Yes, but I'll let you borrow it when you and Daddy renew your vows."

"What's that?" Noah asked.

"I didn't get a chance to tell you," she said carefully not wanting to alert her mother Noah had broken off their engagement. "Mom and dad are renewing their vows."

"You're going to be the best man, aren't you, Noah?" Sarai asked.

Noah's eyes met Jacoby's as he placed the tray in Sarai's lap. "It would be my pleasure."

Sarai demanded, "Where's your engagement ring, Jacoby?"

The room was suddenly charged with electricity.

Noah turned to Jacoby and undid her necklace, slid off the ring, and placed it back on her finger. "Here it is," he said in his deep voice. "And here it stays." He slid it on her finger and kissed it.

Jacoby jumped up and down and threw her arms around Noah's neck. "Noah," she exclaimed, "I love you so much."

He whispered, "I know, Jacoby."

"I promise that I will never keep anything important from you again."

"I know, honey."

"Noah Powers, will you please marry me?"

"Yes, I will." Their lips met and they sealed their mutual promise with a deep, soulful, kiss.

"What's going on?" Abraham said, entering the room and catching the tail end of the conversation. "Y'all are acting like you just got engaged."

"No," Sarai said with mother wit. "They're just recommitting themselves to each other."

CHAPTER 21

The next evening Jacoby, Noah, Claudia, and Rex were on the front porch drinking iced tea. "I'm glad that your mom is okay."

"Yeah," Jacoby said. "She scared us good." Jacoby took Noah's hand and clasped it. "Didn't she, Noah?"

"She scared us straight," Noah added with a slight chuckle. "A crisis can make you realize what's important and make you put away pride and hurt feelings."

"Here comes someone," Rex said.

"I don't recognize the car," Claudia added.

The car stopped in the driveway and Alexandria got out.

"Oh, no," Claudia muttered. "Just when I thought things were getting on an even keel."

Alexandria slowly walked up the driveway. Gone was her swagger and she had a meek expression on her face. "I heard that mom is sick."

The usual surge of hurt that Jacoby felt when she saw Alexandria didn't surface. "She had an episode but she's feeling okay. You can go and see her if you want. Daddy is in there with her."

"I will in a minute. But I need to talk to you."

Rex said, "Claudia and I need to get going. We'll see you next weekend in Miami."

"Yes," Jacoby said standing, and giving farewell hugs. "We'll see you Friday night."

As they watched Claudia and Rex hurriedly leave Noah remained silent.

Alexandria nervously chewed on her bottom lip.

Noah observed that it was the mannerism that he'd seen Jacoby exhibit many times. Two sisters, so alike, yet so different.

"I've moved back to Bunnell," Alexandria said.

Jacoby gave a start of surprise.

"I'm going to stay with Lydia. Your mother doesn't need me in the way." Alexandria took a deep breath. "I want to apologize to you, Jacoby. I purposefully went to Miami to ruin your relationship with Armstrong. I wanted to destroy you."

"Why?"

Again she bit her lip. "I was jealous of you. You're so beautiful and seemed to have everything that I've ever wanted."

"You're beautiful, too, Alexandria. But you don't act it."

"Ever since I was a little girl I knew about you. And I thought that you knew about me, too. Once I found out that you didn't know of my existence it made angry. I felt as if I wasn't worth mentioning."

"Daddy knows that he made a mistake keeping you a secret from me."

"He's apologized to me over and over again, yet I tried to make him pay through hurting you. In the end, I only hurt myself."

"What do you mean, Alexandria?"

"Armstrong was so hateful to me."

"That's his MO, Alexandria."

"He beat me for not being you."

"He beat you because he's an abuser. He was to me," Jacoby said in a forthright manner. "You were witness to that the last night I was at the apartment. What would make you think that he would treat you any differently?"

"I was so hell-bent on hurting you I didn't care." She held her hands out helplessly. "I'd seen brutality before," she whispered, "when I was in prison, so violence was nothing new to me."

"That's a very sad picture you paint, Alexandria," Jacoby said. "I feel that I should also apologize to you. I didn't make things easy for you when you I found out who you were. I hated you on sight." She shook her head at the memory. She swallowed hard before saying, "It's not your fault that you're daddy's firstborn."

"Thank you for that, Jacoby." There was a long pause. She looked at Noah for the first time. "I was sitting in the parking lot when you left Armstrong's apartment. I was scared to death to go inside, but I had nowhere else to go. Once I got there I had a reason to be afraid."

"What do you mean?" Jacoby asked.

"Armstrong pounced on me the minute I got inside. When I got there his face was swollen and he had a black eye. I asked him if he wanted me to get him some ice for it. He slapped me around, and my mouth started bleeding. Then he started throwing things. He broke all the dishes and kicked a hole in the bedroom door. A neighbor heard the ruckus and called the police. They arrested him."

"Good!" Jacoby said.

"I'm sorry about what I did with Armstrong." Alexandria looked down at the ground.

"I didn't want him anyhow." Jacoby's voice was full of warning, "But if you ever try anything with Noah…"

"I won't." She stared at Noah who obviously only had eyes for Jacoby. Alexandria said with frank honesty, "I can tell that it wouldn't work anyhow."

251

"You're right," Noah said, grabbing Jacoby's hand and kissing the ring she wore. "It wouldn't."

Alexandria said with a worried frown, "I never did anything about the beatings from Armstrong so there's no paper trail. I don't know how long they'll keep him in jail."

"If there is a court date and if you need someone to testify on your behalf as to Armstrong's abuse I'm more than willing to do it."

"You would do that for me, Jacoby?"

"Actually, Alexandria," she replied. "I would do it for us."

"Amen." Noah breathed a sign of satisfaction and putting his arm around Jacoby's shoulder drew his fiancée closer.

Author's note:

A subplot in this novel is loosely based on the biblical story of Sarah and Abraham. I've used the original Hebrew spelling (even though they're pronounced the same) to Saraii, just to jazz it up a little bit.

Available on Nook, Amazon.com, and Createspace
Website: http://michelecameronauthor.com
Facebook: aggieauthor@cfl.rr.com
Twitter: michele.cameron16@gmail
Instagram: michelecameron_16

Other Novels Available by Michele Cameron

Skeletons in the Closet
October 2014

Eyes That Lie
September 2013

ABOUT THE AUTHOR

Michele Cameron, a native of Bridgeport, Connecticut, is a graduate of North Carolina A & T State University in Greensboro with a B.S. degree in professional Writing and English Education. Ms. Cameron currently teaches high school English in Orlando, Florida.

Cameron's first novel *Never Say Never* (Genesis-Press, Inc., January, 2008) was given a four star rating. Romance in Color named her the New Face among African-American writers.

Her highly anticipated second novel, *Moments of Clarity*. (Genesis-Press, Inc. October 2008) received a five star rating from Affaire de Coeur.

Cameron has been a featured guest on numerous notable BAN radio stations including, Mr. Media Interviews, Conversations Live with Cyrus Webb, Black Author's Network, I Just Finished, Coffee With an Author, EDC Creations, the morning show, "Who You Calling Old?", The Write Vision with Celeste Kelley, Circle of -Seven with Austin Camacho, and The Literary Diva.

She has written numerous articles on the internet including the websites, APOO Book Club, Affaire de Coeur, Black Author's network, Sormag, and The Book Place.

Cameron's third novel, *When Lightning Strikes*! (Genesis-Press, Inc., August, 2009 followed by *Unclear and Present Danger*, (February 2010). These latest novels received 4.5 and 5 stars respectively. *Eyes That lie* received 4 and 4.5 stars from Affair de Coeur and Romanceincolor.

www.ingramcontent.com/pod-product-compliance
Lightning Source LLC
Chambersburg PA
CBHW070910180626
46817CB00003B/999